THE STEALERS' WAR

Also by Stephen Hunt from Gollancz:

In Dark Service
Foul Tide's Turning

THE FAR-CALLED

Volume Three

STEPHEN HUNT

GOLLANCZ

LONDON

The right of Stephen Hunt to be identified as the author of this work has been asserted by him in accordance with the Copyright, Designs and Patents Act 1988.

First published in Great Britain in 2016 by Gollancz
An imprint of the Orion Publishing Group
Carmelite House, 50 Victoria Embankment, London EC4Y 0DZ
An Hachette UK Company

A CIP catalogue record for this book is available
from the British Library.

ISBN 978 0 575 09214 3

1 3 5 7 9 10 8 6 4 2

Typeset at The Spartan Press Ltd,
Lymington, Hants

Printed and bound in Great Britain by
Clays Ltd, St Ives plc

The Orion Publishing Group's policy is to use papers that are natural, renewable and recyclable products and made from wood grown in sustainable forests. The logging and manufacturing processes are expected to conform to the environmental regulations of the country of origin.

www.stephenhunt.net
www.orionbooks.co.uk
www.gollancz.co.uk

A book tightly shut is but a block of paper.
   – Chinese Proverb

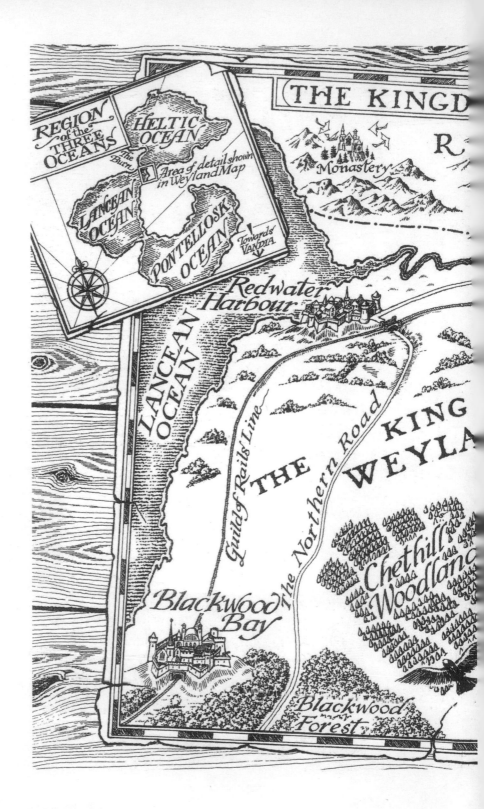

OM OF WEYLAND

O D A L

LibraryHold

Northhaven

NORTHHAVEN
and it's surrounds

White Wolf River

Quehanna

The
Great Gask
Forest

DOM OF
AND

RAILWAY

Great Plains of
Arak-natikh

The Thousand
DUCHIES

Northhaven

RODAL
Hodir-Hanur

HELLIN
Hahellon

Area of detail shown
in Weyland map.

TRESTERER

Heshwick

Navon

O
D
A
L

The
Rodnest
Islands

LARCEAN OCEAN

Midsbury

GIDOR

Ahn

IVAH

Talekhard

Arcadia

Argood

W
E
Y
L
A
N
D

KISH

Tenuthin

RAILWAY

MYSA

Chirk

WEYLAND
and Neighbouring
NATIONS

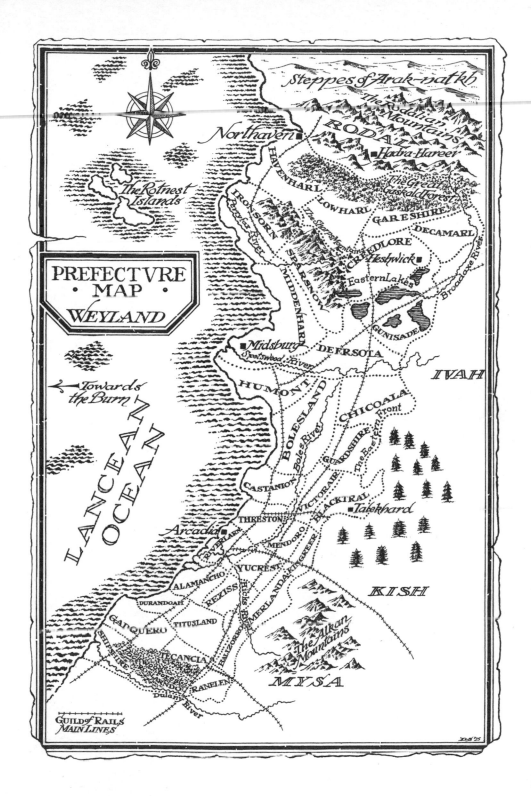

PREFECTVRE
· MAP ·
WEYLAND

Steppes of Arak-nat'kh

Northaven

RODAL
The Roddian Mountains

Hadra-Hareer

The Rotnest
Islands

HAVENHARL

IRONSORN

LOWHARL

The Great
Giskald Forest

GARESHIRE

The Sheeps Mountains

SPARSNOV

Pengis River

MIDDENHARL

CREDLORE
Heshwick

DECAMARL

EasternLakes

Broadaxe River

Towards
the Burn

GUNISADE

DEFRSOTA

IVAH

Midsburg
Spottswood River

HUMONT

CHICOALA
Front

BOLESLAND

The Eastern

Boles River

GUARDSHIRE

CASTANION

VICTORIA

BLACKTRAL

Talekhard

THRESTON

MENDORO

Arcadia

RIVERLARN

YUCREST

ALAMANCHO

REXISS

KISH

DURANDOAH

Hicks River

L A N C E A N   O C E A N

TITUSLAND

GATQUERO

EMERLANDA/KINGSEER

SHIREFIRE

TECANCLA

The Alkan
Mountains

FALIZORN

RANELEN

Dulani River

MYSA

GVILD of RAILS
MAIN LINES

ONE

AN AUDIENCE WITH
THE GREAT KRUL

Lady Cassandra Skar moaned with pain as the nomads dragged her from her horse towards the tent where the King of the Plains awaited her. Of course, the word tent was a bit of a misnomer. It was closer to a palace woven from colourful felt-lined fabric, staked toweringly high with wooden lattices and roof ribs. Multiple tents arranged together like a series of stretched foothills. In fact, as Cassandra gazed at the nomads' faces – expressions ranging from the curious to the openly hostile – she realized that the term *king* might be a bit of a misnomer too. *What would do instead, I wonder? Rag-tag hairy-arsed barbarian war chief lording it over a bunch of roaming savages? Best you keep such suggestions to yourself, lady.* From the way the nomads manhandled her, they clearly didn't see many Vandian noblewomen out here. She didn't take it personally. They clearly hated the other two prisoners in her party even more than her. Sheplar Lesh was a pilot from Rodal, the clans' mountainous neighbours to the south, and as close to an ancestral enemy as the plains people possessed. Although in fairness, they probably regarded everyone with the bad luck not to be born in a saddle among the clans as their ancestral enemy. Kerge was a forest dweller from the far side of the peaks, an oddity that only reminded the nomads that while they commanded the endless steppes, they'd always been beaten back from the rich, prosperous nations on the other side of the mountains.

Cassandra heard Alexamir's shouts of protest ringing out behind her. The love-sick young nomad had promised her his protection. Swore that he would release her if and when she chose to leave for home. *What a joke*. Leave for home? How could she do that with a broken spine and her legs paralyzed by the plane crash? She should have cut her wrists rather than suffer such a dishonour. That was the way of her house. For someone born and trained from birth to rule over millions, Cassandra had ended up not even being able to leave her bedroll unaided. The Vandian Imperium was power and strength or it was nothing. Maybe Cassandra would have ended her life if Alexamir hadn't removed and hidden her dagger. *Or maybe these people will cut my throat and save me the trouble*. Like so much else, it seemed that Alexamir's boasts of his importance among the clan had been somewhat exaggerated. *Or maybe this is how they greet all honoured guests under the protection of one of their so-called greatest warriors?*

She caught a brief glimpse of the witch rider, Nurai, standing by the entrance to the massive tent palace. A look of satisfaction twitched around the margins of her face. *It makes a difference from jealousy, I suppose*. Nurai clearly regarded Alexamir as her property, and would be only too happy to help Cassandra shuffle off this mortal coil; preserving the dashing, insanely reckless nomad for her sole attentions. There wasn't a future Nurai had prophesied where Cassandra's presence among the people of the plains wouldn't end up in despair and the gnashing of teeth and lamentations for the clan. *Maybe that means I'll live a little longer with Alexamir pining after me. Although perhaps the witch rider just foresaw my death here?*

Lady Cassandra was dragged like a haunch of meat, cursing her dead, useless legs, deep inside the palace of tents, ending up in a wooden-frame-vaulted throne room. The throne itself was composed of propellers taken from the planes of their Rodalian enemies, fallen skyguards who had broken every nomad horde to attempt the invasion of Rodal. She gazed up at the man who sat upon the throne. So, this was Kani Yargul, the warlord who had declared himself Lord of Clan Lords. The clans called such a king their *Great Krul*. Cassandra suspected that anyone capable of unifying the quarrelsome, ever-warring clans of horsemen was going to prove an equally great nuisance to the nations surrounding the steppes. Physically, Kani

Yargul looked every inch a warlord. Strapping, even by the standards of the strong Nijumeti tribesmen, perhaps two normal men wide, a shaved head, dark, short beard, narrow eyes, and a notably bulbous nose that had been broken many times. On the warlord's left stood an ancient witch rider, presumably the priestess to whom jealous Nurai owed her training and allegiance. On the right was an even queerer sight. An obviously foreign golden-skinned elder weighed down with the heavy rune-embroidered robes of a sorcerer. The way the robes covered his protruding spine make him look like he might be hunchbacked. His hair was naturally curled in a way that would have made many of the ladies of the Vandian imperial court jealous; a high forehead with dark, brooding eyes belying a superior, erudite manner. The sorcerer looked younger than she'd expect a man of his position to be.

'Hear me, Great Krul. I have given my word to Lady Cassandra, offering her the protection of salt and roof,' said Alexamir, pushing his way to the front of the crowd.

'*Your* word,' said the warlord. 'Not mine. Am I to extend the hospitality of the clans to every beggarly intruder who despoils the grass sea? So much trouble from you, Alexamir Arinnbold. Always. You leave to raid Rodal and prove yourself a man and you come back not with thralls to serve the clan, but with *guests*?' Kani Yargul chewed unhappily on the last word as though it was unexpected gristle on a haunch of meat.

'These two I have taken as thralls,' said Alexamir, pointing at Kerge and Sheplar Lesh. 'But the golden fox I would take as my wife.'

'Then marry the girl as a saddle-wife. Throw her inside your tent and go raiding for more.'

'Indeed,' said the priestess by the warlord's side. 'One saddle-wife is a vexation. Three or four is a goodly number.'

Cassandra pulled against the hands of her captors. 'I am no common prisoner.'

'It is true,' said Alexamir. 'She is the daughter of a princess, granddaughter to the Emperor of Vandia.'

'Another empire?' said the warlord, puzzled. 'I know of the Empire of Persdad to the north. Fine raiding for those willing to brave their legions.' He glanced at the sorcerer. 'What is this Vandia? Have you heard of them, Temmell Longgate?'

'I have, Great Krul,' said the sorcerer, nodding on the other side of the wooden throne. 'The Vandians are now allies of the king across the mountains. They fight in the Kingdom of Weyland's kin war, brother against uncle, for control of the land. Vandia lies far-called to the south, a rich and powerful empire which they boast of as the world's greatest nation. Their forces rarely travel as far north as the Lancean Ocean. I find their presence so close to us to be most disturbing.'

'So, an emperor's granddaughter? It's hard to take a wolf cub without bringing in the whole pack. Still, although they know it not, these Vandians are also my allies. Let them rip each other apart in the south,' scowled Kani Yargul. 'Let their kin war lay a thick red carpet of corpses for us to crunch over when the clans ride. Every dead Weyland soldier is one less for us to face when the time comes.' The warlord stared at Cassandra with his cold green eyes. 'And how much is the Vandian emperor's granddaughter worth in ransom?'

'Nothing,' said Cassandra. 'Not as I am . . . broken. A Vandian noblewoman must be able to fight for her house when challenges are issued. I cannot stand in any duel now. I am worthless to you. My house will expect me to end my life honourably. There will be no gold for you in exchange for my person.'

'At least she is honest,' said Kani Yargul. 'Useless, but honest.'

'She is *dangerous*, Great Krul,' said Nurai. 'She saw what we are building when we rode into the camp. The girl and the rice-eater and his forest man friend, all.'

Yes, that sight had come as quite a surprise to Cassandra. But not as much, she suspected, as to Sheplar Lesh. This was the young witch rider's best chance to have Cassandra executed, and the woman knew it.

'Do you expect this broken girl to gallop south and warn the nations of the Lanca?' said the warlord. He sounded amused, but Cassandra sensed the undercurrent of menace in his tone. 'Have you seen this in your visions, witch rider?'

'I have seen many things concerning this one's presence, Great Krul,' said Nurai. 'All of them leading to dark fates for our people.'

4

Madinsar fixed her understudy with a beady glare. 'Then why have I not seen similarly, my acolyte?'

'The true sight shows many paths,' was all the answer Nurai had to give.

Madinsar pulled her priestess robes in close and eyed Alexamir suspiciously. 'As does the heart. Never confuse the two.'

'This foreign whelp has cast a spell over Alexamir,' accused Nurai. 'How else can you explain his willingness to carry her here, the girl unable even to clean a tent or cook for his family? She is a burden, not a saddle-wife.'

'She was given my protection before her wounding,' said Alexamir.

Even Cassandra thought the justification hollow. There was more to it than that. She had experienced the tenderness with which Alexamir had cared for her when she had been injured. How eagerly he had tried to distract her from her plight and duty. He might be a fool, but he was *her* fool now.

'If a spell it is, I believe it a very ordinary enchantment,' said Madinsar. 'And not one you care for, Nurai.'

'I would ask you to heal my golden fox, Temmell,' said Alexamir.

'I am adviser to the Great Krul,' said the sorcerer. 'You seem to mistake me for some wandering healer.'

'Yet such you were when you first arrived with us,' said Alexamir.

This was clearly not the right response; reminding the strange-looking adviser of his humble origins here. The sorcerer's irritated expression turned to fury. 'I once regrew the arm of the Mark Lord of Simaria after he lost his limb in a joust. Am I now to be the medic to a common mounted thief?'

'Careful, Temmell,' cautioned the warlord. 'It is a fine thing to be a thief among the Nijumeti. To be an unsuccessful thief, however, is quite another thing. Your raiding party took many casualties, Alexamir. And you have returned with a bare handful of thralls and a hostage who has lost her worth.'

'Lesser men would have perished a dozen times where I survived,' said Alexamir. 'We were attacked twice by the Rodalian skyguard, their flying wings swooping down on us, dropping bombs and giving us the bitter taste of their cannons. The golden fox was taken from us and locked up in Salasang. But I broke her out and left the rice-eaters a burning town for their troubles. Then I escaped in one of their planes and claimed two propellers from the rice-eaters' pursuing skyguards. And when these two fools tracked me to recover the girl, I ambushed them and took them as thralls. If any bard was brave enough to travel with Alexamir, people here would be singing for months of my bravery and audacity.'

'Why would we need a bard, when we have you to sing your own songs so well?' asked Madinsar, wryly.

'I dreamt that Alexamir would scale the walls of Salasang and leave the town in flames,' said Nurai, speaking in defence of the reckless young nomad.

'I do not doubt it,' said Kani Yargul. 'You are truly the blood of your father, Alexamir Arinnbold. He danced with death every day until it found him. He tried to get me killed on his adventures a dozen times a season, and this is a hard thing to do, as the spirit of every broken-necked clan lord hovering above my throne will testify.'

'You honour me, Great Krul,' said Alexamir, his chest puffing with pride.

'Do I? The bravery expected of a rider and the recklessness of a clod are easily confused,' said Kani Yargul. 'Sometimes I can barely tell them apart myself. We shall see. Paltry though your booty may be,' said Kani Yargul, 'I shall claim the right of the Krul and take the rice-eater as my own thrall. You have a use for him, do you not, Temmell?'

'Officers of the Rodalian skyguard are rarely brought down on the plains alive,' said the sorcerer. 'I have many uses for such a servant.'

Cassandra winced. *That does not sound good for him.* Although Sheplar Lesh had been prime among her captors after she was seized from the Imperium, the Rodalian pilot had treated her honourably and risked his life twice to save her from the nomads. *You should not show such weakness, lady. One captor less is no bad thing for you.* Except she had no home to return to now. Not as she was.

'You would put him to use against the mountain people, Great Krul?' asked Madinsar.

'And where would you have the clans turn their attention instead, priestess?' retorted the warlord.

'North. Towards the Empire of Persdad.'

'Your ambitions are limited, Madinsar,' said Temmell. 'The nations of the Lancean League are the richest, fattest kingdoms in all the Three Oceans. Poultry left unplucked by the clans for too long.'

'Left unplucked, but not for lack of trying,' said the witch priestess. 'You were not born in the saddle, Temmell Longgate. Wander the camp at night and listen to our ancient songs. Hear of all the Great Kruls who raised their hordes and led them against Rodal, smashed them into the mountains, urged them through canyons and were left with nothing but bleached bones in foreign passes for their plunder. There are countless sagas that end sadly in Rodal. Or perhaps you would prefer those that end in the bogs of Hellin, whole clans drowned in quicksand and never seen again? North lies Persdad, protected only by hills and steppes and mortal men with timber palisades. That is where we should ride.'

'And rich only in wheat and lumber and thick-headed legionaries with blades to protect their wooden walls,' growled the warlord. 'The league lies on the southern caravan routes, littered with trade metals and the bounty of machines and mills, the Guild of Rails carrying treasure in every direction. Ports on the salted sea heaving with vessels packed full of plunder.' He slapped his thick muscled legs. 'This Vandian girl is a sign from the gods. What we seek is seeking us. Her people have joined the kin war in Weyland. Our enemies are disunited. The Lanca turns in upon itself. There is no better time to strike south.'

'You speak wisely,' said Temmell, his eyes gazing slyly at the priestess. There was obviously no love lost between these two, the left hand of the throne as jealous of the right as the reverse was also true.

'No Great Krul has ever breached the Walls of Rodal,' warned Madinsar.

'I am no mere Great Krul,' said the warlord. 'I am Kani Yargul. I shall make the god Atamva weep in envy at how thoroughly my foes are smashed. I will forge a victory crown so heavy that only my own sons will be able to bear its glory without being crushed.'

'Atamva always remembers,' whispered the priestess. Then Madinsar raised her face and looked at the warlord. 'Claim the right of the Great Krul again, my lord, and give me the forest dweller as my thrall.'

'What use do you have for this creature?' said Kani Yargul, staring down contemptuously at Kerge. 'I thought him half a bear and half porcupine, walking upright like a man when he entered my tent.'

'He could dance for us. Or perhaps the high priestess wishes to use the spines from his hide to pick meat from her teeth,' said the sorcerer. 'I hear the care of teeth becomes of great importance when one reaches such an inestimable age.'

'One of a great many nuisances I would rid myself of,' said Madinsar, staring down the sorcerer. 'If I could. This one is a gask. A twisted man, and the people of the forests possess many gifts, including that of dreaming the future. Such a thrall would be useful to me, and of service, thereby, to the clans.'

Kerge looked like he was going to say something, but didn't. Cassandra guessed the gask was going to point out that he had lost his gift of prophetic vision, but on second thoughts had wisely decided to keep his loss quiet lest he end up with a far worse fate. *Poor Kerge. If you could still see the future, you would have never come after me with Sheplar. You would have stayed safe in Rodal and gone back to your shaded city in the trees.*

'I must have something so you must have something,' said the sorcerer.

'As long as our clans grow stronger,' said Kani Yargul. 'So be it. Now bring me my feast. No more talk without action. I have a hunger and I have a thirst.'

He waved away the foreigners and court supplicants. Cassandra was dragged through the crowded tent until Alexamir caught up with her and lifted the weight of her body from the two guards. Nurai manoeuvred through the crowd to make sure she was there too. A knowing look on the young witch rider's face that Cassandra wished she could wipe off by breaking her proud nose. *If I could just take the step towards you, I would.*

'You came back from the raid with three thralls,' said Nurai. 'And you leave the tent with just one.'

'I leave the Great Krul having made two gifts to him,' said Alexamir. 'And the golden fox is the only prize I value.'

Those words struck Nurai like a slap. 'Fools' gold for a fool,' she growled and stalked off.

'The witch rider is right,' said Cassandra. 'I am no prize worth possessing.'

'Her words drip with envy,' said Alexamir. 'But then, what woman would not be envious? I am already a legend among the clans and my saga has only just begun.'

While mine is doomed to end here, it seems. 'And what of me?'

'I gave you my word that you would be free to return to your people if that is what you wished.'

'You gave your word to a different woman.' *One who could walk.*

'You shall be that woman again. I will talk to Temmell. Beg him to heal you. Offer him my life and loyalty if he heals you for me.'

Cassandra felt her heart sink. This golden-skinned outsider, Temmell; he was clearly an itinerant medicine man whose wagon had been seized by the clans trying to cross the plains; an ex-clan slave who had used science and his canny knowledge of herbs and powders to bluff his way into a minor position of power. Not even the imperial surgeons attending the emperor and the imperial family could mend a broken spine. What chance did some travelling peddler who had landed on his feet here have? 'You are wasting your time.'

'It is my time to waste,' said Alexamir. 'Come, I shall take you to meet my family.'

As if I have any choice in the matter. 'I am sorry to hear your father is gone. Does your mother still live?'

'She became one of the Great Krul's wives and lives inside the palace. It is the way of our people. If your friend dies, you take in the wives of your fallen brother. My Aunt Nonna keeps my household. You will like her.'

Cassandra suspected nothing would be further from the truth. Survival out here in the grasslands, cooking, cleaning, finding water, keeping the animals alive that helped feed mouths and give the clans their hides and wool for clothes, leather, saddles and tents . . . that was a full-time occupation. A pampered Vandian noblewoman, raised for power and made a cripple, that was only another burden.

Cassandra glanced behind her to the palace. No sign of Kerge or Sheplar. It was strange, when that pair had been her captors, there hadn't been a day as prisoner in Weyland when she hadn't dreamt of escaping and making her way back to Vandia. But now the pair were thralls, slaves to the clan, she couldn't help feeling sorry for them.

She gazed out to the east, beyond the hills where acres of camouflage netting helped conceal the clans' greatest secret. Perhaps this Kani Yargul would be the first war leader of the hordes to do what had never been done before. Conquer Rodal and push into the rich nations of the south. *So, Vandia is now involved in Weyland's civil war?* The Imperium had come at last to punish the slave revolt in Vandia. Her people were across the mountains in force. Ridiculously close, given the scale of distances the Vandians must have flown to reach Weyland. *Is my mother there? Paetro, Duncan, others from my house?* Almost certainly. Cassandra knew her mother. Nothing in Pellas would stop Princess Helrena Skar from seeking out her kidnapped daughter, punishing the escaped slaves who had humiliated her by snatching the daughter of her house as a hostage. Lady Cassandra had to stop herself from laughing at the irony. All this way and did her grandfather's legions but know it, it was only the indignity of the slave revolt they had left to punish. *With me, there is nothing left to save.* Only to avenge. Better she stayed here among the savage nomads. Lost to her house. Let Helrena Skar think her daughter dead. *For I am. If I only didn't have Alexamir's affections to remind me that I'm alive.*

Alexamir lifted Cassandra on to a horse so she could pass through the camp with more dignity than being carried like a sack of meal.

'You should have let me end my life,' declared Cassandra.

'Then you would have ended two.' It was clear Alexamir would brook no interference with his plans for Cassandra, no matter what her wishes.

There were thousands of similarly sized and shaped tents in the busy encampment, although there was no chance of the nomads getting lost. Each tent's exterior had been dyed or embroidered with unique runes and symbols, prayers for success against rivals and protection against evil spirits. Children played outside while adults cooked on low stone ovens, cleaning weapons and brushing horses, picking stones from their steeds' hooves. She reached a tent, or rather, three connected circular tents formed into a triangular formation. It had been staked on the top of a low hill. Down on the other side was a stream where nomads squatted by the side of the frothing water, beating clothes clean against rocks.

'I return from the raid, Aunt,' said Alexamir, pushing aside a woollen flap acting as a door to the tent.

'Yes. Yes. I heard the cheers from the palace,' said Nonna. 'I shall cook their applause at once to make a fine feast from the great words of such heroes.'

The nomad woman standing inside sniffed, irritated, watching Alexamir bear Cassandra in and laying her down on a simple bed of sheep skins in the corner. Nonna had the same blue tint to her skin as all the nomads. The same twisted blood that allowed Alexamir to walk around Rodal's frozen heights bare-chested. Alexamir's aunt must have been close to her sixtieth year, but she was still a handsome woman, with the muscled tone of a woman a third her age, dark leather riding clothes belted with twin daggers swinging on wide hips. To Cassandra's eyes, Nonna appeared a gladiator born to battle, not a housekeeper. *Perhaps that is the way with all the Nijumeti.*

'And what else have you carried back from your raid? Sheep with no pelts and a stallion that only gallops backwards? A sword hilt with no blade attached, perhaps?'

'This is the Lady Cassandra of Vandia, granddaughter of a rich and powerful emperor,' said Alexamir, a touch too haughtily. 'She has been given my guest oath.'

Nonna bowed ironically in Cassandra's direction. 'Then I live to serve. As *always*.'

'She will be no burden on you. Not for long. Temmell will heal her. I know it.'

'That one? That foreign *degg*? That golden-skinned spell-sucker? Promise him your soul for a saddle-wife if you must. He shall not have mine.'

'My golden fox is to be no thrall or saddle-wife,' said Alexamir, setting matters out clearly. 'She has my protection and we will honour her with all the traditions of roof and salt. She is free to go among us as she wishes.'

Cassandra couldn't help but feel her heart soften at the young nomad's words. Few men in this land or any other would have held to her in this state. *But he has.* Nothing had inhibited his yearning for

11

her. Not being held as a prisoner in Salasang or being shot out of the clouds by the Rodalian skyguard. Alexamir was a savage, a reiver and a common thief, but he possessed the nobility of a prince of the plains.

'How splendid. Then I shall be witness to a miracle of the gods . . . I shall see a fox walk,' said Nonna. She waved her hand indifferently around the connected tents. 'Welcome to your new kingdom, then, Lady Cassandra of Vandia. You will find we have fewer servants than an emperor's offspring is used to, but what we lack in numbers we make up for in spirit.' She snorted and picked up a leather drinking bottle, uncorking it and tossing it to the little-welcomed guest.

Cassandra sniffed at the canteen and then took a gulp, swallowing a pale white liquid that tasted of almonds. It burnt her throat like acid before moving down her gut as a stream of liquid fire. She only just resisted the urge to spit it out again. The young Vandian woman experienced a strange, dizzying warmth coursing through her veins. 'What in the name of the ancestors did I just drink?'

'*Cosmos*,' said Nonna. 'Distilled and fermented milk of the mare. Only the finest. Sent by my sister-in-law from the leavings of the Great Krul himself. Milk of the mare gives a woman the strength to see out the day and work like a devil.' She laughed. 'Drink too much and I shall lose my legs as surely as you have lost yours. Or perhaps I shall go blind first?'

Cassandra proffered the bottle back for Nonna to take. As Nonna reached over, she grabbed Cassandra's wrist and turned it around, inspecting the guest's fingers and hand like a palm reader. 'An emperor's granddaughter, you say? On whose word? These hands are hard and calloused, not soft and coddled.'

'I speak the truth,' protested Alexamir. 'The rice-eaters and men of Weyland held her hostage in the kin war across the mountains. I rescued her. I freed her.'

'Indeed. So, you could not resist stealing a burning brand from the fire,' said Nonna. 'Every day you walk into the tent and I glance up and see you and think you are your father, returned from riding the heavens. Like two peas in a pod, in bad manners, poor wisdom and fine features. Truly you are my brother's blood, Alexamir Arinnbold.'

Cassandra broke the aunt's grip. 'That he may be, but I am Vandian. The Imperium's celestial caste does not have soft hands and fat chins.

We are raised to battle and trained to rule. No house that carries weaklings survives long in the Imperium.'

'Then perhaps your people are not so different from ours, after all,' said Nonna. 'You certainly show enough pride to be a Nijumet. But is it false pride? Never in my day.'

'Your nephew would be dead without me,' said Cassandra. 'I flew the flying wing we stole from Rodal. It was crashing it which broke my back.'

'Indeed? Well, even foul water may put out a fire.' Nonna shrugged and lay a hand not unkindly on one of Alexamir's boulder-like shoulders. 'Yet, where would I be without my Alexamir and his hot air to warm my tent? Winter would have claimed me an age ago.'

If winter tried, I suspect it would end up with a dagger shoved through its eye. This was Cassandra's fate, her future. Worn fabric walls stretched over a wooden frame, her bones warmed by a dried sheep-dung hearth. Before, she had been a prisoner in Weyland. Now she was a prisoner inside her own body. *Where is my escape to be, here?*

War hasn't been kind to Midsburg, mused Duncan Landor, blackened rubble crunching under his feet as he strode toward the military headquarters with his friend Paetro. As sieges go, this city had seen a quick, decisive action. Even the Guild of Radiomen's hold he and Paetro had just left had escaped largely undamaged. But it wasn't the war that was troubling Duncan so much as what passed for a peace which had followed it. After a brief spell of looting, mostly by Weyland's victorious southern army rather than their Vandian allies, both King Marcus' regiments and Vandia's legions had set up camp inside the city's unaffected quarters. And very little that had followed had gone according to plan.

'Have you heard that Captain Aleria's section was posted missing yesterday?' asked Duncan.

'I hadn't,' said Paetro. 'He was no greenhorn; there was a man who knew what he was about. Where was his section dispatched?'

'A rebel artillery column was spotted heading for the Sparsnow line. The captain took a patrol ship out to investigate. The ship was found later, empty. No legionaries, no pilots.'

Paetro grunted. 'There is a road in Vandis where courtesans play the same game . . . Lares Shrine Street. Show a little leg, lure a man into an alley, a flash of knives, and the blockheads were never seen again. Not unless you count the rats in the sewer going after chunks of meat floating by.'

'I hear that King Marcus has declared the rebellion over,' said Duncan. 'He's leaving the capital and travelling on a royal progress through the pacified prefectures.'

'He's as big a fool as the dunces who went visiting Lares Shrine Street's courtesans, then,' said Paetro. 'The northern army hasn't disappeared, they've just scattered. The ones they can keep supplied are hiding out in the wilderness, the rest have buried their rifles in greased rags and are hiding in plain sight in the fields and towns, pretending to be farmers and shopkeepers.'

'There's a lot of wilderness in Weyland,' noted Duncan.

Paetro halted. A line of townspeople marched down the street, a sorry-looking, slowly shuffling rabble, their feet clinking from leg irons welded around their ankles. The group of men and women were civilians mostly, a few tattered grey uniforms that marked some out as parliament's rebels; with a scattering of young children – presumably the prisoners' offspring – following behind the line, weeping and mewling, shoved back by the legionaries' rifle butts when they grew too close. This progression towards the giant Vandian ships landed outside the town was suddenly halted by a group of southern officers in blue uniforms. Duncan wondered if the king's men were going to protest the emptying of Midsburg's quarters by their imperial allies. Supposedly, rebel sympathizers were being resettled to disperse any further support for the exiled pretender, but Duncan understood the prisoners' true fate all too well. Duncan, who had once been taken as a slave of the empire to serve inside the brutally hard Vandian sky mines. *But I earned my freedom through wit and loyalty towards my owner. These fools supported the pretender's rebellion. This is the just price of ending up on the losing side.* Not all the slaves would end up dying inside the sky mines. Some would be put to work tending crops and bringing in harvests to supply the sprawling imperial cities. Others would find themselves toiling as house servants, or workers in the mills and foundries.

Duncan and Paetro drew near to where the southern officers, a cavalry colonel, two majors and a captain, remonstrated with their Vandian allies.

'You are taking too many,' said the colonel. 'You must have nearly two hundred head in this column alone.'

'We have our orders,' said the Vandian commander. 'They come from Prince Gyal himself.'

'And we carry out commands from our *king*,' said the colonel. 'I believe I know where the order of precedence lies between a king and a prince.'

'A prince of the Imperium,' barked the Vandian commander, 'out-ranks a thousand raggedy-arsed local warlords. Prince Gyal speaks as the voice of the emperor here. Now move out of my way, before I decide to add you to the chain gang and ship you out.'

'What is going on here?' demanded Duncan. 'What is the problem?'

'Our trains stand half empty,' complained the colonel.

'What trains?'

'The Guild of Rails' marshalling yard outside Midsburg,' said the colonel. 'We have been bringing in wagons for days, but they wait half empty. I also have quotas to make.'

'A quota for what?' asked Duncan, the answer to his question hanging between himself and his moustached countryman.

'Indentured labour,' said the colonel. 'The mill owners and great estates have placed fresh orders for workers. The rebellion has played havoc with the realm's smooth running. Fields lie thick with weeds and foundries sit idle with cold furnaces after so many were pressed into army service. The rebels must pay for their crimes. Pay with grain from their winter stores and labour from their prefectures.'

'They're to be slaves?' said Duncan. 'In Weyland?' The idea shocked him. There had never been slaves in the kingdom.

'Twenty years' service with full bellies and a dry roof over their heads?' growled the colonel. 'If you want to call these traitors slaves, let me march you out a thousand hungry soldiers fighting on short rations all too glad to head south for the peace of field and factory.'

Duncan merely shook his head and left the officers from the two allied forces bickering over the spoils of war, screeching crows pecking at a corpse's entrails. Vandia had always kept slaves. The richest nation in the world paid for its domestic peace by maintaining as much of its populace as it could in a state of idle distraction, importing foreign muscle to feed and work for the indolent citizenry. But Weyland honoured a different tradition. Its people free and wilfully independent. The wealth flowing into Weyland from the empire wasn't just feeding the southern nobility's coffers, it seemed. It was driving them to ape the empire in other ways. *Well, it'll be the locals' problem, soon enough. Not mine.*

One of the children, a boy who couldn't have been older than nine, tugged at the cloak covering Duncan's back. His pallid face was smeared with tears and dirt and he trembled as though he hadn't eaten for days, which was probably the case. 'Why won't they let me go with my ma and pa, sir? I'll travel with them. I want to.'

Because you're not old enough to sweat in the empire's fields or mills, yet, and be glad of it. 'They'll be travelling a long way. The journey won't be kind.'

'I don't care; I can travel as well as anyone.'

The leg irons would slip off your stick-thin legs if you tried. 'Wait until you're older. That's what you need to do.' Duncan felt inside his tunic and removed a gold coin, tossing it at the boy just as a Vandian legionary marched past and made to cuff the young refugee. The lad sprinted away fast, a dumbfounded expression on his face as he regarded his unexpected bounty.

'You haven't done him any favours,' said Paetro. 'One of the older packrats in the ruins will beat him and steal that coin before he ever gets to spend it.'

'The city's had our steel; it might as well have our gold.' *The saints know, it's all I have to give. What the hell's happened to Weyland and its people? My family not least among them? This isn't my country anymore. I lost my home the moment I left.* 'I hope the pretender and his rebels roast in hell, starting a war they couldn't hope to win. This misery and devastation, it's all on their heads.'

'Civil wars are just like any other kind,' mused Paetro as they walked away from the prisoners. 'They start from many causes, but they always end with one winner and one loser. Oft as not, not much difference between the two.'

True enough, old friend. Duncan thought of the corpses littering the land beyond the shattered city walls. Weylanders loyal to King

Marcus mingling in the mud next to the pretender's rebels, Vandians dotted around the thick artillery-churned mud, lying between the locals. *Hard to tell them apart, now.* Looters crept out after dark to fight the crows for what the dead soldiers had to give up. A few coins and keepsakes. Rifles and pistols had already been stripped by medical orderlies checking for anyone left alive. Wounded traitors were bayoneted where they lay, on the orders of the officers commanding the Army of the Boles. That was the price of treason these days in Weyland. Not that Duncan needed to be reminded when he reached what had recently been Midsburg's rebel parliament building. Bodies still hung from lampposts more or less intact. The nearest wore a once-fancy grey uniform, its tunic's yellow piping spattered with dried blood. Field Marshal Samuel Houldridge had once been supreme commander of Weyland's forces, but he had made the equally supreme error of supporting the pretender's claim to the throne, rather than King Marcus'. Houldridge's corpse had been discovered bled out in front of the assembly building after the siege, unable to feel the rope around his neck when it hoisted him high for all to see. But the forms had to be observed. Duncan suspected the same couldn't be said of the rebel assemblymen swaying in the wind on lampposts down the street. The politicians who had stayed; or the ones caught fleeing the city, attempting to reach Deersota in the east or the Sharp Mountains to the north. If King Marcus ever recalled parliament, it would be a long time before he faced what once used to be called the 'loyal opposition'.

A well-armed sentry post of Vandians and Weylanders checked Duncan and Paetro's papers before admitting them to the old assembly building. What had once been the rebellion's headquarters now served its conquerors. With the siege over, the various army followers and courtiers mingled freely with officers and nobility from two nations inside the building. And three of the women in the main chamber encapsulated Duncan's plight right there. His countrywoman Adella Cheyenne, a local beauty whom he had once loved, and who had betrayed him to take up with Baron Machus. Princess Helrena, mistress of Duncan's house, whom he still loved but who had forsaken him for the necessity of a future political marriage to Prince Gyal. And Leyla Landor, his father's ridiculously youthful and spirited new bride, whom he felt little for, but who was the only one to console him behind Benner Landor's back, the one woman who seemed to appreciate Duncan for who he was.

Paetro moved through the chamber to locate Princess Helrena while Duncan halted briefly to converse with his father. Benner Landor wore the blue uniform of a colonel of the Royal Artillery with a pleased, proud superiority that came naturally to the landowner. You wouldn't have known that before the rebellion, the closest Duncan's wealthy father had got to a cannon was walking past the unused wall guns mounted along the ramparts of Northhaven's old town. *Yes, this has been a good war for old man Landor*. He had been elevated to the nobility for his support in the war; the self-made man made respectable at last. His young new wife had seen to that.

'Have you heard the news?' Benner Landor growled at his son. 'We are to travel home to Northhaven. The Army of the Boles is to be garrisoned in the prefecture while we pursue the last few outlaws and seek to dig the damnable pretender out from the burrow of his exile.'

'It's not my home anymore, Father,' said Duncan. 'I will be returning to the Imperium when the Vandians depart.' *And the sooner, the better*.

Benner sounded hurt. 'You don't want to see Hawkland Park again?'

'If the empire requires it . . .'

Benner shook his head, sadly. 'I wish you would reconsider leaving.' He turned to look for Leyla Landor, signalling his young wife should come over, calling out. 'Talk sense to this lad, Leyla. He seems to heed your counsel these days far more readily than mine.'

'You don't need me. Not anymore,' said Duncan. He watched the young wife walk towards them. Leyla might not spark anything approaching true love in his heart, but by the saints, she could certainly raise his ardour. Her walk, the way she slipped through the crowd, her sensual voice and manners. There wasn't a thing about Leyla he would change except the old gull she had chosen to marry. 'The House of Landor has a new mistress of the estate and a new heir.'

'But it still holds our old welcome for you. Has your time away from our country changed the boy I knew so much?'

Duncan held back from pointing out that Benner Landor had rarely

18

spent time with either of his two children. Too busy with the affairs of the house. 'Perhaps time has. And Weyland won't be the same country after the rebellion has been crushed.'

Leyla drew close and curtsied towards Duncan and he returned a shallow bow, having to tear his eyes away from the way she seductively brushed folds from her purple velvet and cotton day-dress.

'You're wrong about the nation, too,' said Benner Landor. 'Our tenant farms still need administering. The land will require seeding and ploughing and hard toil across the seasons. There will be even more contracts coming our way to supply grain fuel to the skyguard's new squadrons. Whatever animosities the rebellion against the king sparked, they will be buried with the final few outlaws and traitors.'

Duncan's father believed the southern newspapers' propaganda a little too readily. The rural north bred hard families who lived equally tough lives. They wouldn't bend their knees so readily in front of conquering southern armies. If anything got buried after the rebellion's end, it might well be a dagger in the spine of those who had supported the king a little too readily.

Leyla observed her husband as he walked off towards the general, a look of mischief crossing her face. 'You could stay with us.' She leant in to rub the inseam of Duncan's trousers unnoticed by the others in the room. 'I will always have a *special* place just for you.'

'You knew the time would come when I put Weyland behind me and returned to the Imperium.'

'And things shall be so boring at Hawkland Park without you, Duncan. Peace will arrive and Benner will return to his tedious clerks and crops and bills of lading.'

'Such tedium is where the house's fortune is found. But my father will be Lord of the Northern Marches or whatever title it was King Marcus promised him for his support in the war.'

'And what will I do while Benner glories in his newfound reputability?'

'You could start by increasing the bounty on the head of Nocks. There's still been no sighting of the creature since the fall of the city.'

Leyla sighed, as though it had been she who had suffered a great betrayal. 'I don't blame Nocks so much as I blame your sister . . . she seduced Nocks and goaded him into trying to murder you. Nocks

19

was always the most loyal of man-servants before Willow dangled the promise of her body in front of him like a fancy lure to the trout.'

'The law will catch up with my sister.'

'And when are you and I to catch up?'

'Don't you have a son to raise? The House of Landor's new heir.'

Leyla giggled. 'How provincial of you, Duncan. A true lady doesn't bother herself with the minutiae of childcare. That's what all those wet-nurses, governesses and tutors are paid for. Young Asher will be educated at a grand southern academy inside the capital, alongside the children of the rich and the high-born. I refuse to bring him north after the war ends; he would be completely corrupted in base company.'

'I didn't turn out so bad.'

'You ran wild like a ruffian by all accounts,' said Leyla, squeezing his arm. 'But then, perhaps it's the rogue in you that calls out to me. Do I have to point towards your sister's behaviour to illustrate the disadvantages of being raised alongside sordid commoners?' She nodded towards Paetro. 'Willow betrayed and abandoned your Vandian soldier friend during the siege, didn't she? Left him for dead and fled with that outlaw Jacob Carnehan, all the while scheming for Nocks to put a bullet in your back.'

'I'll provide a proper education for Willow after she's tracked down. It won't be long before Nocks and Willow run out of rocks to hide under,' said Duncan. *Damn my sister.* Duncan had given Willow a second chance to make up for her betrayal of him inside the empire and how had she repaid his soft heart? She had sold out her entire family, betrayed them all – her new husband, her father and brother and step-mother. And for what? To run off with that fool Carter Carnehan and his murdering pirate of a father – to help the rebels turn against their lawful king? *Well, I won't be stupid enough to give Willow another chance. The best she'll get from me is being turned over to her rich dolt of a husband for chastisement.* He supposed Viscount William Wallingbeck would allow Willow to give birth to his new heir before he handed his treacherous wife over to the magistrates. Pleading your belly was a well-known legal ploy to escape justice inside a courtroom. *But not this time.* Willow had murdered a servant down south in a fit of pique, as well as plotting to slay Duncan while she betrayed the loyalist cause. *May the saints give me the opportunity to watch Willow pay for her crimes before I quit this place.*

'I don't see Viscount Wallingbeck here. How is his lordship dealing with my dear sister dishonouring her marriage vows?'

Leyla frowned. 'Less than happily, it is fair to say. He is the officer who led the cavalry charge which broke the back of the pretender's forces defending Midsburg. William should be being celebrated as a war hero. Instead, he is being laughed at as a fool who let his wild wife run away to join the rebellion, absconding with his unborn son in her belly. The viscount comes from a proud and ancient line. Mockery is not what he enjoys being served. *Lady* Wallingbeck will find very little to enjoy about their reunion when the time comes.'

I'm surprised the boorish dolt even noticed she'd slipped away. 'He'll have to fight the constables for her attentions.'

Leyla waved a finger in the direction of Princess Helrena and Prince Gyal. 'Over to your mistress and offer her a little honey to keep her sweet. When you need to make more, you may re-visit my flower. I will be passing the Blue Shutter Hotel in my horse trap at the usual time this evening.'

'And I thought that being at the front of a column storming a city wall was dangerous enough.'

'My horses require their regular gallop, as do I.'

'What if my father notices your absence?'

'Oh, but Benner has other interests. Our quarters are covered with plans of how he will develop the prefecture when we hold North-haven again. Between him and Prefect Colbert, they are dividing up the wealth of the north. At least on paper.'

'How little things change,' sighed Duncan.

'While others don't . . . you are still a Landor. It is your obligation to fill in for the head of the house. And I have some most interesting *duties* planned for you.'

Duncan bowed towards her. 'Then I am obliged . . .' She left his side for Benner Landor's, and Duncan couldn't help but notice the envious male glances following her from among the rest of the officer corps. *Damned if she'll lack for company when I'm back in Vandia. What a fool my father is. He orders the finest meal in the restaurant and leaves it uneaten while he jabbers on about government contracts and the house's coffers.*

Duncan made to join his friend Paetro but was halted by the one woman he didn't want to talk to this afternoon. Sadly, as always, the duplicitous Adella Cheyenne had schemes of her own.

'What a delightful lady the new mistress of Hawkland Park is,' said Adella. 'And what a delightful fool the great Benner Landor must be. Or perhaps not – as I hear that the new Lady Landor's recent birth has rapidly made your position as heir redundant.'

'You know nothing about Lady Landor,' snarled Duncan.

'How protective of you. How gallant. Why that look? It's almost as if you don't like seeing me here.'

'Maybe I don't like being reminded of my mistakes.'

'You don't like meeting me because I cause you to remember that you're no different from me. Just hanging on to a different set of coattails, is all.'

'I have earned my position here. While you were sitting on picnic blankets on the hills above Midsburg swapping gossip and cold meats with Vandian courtesans and southern courtiers, I was in the thick of the siege.'

'Then more fool you,' said Adella. 'Although that tiresome slaughter has bought me one small advantage. I suppose it is only fair for the people of Northhaven to see me one last time before I travel back to the Imperium.'

Adella made it sound as though she would appear above their old town like an angel descending from heaven, a halo of holy fire burning brilliantly around her. 'Yes, that's just what they've been waiting for.'

'Sour grapes?' Adella laughed. 'Well, why not. You family holds title to almost every other crop in Northhaven. I warned you when we met in Vandis . . .' She indicated Prince Gyal and Princess Helrena across the chamber, deep in conversation while Paetro stood by, waiting for his chance to report. 'Your precious princess would discard you like a hound dropping a bone just as soon as some real meat presented itself.'

'And what does that make you? One bone among many on the baron's table.'

'There are few males among the celestial caste who do not keep a harem,' said Adella. 'It is the empire's way. Many heirs make for a strong house. Unfortunately for you and your princess, the same

22

custom does not apply for a female head of house. Helrena Skar will be Prince Gyal's wife, perhaps an empress for an emperor, and what then for poor Duncan Landor?'

What then indeed? 'You forget, I am a free man now. A citizen.'

'Oh, but aren't there an awful lot of them in Vandis? Clogging up the capital's streets and avenues. You must have noticed how thick the unruly mobs run as you flew over them in your lover's helo?'

'I'm sure your view is better next to the baron – at least, it is when you can push your way to the front of the cockpit through all his other concubines.'

Adella rubbed her belly. 'My child is due to be born in a few weeks. The baron always favours wives who present him with strong children.'

Duncan located the brutish baron in the crowd. Duncan had reason to loathe the coarse Vandian noble even without his removal of Adella from the sky mines. Baron Machus's treachery had nearly led to Cassandra being kidnapped by her dangerous grandmother. *There's a man who appreciates a fresh bone to gnaw.* 'You deserve each other.'

'Keep your hypocrisy. I did what I had to do to survive, Duncan. If you want my advice, you'll remain behind in Weyland, *free* citizen. Help old man Landor run his house and count yourself lucky to have ever escaped the sky mines.'

'Your counsel is the last thing I need. I'm not heading anywhere until I rescue Lady Cassandra.'

'And don't you think that celestial class brat's better off staying in Weyland, too?' pouted Adella. 'Even as a hostage? Prince Gyal won't be happy with another man's leavings clogging up matters of imperial succession. The first child sired by Prince Gyal that drops out of Helrena's womb might as well be carrying an execution warrant for the silly girl.'

'Protecting Lady Cassandra is my business.'

She laughed. 'Really? One way or another it's a trade that's going to get you killed, I think. But then, you're one of the high and mighty Landors. I'm sure you know what you're doing.'

'As you did, you mean, when you betrayed the escape attempt inside the sky mines?'

'Don't appear a bigger fool than you already are,' said Adella.

'Nobody truly escapes from the sky mines, even if you don't die in the attempt. Look around you, count the Vandians and their legions and their warships and fleet. Sent to punish their slave revolt. Perish in the Imperium, or die later. That's no choice at all. I chose to live, as did you. You can't forgive me because you can't forgive yourself. But I don't suffer from such a weakness.'

Duncan snorted. Adella was right about one thing, he had been a fool, once; at least as far as she was concerned. *To think that if the skel slavers hadn't struck Northhaven, I might have ended up marrying her.* Duncan had experienced a few narrow escapes on the battlefield, but none so narrow as escaping this woman. 'We'll lay on one more picnic for you and your useless friends. It might be a little chilly along the border, but I'm sure the camp followers will dress up warm.' He stalked away without a backward glance. Paetro stood stoically, waiting for Princess Helrena to free herself from the company of the mission's commander as he held forth. *The prince almost enjoys the sound of his own voice as much as my father likes to drone on about the Landor fortune.*

'It is a delicate balance to maintain,' said Prince Gyal. 'If we flood the slave auctions with too much produce, we will depress prices and many of the market owners' houses will turn against us. Perhaps we should make gifts of the slaves to buy wavering allies? We could announce it on the victory podium after we march down the Grand Avenue.'

Duncan resisted the urge to glare openly at the prince. *Being crowned emperor is all that matters to him. Not Helrena. Surely she must see that?*

'Any friend who can be bought is only waiting for a better price to be your enemy,' said Princess Helrena. 'And your plans for a triumph in the capital are premature. The rebels still hold my daughter hostage.'

'*Our* plans,' said Gyal. 'And I have not forgotten the bargain we struck. The local rebels will scramble to hand over Lady Cassandra soon enough. She is the only bargaining chip they possess to save their skins.'

'I would not underestimate the Weylanders. These rebels you dismiss so easily led the only successful slave revolt inside the empire in a thousand years.'

'The stain of which has been well avenged here,' said Gyal. 'Their supposedly proud rebel capital fell in a day, and how could it be otherwise? Armoured legions and helo squadrons and electric rifles against horsemen with sabres and a few primitive holster guns. When ice meets a fire there can be only one result... ice melts away and drains into the soil.'

'Melt enough ice and you may drown in it,' warned Helrena.

'You are over-cautious,' laughed Prince Gyal. 'A trait you must overcome when you rule by my side as empress. This campaign will prove as a glorious example of how far Vandia may project her power no matter what the distance from the empire. The Imperium's borders have remained static for far too long. There are countless nations out here awaiting annexation, like grains of sand on a beach. We shall create a vast outer ring of imperial provinces and reward our allies with governorships of the new territories.'

'And create a thousand potential emperors and breakaway rival empires in one stroke?'

'Not if we also expand the legions and fleet in line with the Imperium's expansion,' said Gyal. 'And by so doing, provide the hostile caste commoners choking our rabble towers with something to do other than demand expanded food allowances while clamouring for ever more lavish kino screen entertainments. Let them fight instead. Let them be rewarded with land for military service. We shall lance the boil of our overpopulation and drain it away like pus.'

'You have grand dreams for someone who has yet to occupy the diamond throne.'

'Grand dreams are the only kind worth having, my love. They shall carry us to the throne and keep us there.'

Prince Gyal took himself away to give Baron Machus the benefit of his endless wisdom, while the princess turned her attention to Duncan and Paetro. 'So, gentlemen. What news of my daughter from the Guild of Radiomen?'

'We've spread word among the traders of the reward we're offering for the little highness's safe return,' said Paetro. 'No doubt they'll prove as eager for a taste of it as the local bounty hunters.'

'Perhaps a little too eager,' said Duncan. 'We're already being flooded with dubious sightings of Cassandra. Any young woman on

25

the road is fair game to being detained, snatched or just reported in the hope she might make her kidnappers rich.'

Paetro shrugged. 'True enough. And with the southern armies sweeping across Weyland's northern prefectures, there are a lot of female refugees on the move across the Rodalian foothills.'

'The local king will reclaim his land soon enough,' said Helrena. 'Prince Gyal intends to fly the fleet north. He will give these Rodalians a simple choice. Surrender Lady Cassandra and the pretender-in-exile or face the imperial hammer.'

'I'm not sure that's wise,' said Duncan. 'The Rodalians are a proud, quarrelsome people. They rarely take kindly to being told what to do.' *And they might have been a lot more receptive to such a demand if that idiot Prince Gyal hadn't hung Rodal's leader in Arcadia when he dared to challenge the imperial presence here.*

'The prince has command of the expeditionary force,' said Helrena. 'While I still linger in disgrace for allowing the slave revolt to start inside my holdings. Gyal will, as always, do exactly as he pleases. But so long as his campaign results in Cassandra's safe return . . .'

'He needs your support to claim the throne, my princess,' said Paetro.

'And I am sure he considers making me his empress ample compensation for our alliance,' said Helrena. 'This military campaign is Gyal's game. We must play as his pieces if we are to survive and prosper.'

Paetro stared coldly across at Baron Machus and the prince, no doubt remembering how easily Helrena's cousin had once betrayed them and switched his support to Gyal. 'I do not care for those we must share the board with.'

'Nor do I, Paetro Barca. But the easiest path to destroying your enemy is to make him your friend. That is the only option fate has left me with. Send word to the captain of my flagship that we will be departing shortly. He's to make room in our holds for King Marcus' levies as well as our legionaries. Gyal has agreed to fly the Army of the Boles up to the northern border.'

'There isn't much of a rebel force left in the field to surprise by such leapfrogging,' said Paetro.

'All for the good, then. But I trust the threat of regiments moving along the border will not be lost on these quarrelsome mountain tribes,' said Helrena.

More like poking a mountain lion with a stick. Duncan watched Paetro exit the room on his way to their massive Vandian vessel of war squatting outside the city. 'I wish it didn't have to be this way.'

'Our feelings are of little importance. If the family is to continue, if the house is to survive, I must be empress. A union with Prince Gyal is the most unwelcome price I must pay? Then perhaps I should count myself blessed?'

'And what would a worse price look like?'

'A blood price, of course. The lives of millions of loyal citizens under our house's protection back in the Imperium. Cassandra's, yours, Paetro's, Doctor Horvak's. Blood is always the currency you wager with inside Vandia. I still need your loyalty, Duncan. There are a hundred ways for us to fail and fall. Weyland was your homeland once. I need you to help me navigate these shoals.'

'And after we rescue Cassandra?'

'Then we shall return home and we shall see.'

'I am not sure I even know what victory would look like anymore.'

'Gyal intends to use the diamond throne to expand the empire and keep it growing for all eternity – or at least, as long as his reign may last. I have other plans. I would use the throne to change Vandia for the better. Perhaps the world too.'

Duncan thought of the dangerous head of the Imperium's secret police, Apolleon, and Doctor Yair Horvak labouring away for the house, and the oddly matched pair's strange, mysterious schemes. 'You're keeping curious bedfellows to achieve your aims.'

'You know I would keep you to warm my sheets. But if Gyal discovered it . . .'

Duncan understood. Helrena openly flaunting a lover would be seen as a weakness on the part of Prince Gyal. And all such weaknesses had to be ruthlessly destroyed, if not by the prince, by his many allies. 'You're protecting my back.'

'As you still protect mine. Sharp eyes, Duncan. Daggers often multiply within victory's shadow.'

Duncan gazed around the chamber. Prince Gyal. Baron Machus.

Adella Cheyenne. His grasping dunderhead of a father. *Yes, and with allies like these . . .*

Leyla waited for Prince Gyal to finish with the baron before she slipped to his side, carrying him a glass of sweet white wine from one of the tables at the room's side.

'I understand that you have developed a taste for ice wine, Your Highness.'

'Blood-red has always been the fashion inside Vandia, Lady Landor,' said Prince Gyal.

'You have good tastes. Ice wine is one of the few good things to come out of the north these days.'

'Not the only good thing, surely? Your house is one of the northern loyalists taking a stand against these rebels.'

'I came out of the south before I married into the north,' said Leyla.

'Well, we shall travel back to your home together,' said Gyal. 'And make an end of both our nation's troubles.'

'Will you present my own home back to me as a gift, Your Highness?'

'King Marcus enjoys the Imperium's trade and favour. At the far end of the caravan routes, that must be considered the most rare and valuable of our gifts.'

'The king is well aware of his fine fortune when it comes to his allies,' said Leyla.

'It is a rare thing to understand what is on a king's mind,' said Gyal. 'I had heard that you were well acquainted with court life in the capital, once. A player in Arcadia's theatres?'

'More of a singer,' said Leyla. 'I am sure that our stages are very humble compared to the theatres in Vandia.'

'The Imperium also prefers its entertainments blood-red. Nothing entertains the mob so much as seeing high-caste nobles murdering each other in duels.'

'How shocking,' said Leyla. *And how exciting. I can think of many Weylanders at court who would benefit from gutting each other with sabres.* 'And you allow that?'

'Allow it? We encourage it. The only thing more dangerous than opposing Vandia is to hold it,' said Gyal. 'Those who fall to their opponents' blades keep the bloodlines pure and strong. And the empire must always stay strong to repel its enemies. To possess so much wealth is to suffer the envy of the world.'

'And is your emperor allowed to be challenged to arms?'

'A challenge must be between equals. An emperor has none.'

'And an empress?' said Leyla, innocently.

'The same custom holds. However, some of the best duels in the arena are between celestial caste women. The head of a house in the Imperium must rule through force and resilience, irrespective of gender. It is my observation that women rarely fall short of the challenge.'

'Most refreshing,' said Leyla. 'In Weyland few object to a woman thinking for herself, but only so long as she is thinking of a man. I do so admire equality of manners. That explains it . . .'

'Explains what?' asked the Vandian.

'Why Princess Helrena appears so radiantly satisfied. She always keeps a few particular favourites to keep her attentions engaged.'

'*Particular* favourites?'

'Surely you must have noticed how Helrena's face lights up when my husband's son Duncan is around? He serves her *very* diligently, but then, I would expect nothing less of him. I understand that in Vandia your rulers are expected to keep a harem? Hundreds of partners to enliven the high-borns' existence. I suppose it must be considered bad form to have favourites when you reach such an exalted position?'

'Diversion was never the purpose of the harem,' said Gyal, his expression turning dark. 'It is maintained so the imperial bloodline can fill the houses of the empire with strong leaders. It gives the powerful a fair chance at claiming the Diamond Throne when next it sits vacant. A carrot to dangle in front of our allies . . . the opportunity for foreign daughters to become part of Vandia. It is the reason why so few empresses ascend the throne alone. A single woman is limited to a single womb. An emperor can gift the Imperium with thousands of vigorous rulers.'

'Oh dear,' said Leyla. 'So in the end it's all about duty and obligation? King Marcus seemed much taken with the idea when last we talked. I suspect he will be rather disappointed when he discovers your splendid institution is more about the lineage of the realm and less about amusement.' *Not that it'll put the rutting goat off. And nor should it. Not when Marcus has promised me the job of selecting the noblewomen to fill it. What kind of entertainments would I turn to if I didn't have the powerful and high-born simpering and kissing my feet for a chance at making their silly bitches the mother of the next monarch?*

Gyal stared icily towards Princess Helrena and Duncan. 'Disappointment is part of life. It comes to us all.'

Leyla took a glass of ice wine from a passing servant and pressed it into the Vandian prince's hand. *And what a pity when it comes visiting Duncan Landor. That will only leave a fugitive rebel girl wanted for murder and one stupid old man standing between me and the House of Landor's wealth.* Leyla smiled happily. 'Let us trust that a few good things may enter our lives, Your Highness.'

There were many days, Carter Carnehan mused, when he'd sell what little he possessed for the chance of solitary confinement. The rebel skyguard pilot he shared a cell with seemed to have two moods. Sardonic, or icily condescending and distant. Sometimes she even combined them together to make a third mood. He wasn't sure what to call this third state, although Carter had been given plenty of time to consider the matter. Beula Fetterman had escaped from a prisoner-of-war camp down south to end up in Midsburg, flying missions for Prince Owen against the usurper's forces. *I bet when it came time to draw lots to see who was to escape, the soldiers in the camp fixed it so her name came out first. Just to be shot of her.* Sadly, the hard stone walls which separated Carter and Beula's cell from the rest of the Rodalian capital were thick enough that her manners hadn't yet irritated the guards enough for them to transfer her over to someone else's care. *The day will come, though. The day will surely come.* It might have come faster if the guards assigned to imprison them had been able to speak trade tongue rather than the local mountain dialect. But the authorities clearly didn't want unauthorized communications passing between captors and prisoners.

'Another day in paradise,' said Beula. She idly tossed pebbles that had come in with the guards' boots into an empty wooden rice bowl at the foot of her bunk. When she was out of ammunition, she emptied the bowl and started again. The irritating thud-thud-thud of the pebbles landing was just the smallest part of her charms.

'We're lucky to have made it to the prison in one piece,' said Carter.

'You keep on saying that.'

'Only because it's true.'

It had taken the hurried appearance of Nima Tash, the daughter of the murdered Speaker of Rodal, to calm the patriotic crowd down enough for Carter and his quarrelsome pilot to escape being lynched. Before Nima had come into sight, the mob which greeted Carter's landed plane hadn't seemed particularly willing to understand that there were two sides fighting in Weyland's civil war, and he hailed from the faction that *hadn't* executed the Rodalian political leader in a fit of pique. While Carter might have been spared being torn apart, he had traded his liberty for internment. *With her.* They were well treated enough. A mattress apiece in their dry if windowless cell. Warm food and enough of it not to go hungry. Even a separate privy in a side-chamber off the cell. What Carter didn't have was any news of how matters were progressing beyond the border, and that was torture enough.

'I wonder if Midsburg is still under siege?' said Carter.

'Of course it isn't,' said Beula. 'King Marcus and his armies reached the city and declared a national holiday, pardoning every rebel soldier north of the Spotswood line who ever supported parliament in raising arms against him. He's real generous like that.'

Carter still lived in hope that Sheplar Lesh would turn up outside their cell one night. The Rodalian aviator clutching a copied set of keys to release Carter, giving him the good news that Lady Cassandra was locked securely away inside Hadra-Hareer, their old gask friend Kerge watching the hostage like a hawk. Now that the empire had entered the civil war on the usurper Marcus' side, Prince Owen required the imperial brat for whatever leverage she was good for to regain his rightful throne. *I need to find the girl. To get my father back. To bargain for Willow's freedom.*

'Sheplar must have heard we're locked up here,' said Carter. 'Hell, half the city came down to throw rocks at our aircraft.'

'They weren't aiming at my kite,' said Beula. 'They were aiming at *us.* And your so-called Rodalian friend's showing more good sense than we ever did. Flying unannounced into the mountain kingdom like a pair of trusting rubes.'

'I might have done things differently if I had known the country had closed its border. But strangely, King Marcus and his Vandian butchers didn't see fit to consult me before they stretched the Rodalian First Speaker's neck. I'll be sure and have words with the usurper next time I'm at his court.'

'Do that. And while you're there, get a pardon for us and a steak sent up from the palace kitchens.'

'Bloody and raw.'

'And while you're at it, give me a damn night's peace. You were yelling again last night.'

Was I? All of Carter's dreams in Rodal seemed to be bad ones. His mother dying in the slavers' raid on Northhaven. The dead faces of all the friends he had left behind in the sky mines, bones in a volcano-blackened landscape full of them. More corpses from the rebellion at home, soldiers he had known and fought alongside. All of his nightmares suffused with the worries of what was passing unknown to him beyond these ancient walls. His father and Willow. Carter ignored the pilot and gripped the iron bars that ran from floor to ceiling at the front of the cell. The corridor outside was illuminated with the same diffuse, slightly gossamer light that infused much of the city. The bulk of Hadra-Hareer lay deep within the mountains, relatively little of the Rodalian capital exposed clinging to the canyon walls outside. If Carter lived somewhere winds tore through narrow passes to reach many hundreds of miles an hour, he supposed he would have burrowed into the safety of the rocks for his home too. Not for nothing was this area of Weyland's northern neighbour marked on maps as the Valley of the Hell-Winds. Their Rodalian captors had constructed mirror arrays in the cracks and crevices at the top of the mountain range, capturing bright sunlight and spreading it through the safely buried city. There were chimneys too, clinging to the crevices, where cold fresh air came inside at incredible velocities, slowed in granite buttresses and then dispersed across Hadra-Hareer's chambers and man-made caverns. Carter might not be able to see the daggered mountains outside, but he could hear when the winds were roaring. The corridors' air vents rasped like soft voices always just beyond understanding, hurricane forces tamed to sing their alien tale. It was little wonder Rodalians worshipped the spirits of the wind. To live in any Rodalian city was to wake up with their whispers and go to sleep listening to the same. Down in Northhaven, they said traders who visited the mountainous country sometimes went mad from the spirits' singing. *And they didn't have Miss Fetterman to contend with, either.*

'I need to see the Weyland Ambassador,' shouted Carter. 'I know there's an embassy in the capital. Give me some news, damn you. A newspaper, anything.'

There was a rattling from the end of the corridor as the door opened. A soldier Carter didn't recognize strolled in, gazing at Carter angrily through the cell bars. 'Visitors,' said the guard in trade tongue. For a moment Carter thought he had imagined understanding the word, so long was it since he had heard anything apart from Beula's snide asides.

Two more soldiers marched down the corridor and Carter wondered if he was dreaming when they stepped aside. His father, Jacob Carnehan. *Alive. Safe. Here!*

'Sweet saints, is it really you?'

'I'm no mirage,' said Jacob, thumping his legs by way of proof. 'It's damn good to see you, Carter. I've been in Hadra-Hareer a while, but on fairly thin sufferance it has to be said. I wasn't allowed to send word to you that I had arrived, let alone visit you.'

'You have to get them to release me,' begged Carter, fighting down the urgency in his voice, struggling to stay coherent. 'I need to get to Midsburg. I'm on a mission for Prince Owen.'

'I know all about your mission. I'm sorry, but it's failed. Lady Cassandra's not in Rodal anymore. And the siege of Midsburg is over. The city fell within days to Bad Marcus and his Vandian friends. It was like a wall of sand trying to stand against the tide. Most anyone who got out alive is in Hadra-Hareer right now.'

Carter rocked with the terrible news. 'Then the war's over? We lost?'

'I didn't say that. Prince Owen is alive and here inside the city. The National Assembly's army is dispersed across the north of Weyland

and fighting the usurper's forces. Not in formal regimental actions, but ragged hit and run raids. Burning southern supply columns, blowing bridges and slitting royalist throats at night, then withdrawing into the forests and hills before the usurper's skyguard show up to pound our boys.'

'Oh, that's good news,' announced Beula lounging from her bunk. 'So the north doesn't have an army anymore? It has a band of bandits. As if we didn't see enough of them before the rebellion started.'

Jacob stared coldly at the woman. 'This is your pilot?'

'A pilot needs a kite to be called that, old man. Right now, I'm just Prisoner Number Two on this cursed mission.'

'I wouldn't pay much attention to Flight Captain Fetterman,' said Carter. 'She's still a little miffed that our greeting in Rodal was nearly being stoned to death.'

'Our welcome wasn't much friendlier,' said Jacob. 'Rodalian politics got a lot more fractious when the Vandians decided to use Palden Tash's neck as an example of what happens when you sass the Imperium in public. His murder had the desired effect. No nation in the Lancean League wants anything to do with the rebellion, except maybe Rodal. Half the Rodalians wants to avenge the insult to their nation's honour. The other half wants to leave Weyland's civil war well alone; allow us to murder each other until we run out of bullets.'

'Maybe they should, at that,' said Carter. 'I thought you were dead or at best rotting in chains inside the usurper's dungeon.'

'I got a taste of Bad Marcus' hospitality, but our friend Sariel had other ideas,' said Jacob. 'He sprung me out. Not that his help doesn't come with a price, but I'll tell you about that later.'

That sounds ominous. 'You're going to get me out of here?'

'Us,' said Beula, pointedly.

'I'm working on it.'

'Damn, but it'll be good to see Sheplar, Kerge and Tom again.'

'They never reached the capital,' said Jacob. 'Lady Cassandra was seized in a nomad raid and carried away into the plains. Sheplar and Kerge went after her. Nothing's been heard of them since.'

Carter winced. *Lady Cassandra and her house sweated me and mine as slaves inside the empire's sky mines. Maybe her ending up keeping a bunch of savages' goats fed and watered is just the world's way of levelling the score.*

Damned if I'd wish such a fate on Kerge and Sheplar, though. 'Well, those two survived the worst of Vandia. What's a few barbarian horsemen compared to taking on the Imperium? Did Tom make it out of the siege?'

'He came down with a bad case of working for the usurper,' said Jacob. 'He didn't recover from it, I'm happy to say.'

Carter couldn't keep the shock from his face. 'Tom betrayed us?'

'He was never with us . . . one of the king's intelligencers all the time. He arrived at Northhaven with the usurper's orders to rescue Lady Cassandra. Tom Purdell was the reason Bad Marcus knew what the rebellion was doing every step of the way. Purdell tried to assassinate Prince Owen. Missed by an inch, although he murdered Assemblyman Gimlette in the attempt and left Anna Kurtain badly wounded.'

'Son of a bitch!' Carter thought of all the times he had helped his brother guildsman. The travails and troubles they had shared together. *And all that time he was really Bad Marcus' man?* The scale of the betrayal left Carter sick to the stomach.

'Purdell's dead?' said Beula. She seemed to be having as much trouble believing what she had heard as Carter.

'Flight Captain, I'd have to say he most surely is,' said Jacob. He turned to speak to the Rodalian soldiers in their mountain tongue. Carter knew his father had spent many years in a church monastery inside Rodal, and he jabbered proficiently enough in the guards' language. About the only word Carter recognized was his father frequently invoking the name of Nima Tash, the local noblewoman who had saved them from a lynching. The conversation developed into a heated argument before one of the guards set off down the corridor. Jacob pointed his hand down the passage. 'Let me introduce you to the person who was good enough to stick a bullet in Mister Purdell's treacherous heart.'

A figure pushed her way into the prison corridor, a woman who hadn't been out of Carter's thoughts for the best part of a year. 'Willow!'

'Carter!' There were tears in her eyes. 'I've been waiting so long for this. Every day being turned away outside the prison.'

How long has she been here? 'It's so good to see you alive.'

'Alive, but . . .' Willow's pulled her coat aside so that Carter could see it had been warming a pregnant belly beneath. Carter's heart sank and he tried to keep the look of surprise from his face. Of course Viscount Wallingbeck would have consummated his forced marriage to Willow as quickly as possible. The viscount wanted to get his hands on the Landor dowry as much as Benner Landor wanted a titled son-in-law; as much as his conniving new wife wanted to clear the house's succession for her own child. And nobody wanted a penniless low-born son of a pastor in the way. *Nobody except Willow.*

'Please forgive me,' said Willow.

'I'm the one who needs forgiving,' said Carter. He reached through the bars and clasped her hands in his. Every bit as warm and soft as he remembered. 'I should have been there protecting you. I travelled all the way down to Arcadia to prevent you from marrying that southern bastard, but when the war broke out, I was swept north; Bad Marcus' armies hunting after us like a cat after a rodent.'

'I never married Wallingbeck, at least not legally,' said Willow. 'My infernal family drugged me until I could barely stand, then presented me with a marriage certificate from a bribed priest with a forged scrawl on it instead of my signature.'

'Parliament might be in exile, but our assemblymen have declared Owen the lawful monarch,' said Jacob. 'He's annulled the whole shambles.'

'But he can't annul this,' said Willow, sadly rubbing her pregnant belly. 'The viscount forced himself on me. I wouldn't have—'

'You never have to explain anything to me, Willow.' said Carter. 'Not for this, not for anything. I failed you as completely as a man can. I meant to rescue you, but here you are, saving me from imprisonment in a Rodalian prison instead.'

'The lady's getting mighty practised in it,' said Jacob. 'If it wasn't for Willow's steady aim, I'd have a meat cleaver through my skull courtesy of Tom Purdell and his gang of traitors.'

'That animal Purdell deserves to burn in hell,' said Willow. 'Along with my family for forcing me into the viscount's hateful hands. And may Leyla Holten be waiting at the bottom of the gallows steps to receive her punishment first.'

Willow spat the words with a vehemence quite unlike her. *What's surviving this bloody war done to her?* 'You're free,' said Carter. 'Back with me. That's all that matters now. Just get me out of here and I swear I'll never let you down again.'

'We're pushing to get you released,' said Willow. 'There's to be an election for a new First Speaker. There is a pro-war faction and an isolationist faction at each other's throats over the future of Rodal. Nima Tash wants revenge for her father's murder and is on Prince Owen's side. She's our best chance of getting you out of here. Her family's enemies are opposing your release just to tweak her nose.'

'Miss Tash arranged for Prince Owen's official asylum here. But the isolationist faction is led by a politician called Temba Lesh,' said Jacob. 'He'll cut you loose all right. Cut us all free and prod us across the border at the end of a bayonet, straight into the hands of Bad Marcus' army.'

The guards started to jabber in Rodalian, while Willow and Carter's father were pushed back down the corridor, Willow trying to reach back to Carter's outstretched palms.

'I'll see you free of this place,' called Jacob Carnehan. 'Just wait.'

Waiting is all I can do here. 'I know you will.'

'I love you, Carter,' shouted Willow.

'I—' but Willow had been led out of sight. *And I love you.* He clung on to the memory of her face, her red hair, her pretty earnest eyes. *Willow's escaped from our enemies. That's all that matters. The war and the rebellion can rage on, but as long as I have her, I have my own peace.*

Beula snorted when she heard the heavy wooden door swing shut down the corridor; silence except for her barbs. 'I always wanted to be a pawn in a contested election. So much more entertaining than flying.'

'My father will keep his word.' *One way or another.* Carter hoped that Nima Tash and her allies prevailed, because otherwise their Rodalian captors would find out exactly what his father was capable of. Jacob Carnehan had crossed a world and faced down the Imperium to free his son. What he had become scared Carter because there was very little left of the man who had been his father an age ago.

'So that's the great Jacob Carnehan. Or should I say the outlaw *Jake Silver*? Still alive after all this time. Is it true what the southern papers say about him?'

'I try not to read their lies.'

'That he's a wanted killer who escaped across the sea to the Burn. Led mercenary armies over there and killed more souls than the plague.'

'We're all outlaws now, as far as the usurper is concerned.'

'Ain't that the truth. But some of us a little more so than others. Is your pa's brother really that murdering pirate, Black Barnaby?'

'All I can say is that he never came to dinner at Northhaven.'

'That's having a black sheep in your family, all right. Well, this is surely what I would call a turn up for the books,' said Beula. She seemed determined to spoil Carter's joy at seeing Willow again. 'You fly all the way out here for the enemy emperor's granddaughter, and you end up letting her slip through your fingers. Instead, you discover your own girl complete with another man's bun warming her oven.'

'If that's your maternal instincts coming out, you can keep them.'

'Oh, I chose flying with the skyguard over a family. If you want my advice, you should ditch the rich girl and let her raise her brat on the viscount's tab. Head out for a country without a dog in this fight. Hellin has got more than enough bogs for a wanted man to hide in until the rebellion's long forgotten back home.'

'That's your advice?' *You should take it yourself. A swamp would suit your nature.* 'You're hardly much of a judge of character,' said Carter. 'You broke out of a prisoner-of-war camp with Thomas Purdell.'

'Yes, your *good* friend. And I also escaped with Assemblyman Gimlette,' said Beula. 'Who, from what your father said, helped prevent Prince Owen from being assassinated.'

'I wouldn't hold your breath for a medal when we get out of here.'

Fetterman laughed. 'What the hell would it be worth anyway? The war is over, Northhaven. Midsburg's fallen. The hostage we were sent to bring back from here is now a saddle serf with a horde of blue-skinned barbarians. King Marcus holds the nation under his little thumb and we're bottled up in exile with a country full of rice-eating mountain goats who might yet decide to hand us back to hang in Weyland if the wind blows the wrong way. And there's a *lot* of wind in Rodal.'

And a lot of it in this cell, too. Willow was free and safe and would

38

soon be by his side again. If that was as good as it got, Carter would live with it and offer up a prayer of thanks every morning. *Luckiest damn man in the nation*. It's just that this foreign bolt-hole wasn't his country. And by the sound of it, neither was Weyland.

TWO

SHADOWS IN THE DARK

Leyla Landor gazed up at the dark sky, full of glittering stars as cold as the night air. She had just left the hotel with Duncan stretched out sleeping between the silk sheets. It was hard work keeping your options open. If Benner was by chance hit by a cannon ball in the dying days of the rebellion, then Leyla might be required to convince his dolt of a son to marry her far faster than the propriety of a widow's weeds might demand. *Yes, all in all, hard work. And what is the rest of this night's business but keeping my options open. Or perhaps, choking them off?* Leyla stood waiting in Midsburg's business district, three-storey office buildings with dark windows unlit by lantern or candle, a district that would stand emptied of clerks at this time of night, even if its workers weren't languishing in chains somewhere awaiting their just punishment for failing at the game of rebellion.

A shadow emerged from a dark passage between a warehouse and a shipping agent. Nocks' reedy voice sounded as irritatingly dissatisfied as always. 'You could have picked somewhere outside the city walls, eh. What's left of them standing at any rate.'

Light from a public oil lamp fell on the squat man's face. The scar split the hard, mean features like a river, but Leyla never had a problem looking him straight in his glinting rodent eyes. Nocks was a murderous, uncouth killer, but he was very much her creature. Not out of love or even his fumbling lust which she occasionally satisfied, but out of grim necessity. King Marcus had passed the care of this mongrel wolf to Leyla, and Nocks complemented her own skills well enough. A little brawn to flex alongside her cunning and wiles.

'Nobody's looking for you very hard,' said Leyla. 'I've seen to that.'

'So, you're still the king's eyes in the north. But what about me?'

'King Marcus is travelling up here to stamp his authority on the retaken prefectures,' said Leyla. 'And I can tell you that he is less than happy at the ease with which Jacob Carnehan and the pretender Owen Hawkins managed to escape the siege and flee north.'

'You can't hang that failure on me,' said Nocks.

'Oh, I am well aware,' said Leyla. The cold corpse of the king's assassin, Thomas Purdell, discovered in Midsburg among his dead agents spoke volumes of how that particular debacle had ended. 'But you are still to hang if the law catches up with you. For trying to murder my darling husband's son.'

'On your orders, you sly bitch.'

Leyla slapped him hard, but the squat brute hardly moved. It was like striking granite. 'You answer to me, Nocks. The very day you forget it, you will find the court gallows waiting for you.'

'Then maybe I'll sing a little song of my own before I stretch, eh?'

Leyla stroked his face, a touch of silk to remind him how harsh the leather could bite by comparison. 'You're a cold-blooded butcher, Nocks. But you're not an unintelligent one. The realm isn't large enough now to escape from King Marcus should you turn against him.'

'You'd know all about that.'

'I am more than the king's mistress now.' *And I will be more yet, through careful planning and application.* 'But not if you continue to fail me.'

'Duncan Landor got lucky. I was about to put a bullet in the boy's back when his friend Paetro turned up and stopped me.'

'Yes, that idiot Captain Purdell couldn't even slit the Vandian's throat successfully. Although I understand Paetro's body now carries more scars than skin. Purdell's fondness for torturing his victims rather than a quick, efficient finish always was the man's weakness.'

'A good scar reminds you to be more careful next time,' said Nocks, rubbing the split in his face.

Yes, you're a living advertisement of that. She knew he blamed the rebel pastor Jacob Carnehan for his wounds . . . a loathing as deep and passionate as any man felt.

'Scars aside,' growled Nocks, 'I'd still rather have the imperial bastard Paetro planted rotting under the dirt.'

'I have turned your failure into what success I could,' said Leyla. 'Paetro returned with news of Willow Landor's betrayal of him – helping that infernal outlaw pastor escape; how easily Willow broke her oath and betrayed the royalists to join the rebels. It was a simple enough thing to convince Duncan that your attempted murder of him was just another part of his wayward sister's schemes.'

'Well bugger the lot of them. I need a royal pardon,' said Nocks. 'I had to flee Weyland once before, one step ahead of the executioners. I'm too old to sign up across the sea in the Burn as a mercenary.'

'And a pardon you shall have, my loyal little beast. Just as soon as you've redeemed yourself.'

'You still need me to slip a dagger in that prig Duncan Landor's back? I'd be glad of the job, but he knows me well enough to never let me close again.'

'Duncan's demise is already arranged,' smiled Leyla. 'The commander of the Imperium's expeditionary force, Prince Gyal, has been made aware that Duncan is cuckolding his empress-to-be. While the rebellion is crushed, I expect Duncan to be assigned some very dangerous missions in the thick of the fighting. Just as many as it takes to give him a hero's funeral.'

'So what do you need me to do? Stand over the rich boy's grave and clap as his coffin's lowered into it?'

'The House of Landor has *two* heirs who stand to succeed before my son. I removed one of them by turning Willow Landor into Lady Willow Wallingbeck. But when the viscount divorces Willow for fleeing the marriage nest I kindly prepared for them, the silly girl will become an heir to the Landor fortune again.'

'You want Willow dead?'

'I want her *destroyed* for her treachery. She's hiding in exile with her rebel friends. Bring her back to me. Willow must give birth in her husband's estate. I owe Viscount Wallingbeck the squalling brat of an heir I promised him. After that, the gallows for high treason will be a fitting fate.'

'Willow's in Northhaven?'

'Not anymore. Rodal. The rebel leadership has taken refuge inside the Rodalian capital,' said Leyla. 'The borderland is full of rebels and refugees fleeing the advancing southern armies. Remove a rebel uniform from a corpse and you'll be able to pass over to the other side in the confusion easily enough.'

'Well, you are Willow's step-mother,' laughed Nocks. 'Dare say you know best.'

I do try hard to arrange a convenient end to matters. Leyla noticed the deadly look in her odious little manservant's eyes. *Hatred, not lust.* 'I need the scandal of Willow's betrayal erased. Settling scores with Jacob Carnehan and the pastor's son can be attempted in your own time. Although I suspect King Marcus and his imperial allies will finish the job long before you get around to it.'

'Those two are an itch that needs scratching,' growled Nocks.

'If it helps, think of the agony Carter Carnehan will endure after you abduct his lady-love and return her for chastisement. And if Carter pursues his unsuitably high-born woman south, then no doubt Father Carnehan will follow his son as he did before. Wouldn't you prefer the chance to finish your business with the Carnehans personally, rather than hearing second hand of how they died on the sharp end of a royalist bayonet?'

Nocks nodded and Leyla knew she had her little beast back on the leash again. She reached behind his neck and scratched the back of his hairy, thick neck. *Yes, I always know best.* 'Isn't that better?'

Duncan hadn't visited the town he had been born in for years. The young Weylander had imagined a variety of greetings upon his return to Northhaven, and every one of them had all been happier than this. He fought desperately to hold on to the reins of his horse as it panicked, rearing wildly into the air with a hail of burning timber coming down around him. A fireball expanded out from where the bridge across the White Wolf River had been up until a few seconds ago, the horsemen crossing it incinerated along with their gun carriages. Duncan barely had time to take in infantry columns staggering away from the inferno, blue uniforms shredded or ablaze, before a volley of fire opened up on the road from the woodland to their left. *That would have been me if I had been at the head of the column.*

'Take cover!' yelled Duncan. He didn't wait to see if the high and mighty officers of the Army of the Boles were heeding his advice. Duncan's battle-trained mare recovered its nerves, and he spurred her towards the cover of a drainage ditch and low stone wall running along the wheat fields on his right. He pulled her down behind the stones and a granite marker indicating the town of Northhaven waited a mile away. It was topped with the arms of the House of Landor. The irony of its presence was reinforced when 'Colonel' Benner Landor came sprinting towards Duncan, just ahead of a hail of bullets, his father's steed left fallen across the Northern Trading Road. *Look, Father . . . we can die on our own land.*

'Bandits!' Benner Landor yelled towards the trees. 'Filth! You'll hang for this. I'll see every one of you swinging from a tree!'

Duncan pulled his pistol out from its holster and fired blindly into the tree-line. Branches wavered in the volley of counter-fire, but it might just have been the chill wind making the leaves sway. 'I don't think they know who you are.'

'On my own acres,' growled his father, as though the shame of being ambushed here was worse for the powerful Benner Landor than any of the wounded soldiers lurching away from the river's fast-flowing rapids.

All the way down the road their regiment took cover where it could, returning fire into the woodland. Behind walls. In ditches. Lying flat in wheat fields. Their ambushers could be inside the trees or the thick bush below or they might have already retreated, vanishing into the wilds like malicious tree sprites. Duncan was glad that Paetro and Helrena had stayed with the Vandian fleet, the Imperium's great ships landed in river flats to the east. Legionaries were felling trees for miles around, constructing fortified landing fields, camps and barracks for their forces. *Nobody from the Imperium to witness my countrymen's incompetence.* This was still an army of hastily-formed amateurs. Bullets cut down fleeing southern soldiers trying to gain the field wall. *Nope, our bushwhacking friends haven't pulled back yet.*

An officer came crawling towards them, using the cover of the wall, pieces of flint flying from the stone above his wide-brimmed hat.

Hugh Colbert was Northhaven's prefect. He'd worn the additional title of General of the Army of the Bole easily when it seemed like advancement under the king's patronage. Less easy now, though, with the politician crawling behind a field wall crumbling under heavy fire. Mud from the soggy ditch concealed the three gold-embroidered stars and wreath on the high collar of his blue double-breasted coat, but it couldn't hide his temper.

'I was told our path into Northhaven had been scouted and declared clear of marauders,' barked Colbert.

'It was,' said Benner Landor. 'The skyguard flew over this road only two hours ago.'

'And the pretender's supporters move at night,' said Duncan, fighting to keep the exasperation from his voice. 'Rarely in numbers large enough to count from the air.'

'Move our cannons behind the wall!' yelled Benner Landor down the road. 'Load for grapeshot.'

Duncan's father appeared content to benefit from shelter denied his artillery-men. Out on the road soldiers struggled to hold the horses steady as nearly invisible snipers aimed shots at gunners and the trains of horses bearing each artillery piece. The royalist army's heavy pieces had been crossing the bridge, leaving the survivors with relatively light gallopers and six pounders. *Small mercies. We stand a chance of getting them behind cover.* Bullets whizzed like angry hornets through the air. They were starting to be lost in gun smoke coming from the southerners, rifles loaded with shot after shot and emptied into the woods. Ammunition carriages were dragged off the road and unceremoniously dumped around the artillery, left halted in the mud as wagoneers forced their horses to lie down. Some soldiers loaded their cannons even as the artillery pieces were manhandled back behind the flint wall, charges and ammunition canisters rammed into place, and then the cannons bucked, discharging deadly clouds of grapeshot into the woods. Birds erupted for the sky as tree trunks splintered, their calls lost beneath the explosions. Duncan's ears rang from the detonations. The nearest cannon was less than twenty feet away, rocking in the mud ditch, thick waves of dark, acrid powder smoke pouring out of its dark iron barrel and enveloping Duncan's position. Its crew didn't bother cooling the barrel with water; they rammed another load into place, trimmed the fuse and set the six-pounder off again.

With the noise of the artillery fire, Duncan only noticed the cavalry company cantering behind the artillery when it was nearly on top of him, its riders and mounts seemingly unconcerned by the cannons' thunder. He groaned as he noted the officer at the fore was Viscount Wallingbeck.

'Hold your fire!' called Colbert, his command shouted on and passed down the wall.

'Chased down many a fox through woods far thicker than this,' Duncan's brother-in-law hooted. 'And rebel vermin don't dig warrens to escape into.' Viscount Wallingbeck spurred his horse forward, hurdling the wall and galloping towards the dark pines, yelling as his carbine tore bark off the trees. The nobleman was followed eagerly by his company, shredding their way through the undergrowth with heavy steel cavalry sabres and from the sound of it, riding down anything they encountered below their mounts' hooves.

'Forward the cavalry!' came the infantry's cries from behind the wall. *General Colbert's infantrymen rediscover their spirit quick enough when someone else shows up to do the dying for them.*

'Noble blood,' said Benner, approvingly. 'Quality of birth shows through every time.'

Pity it didn't rub off on the viscount's wife. It wasn't beyond the bounds of possibility that Willow Landor was one of the rebels just aiming pot-shots at them from the woods.

'A solid fellow,' said Colbert. 'A yard of sharp steel is a fitting last meal for those traitors.'

Duncan suspected the majority of their ambushers possessed the good sense to pull back when they noticed cannons being loaded with grapeshot. Those left firing were only holding fast to slow the pursuit; but the rebels hadn't counted on the reckless abandon of a brute like Viscount Wallingbeck riding with them. Colbert didn't order the infantry in after them. Once the cavalrymen had the bit between their teeth, anyone around them was likely to be ridden into the mud and sliced at, friend and foe alike. A strange silence fell down the length of the road. Their column left as spectators. The creaking of cooling cannon barrels, shots and yells muffled by the undergrowth. Sentries were picketed just inside the trees to ensure their ambushers didn't try to circle back. Wisely, in Duncan's opinion, the artillery was left behind the wall in case they were needed to clear for action again. The road was emptied of corpses and dropped supplies, wounded soldiers attended to, horses calmed and wagons put back into some sense of order. Wallingbeck and his men emerged from the dark shade of the trees ten minutes later, a disarmed sergeant in a rebel uniform stumbling before them. A boot against his back from one of the riders sent the prisoner into the arms of the infantry.

'This is all we have to show for the fight?' demanded General Colbert. 'A single damnable outlaw?'

'There're more bodies dead back there,' said William Wallingbeck. 'Not enough to account for the fire the column took, I'd say. With your permission, we'll ride around to the eastern edge of the woods and see if we can flush out any of the pretender's grouse that attempt to fly that way.'

Colbert nodded and the horsemen rode off whooping, waving their sabres in the air.

'I know you, man,' said Benner. 'You work for the Avisons as an estate manager.'

'Not anymore,' spat the captured soldier. 'Now I work as a pig slaughterer. Southern pigs and the traitors who support them.'

Duncan's father might be an amateur officer, but he had a memory like a steel trap when it came to the business of the house. Particularly as it related to people who worked for commercial rivals inside the prefecture.

'Not one of mine,' said Benner, taking whatever consolation he could from the fact.

'Long live the assembly of the people and the people's king. May maggots feast on the usurper's bony arse.'

'You stand condemned as a rebel by your own detestable words,' said Colbert. 'Hang him.'

'I wear a uniform. I'm a soldier. I demand the common conventions and protection of the Lanca.'

'You are nothing but a bandit in grey rags, sir. The outlaw pretender you serve has fled the nation and you shall suffer the same sentence as Owen when we capture him.'

'Hang him in front of the town,' said Benner. 'Raise him like a standard on the flagpole for everyone in Northhaven to see the cost of rebellion against the king.'

'A capital suggestion,' said Colbert. 'And he won't be the last example that needs setting. By the saints, Benner, if you had not rebuilt this city after the slavers' raid, I would burn a street for every soldier lying dead on the road here today.'

Duncan's father looked pale enough to faint. 'I am grateful for your forbearance, Hugh. I still have loans on the majority of the properties. The cost of building a new cathedral was enough to bankrupt a lesser house than mine.'

'Well then, we shall have to make sure it's the rebels who pay for the cost of meeting their treachery,' said General Colbert. 'We'll root them out; confiscate land and title deeds from every traitor who put the king's treasury to such cost.' He looked meaningfully at Benner. 'Such reparations are King Marcus' due. And the king's allies in the north.'

'Our due,' agreed Benner.

'And how will the rebels pay?' asked Duncan. 'When you throw the defeated off their land and cast them out of their stores and premises?'

'With their labour, of course,' said Colbert. 'The new mills in the south are hungry for indentured labour. And the estates up here will be far more profitable without greedy field-hands constantly grasping and griping in the cause of unreasonable wages, threatening to down tools at every opportunity.'

Benner nodded. 'It is good to see our Prefect still remembers the problems of the region.'

'When an ungrateful hound bites the hand that feeds it, you kick it quite thoroughly and place the dog on a shorter leash,' said the general. 'We have been over-kind for too many years, and our forbearance has been interpreted as weakness by the rebels.'

Duncan watched the struggling Avison man held by two soldiers as a noose was fitted around his neck by a third trooper. He suspected the nobles' so-called kindness wasn't a mistake that would ever be repeated. Not as far as Northhaven and its people were concerned. *This isn't your business. Northhaven is no longer your home. Forget that and you'll end up back here shuffling trade papers for old man Landor like a glorified clerk until you're old enough to need a walking stick. Vandia is where everything that matters to you belongs now.*

Colbert mounted his horse, drawing his sabre to point it down the river. 'March east to Little Bridge and ford the river there. Check for powder charges *first*. When you've crossed, secure the airfield so we can start landing our skyguard.'

Crossing Northhaven's town limits was a surreal experience for Duncan. The last time he had seen his home was through the grubby glass porthole of a slave carrier, circling the burning town from a few thousand feet, jostling with his fellow prisoners in a crowded slave hold for what they all thought would be their last ever glimpse of home. *I suppose for many of them, it was.* But not for Duncan. He had risen to become an imperial citizen. Past all the fools and doubters who had only seen a spoilt, pampered, useless and largely ornamental heir to the House of Landor. Past all the jealous townspeople who had considered Duncan's capture as a slave his just deserts for lording it over the rest of them for so long. From what he had seen of his devastated town, left burning by the slavers' incendiary bombs, Benner Landor had done a grand job of rebuilding Northhaven when Duncan was far-called inside Vandia. The old, narrow, wooden streets that once sprawled up the hill towards the ancient fortified citadel of the old town, had been rebuilt as wide open boulevards flanked by four-storey stores, apartments and businesses, backed up by suburbs which sprawled across twice the area they had replaced. There was even a full-sized stone cathedral risen on the outskirts of the town. *No wonder my father was so worried about all of this being damaged in a siege.* Part of Duncan couldn't help but resent Northhaven. Benner Landor's duty to house and staff, the best excuse his father had to avoid joining the rescue expedition which had ventured after the slavers. *Leaving me and Willow to rot wherever we ended up. Replacing our mother with Leyla and his son with a fresh new heir. It would serve him right if he saw the fruit of his crippling loans go up in flames and smoke again.* Jacob Carnehan had risked his life to save his son Carter, Willow and every other Weylander left alive in the sky mines. *And he was just a common pastor who turned out to be a murdering bandit hiding out from the law.* Would Benner Landor have survived the hard, long, dangerous journey from

Weyland to Vandia? Unlikely. Even Jacob Carnehan had arrived at the far end driven half-mad from the voyage, stripped down to the true, ragged core of the killer he had once been. But then, by rights, everyone in the expedition should have died. Because that was what family did for family. *They put their necks on the line for those they love.* Duncan snorted to himself. *But not me. I've got a treacherous sister who wants to stick a knife in my back and a father who'd sooner shuffle trade papers in the warmth of his mansion than try to save his own children.*

Duncan glanced back towards the landau. The open carriage rattled up the hillside avenue drawn by a pair of white mares. His father putting Leyla Landor on display was an all-too-obvious way of flaunting the fact Northhaven's richest family had returned to take charge; the hard-faced blue-uniformed soldiers lining the streets the guarantee of the king's imposed peace. Sitting in the facing seat of the open carriage, Adella Cheyenne appeared happier about returning to Northhaven than his father's new wife. *There's an irony for you.* When Adella had been a common town clerk's daughter with an eye on snaring Duncan as her future husband, Benner Landor couldn't do enough to keep the young woman out of the way of his son. Now that Adella was one of the favoured courtesans of a powerful Vandian nobleman, she was permitted to ride alongside Leyla Landor. The sight of captured rebel bodies swinging from lampposts didn't seem to be enough to rub the sheen off Adella's return, at least, not in her eyes – affecting all the pomp and majesty of a queen returning to her kingdom. William Wallingbeck had done a thorough job of sweeping the town with his cavalry. Duncan's brother-in-law had handily discovered enough traitors to decorate the streets all the way up the hill to the gatehouse of the walled old town. *I wonder how many of them were actually rebel supporters, and how many the result of old grudges and family feuds being settled?* It seemed unlikely to Duncan that those actually involved in the rebellion would have hung around to see how forgiving King Marcus' forces would prove to be. There was a lack of males of fighting age along the town's streets, along with an awkward predominance of surly pensioners and frightened mothers with trains of young children clinging to them. That suggested that anyone with trouble in mind and treason in their heart was hiding out in the wilds somewhere. The pinched faces and hungry expressions of the townspeople indicated a serious lack of backs labouring in the Landor fields, too.

Benner Landor glanced about the street, sitting a little too stiff and proud on his horse. Duncan's father appeared unsettled. *You've noticed how many of your tenant farmers are absent, too. No rents, no crops, and perhaps daggers in the dark creeping towards Hawkland Park. You'll need to hire a lot more sentries at the estate, Father.*

'You've done a fine job of restoring order, William,' said Benner Landor.

Wallingbeck patted his sheathed sword. 'No sand left in 'em. All their fighting spirit's fled. But that's the best you can expect when you set copse-cutters, cattlemen and shepherds against a gentleman in the saddle with a foot of sharp steel and a carbine, eh?'

'They're a disgrace to the prefecture,' said Benner. 'I would hardly credit it. I travel away to stay at the court for a season, and in my absence the whole territory is wrecked by treason.'

'It is not your fault, my darling,' called Leyla from the carriage. 'The people here were led to ruin by our traitor of an assemblyman, Charles T. Gimlette.'

Duncan held back a snigger. *And is he by chance related to the same plump fool whose votes were purchased with Landor money for decades?* From the sound of it, the politician had found himself on the wrong side of the conflict purely by dint of his party membership, ending up as one of many arrested when the king sent his guards to disband parliament. Gimlette had escaped, only to die ignobly in the siege of Midsburg. *The only thing Charles T. Gimlette led was his way to the nearest restaurant with an expensive menu. Who'd have thought being a paid lackey of the House of Landor would turn out to be such a dangerous profession?* Certainly not their ex-assemblyman.

'Where is everyone?' demanded Adella. 'There should be more people out on the streets to welcome us.'

The lack of citizens on the streets wasn't the only disquieting thing about their victory procession. It was a chilly day. Half the town's chimneys should have been giving out smoke, but they were largely standing cold and still. Either Northhaven didn't have wood chips to burn or enough people who needed to stay warm.

Leyla gave Duncan a sly look from the landau that seemed to

suggest she found the company of the baron's mistress as irritating as Duncan did.

'I think they're a little shy today,' said Duncan. 'Bayonets and rifles can be terribly off-putting. Especially to copse-cutters and shepherds.'

'They'll need to get used to it,' said Benner, failing to acknowledge his son's sarcasm. 'The Army of the Boles is to be garrisoned here until the pretender and the remaining few bandits are captured and executed.'

Peace isn't anything the Landors can buy with our money, Father. Luckily for Benner Landor, the house could rely on brutes like Viscount Wallingbeck to pay with steel. They reached the old city's main gatehouse at the top of the slope, its heavy wooden doors left open and a metal portcullis raised, the ramparts of the high stone wall patrolled by southern soldiers. An anxious committee of notables awaited them in the gate's shadow, flanked by royalist troopers, but no faces Duncan recognized. Not the old mayor or high sheriff or anyone from the town council. The most senior of the party was a weary-looking man wearing a bishop's vestments, a white circular cape and tunic and a heavy mitre on his head. *He must have come with the cathedral.* In Duncan's day, the only churchman in the town had been Pastor Carnehan. *I don't know these people and they don't know me . . . not even as Benner's son. A visiting traveller would receive more welcome on market day. I'm as good as a stranger here now.*

'Bishop Kirkup,' said Benner Landor. 'I am glad to see that you at least have survived the rebellion unharmed.'

The bishop seemed to understand well enough who had paid for the heavy stone of his cathedral and the living of the new seat. 'The saints be thanked for your arrival. You have liberated us from an unholy terror, Squire Landor. I preached for peace, passing on every urging from the church authorities in Arcadia, but there were too many hotheads here ready to declare in favour of Prince Owen.'

'The pretender you talk of is no true prince,' said Prefect Colbert, coldly. 'Only an outlaw traitor who conspired against the nation with raiders from the Burn. Owen Hawkins was cast out by the royal family for his crimes and, as his revenge, the pretender led the realm to rebellion and ruin to satisfy his malice. Rule has now passed to the upper house. In Northhaven, to *me*.'

'Then the day I prayed for has arrived,' said the bishop. 'You must cast aside your general's uniform, be our prefect once more and the north shall again know peace and serenity.'

'And my husband is no mere squire, nor a colonel of the royal army,' said Leyla. 'King Marcus has elevated Benner Landor to the peerage for his help in crushing this treason.'

Leyla wore her pride on her sleeve like fresh lace, but Duncan suspected her words wouldn't do Benner Landor any favours. Tales of old man Landor's 'succour' would find their way back to everyone conspicuously absent from these streets. She was unwittingly painting a target on her husband's back for every disgruntled peasant with a birding rifle to take a shot at.

'Then *Lady* Landor, we await your return to the prefecture with eagerness.'

'Do not count on our presence at too many of your services, Bishop,' said Leyla, grandly. 'The court in Arcadia awaits our return equally as eagerly.'

'But my dear,' said Benner, 'the business of the house and our wealth resides in Northhaven.'

'We shall talk about it later,' said Leyla. 'In more private surrounds.'

'It is the business of Northhaven which worries at me, Lord Landor,' said Bishop Kirkup. 'Our people have gone hungry for months now in the town and district. We were hoping—'

'The supplies that follow the army are reserved for those loyally fighting for the king,' said the prefect. 'If there is any insufficiency of crops from the farms, it is because too many traitors have been clutching rifles in their hands the last few seasons instead of seed drills and hoes.'

'Our winter stores have been stolen by soldiers from both sides and the Guild of Rails has not shipped supplies in, even where they are bought and paid for.'

'We will deal with the pretender and his bandits . . . there will be no more thefts of goods. Now that Northhaven has returned under lawful rule, contracts and shipments will be honoured once more. These hungry people you speak of need to tend to the business of making an honest living and their living shall return to them again. If any family starves here, it is because too many of its members are filthy rebels. The same cowardly dogs who set upon us as we approached the town. This was a prefecture of farmers before the rebellion. Only a fool fertilizes weeds in his field. Do I look like a fool to you?'

'No, Prefect, clearly not,' stuttered the bishop.

'Excellent. Then I trust my headquarters will not be troubled by beggars while we root out the last of the brigands here. We shall treat panhandling as an admission of service with the pretender's rebels.' Hugh Colbert reached out to seize the boot of one of the executed men and set the corpse swinging from the lamppost to indicate the fate of such disclosures. 'This is how a farmer deals with a weed. He yanks it out of the soil that nurtures it so it no longer threatens his fields. It was the assembly's failure to make this clear which led to their corruption, demise and the blight which swept the realm. Better that weeds die rather than the harvest.'

'Then we shall work the soil together in humility,' said the bishop, hesitatingly accepting the lack of aid. He appeared less than happy about it, despite his words.

Working the soil together. 'That I'd like to see,' muttered Duncan. It was clear that neither the prefecture's new master nor the prince of the church knew the front end of a sickle from the back.

Adella recognized one of the welcoming committee. Duncan remembered she used to help her father, the chief clerk of the town council. 'Mister Gilbert, an officer from the Army of the Boles visited earlier to bring word of my arrival to my mother and father. Where are they?'

'Word arrived, Miss Cheyenne,' said the councillor, 'but I fear there was nobody to deliver the happy news of your safe return to. Your parents haven't been seen inside the old town for a few days, now.' He raised his hands in a conciliatory gesture. 'When the royal army was heard to be advancing north, many people feared a conflict with the—' He paused a second to find the right words. 'That is to say, between, the rebels and the king's forces. Plenty have relatives and friends in the countryside where they can expect a welcome. They fled the city for fear of being caught up in a siege.'

Well, that's a polite way to say they left terrified of meeting with the king's rope. It wouldn't have taken much to spook her parents. Duncan remembered Adella's father as permanently on nerves, a highly strung disposition hardly helped by well-warranted fears that Adella's plans to marry Duncan would bring the House of Landor's wrath down on his family. Despite everything, Duncan couldn't help but feel sympathy for Adella, the crestfallen look on her face. *She might have sold us out to escape from the sky mines, but her folks were okay.* The parents deserved to know that their daughter had not only survived the slavers' raid, but prospered, in her own stony-hearted way.

'The chief clerk is not my main concern,' said Benner Landor. 'Where is the mayor, where is the high sheriff of the district police?'

'All gone, my lord,' said Gilbert. 'The mayor disappeared a couple of days ago. The sheriff died at the outbreak of the – the rebellion. There was fighting between the territorial regiment and the constables over who the town should declare for. Fighting between the services and fighting between factions inside them. It was only settled when the fort at Redwater joined the rebellion and sent ships with marines up the river to assist the–'

'Spare me the minutiae of this region's lapse into treason, man,' barked Prefect Colbert. 'Fled and dead. That's all I need to know,'

Mister Gilbert shifted uneasily on his boots. 'There's a ballot scheduled to elect a new sheriff as well as a new assemblyman.'

'No longer necessary. The upper house rules alone. There will be no reformed national assembly; that ground has been well and truly poisoned. I am appointed prefect by the grace of King Marcus, and all local positions are to be within the gift of my office.'

Viscount Wallingbeck hooted with laughter from his mount. 'General, I fear you'll struggle to find an honest Weylander to appoint inside this nest of vipers.'

'Please, do not even consider my husband,' called Leyla from her carriage. 'Benner is burdened enough as one of the new peers of the realm. He does not need to be bothered by any additional piffling duties. I do not wish to spend my days watching petitioners arrive at Hawkland Park to beg for mercy for their drunk, incarcerated cousins, or whining about flour shortages and broken drains in the old town.'

'Quite so, my lady,' said Prefect Colbert. He looked at the old clerk. 'You there. Gilbert, was it? You at least have demonstrated manners and a small measure of moxie in emerging from the town hall to greet us, rather than bolting off like a startled jack-rabbit. You shall be mayor.'

'Me? But my lord, I'm just all who's left.'

'A more than adequate qualification, *Mayor* Gilbert. Keep the leaves out of the drains and the business of the town hall inside the hall rather than irritating people of quality, and you will hold your job for life. Fail in your duties and it will be a very *short* tenure. Now, for a sheriff. An outside appointment would be best.' Colbert looked over at Viscount Wallingbeck. 'What's the name of that large lump you keep to flog deserters?'

'That would be Lieutenant Donald Blood of the provost-marshal's staff,' said Wallingbeck.

'Still alive is he? Yes? Excellent. He shows the making of a fine law officer, and holds an amusingly suitable surname for the post, to boot. Tell Blood he occupies the post when you next see him. I shall retire to consider all other appointments. Any of you with a living supplied by the state who wishes to keep their trade will be expected to inform on at least one known rebel sympathizer inside this district.'

'The bishop declares his parishioners need food,' said Leyla. 'Why not offer a soldier's rations to anyone who turns in a rebel sympathizer inside Northhaven? A week's worth of rations for information leading to the capture and execution of any bandit plaguing the territory's highways.'

'An inspired suggestion, Lady Landor,' said Prefect Colbert. 'Mayor Gilbert, I expect to see posters promoting the army's generosity on every street corner by the end of the day. Are you certain you're not minded to accept the position of high sheriff of Northhaven yourself, milady?'

'I regret that King Marcus requires my advice more than the constables of Northhaven,' said Leyla.

'And who are we to deprive the king?'

Duncan looked up at the pale dead faces swinging from their makeshift gallows as the procession rode through the city gate. Like statues. Cold, dead, marble. He didn't recognize any of the dead and he was glad of it. *The sooner I return back to Vandia, the better.* This wasn't his town, his people, his family anymore. They were as dead as every hung rebel.

Cassandra could see Alexamir was excited about something beyond the household's normal routine. She turned to watch the nomad from her seat at the small wooden table, its surface covered with chopped root vegetables for the elderly mistress of the tent. Usually Alexamir entered the tent at this time of day to carry Cassandra out, hauling her up into a horse's saddle. Then they would go riding across the plains. It wasn't easy to control a steed by reins alone, without the use of her legs to reinforce control, but Cassandra managed. In truth, she lived for their daily rides. It was the closest she came to being mobile again, able to travel where she wished, a tug on the reins in any direction she cared to head. In the saddle she wasn't half a woman any longer, she was part woman and part horse, living in the traditional Nijumeti manner, just as they had for centuries. She could race, halt, touch the horizon and speed through the wavering grasslands as fast as a crossbow bolt, the wind on her face and the rain in her hair.

But today, just seeing Alexamir's expectant expression, Cassandra knew a canter through the endless steppes wasn't to be her lot. 'What is it?'

'Temmell has said he will give us an audience today.'

Despite Cassandra's broken back, she felt a shiver pass down it. There was something she didn't like about the trickster. 'For what purpose?'

'Temmell has agreed to take a look at your spine, to see if there is a healing he might work on you.'

Is it impossible? No. 'I wish there was,' said Cassandra. 'But I fear you will be disappointed. Your clan sorcerer is little more than a travelling medicine peddler. What your people see as sorcery I see as tonics purchased in far-called lands, where the state of medical advancement is higher than the herbs picked by your own healers.'

'You are wrong, golden fox. Temmell is a true sorcerer. The Great Krul has risen to be chief of all the clans by relying on his magic and counsel.'

'But he's a foreigner. He arrived in a travelling doctor's wagon, didn't he?'

'Temmell wasn't born in the saddle, that much is true, as anyone may see from his golden skin. He came to us as a traveller, half-mad from the journey and the long sun and the dry winds. Those so-touched are holy, their minds stirred by the gods. Gods who sometimes choose to mix their souls with common mortals so that we may hear the tales of heaven on the plains.'

Cassandra grimaced. It was no wonder the witch riders of the clans resented the interloper. Magic that was considered more powerful than theirs? 'And Temmell believes he can cure me? Something that would be beyond even the best imperial surgeon?'

'He says he will examine you and see what he may do.'

Well, that at least will be free. Cassandra was fairly sure there would be potions available to work their magic on her. But only to be had very far away and at great cost, so she and Alexamir would have to wait an age for them to arrive. Long enough for Temmell to make his fortune and clear off to lands where his face was as fresh as his new marks' gullibility. This was a strange predicament. Cassandra needed to humour the clans' superstitions for Alexamir's sake, but she feared whatever hopes he harboured would only be used to pick his pocket. 'So then, let's see the man. It won't do to keep the great and powerful Temmell waiting.'

Alexamir picked Cassandra up from the table's seat and began to walk to the tent's entrance, but she faltered. He put her back down on the bed furs.

'What is it?' asked Alexamir. 'Speak your mind.'

'This is hopeless. Me; my injuries. Bad enough that I am a foreigner here. Now, a cripple as well. My situation is not one that you should be risking your reputation for. I have seen the way the other warriors look at you. And me.'

'It is my reputation to risk.'

But Cassandra didn't want that. For him to tie his fate to such a forlorn hope. *To me.* 'What price will that trickster ask of you for healing me?'

'I have told you, Temmell is a mighty sorcerer, not some travelling conjuror. I have seen him call upon the gods and work miracles.'

Yes, but miracles are even more expensive than healings. 'How can you want me like this?'

'The wind blows because it does. The sun rises because it does. The nights are cold because they are. You Vandians think too much.'

'Perhaps that is true.'

'Thoughts are clouds; fulfilment is rain,' said Alexamir. He rested himself by her side in the warm bedroll and kissed her.

'Is there a rainstorm brewing now?' asked Cassandra, returning the kiss.

'Yes, I sense a mighty storm.'

Indeed, it was a hurricane. One that almost lifted the rafters off the nomad tent, as their clothes fell across the rugs of the dry mud floor. Cassandra might not be able to walk, but she felt the warrior's body like the weight of boulders as they rolled in the bedding furs. Her body was so soft in comparison; she might as well have been warm clay on the potter's wheel. Even at the height of her training in the Vandian fencing rooms, she would have been pliable in contrast. That was one of the differences between Vandian and Nijumeti anatomy, but not the most interesting one by far. Though perhaps that was just the more basic difference between male and female, whatever their nation and race. It was a difference she was determined to enjoy. Luckily for Cassandra, for a people who could ride a week in the saddle and then fight a pitched battle at the other end, stamina was not an issue. By the time the storm abated, she was soaked in sweat and not fit to crawl to the tent's entrance, let alone visit some grass sorcerer to plead for her health.

'I wonder if your clan's sorcerer would mind if we visited tomorrow?' sighed Cassandra.

'I would lay here with you for a full season,' said Alexamir, 'until those who rode past outside called me Prince of Idles, rather than Prince of Thieves. But that will not heal you again, and that is what I would have.'

'You heal me,' she insisted. 'Just by being here.'

Alexamir gathered her clothes from where they had been thrown around the floor and placed them by her side. 'I will carry you forever ... but I can only carry you so far. For the rest of the journey, I fear we must both place our faith in Temmell.'

Cassandra kept her misgivings to herself and tugged her clothes back on. Old Nonna returned to the tent just as Alexamir scooped the now redressed Cassandra out of the bedding furs. She glanced at them both and wrinkled her nose. This old woman could see through to the truth of a situation like a hot blade parting butter. 'What is this? Courting? It is time to prepare supper, not time to smell wild tulips on passion's slopes.'

'We need to leave for a while, Aunt. But the journey will take us no further than Temmell's presence.'

'In that case, take a dip through the stream on the way back, Alexamir Arinnbold. I will not share my tent with the stench of that gold-skin's dark sorceries.'

'His power is pledged to the Great Krul,' said Alexamir.

'Am I so old that I am blind, boy? That much I know. But you borrow such forces at your peril. Never in my day.'

'He will help heal Lady Cassandra,' protested the strapping nomad.

Nonna turned her beady eye firmly on Cassandra. 'You think so? He has a right to cure who has a heart to help. Where is the heart in that foreign-born goat? You will struggle to find it.'

'Temmell's heart has been filled by the gods. He is wise.'

Nonna shook her head in dismay. 'What you call wisdom I call cunning. Temmell lusts after the souls of others to fill the void the gods carved in his own. Already the rogue has his tendrils into Kani Yargul. Nothing good will come of you owing that creature a blood debt.'

Cassandra suspected nothing at all would come of this, but she didn't wish to disappoint Alexamir. Better he found out the trickster's limits himself.

'Do not listen to Nonna,' said Alexamir as he carried Cassandra to a horse outside. 'Where Temmell is concerned, our clans' women give too much weight to Madinsar and her witch riders.'

'You believe the witches speak from jealousy?'

'It is more than a matter of envy for Madinsar,' said Alexamir. 'Hers is the hatred of blood feud. Madinsar was mother to a young man called Chinua. Chinua rode as head of one of the clans which opposed Kani's rise to be Krul of all Kruls. Chinua was slain by Kani Yargul in combat. They rode out into the hills to settle the matter between themselves, and Kani came back with Chinua's head in a sack.'

'Then surely Madinsar should hate the Great Krul? His was the blade that murdered her son.'

'You do not understand our ways. It is natural for clan leaders to desire to be Great Krul of all the clans, just as it is natural for other clans to resent a fledgling king like an unbroken horse resents its first rider. Few men ever manage the feat. As soon as one Krul looks like uniting enough clans to become a danger to the rest, the remaining leaders fear for their power and join forces to unseat the Great Krul. It was Temmell's advice that helped our Great Krul gain his seat – setting one clan against another, forging and breaking alliances with a skill unsung in our histories. Without Temmell's magic, the Great Krul would not sit on his throne and Madinsar's son would still live.'

In other words, they blamed what they could not understand, rather than that which was familiar. The witch's attitude didn't seem particularly sensible to Cassandra. In the Imperium, you blamed the head of a rival house for your setbacks, not the enemy's advisers, who were expected to be the best that could be bought. *Well, you'll spend the rest of your life with these people, lady. You had best learn how they think sooner rather than later . . . prejudices and superstitions included.*

To Cassandra's surprise, she and Alexamir headed away from the tented city first, leaving the camp's outskirts behind them. Instead, they set their horses in the direction of the shocking sight which had greeted Cassandra on her arrival here. Out on the plains, between a series of low, rolling hills, lay a great litter of aircraft remains, a veritable graveyard of the huge merchant carriers that had once criss-crossed the heavens. Cassandra had camped in a few of the carriers' wrecks on the way here, rotting canvas and wooden fuselage like the bones of whales. The lack of high altitude trade winds here, the stretch of the plains, and the dearth of friendly cities willing to sell fuel to aircraft made Arak-natikh a fiendishly difficult crossing. Many were those who ran out of fuel and crashed. But these wrecks before her now were different. Newer, not yet decayed down to uselessness. Everything hid under a sea of camouflage netting. The usual fate of downed carriers was to be stripped of metals. Such plunder ended up as nomad spearheads and blades. But the scope of industry under the netting indicated a different fate for these crashed carriers. As they drew closer, Cassandra's ears echoed to the banging of blacksmiths' anvils, the acrid smell of furnaces making her horse whinny. She passed scaffolds erected around aircraft, seamstresses cutting away and storing the fabric fuselage, carpenters carefully sawing through plywood frames. Trains of horses dragged away the fruit of the nomads' labour on wooden sleds. These merchant carriers had been virtual city-states of the air. Such work was beyond the ability of one or two clans. Only a Great Krul could muster the resources to build this . . . an aircraft works in the heart of the plains. Stripping downed craft and rebuilding the frames as smaller, more manageable craft. Some of these crashed carriers were six-hundred rotors large. Six hundred engines available for repair and re-use. That was a lot of blades and crossbow bolts to forsake. But none of Arak-natikh's neighbours would believe the nomads capable of fielding a skyguard of their own, not in a thousand years.

All this certainly explained Alexamir's familiarity with, and lack of fear around the kite they had stolen to escape Rodal. *What's Temmell's involvement in this place, I wonder? Is this part of his grand strategy for the grass king?*

'Temmell is working here today?' asked Cassandra.

'Today. Every day. There is little the sorcerer does not know about the creation and flight of these wooden pigeons,' said Alexamir.

'Your man seems very versatile in his magic.'

'He is Temmell,' said Alexamir, as if that should answer everything.

Those are his words, not yours. A suspicion arose in Cassandra. 'You've been trained to fly, haven't you?'

'I have only started to learn,' said Alexamir. 'I am not yet such a fine flier as I am a rider. But the day will soon arrive when I am master of the air. After all, the rice-eaters easily swoop on their cold winds, and they are a dull, mealy-mouthed people. Should not the mighty Alexamir be able to fly a thousand times better than the most skilful Rodal has to offer?'

'There are no winds to catch out in Arak-natikh.'

'We have horses to ride here,' said the nomad.

Of course you do. So where will the clans be riding its new wooden pigeons, I wonder? 'I can fly as well as anyone.' *Just not with pedals anymore.*

'I have seen you fly and fight in the air. I know that is no boast. But with Temmell's blessing, you shall again climb into a wooden pigeon using your own legs.'

'I'm not one of these crashed merchant carriers, Alexamir. It will take more than a little sawing and sewing to give me back my mobility.'

'We shall see.'

They came across a building in the centre of the works that resembled a circular wooden long-hall, built entirely out of salvaged planking. Canopies and awnings were pegged out around it, shading tables and blueprints from the sun. Scribes sat at some of the tables, balanced on long benches, working quietly at their scrolls and ledgers. From what Cassandra had seen so far, the ability to read and write was a rare skill among the nomads. *Being able to design and build aircraft an even rarer one, though, lady.* Alexamir enquired within the building for Temmell, and finding him elsewhere inside the works, left Cassandra sitting on her horse while he trotted off to bring the sorcerer back. The grass was brown and dry in the mottled shade of the camouflage netting, but Cassandra's mount chewed at it happily enough. She saw the door to the long-hall swing open. Out of it emerged Sheplar Lesh, his legs slowed by a heavy length of weighted chain between his ankles. His hands were free, though.

Sheplar started as he saw Cassandra up on her steed. 'When I saw you on the horse, for a moment I thought . . .'

'No. I am still broken. In the saddle is the only place where I am half-useful.' Cassandra nodded down towards the skyguard's leg-irons. 'But I see I am not the only one here with restricted mobility.'

'The usual fate of foreigners who come across this works by accident is death,' said Sheplar. 'But they hope to use me. Helping them build flying wings in the style of Rodal. Training their blue-skinned barbarians to fly.'

'You will not have a choice in the matter.'

'I always have a choice. I do not fear death.'

'The Nijumeti will not hesitate.'

'Neither will I.'

'So, it seems our positions are reversed,' said Cassandra. 'You were once free and my jailer. And now . . .'

'You think yourself freer than I? There are plenty of Rodalian women here taken as saddle wives in nomad raids. Some of them are out on the scaffolds unpicking the carriers. Talk with them of their so-called freedom and see how they feel about the matter.'

'I have Alexamir's word.'

'The word of a Nijumeti? As cheap as grass, here.'

'Alexamir has proven his words with deeds. Besides, I have nowhere else to go, Sheplar Lesh. I have no place inside the Imperium anymore, nor my house. Not like this. By Vandia's code, I should end my life. I have lost my home as surely as you have lost yours.'

'I am sad you believe that is your path. I still have hope.'

'Hope of what?'

'To escape and carry word back to Rodal of the Great Krul's secret schemes out here.'

'I do not think much of your chances.'

'Help me and they will be greater.'

'I am no use to you and your friends back in Weyland as a hostage now. The emperor will not pay a single copper coin for the return of a cripple such as I. West is as good as east to me, now. I shall stay here.'

'I hope you change your mind, little bumo, for both our sakes. When you do, seek me out.'

'Another lost hope.'

She watched as the Rodalian was marched off towards the furnaces by two bare-chested smith's apprentices where a half-disassembled engine lay spread across the grass. The Rodalian passed Alexamir, who arrived riding alongside Temmell. Alexamir swung off his horse and helped Cassandra dismount from hers, carrying her inside the wooden round-house. Cassandra noted how tight Alexamir held her. How warm his hands were. *Not much recompense for losing my legs, but it's something.* Inside, she stared up at a roof lined with transparent canopies from the downed carriers, admitting a flood of light. Wooden aircraft models rotated from the rafters, turning on the ends of lines. A distillery bubbled against the wall, extracting fuel from sacks of grain. There was a bitter oily stench to the room which suggested the nomads had yet to develop an effective method of mass-producing engine grade ethanol.

'So,' said Temmell, 'what business do we have this day, Alexamir? Are you here to demand to be made a squadron leader of the Great Krul's new skyguard again? Such matters are out of my hand, as I explained to you last time you sought me out here.'

'It is your sorcerous mastery over flesh that I would have you grant me, mighty Temmell. We spoke of it the other day. Do you not remember?'

'With so many calls on my time, how could I be expected to?' said Temmell, gazing at Cassandra as though he'd come across a lost pair of socks. 'Ah yes. The far-called daughter of Vandia.'

'You speak of the woman who will be my wife.'

'So you say.' His intense eyes twinkled at Cassandra. They were grey, like slate, and flecked with the same gold as his smooth skin. 'A fine woman. I note she has the beauty of the Vandians. It is common variety inside the empire. But then, the Imperium steals so many fine-looking young slaves of both sexes from the world, as well as taking the cleverest minds. It is as though Vandia is determined to breed a race of gods to enjoy its wealth.'

'You are a healer as well as all of this?' asked Cassandra.

'*This*?'

'This aircraft works. Matters of flight. Your scheme, I presume.'

'You have seen the Great Krul. What do you think? And there is very little I do not understand about matters of flight,' said Temmell. He threw back his cloak and what Cassandra had first taken as a hunched back unfurled into a pair of white feathered wings.

Cassandra gaped at him in amazement. *No wonder Nonna called him a creature.* 'You can fly!'

'You might say it comes naturally to me. At higher altitudes, where gravity's touch bears down as light as the weight of the air itself, I soar. Taking off from these grasslands is usually the issue. But give me a mountain slope with a good headwind . . .'

Cassandra had heard such flighted peoples existed, but the empire had never conquered a province with a population so many twists of the spiral removed from the common pattern. It was little wonder the superstitious nomads had spared this curious traveller, instead of cutting his throat. A greater wonder Temmell hadn't ended up being displayed in a cage as a freak before he got here, however.

'My wings were a gift,' said Temmell. He rubbed his dark curls with a measure of frustration, folding his wings back on themselves, making them small enough to cover again with his cloak. 'Some days I even come close to remembering from whom.'

'Do remember now the healing we talked of yesterday?' said Alexamir.

'Yes, yes, that at least is not presently fogged,' said Temmell.

Cassandra gazed at the traveller with a degree of trepidation. *Is he mad? He truly is insane if he thinks he can fix me.*

'You look like someone I knew, once, Vandian. Was it the Duchess of Ayak, or perhaps one of my daughters? My loins have produced so many children over the years.'

'I knew my father before he died. And you are not he.'

'Your father died badly, I can see that in your eyes.'

'My father died a hero of the empire.' *Betrayed by my grandmother for the crime of loving my mother.*

'Yes, one of my daughters. But which one? So many names.'

Alexamir lay Cassandra down on a cot in the corner of the room, rough woollen blankets that had seen better days making her neck itch. 'You would want to heal one of your daughters, would you not?'

'No, no,' muttered Temmell. 'Not one of mine. Not Gisi. Not Ashavani or little Missa.' For a moment she thought the mercurial traveller would refuse to inspect her, but Temmell's moods seemed to change with each second. He drew closer, kneeling by the cot. 'Roll over Vandian. Expose your spine for me so I may make my diagnosis.'

Cassandra pulled herself over and lifted up the linen tunic. She craned her neck to see the trickster rub his hands together. Then Temmell placed both palms flat against the bottom of her back. His golden skin felt as smooth and cold as porcelain, and she grunted as he pushed against her vertebrae.

'Yes, I feel the break. Just here. This was no riding accident.'

'My flying wing was shot to pieces,' said Cassandra. 'We crashed escaping to the steppes.'

'You can fly? Alexamir spoke the truth to me, then. You are of the celestial caste. You are far too young to be any pilot of the empire's legions.'

'I was trained to fly a helo, flying wing and patrol ship,' said Cassandra. 'By the finest aces of the legion. And I *am* granddaughter of the Emperor Jaelis Skar.'

Temmell chortled. 'Yes, but there are so many of those rattling around the harem's corridors. For all of Vandia's size and power, it is just another family business. But at least you were born to the right family for your empire. The only one that counts. *Currently.*'

'You know a lot about us, for a race I have never seen or heard of inside the empire.'

'Oh, I have forgotten far more. You might say I am as broken as you in my own way. But I still retain fragments. The knowing of things is a more reliable blade than any Vandian duelling dagger.'

'You have the power to heal her?' asked Alexamir. He sounded even more desperate in the need for a cure than Cassandra. Despite herself, Cassandra felt surprised. Her mother Helrena had cared for her. Duncan and Paetro and Doctor Horvak had protected her and would have given their lives for her. But Cassandra had never experienced a passion for her like this inside the empire. Any suitors there would have seen only the wealth of her house's sky mines, the blood imperial of the match. But Alexamir had risked his life to rescue her from Rodal, not for her position or her house or her wealth. Just for who she was. And he had continued protecting her when she was as much use as a chocolate cauldron on a camp fire. *That's a rare thing to find in the world, lady. Perhaps a once-in-a-lifetime discovery.*

'As far as healing, the proof of the pudding will be in the eating.' Temmell pointed to a table covered with scale models of flying wings, like a particularly messy counter of a child's toyshop. 'Pass me that wooden-handled chisel.'

'You mean to carve my golden fox?' Alexamir sounded shocked.

Temmell grinned as he took the tool from the nomad, unscrewed the handle and passed it to Cassandra. 'Indeed I do, but not with this. Bite hard on the wood, my little celestial caste beauty. Otherwise, you shall lose your tongue before you ever regain your legs.'

'This will hurt?'

'Excruciatingly so. Nothing is without cost. I would offer you a good swig of that foul sour milk whisky the clans produce, but I need your flesh unpolluted for this work.'

'I am used to pain,' said Cassandra, with a bravado she had to work to feel. 'I trained every day in the duelling hall.' *Besides, I feel little below my thighs, sad to say.*

'Ha. A connoisseur? Let me introduce you to my wares, then.'

Cassandra was about to ask why the trickster was not going for any of his travelling potions or at least a surgeon's bag, but instead the man lay his hands back on the bottom of her spine. The sleek golden hands seemed to flatten, almost melting into her skin, joining with her body. And then Cassandra discovered the strength of the sorcerer's *wares*, only just managing to fumble for the wooden handle, squeeze it into her mouth as a shock like a bucket of acid tossed over her began to eat into her flesh. She screamed through the wood, an undignified trail of drool soaking into the woollen sheets. *Nothing like this. Never!* Cassandra had been trained for pain tolerance using shock foils, thin sabres with pliant metal blades charged from a rubberized hilt battery to deliver agonizing cuts. A bare handful of practice cuts were enough to render a bull-sized guardsman a semi-conscious wreck on the floor. Cassandra might as well have trained with a feather duster for all that it had prepared her for this.

'Hold her down!' commanded Temmell, bearing down his victim's spine with all his weight.

Alexamir grabbed Cassandra as she thrashed insanely. Despite the nomad's bulk, he was hard-pressed to stop her flailing off the cot. *How can I twist so much?* A minute ago and she was barely capable of crawling unaided across the floor. 'You are killing her, Temmell. In the name of Atamva, show pity!'

'I am killing what is dead inside her,' growled Temmell with a cold detachment. 'It is only the fire of life her nerves experience. New, beautiful fresh life.'

'Please!' called Cassandra through the wood; she had gnawed it to splinters. The word came out as a spittle-flooded *Leaze*.

'Something new for you, today,' said Temmell. 'Something new for the world.' The heat from his two-handed touch forked down across her spine and into her calf muscles, setting them twitching as though in a fit. They hadn't stirred for so long, and now, *this*. Temmell chanted in a language that Cassandra didn't recognize, oddly lyrical for a tongue that sounded so short and guttural, his head nodding as if trying to find a rhythm to match his so-called patient's pain.

Cassandra felt as though she was tied between a train of horses, that being ripped apart was her punishment. She tried to pass out, seeking the blessed relief of oblivion, but it was denied her. Screams echoed through the hall and they were hers. No one came to end them. Until they were over. For a moment the absence of pain seemed another trick, but she was left quivering across the cot, the woollen sheets so soaked with her sweat that she might have come from a bath untowelled.

'Cassandra,' said Alexamir. She wasn't sure if he had ever called her that before. It was as though she was reborn here. 'Can you move your legs?'

'Try, Vandian,' said Temmell. 'Swing them off slowly over the side and bear your weight upon them.'

She tried and, amazingly, her flesh obeyed. Hesitantly at first, then more smoothly. *How many times have I woken and forgotten my condition?* Attempted to move and found herself flailing as wildly as a beached creature of the deep sea, shored hard. Alexamir lifted her up under her arms, but not to carry her. *To support me!* Cassandra was standing. After all this time. Something so simple. She moved a leg forward and it obeyed. Her muscles felt like swinging stone and followed as slowly.

'You see,' said Temmell. 'Am I not the greatest force upon this world, equal to the gods? Lucky you are, Vandian, to have fallen in with my company. There are few in all the lands of the people capable of such a feat.'

'Feat. This is a gods-sent miracle.'

'Walk around the tables here, bear her up Alexamir Arinnbold. Her muscles have grown stiff and weak for so long without exercise. You must walk her like a young colt, with you as her training rope.'

'How does it feel?' asked Alexamir.

Cassandra tottered trying to stay upright. Every step felt like wading through treacle. 'Like freedom.'

'Keep going,' urged Temmell. 'The more exercise her muscles have now, the better.'

Cassandra did hesitant laps around the model- and plan-littered tables, her flow of blood circulating at last as it was meant to. Just as she was thinking of stopping and resting, a feeling similar to pins-and-needles began to spread across her legs, a sudden flare of pain, and she was felled towards the floor as effectively as a puppet whose strings had been severed. Alexamir lunged and caught her before she hit the side of her head against a table. Cassandra stared up accusingly at the trickster.

'Freedom has a cost,' noted Temmell, coolly.

'What is happening?' demanded Alexamir.

'I said she would walk again. I did not say for how long.'

'The healing has not worked, has not taken?' Could Cassandra bear the pain again for a second attempt? *I'll have to.*

'It has worked perfectly,' said Temmell.

Alexamir angrily faced the sorcerer. 'How can you say that?'

'Because this is what I intended,' said Temmell. 'She will walk for ten minutes each day. Tomorrow she will have another ten minutes at the same time. The day after that, another. A pie-maker gives out a free taste of his wares. He does not, however, give his pies away for free.' He smiled at Cassandra. 'However pretty the customer doing the pleading.'

'You must heal her. Forever. Permanently.'

'Must?' said Temmell. 'I have found in the world there is very little I *must* do. If we shall talk about *musts*, let us first talk of their price. And who is to do the paying.'

'What would you have me do?' snarled Alexamir.

'Oh, I don't know. Conquer the world. Climb a distant mountain and bring me back a rare extinct flower for one of my potions. What *can* you do for me, Alexamir?'

'Whatever I have to do.'

'How pleasing. I do have something in mind as it happens. For too long you have boasted about being the greatest thief of all the Nijumeti. The women of the clans have heard this, so too the men. So oft and forcefully have your boasts been repeated that now even I, Temmell, the keenest mind of this or any other generation, have been taken in by them. I have something for you to steal, Prince of Thieves. An item worthy of your self-appointed and self-regarded title.'

Cassandra waited expectantly along with Alexamir to hear what it was to be. *Temmell may not have been born to the clans, but he can certainly bluster with the best of them.*

Alexamir could no longer suffer the suspense. 'What, Temmell? Name it. Let me hear your price.'

'It is access to the master copy of the Deb-rlung'rta, a book to be found in the Rodalian capital, Hadra-Hareer.'

'A *book*,' said Alexamir, as though he had been asked to steal a cup of horse piss from the stables of the Rodalian First Speaker.

'If you're growing bored of life out here, I can recommend a hundred titles from my house's library,' said Cassandra.

'The Deb-rlung'rta isn't to be found in the shelves of any Vandian house, however well-appointed their library,' said Temmell. 'It is the master codex of the wind priests. It details the tidal openings and closings of Rodal's wind dams, the tables for how the priests should react and coordinate against the weather and which spirits of the air need summoning.'

'A book of spells,' said Alexamir, with some measure of understanding.

'A chapter or two is taken from it and contained in every wind dam and temple, as well as the skyguard stations, detailing local conditions. But the complete compendium for all of Rodal only exists in one place . . . the great temple at Hadra-Hareer. It is updated every year, chapters copied by hand by scribes and illuminators, then sent by flying wing to all the temples and stations of the skyguard.'

'Look at Alexamir!' shouted Cassandra. 'Do you see a Rodalian standing there? He's a blue-skinned horseman, their ancient enemy. You're not sending him to steal for you. You're sending him to die.'

Temmell stared coldly at Cassandra. 'How touching. I had always wondered if a cat feels any real affection for the hand that feeds it, or if the relationship was only an accommodation. The mysteries of cats are beyond even the Astounding Temmell. Less so, those of people. Do not fret, little Vandian, my power stretches far further than a severed spine. I have a glamour to cast upon your Prince of Thieves before he is to prove his title. It will change his skin colour to a nice pallid tone and soften his noble brow and features towards the Rodalian.'

Alexamir appeared shocked. 'You mean to change my face?'

'Only temporarily. Perhaps a little too temporarily. Once my spell is cast, you will need to travel and be brisk about your business. Without reinforcement by me, your face will soon return to its true-blooded steppes form. And it would not do for you to lose your disguise while surrounded by citizens of the Valley of the Hell-winds. A plane will be allocated to you along with one of our budding aviators.'

'The Great Krul will never allow this,' said Alexamir. 'If one our wooden pigeons is seen and reported, all the enemies of the clans will know of our new might.'

'Yours?' sneered Temmell. 'I think you claim too much credit, even for a Nijumeti rider. It is not my thunder I require you to steal. Kani Yargul can be made to grasp the value of this prize. To understand the winds of Rodal is to *control* Rodal. I am not building the first skyguard in the history of the Nijumet to watch it torn apart in storms summoned by the cursed priests of the wind temples.'

'Do not go,' Cassandra begged Alexamir. 'Not for me. Healing me is not worth it.'

'You are wrong,' said Alexamir. 'It is. To me. And the cost is mine to pay.'

Cassandra shook her head. 'If this book is irreplaceable it will be impossibly well guarded.'

'You are half correct,' said Temmell. 'Impossibly well-guarded, naturally. But hardly irreplaceable. The knowledge that comprises the Deb-rlung'rta exists in piecemeal fashion inside the skull of every priest in every temple in the heights. They could come together in convention and put it back together like a jigsaw.'

'Do not steal it, Alexamir. You steal only your death.'

Temmell laughed heartily, the first sign of true amusement Cassandra had heard from the man. 'Oh, I do not require Alexamir Arinnbold to merely *steal* the Deb-rlung'rta. That is hardly a feat equal to the talents of the Prince of Thieves. He is to break into their great temple, copy the text and leave it resting in place. Seemingly undisturbed by all fingers save those of a few grubby log keepers and scribes. They must not know we have a copy until it is too late.'

'I will do as you bid,' said Alexamir. 'I would do it if this spell book was resting in the dark hall of Kalu the Apportioner himself using the tongues of a thousand demons as its cushion. How am I to copy this book, though, when I have not been taught a scribe's reading?'

'Open the book and stare well at each page. The first enchantment I shall cast over your features. My second will make your mind a copy-book. I shall lift the impression of the script from your mind when you return.'

'You may change his face,' pleaded Cassandra, 'but you can't change the man. His manners, his accent ...'

'I see that the celestial caste's education still includes the arts of spycraft. Have no fear, little Vandian, my glamour will alter the muscles of his throat. I'll have him singing like a born rice-eater quickly enough. And as for manners, well Alexamir is an intelligent young man and, I have noted, a very fast study. He will prosper under my tutelage. Slow wits do not last long in my service.' He turned towards the nomad. 'I must minister to your golden fox and ensure my healing has taken. Ride to Kani Yargul and ask him to grant me a private audience before supper. Then return and carry away the Lady Cassandra. Your training for your task begins this evening.'

Alexamir exchanged a worried glance with Cassandra. She listened to Alexamir's galloping steed as he departed, before glaring at the trickster from her cot. 'You are using him.'

'We are using each other. On such transactions are the foundations of civilization laid.'

'If you call the clans civilization.'

'I call them an opportunity. One not to be wasted.'

'You don't need to supervise my recovery. Whatever you did to my body, you're sure enough of its effects.'

'You have caught me out. I don't need to supervise your condition,' admitted Temmell. 'But I do need to discuss your fears. And it is better that the Prince of Thieves is not distracted by them. His success will require a fierce clarity of purpose.'

'Fears? You believe I am afraid of you?'

'Only a stupid person would fail to be. And you, I think, are far from dull-witted. But it is not your fear of me that is my concern. It is your fear of Alexamir's success ...'

Cassandra tried to laugh. 'So, you believe I fear walking again?'

'No. It is the duties that are attendant upon your healing which you fear. When you have your spine unbroken, you will be able to walk. And where might you walk to, little Vandian? Naturally, you will follow all those lessons of duty and honour to your house and emperor and Imperium. Such heavy baggage. It is little wonder that you lay sprawled there, barely able to crawl with all that weight upon your young back.'

Cassandra attempted to reply, but something within her choked the words. She had to gather herself back together before she could speak. 'Alexamir gave his word, his blood oath. He will show me the life of a nomad and then I am free to choose to return to Vandia at any time.'

'As you *choose*. Of course you fear me. I can smell the terror upon you like a scent, like an expensive perfume from Ortheris. But you fear having to choose to abandon Alexamir so much more.'

Tears rolled down Cassandra's cheeks. 'Leave me be. This is no healing.'

'The truth is always healing. Just not for your Prince of Thieves. He may not bring me back the Deb-rlung'rta if he knows it is also your passage home. Or perhaps he will . . . the honour of such savages! But the hesitation and conflict such a truth will cause in him is as great an enemy as a city filled with half a million ancient blood-foes of the Nijumeti.'

'Leave me alone!'

'What is the saying in Vandia? *Family. House. Empire.* No place for a low-born nomad in such a philosophy. Oh, I will fix his golden fox's mangled legs. But you're not going to hobble away from Alexamir until I have a copy of the Deb-rlung'rta sitting safely in my hall.'

'What kind of man are you?'

'I wish I knew. Truly I do. It would probably be kinder to Alexamir if he died from the charge of a temple guard's pistol before you break his heart. But you wouldn't want to see his death come to pass. So keep your mouth shut around him, little Vandian. Let him survive to return with my prize. Then you may allow the grand sweeping tragedy of your life to play out as it will.' He turned before he left the chamber, giving her an ironic bow before he exited. 'My lady of the Imperium.'

Cassandra was left to her worries, whirling around her like a murder of crows, pecking at her. Sometimes it took another's viewpoint to crystallize who you were and what you truly felt. She loved Alexamir, but she could not tell him. Because the trickster was correct. When Cassandra could walk, she would have to walk away from him. There was no place for Alexamir in the Imperium and no place for her here. *Let him fail, but return alive. I will stay like this. Ten minutes a day and broken for the rest. Let that be my fate, please.*

Her brooding was interrupted by the swinging of the hall's wooden door. A man entered. Not a Nijumet, that much was certain. Pale white skin, a narrow face and thin black moustache. He looked like a trader; thick, high leather riding boots, worn leather trousers and a heavy furred green jacket good for sleeping out on the plains. No slave, either. Not with a pistol holster belted near his left side, a flared ornamental barrel jutting out. *Meant to be fired from a wagon or saddle, if I'm any judge.*

The traveller noticed Cassandra lying down on the cot and his eyes twinkled with mischief. Cassandra guessed his thoughts. 'I'm not one of Temmell's saddle wives.'

'I don't think the man has any. And you're no mountain maid. Kishian or Persdad?'

'Neither. Shouldn't you be wearing ankle irons?'

'I'm more use to the Nijumeti able to run as free as a jackrabbit,' said the trader. 'I am Brean Luagh of the very fine nation of Hellin.'

Hellin? 'I have heard of your country. You're the only people who trade with the nomads.' *These are the traders Alexamir said would take me back to the league and the nearest Guild of Radiomen's hold, if I decide to leave. When, lady, when.*

'Well, some of us do and some of us don't. Business can run awful tricky out here at times. It takes a special person to rub along friendly-like among the clans.'

'A skill you possess?'

'Along with a few wagons filled with barrels of rubber. Very useful stuff, rubber.' He winked at her. 'Not many rubber trees out here in the steppes. Not many trees at all, really. Rare stuff here, you might say.'

'So you bring it out of Hellin.'

'I can see you've never visited my country. I'm a poor bog-walker, and a poor bog-walker likes a good piece of marsh. It's versatile stuff, marsh. Slippery, sucking, complex soil. Good for drowning every horde to wander in from the steppes. And the ones who don't get sucked under the bogs end up dying from the bites of our very friendly snakes and insects. Poison and fever and marsh. And Brean Luagh. At your service. But no rubber trees. That I source from Morynia. Is the master of the house in?'

Cassandra nodded in the direction the trickster had left.

'He's particular about people disturbing him in those rooms. Who knows what he does in there, eh? Would you be so good as to tell Master Temmell when he reappears that Brean Luagh is in town and requests the pleasure of his company for a little haggling? Are you sure you're not from Persdad?'

'Quite.'

'Temmell is an interesting fellow; a golden eagle among grass mice. Have you ever met anyone like him out your way?'

I don't recall mentioning what my way is. 'People are different wherever you travel.'

'And isn't that what makes the journey so interesting? Well, there it is. Might I have your name, it seems awful distant to be leaving without knowing it?'

'Cassandra.'

'A name as lovely as yourself. I shall bid you a farewell, then, Cassandra. Perhaps we shall meet again before I take my leave of the Nijumeti.'

Cassandra shrugged. 'I'm not going very far.' *At least, not much further than a ten-minute walk.*

Cassandra was back inside the family tent when Kerge appeared at its opening. 'Where is the manling, Alexamir?'

'Away at council with their grass king and what passes for a court sorcerer in these parts,' said Cassandra. *Training him to commit suicide for me.* 'You are not chained?'

'Madinsar does not chain her servants. She would see a thrall attempting escape the day before the slave knew of it themselves.'

'She has the future sight you possessed?'

'Madinsar has it,' admitted the gask. 'I never thought to meet a common-pattern female with our people's talent, but she possesses it. As strong as any among the Elders of Quehanna.'

'You almost sound happy about your discovery,' said Cassandra.

'She is working with me, helping me recover my golden mean.'

'That sounds uncommonly kind of her.'

'Naturally, it is for her benefit rather than my own,' said Kerge. 'Madinsar wishes to regard the branches of the great fractal tree. She seeks to shape it, as I once did.'

'Then you are a pawn on the game-board rather than a patient on the surgeon's table.'

'You may see what Madinsar is yourself. She wishes to meet with you.' Kerge glanced around the empty tent. 'Is the old womanling not here? The nomad's aunt?'

'Nonna is out penning her goats before nightfall and the wolves come prowling,' said Cassandra. 'I am no slave here, Kerge. My status is that of tent-guest. You do not need to ask any permission save my own.'

'Then you will see Madinsar?'

'Only if you carry me to the pony tethered outside.'

The gask bore her outside, the spines of his skin resting uncomfortably against hers. After a short ride in the cooling night air, they entered Madinsar's tent together. It proved to be a place of bright colours; a soft richness about its incense-scented space, cushions, rugs and blankets. That surprised Cassandra. Tapestries hung from the roof, ancient stories told in pictograms, works that must have taken multiple lifetimes to weave. Cassandra could see this place belonged to a person of importance among the Nijumeti. Unlike Alexamir's tent, the witch rider's was lit by a chandelier studded with orange sun crystals. Left outside for a day, the crystals absorbed the day's light, and then gently emitted what they had stored when placed in darkness. The wheel twisted above her, pulsing softly in rainbow hues which added to the ethereal quality of the tent. *Yes, all the trappings of a holy place.* The high priestess of the witch riders emerged from an antechamber to welcome them. A slight smile pulled at the corners of Madinsar's mouth. 'Welcome, Lady Cassandra Skar of Vandia.'

Cassandra glanced around. 'Is Nurai not here?'

'She travels away from the camp presently.'

'Good.' *I have enough problems in the camp without Alexamir's old admirers trying to find extra ways to kill me.*

'Nurai has loved Alexamir Arinnbold for as long as she has known him,' said Madinsar. 'You can understand how unhappy she feels at your presence here.'

'She claims to have seen my future.'

'Only clouded dreams. It is never a good thing to see your own fate too clearly. Happiness is blindness. Witch riders are rarely happy. It is the curse of our gift.'

'Are you happy?'

'Happy?' Madinsar snorted. 'Worries lap around my mind like the waters of the salt sea. Such waters leave me no room for personal concerns. I have seen dark futures, terrible futures. The end of all things.'

'Pieces decay: the board is eternal.'

'A wise enough saying. But I have seen the board on fire. Many of us have. And not just here.' She glanced at Kerge.

'That is the truth,' said the gask. 'Our elders have scryed disturbing glimpses of what may come to pass. It is as though the branches of the great fractal tree narrow before us. The paths diminishing down to a single, terrible, lonely future. An autumn followed by winter. Darkness eternal.'

'When witch riders talk of this, we are called foolish old women too close to death, women who dream only their own end,' said Madinsar. 'But now I discover that the tales of a forest people beyond the mountains are true. Males and females with the dream-sight. And I find the witch riders share the same dreams with the gasks, or should I say nightmares.'

'The world is filled with wars and conflict and death,' said Cassandra. 'I don't need your gift to understand that. Just reading any one of a thousand history texts is enough.'

Madinsar shook her head. 'Our gods do not give us the gift of future-sight through the gasks' forest, but through the stream with a million tributaries. Kalu the Apportioner's stream. And you are right, its waters bubble and froth with the rapids of mankind's passions. How could it be otherwise? But witch riders do not dream of rapids. We dream of nothing at all. It is a darkness more absolute and terrifying than anything an ungifted could understand. Imagine you woke one morning and discovered the sun has not risen and there were no more stars in the sky. Only cold and endless winter. The grass of the plains turned black, the very air we breathe as thin and frozen as daggers. This is our future.'

'It is close to what I saw before I lost my gifts,' said Kerge, miserably.

'You have not lost the gift,' said Madinsar. 'There is a rock slide in the water damming your flow. The rocks belong to you. They are yours to remove.'

'I am trying.'

'Rather, we are chipping at them together,' said the witch rider.

'Nurai claims I will bring death and misery to the clans,' said Cassandra.

'Misery to her, perhaps. Maybe to us all. I dream of defeat to the south of the steppes, or victory north of the plains. Your friend Temmell means to smash us upon the peaks of Rodal. Matters will not end well there for our people.'

'Temmell is not my friend.'

'I sense his scent upon you, girl. Like the brand of ownership on a steer. He has burnt into you and do not deny it.'

'Temmell says he will heal me.'

'As I heal a roast chicken by digesting it and making it part of my flesh?'

Cassandra snorted. 'I am not yet healed.'

'I need no gift to see that. The gask carried you in here, girl. Let me carry you out.'

'Temmell's cost I understand. What is to be *your* price?'

'Yet to stand revealed to me. But we will need to pay its tally . . . all of us who are willing. Even those who are not. A dead river has only one course.'

'That sounds terrifying,' said Cassandra.

'Then you sit upon my seat, now, girl. It may soon be impossible to choose between life and death. We may only be able to choose what we are willing to die for. Or *who*.'

'I shall try to give you your answer when you fully have your question,' said Cassandra.

'Yes,' sighed Madinsar. 'I am sure you will.' There was a measure of sorrow in her voice heavier than anything Cassandra had heard before. Madinsar lifted Cassandra up from the cushions, assisted by Kerge. Together, they bore her back to the pony tied outside.

Brean Luagh approached his line of covered wagons. He attracted a hopeful bob of the head from one of his men perched on the driver's seat of the lead wagon. There was a fire to the side, the rest of the traders and his family warming an iron pot filled with vegetables and local game. The driver had a rifle nestled in his lap like a cat for the stroking. Mael was a cousin. Not a particularly clever one, it had to be said. *But you have to work with what you are given.* 'Do we have a price for the goods?'

'That we do not,' said Brean. 'The golden eagle is off with his beakers and experiments. But we'll make a deal soon enough. After all, how many other traders do you see out here? A profitable trip, the gods willing.' Brean walked around to the rear of the wagon and untied its canvas cover before hauling himself into the back. 'Keep your eyes peeled. A little warning if one of our Nijumeti friends comes around wanting to swap goats for guns.' He yanked the bales aside, exposing a pile of wooden crates. These he dragged back, exposing the wagon's floor. Brean removed a small steel key from the ammunition pouch on his belt, slotting it into what looked to be a knot of wood. A turn to the left and the hidden mechanism answered with a click, the concealed panel lifting up an inch. He slipped his fingers below and slid the small hatch fully up.

Mael stuck his head through the wagon's front curtain. 'You'll be bringing the guild-mark down on our heads one day with that contraption.'

'Only natural for the Guild of Radiomen to be a little miffed,' said Brean, removing the brick-sized radio set. 'Them with holds filled with batteries and secrets and us with the whole caboodle squeezed down to this. Hardly seems fair . . . to the likes of them.'

'Miffed won't be the word for it.'

'Don't worry, boy. Have a little faith in King Marcus and his far-called friends. If I'm any judge of character, the long guilds won't be "long" for this part of the world.'

'What are you saying, Brean Luagh?'

Brean activated the radio, just as the Vandians and Weylanders had shown him. His answer a swine-like squeal of static. 'Why, that in a fight, you always back the man carrying the biggest blade.' He lifted out the code book and located the day's date in the table, along with the associated pass-codes. 'So let's find out how much the biggest blade is willing to pay for the safe return of an emperor's grand-daughter.'

'The lass with the price on her head is here?'

'No, you great idiot, the other girls. Her three beautiful noble-born sisters we're expected to report for bleeding free.'

'No need to be offensive,' sniffed Mael.

'What a sensitive soul you are today. The high-born lass is out in the aircraft works with Temmell himself.'

'Never thought the young wizard was particularly interested in the fillies.'

'You'd make an exception for the granddaughter of the big man, though,' said Brean.

'She looks like her picture?'

'That she does. A little sadder, perhaps.'

'I'd be sad out here.'

Brean snorted and tried the radio, fiddling with it for as long as he dared, but he couldn't raise anyone at the other end. *This machine is meant to be simple to use.*

'Is it broken?' asked Mael.

'No. We're just too far out,' sighed Brean. 'Too many mountains in the way to the south. They warned me it might be the case.'

'Maybe we could raise one of the Guild of Radiomen's holds in Rodal,' said the driver, sarcastically.

'A fine idea,' said Brean. He turned the radio set off and slipped it back in its compartment and concealed it once more. 'Would you not mind passing on this little message for us. Who to? Why the very same king that's been hanging Rodalian leaders for their impertinence.' He laughed. 'This box of tricks will work better when we're rolling close to the border back home. A bit of patience and we'll be fine, rich gentlemen by journey's end.'

'Let's leave now. Sod the Nijumeti. We can grab the lady and take her with us.'

'You must be joking. You're getting greedy, Mael Luagh. It's not a single clan we're selling to out here, it's the horde. That means the whole damn lot of them. Mean, saddle-born rascals, with a fine talent for mayhem. And Kani Yargul doesn't have to catch us to make things difficult. He just has to let the Marsh Lords know how grateful he is to the Luagh boys for all our ball bearings, rubber straps and barrels

81

of engine oil. When the first nomad comes a-flying over Hellin, we'd have a bigger price on our heads than the emperor's granddaughter.'

'So we're to be informers?'

'A dirty word. I prefer to think of it as facilitating a joyous family reunion. If there's anything more disagreeable than a clan horseman, it's a *disappointed* clan horseman. Business as usual for us in the camp. Then we clear off. Nothing out of the ordinary to tip off our trading partners. I don't know how friendly those imperial fellows with the big steel aircraft are going to be when they come calling for Lady Cassandra. She looks to be a tent-guest rather than a saddle-wife, but who knows how hard these far-called boys will land? Them with their big guns and habit of chiding anyone in the vicinity with a noose. It wouldn't do for any unpleasantness to be blamed on a few innocent lads out of Hellin.'

Better this way. Put any bloodshed behind us, and the mound of imperial gold before us. Yes, this could be a very profitable trip by the end of it. And filthy rich in a while, is still filthy rich.

THREE

DEMON OF THE NORTH WIND

The high, echoing debating chamber of the Rodalian Speakers had been witness to many arguments over the centuries, but none as important as this one. At least to Jacob. Council wasn't in session. This was a private meeting between the Weyland exiles' leaders and the Rodalian forces competing over their future. Jacob could tell that Temba Lesh hailed from the same family as Sheplar. An ungainly man of sixty-five years with rubbery features and a short white brush of hair who seemed to lean unnaturally forward like a bird, even while seated at the stone table in the centre of the chamber. A carrion bird, as far as Jacob was concerned. *At least, that's what we'll be if he has his way. Thrown back to Bad Marcus to fight for our lives for the Vandians' amusement.* Nima Tash was a different matter entirely. Like a jasmine-scented porcelain doll of how outsiders depicted female Rodalian beauty. But the young daughter of the murdered Rodalian leader was far from fragile. She was as tough as tempered steel and it would be a fool who bet against her claiming her father's absent seat. *Out of the two of them, I reckon I'm glad she's the one backing us.*

'Your supporters used to argue heatedly for remaining removed from Weyland's recent difficulties,' said Temba Lesh, his head bobbing in Nima Tash's direction.

'That was before my father was hanged for daring to speak against the Vandian presence inside the league,' said Nima. 'Hanged in front of our embassy party, despite carrying an ambassador's papers and supposedly being under the royal palace of Weyland's protection of salt and roof.'

'The Imperium does what it likes,' said Jacob. 'They don't bother with diplomatic niceties. You don't bow fast and deep enough to them; they'll call it a discourtesy and take your head off.'

Temba thumped the table. 'And yet these are the very people you have goaded inside the territory of the Lanca.'

'You want to complain about it,' said Jacob, 'I'd suggest taking the matter up with King Marcus. He's the Imperium's man in Weyland, not us.'

'This is precisely why we should not get involved any deeper,' said Temba Lesh. 'It was a mistake to try to mediate in Weyland's civil war. Blood must out and it was never ours to risk or spill. A mistake that cost the previous Speaker of the Wind his life.' He pointed accusingly at Nima Tash. 'You have allowed your grief as a daughter to overwhelm your duties as a Rodalian speaker. Just allowing these foreigners exile among us is a grievous provocation.'

'Spoken like a candidate to be the next Speaker of the Winds,' said Nima.

'I reckon Miss Tash knows how to count,' said Jacob. 'And she's got eyes to see. You think that Marcus will be happy only holding Weyland after he's pacified it? A madman like Bad Marcus is either adding to the pile of loot to divide among his supporters, or he's growing nervous that someone's going to steal his share. The usurper's not the sharing kind. And with the skyguard and new weapons provided by the empire, Marcus doesn't need the Walls of the League anymore. Rodal is just another bird clucking for the plucking.'

'I do not *wish* to be involved,' said Nima, 'but as General Carnehan says, we are. And it is better that Rodal joins the fight while we still have allies in Weyland to assist us.'

'Allies? This man Carnehan is a danger to us all. His presence among us is an insult. He fled crimes in Weyland, and then served across the ocean as a Burn mercenary. He is a wanted fugitive across the border under his true name.'

'I know how to fight,' said Jacob. 'And I know how to win. If there's any other qualification to being a commander, it doesn't belong on a battlefield.'

'We are not yet a battlefield,' spat Temba. 'Rodal is a sovereign nation. We make our own decisions in our own parliament.'

'We had a parliament too,' said Prince Owen, entering the council chamber. He was accompanied by Anna Kurtain. The dark-skinned woman glanced coldly at Jacob. She still hadn't forgiven him for shooting the prince in the leg in Midsburg. Or maybe she was still pissed Jacob had used her as a hostage to guarantee the prince's signature on his commission as commander of the northern forces? *The assembly needs its standard to rally around. Damned if I was going to let the boy stay behind for some suicidal last stand.* Prince Owen limped forward on a cane before speaking again. 'The national assembly was dissolved in Arcadia by royal decree.'

'And smashed a second time at Midsburg after the north rebelled,' said Temba. 'Your rebellion has failed, Prince Owen. And I address you by that title only as a courtesy. Your uncle has almost complete command of your country. The national assembly's army is scattered and royalist soldiers are everywhere. I understand that King Marcus and his forces call you "the Pretender". Are you pretending to still be in the field with a chance of victory as well?'

'Damn right our army's scattered,' interrupted Jacob. 'I was the one who scattered it. As long as the empire's legions are still in the field, it's suicide to meet the usurper and his allies in the open. We're playing hit and run. Cutting the usurper's supply lines, cutting his men's throats and melting into the wilderness.'

'So then,' said Temba. 'A bandit war fought by a man very close to being one himself? We do not need to give sanctuary to brigands. We do not need a prince without a throne as an ally. There are dozens of houses across the border with tenuous claims to Weyland's throne. If you dig back far enough in my ancestry, you'll probably find some within my line's blood.'

'That's only because our two nations have stood together as allies for as long as we've been able to call ourselves countries,' said Prince Owen. 'We've fought alongside each other against nomad hordes and pirates and every invader who ever threatened our peace, the peace of the Lanca.'

'The articles of the Lancean League are clear enough,' said Temba. 'No interference in civil disputes. I have no more claim to tell Weyland who is to be its king or government than you have to tell Rodal who should be the next Speaker of the Winds. We will decide our coming election by ballot.'

'While we decide ours with bullets,' said Prince Owen. 'I respect your wishes to stay out of this hideous conflict. When the fight was over my claim to the throne and my uncle's, Rodal had a chance of neutrality. But the arrival of the Vandians has changed everything.'

'So your self-interest would have us believe.'

'It is true,' said Nima. 'I stood in Weyland's capital with my father. I saw what the Imperium is doing in Arcadia. You did not.'

'These Vandian forces are far-called, operating at the end of their range. Or do you deny that intelligence? The Imperium will grow bored here quickly enough. They are like the Kruls out on the plains. Savage children, but with better toys. A few raids to make a name and strike fear into the other clans, and the nomads retire to tend to their horses and their tents. Vandia is no different. The empire has no true interests to defend here.'

'The Imperium was paying skel raiders to attack Weyland for slaves,' said Jacob, 'and making Marcus rich for looking the other way. The only reason the Imperium is here is to punish the slave revolt our Weylanders sparked when we escaped. The Imperium has to save face back home. Vandia's like any bully. It can't let someone punch it in the nose and walk away. It does that, every other victim's going to wonder if a punch in the nose is an easier price to pay than regular tithes of flesh and silver to the emperor. And there's a hell of a lot of victims around the empire . . . millions of slaves who help keep it rich and every neighbour unlucky enough to feel the imperial boot on their throat.'

'Our skyguard is the skyguard of Rodal first and the League second. We would never try to enforce justice across the world. Such a task is clearly impossible. There are thousands of nations that are prey to better armed and more aggressive neighbours. Are we to intervene across Pellas? Let the Imperium fight and grow bored with fighting. Let the Imperium fill their slave markets with raids far-called from here.'

'The Vandians may clear off in a year or so,' said Jacob. 'But Bad Marcus isn't going anywhere. He's got a taste of the Imperium's wealth and what it can buy. He'll be their puppet here until he dies, and after that, the country will be passed down to his children. You'll be stuck with his rotten clan on the throne for generations.'

'King Marcus cannot fight the entire League. That would be madness.'

'What the hell else do you call his lust for absolute power?' spat Jacob. 'You're right about me, Temba Lesh, I did serve as a mercenary officer in the Burn. And I've dealt with a thousand rulers like Marcus. Dukes and barons and princes and queens and emperors. Their titles were a mixed bag, but there was only a hair's difference between the lot of them. Some of them I served, and a good many more I slew. You want to understand what you're facing now, you take a ship across the ocean and serve in the free companies for a couple of decades. Eat blood and dust and then come back here. You'll know the usurper for what he is and what he's capable of.'

'I cannot make another nation free,' said Temba. 'Only your people can do that. If you truly suffer a tyrant, throw him out. If we cross the border and fight for the north, then millions of Weylanders in the south will hate us and call us invaders. There will be blood between our two lands for generations.'

'There'll be blood,' said Jacob. 'The only mistake is being afraid to choose how and when it's spilt.'

'Rodal is not your sabre or your knife or your rifle. If I am elected Speaker of the Winds, your exile among us will be at an end. Our borders will remain closed for as long as chaos divides your nation. You will have your blood and your feud. But not one Rodalian life will be shed on either side of Weyland's civil war.'

'You're a stubborn fool,' said Jacob.

'Were you called Quicksilver across the ocean for your words? They flow so easily.'

'For deeds, not words. Hesitation's a lot like death,' said Jacob. 'It's always punished on the other side of the water.' *Just like good intentions.*

'The mountains break everything,' said Temba Lesh. 'That is an old saying *here*. I shall leave you to your council. There is nothing more from me that needs saying.'

Prince Owen watched the elderly Rodalian politician rise proudly and leave. Then he turned to speak to Nima. 'I need to know what your chances are of being elected Speaker of the Winds, Madam Tash?'

'In truth, both sides are too evenly balanced to call,' said Nima. 'Many among us thirst to avenge the indignity of my father's execution, the stain of dishonour. To have Rodal's leader murdered for daring to speak his mind while under diplomatic immunity inside the territory of a trusted ally . . .'

'I've had a good few pieces of paving hurled my way on the streets here for the crime of being a Weylander,' said Jacob. 'I know how furious your people are. We need to remind them that it was a Vandian noose around your father's neck, not a Weyland one. How much support can Temba Lesh muster?'

'Enough. Cooler heads and wiser council,' said Nima. 'Our two countries have been allies for so long, there are many who can imagine no conflict between us.'

'They'll imagine it well enough when the usurper and his imperial paymasters turn up here.'

'You do not need to convince me,' said Nima. 'I saw what we face. There is not a day that passes when I do not go to sleep weeping over my father's murder: but my support is not yours for personal revenge. I would not waste one Rodalian life on the conflict across the border if I thought your troubles would stay confined there. It is my judgement that King Marcus is not sucking in Vandian resources to build armoured regiments and a powerful new skyguard because he wants to mount fine parades in Arcadia and impress the crowds with fly-pasts. The plague that sickens you will sicken us soon enough.'

'You will win the election for leadership of your government,' said Prince Owen. 'And we shall fight the sickness together.'

'We're not fighting it hiding out here,' protested Anna Kurtain.

'I agree,' said Prince Owen. 'We should be across the border, carrying the fight to the usurper.'

'The fight is ongoing,' said Jacob. 'The north's loyalty is still yours.'

'But I am not there to be seen leading our people.'

'Do you know how large the price on your head is now?' said Jacob. 'Marcus understands if you die the rebellion dies with you. You're barely safe here in Hadra-Hareer. You tried it the old field marshal's way and all you got for your trouble was a crushing defeat at Midsburg. We can't mass forces for regimental actions in the field. The usurper controls the air and the sea now. He probably would have even without the Vandians showing up to lend him their imperial legions. So we bushwhack blue-coats, and bleed them, and make them pay for every step they take over the Spotswood River.'

'I can never win the throne like this. All you have to offer our people is endless war and suffering.'

'All we need to do is outlast the south,' said Jacob. 'They'll get bored soon enough and come after us here. Rodal is where you'll see your regimental action. We'll man the Walls of the World and break them against us like we're shelling walnuts.'

'Outlast the south? Have you not seen the reports coming across from Weyland? My uncle is seizing northern cities and stripping them of citizenry – shipping people across the Spotswood River to work as indentured labour in his supporters' mills and manufactories. Vandia is claiming their share of our people's flesh, too, taking thousands as slaves. We have to sally out from here and show the people of the north we can protect them. If we do not, we will lose all support.'

'Every man and woman taken for a slave leaves a dozen behind with hate burning in their heart.' *And I should know because it's a mirror of mine.* 'We can use that hate. It's as good as bullets in the coming fight. We wait the south out and they'll advance on us here.'

'How can you be so sure what they will do?' said the prince.

'Because I'm going to keep on jabbing the wasps' nest until the south comes buzzing at us. You need to ask the assembly-in-exile for permission for us to start blowing the Guild of Rails' lines.'

Owen stared at Jacob as if he had gone insane. 'And the long guilds will place the guild-mark on the whole nation, withdraw entirely from Weyland.'

"That's exactly what I'm counting on. Bad Marcus can only move so many troops around using his skyguard. The rest have to travel by sail and rail. When the Guild of Rails stops running trains across Weyland, we'll sink ships to block the northern harbours and make the usurper march every step of the way.'

'A body cannot survive without arteries,' said Nima, her look of shock a mirror of the prince's.

'Right now, it's the usurper's flesh all the way to Arcadia,' said Jacob.

'And after the war ends?'

'That'll be a good time to mend fences and sow a new harvest.'

'I will not destroy my realm to save it!' shouted Prince Owen.

And with me in control of the northern army, you won't have to. You're too weak to rule and too strong to be ruled, my prince. That's what I'm in command of the army for.

'There is a name for such a wicked strategy,' said Nima. 'A scorched earth policy.'

'I learnt my trade in the Burn,' said Jacob. 'How do you think the lands across the ocean picked up their nickname?'

'I forbid it,' said Prince Owen. 'And the assembly will never permit it.'

We'll see. 'You'd be surprised what the assembly will support. Take Augustus Sparrow for example.'

'The speaker of the house is a good man.'

'Your good man's working real hard to arrange a royal marriage between Weyland and Ortheris.'

Owen recoiled in shock. *No, I didn't think he'd told you.* The prince made to stand up, but Anna stopped him. 'I am not a piece of royal chattel to be bartered away.'

Jacob pointed over the table towards Anna. 'Marrying a commoner is for peace-time, Your Highness, when the newspapers need to be kept happy with stories of pleasant royal progresses. If Ortheris could be convinced to support the rebellion, we'd open up a second front at the other end of the country. There's a lot of soft underbelly down in Gadquero and Ranelen. Under-defended prefectures with the southern army getting rowdy up here. You want to be King of Weyland, you'll put your people's needs before yours.'

'You dare to lecture me?'

'I dare to point out, *Your Highness*, that we need to do whatever we have to, to beat the usurper and send the Vandians packing back to their far-called empire. If you don't have the stomach for it, you might as well pardon the usurper for assassinating your parents, gift him your throne and head off into exile somewhere a lot further away than Rodal. Southern end of the Lanca is nice and civilized, I hear.

Good climate. You hide far enough away, your uncle's knives probably won't even track you and Miss Kurtain down there.'

Owen glared at him. 'What you suggest is insane. You would put an end to our kingdom to save it.'

'I know what Bad Marcus is willing to do to hold on to the throne. I've had a bellyfull of it. I need to know what you're prepared to do to take it from him.'

'I will talk to the assemblymen and you will have your answer.'

Jacob shrugged and stayed seated as the prince and his bodyguard left the chamber.

'You should not talk to Prince Owen like that. It is dishonourable for a master to be spoken to in such a way by one of his servants,' said Nima.

'The boy was a Vandian slave in the sky mines for most of his life,' said Jacob. 'He should know better than anyone how hard it's going to be to beat Bad Marcus and his imperial allies.'

'He is trying to do the right thing for his people.'

'This is a war, Miss Tash. Hard and dirty and grim. It's bloody and ugly and I wouldn't trade a single rusty bayonet for the prince's good intentions.'

'I see how the cost of it weighs on him,' said Nima.

'I do too, and not only for the prince. You've traded sides in this mountain parliament of yours to support war over peace. There are plenty in Hadra-Hareer calling you worse names than they call me. If it had been you supporting staying out of the war rather than that old man, your father's vacant seat would be yours by now. You'd already be Speaker of the Winds.'

'Power has no meaning to me, beyond how it is used to help my people,' said Nima.

'It seems I'm surrounded by honest, well-meaning folks,' said Jacob. 'After Prince Owen escaped from Vandia, he made similar noises instead of slipping a dagger in his uncle's back. He hesitated and here we are. Blood feud and civil war.'

'Prince Owen chose to seek justice rather murder.'

'No, he chose murder. A whole nation's worth rather than getting his hands dirty with just the one.'

'I wish Sheplar Lesh was back here with the Vandian girl,' sighed

Nima. 'We could end the murder. We could use the Lady Cassandra as a bargaining chip to open negotiations with the Imperium. If we handed her back to the empire as a sign of good faith . . .'

Jacob snorted.

'You find my words amusing?'

'The emperor doesn't give a shit about his missing granddaughter, beyond the slap in the face of imperial power her being held as a hostage represents. We could hand Lady Cassandra back smiling and happy, or we might send her back one finger a time in a diplomatic bag, and Vandia would press ahead what it's planning to do here all the same.'

'But you took her hostage? If you think that, in the name of the spirits, *why*?'

'Lady Cassandra's mother is Princess Helrena. Daughter to old Emperor Jaelis himself. It was the slavers working for her who buried my wife and stole my son. I wanted to give the woman a little taste of what she gave me.'

'Merely for revenge?' Nima shook her head slowly, sadly. 'Sometimes I do not see why Sheplar followed you to Vandia.'

'Sheplar didn't follow me, he followed his honour. He was charged with protecting Northhaven and that duty flew as far-called as the taken. Same reason he's out there in the steppes, trying to hunt down the little lady.'

'If what you believe is true, Sheplar and his gask friend are risking their lives for nothing.'

'Man has a code. I wouldn't call that nothing.'

'And what do you have, Jacob Carnehan of Northhaven? Or should I ask that question of General Quicksilver?'

'A reputation, Miss Tash. Never defeated on the battlefield, no matter what the odds or who the enemy.'

'You lost at Midsburg.'

'Oh, that was the prince and his old field marshal's battle. I can only claim the few slit throats that Temba Lesh seems to take such offence at. But at least the right side is dying now.'

'I do not care for your methods or your reputation. Skor Khrom,' muttered Nima, ancient words to ward against ancient evil.

'Nobody ever does. Until a couple of thousand bad sons-of-bitches

with blades and guns turn up like evil always does. Then I'm everyone's friend; until the very last day of the battle, when memories
get awful vague on who it was who won the day and put the villains
under the dirt. I'm the wretch that buries the night-soil, Miss Tash.
You and Prince Owen can be as sniffy as you like about it, but I'll ask
one favour of you. Let me bury the shit good and deep for you before
you start holding your noses.'

Jacob followed the path to its end. There had been a wooden handrail
to the right, once, protecting travellers walking the winding mountain
trail from falling into the cloud cover drifting below. Now, much of
the path lay broken, vanished from rock slides and erosion. Half an
hour's careful trekking from Hadra-Hareer. The single-storey pagoda
perched at the end of the narrow track was in a better state. An open
stone turret with a wooden roof decorated with elaborate carvings.
Jacob could hear the wind thrashing against it like a drum as he
approached. The man inside was holding on to the stone wall, his
eyes fixed on the peaks opposite.

'This is not a path that many foreigners find comfortable walking,'
said Temba Lesh. 'It is treacherously icy. If you misjudge the winds'
timing, they will catch you and throw you into the air like a hound
playing with a bone.'

'I spent a good few years in a monastery at Geru Peak,' said Jacob.
'I'm almost part mountain goat now.'

'I have heard of the place,' said Temba. 'Your monks do not find
many converts here. Our spirits of the wind blow louder than any call
from the strange saints buried inside your religious texts.'

'Don't tell anyone, but they never really looked too hard. Geru Peak
was a place you went to be with your own thoughts, mostly. Just the
mountains and the sky and the sea.'

'Strange things wash up on the tides below their cliffs.'

'Don't they just,' said Jacob. *Like a half-dead war leader escaping his
former trade.* 'Although a lot of what you hear down that way is just
stories.'

'Where we stand now holds a tale,' said Temba. 'Would you like to
hear it, before you try to convince me again to sacrifice my countrymen in your hopeless foreign war?'

'Why not?'

'This place is called the Pagoda of Chesa and Senge. It features in one of the ancient legends. They were two lovers, whose families disapproved of their relationship. Senge, the boy in the tale, was set a series of impossible feats to achieve, to win the hand of Chesa. Neither family wanted a union, and they thought the unachievable nature of the tasks would ensure his failure. Senge defeated countless enemies – the Great Krul Michka, Spear of the Steppes, wicked wind spirits, many ghosts, as well as hordes of strange creatures from the high mountains. He did this with Chesa's secret help, however. When Chesa's assistance was discovered, she was sentenced to death by her own mother. So Senge defied both families by rescuing Chesa from her home in Hadra-Hareer. The two lovers fled here to this pagoda, pursued by soldiers from both families. They prayed to the winds to save them, but the winds could only summon enough force to rescue one lover. Senge prayed for Chesa to be saved. Chesa prayed for Senge to be saved. The winds blew them both high into the air, and rather than allow one to live heartbroken without the other, both were impaled on the same peak and their souls joined with the wind so they could live together in eternity. That is where the Che'senge Wind comes from. If you listen quietly, that wind sounds like the boy and girl whispering to each other.'

'And I feel a lesson blowing in behind that old tale . . .'

'You may beat the odds and even achieve the impossible, but trying to live solely for another leads to misfortune. In the end, the mountain breaks everything.'

'Family before self, nation before family and pride before a fall. The mountain breaks everything,' said Jacob. 'You said the same in your council chamber. I must have heard those words a thousand times when I was in the monastery in Rodal. It's a good saying, mostly because it's true. Every Rodalian city a fortified citadel hanging off the crags, most of your streets buried deep below the rocks. Some on heights so high attackers need air masks to assault them. Gales driving strong enough they make hurricanes a breeze by comparison. Thousands of miles of winding canyons and hidden valleys and towering bluffs with countless ambush points. Rodal, always the indestructible Walls of the League.'

'And we will not abandon those walls to venture out and die in a fight that's not ours,' said the old politician.

'You won't have to,' said Jacob. 'I know that Rodal's not a country. I always knew that. It's a killing ground.'

'King Marcus will not venture here. Neither will his imperial allies.'

'They just need the right encouragement,' said Jacob.

'You are a most dangerous man. A killer.'

'I tried to be a better man,' said Jacob. 'I left. I changed. I hid.'

'There are many things a man may hide from,' said Temba. 'His true nature is sadly not one of them.'

'Maybe you're right,' said Jacob. *But I tried so damn hard, didn't I?*

'I understand your wife died in the slavers' original raid on Northhaven?'

'Mary Carnehan was her name,' said Jacob. 'Lord, how I loved that woman.'

'You must have, to have attempted to change for her.'

'I had already changed when I washed up back in Weyland,' said Jacob. 'I'd had my fill of fighting for rulers who made Bad Marcus look like a charity warden. I just wanted peace. To be left alone. The peace of church vows and a quiet life. I guess I stayed changed for Mary and our family, though. When Mary died, it didn't take long for me to dig up my pistols and my old habits.'

'You still have a son to live for.'

'Interned inside a cell in the city.'

'When you leave Rodal, Carter Carnehan will leave alongside you, that I promise. Pellas is a world without end. There's always somewhere else you can travel to.'

'You can never run away,' said Jacob. 'It took losing my wife and old life to teach me that.'

'But you can,' insisted Temba. 'Your only anchor is the weight of revenge. Cut it free.'

'If the skels' slave raid had just been a random attack,' said Jacob. 'I might have been able to walk away from Mary's slaying. But discovering Bad Marcus sold my last surviving child like he was no better than poultry at market . . . finding out Marcus was responsible for burning my town and murdering Mary for Vandian gold? My own king. The same government that was meant to protect us. How could I possibly walk away from a sin as black as that?'

'Sins are for the gods to punish, not men. You chose to live by a vow of peace once before. You may do so again. The way out is yours.'

'Saints and God,' said Jacob. 'They made me into a hammer. They gave me the times that forged me. Now, all I'm being sent are nails. I'm meant to be here.'

'Not in Rodal,' said Temba Lesh, leaning out over the ledge and feeling the cold air against his face. 'No. Not here.'

Jacob shrugged. 'Your heart is in the right place, Temba Lesh. Just like Prince Owen. Working for peace when the times only want to give you war. Thinking there is a deal to be done. That the usurper can be eased out of his stolen throne by reason and right alone.'

'Follow your leader's example,' said Temba. 'That is my suggestion. Seek the way of peace.'

'I tried it the prince's way,' said Jacob. 'I got a civil war instead of a quick coup and a bullet in the back of Bad Marcus' ugly head. I followed Prince Owen a second time and left a quarter of the National Assembly's army dead in the smoking ruins of Midsburg.'

'You are sworn to him,' said Temba, sounding horrified. 'Your words sound close to treason.'

'I made a vow over my wife's grave,' said Jacob. 'I didn't give it to any whelp of a boy.'

Temba pointed down the path. 'Go from Hadra-Hareer. Leave!'

'As you like it. But you had better understand that Prince Owen is merely the standard the rebels follow,' said Jacob. 'I'm the lance the standard's attached to. And a lance is only meant for a single task.'

'Skor Khrom,' spat Temba.

I've heard that before. 'Not any Rodalian insult I know.'

'It is not a curse. Skor Khrom is the Demon of the North Wind,' said Temba. 'One that takes human form and moves among the people, sowing hatred.'

'Hatred I've got aplenty, but I'm saving it all for Bad Marcus and the Vandians.'

Temba shook his head and turned his back on Jacob. 'You are an oath-breaker, with contempt in your heart for your own master. Duty and service and honour. This is everything.'

'No. That would be victory,' said Jacob. He seized Temba's legs and pulled them up, tumbling the old politician forward, screaming, across the edge of the pagoda. Jacob leant over the stone parapet and watched the body bouncing off the ragged cliffs, tumbling through the air to be swallowed by the white river of clouds running below the peaks. *The mountain breaks everything.* It would smash Bad Marcus and the Imperium too before long. Jacob heard a voice whispering on the wind, but it wasn't the Rodalian's pair of tragic lovers. It was Mary, his wife's weary, disappointed voice. *You didn't have to do that.*

'I've missed hearing you. You've been gone so long. He was just one man. Old and stubborn. Nima Tash will win her election now. Prince Owen will have all of Rodal on his side.'

You're a fool if you think he'll be the last corpse.

'The enemy were coming here anyway. Temba Lesh was a dead man walking. The trick is to make Bad Marcus and his friends arrive on my timetable, not the enemies'. One fool dead to save a nation, maybe two countries. I've made far worse bargains in my time. I can beat our enemies, Mary. It's the only thing I know how to do.'

You knew more, once.

'I did. You saw it, too. But you're gone. You're dead.'

My love, so are you.

'That's as maybe. Hell if I'm going the rest of the way without company. Bad company.'

Don't get Carter killed. Please. Take our son and leave here. Travel far away and save him.

'Sariel has plans for Carter. He'll be free enough and far from here. The boy won't need to see the worst of what I'll have to do.'

I will, though.

'Jacob Carnehan will be resting alongside you soon enough, Mary. I promise. But first, Quicksilver is going to fix what's broken.'

Not everything.

'No. Not everything.' A lance, impaling Bad Marcus. Driving into the glory and pride of the Imperium again and again and again. His enemies' dead corpses littered across the valleys and canyons of this hard, cold land. The Walls of the League. Every invader the Lanca had ever faced in the north had met their end here. Quicksilver had just one more foe to add to the tally. 'I can't have peace, Mary. So I'll have to settle for war. Bad Marcus wanted it; he practically begged for it. He spat in my face and he as good as spat on your grave. So I've arranged a fine old war for him. It won't be like the Burn, but I reckon it'll do.'

Jacob walked back down the treacherously icy path. Whispers chased his every step. Mary and Temba Lesh and maybe the long-dead voices of Chesa and Senge. It sounded like 'No more, no more.' Jacob shook his head. *Sigh all you like. There'll be new ghosts here soon enough. Enough company for everyone.*

Paetro walked down the street of Northhaven's old town alongside Duncan. Now that the southern army had claimed its victory here, the Vandians had landed their giant capital ships around the airfield outside the town and on the banks of the White Wolf River. The flats were filled with the hammering of the Imperium's new barracks being raised. The chop of helo rotors as the empire's attack craft drifted up and over the town's homes to patrol the pacified territory. Following the arrival of the Army of the Boles in the previously sleepy backwater, the township's malnourished, depleted population had been further stunned by the Vandians' overwhelming show of force. Enough metal in a single patrol ship to make any citizen a wealthy man. Helo squadrons and rocket-driven craft and capital ships capable of swallowing a sea-borne frigate without indigestion. Tanks rolling down ramps, each as large as a mobile fortress and resembling them besides. The tramp of thousands of legionaries' boots marching in unison. Technologies that made the Weylanders look as advanced as the nomads of the steppes; numbers that made the locals feel like strangers in their own homeland.

'Workers are a lot like house cats,' said Paetro. 'They get nervous and jittery when a new master or mistress is forced on them. Soon as they know they're going to be watered and fed as regularly as the previous master, they'll settle down.'

'The man Prefect Colbert appointed as new sheriff is an army officer called Donald Blood. His nickname in his regiment was "Flogging Blood".'

'So the locals are getting the boot rather than the food bowl,' said Paetro.

'There are supplies enough for anyone who turns in rebel fighters and sympathizers,' said Duncan.

'Divide and conquer? Nothing like it for showing your contempt and seeding self-loathing among the defeated. There're only two good ways to deal with your enemies, lad. You make them dead or you make them your friend. Putting your shoe leather on a man's throat and kicking him every now and then to help you feel better is a sign of weakness, not strength. Sooner or later, the most docile, conquered serf is going to get tired of the beatings, snap and come at you. When a worker's crazy like that, they don't care if they live or die.'

'I think the royalists are still enjoying the feeling of victory.'

'Well, that's a feeling for children who enjoy taking a magnifying glass to ants,' said Paetro. 'They had better start acting like war leaders, or they'll lose everything they've won.'

'It'll be my father and his friends' problem. Not mine.'

'Right enough. This town is the final stepping stone for us,' said Paetro. 'Prince Gyal has everything he came for now. He's got a victory fit for a fine triumph in Vandis: the slave revolt avenged; holds filled with so many prisoners that he is going to risk flooding the slave markets back in the Imperium.'

'So we just need Cassandra back safe,' said Duncan.

'That *we* being you, me and Helrena,' said Paetro. 'Prince Gyal only needs the little highness as a wedding gift for Helrena.'

But of course, mused Duncan, *his true wedding gift will be the imperial throne*. Like the wanted posters in the constables' office used to read, 'Dead or Alive'. And if Cassandra turned up dead, that would be just too bad as far as the scheming Prince Gyal was concerned; and no doubt a lot cleaner for his future offspring and the imperial line of succession.

Paetro patted the short-sword hanging from his black leather belt. 'We'll make time this afternoon for a training spar.'

'Sometimes I think you're training me to duel as hard as you used to train Lady Cassandra.' The muscles in Duncan's arms ached at the gruelling memory of their last session together.

'I'm training you for war, lad, not duels. This one or the next.

Most of our house's guardsmen served in the legions, same as I did. Decades of service. Your training is as good a substitute as you're likely to receive.'

'Northhaven had a territorial army company where I learnt the basics.' *Along with Carter and all the prefecture's other young bucks.* Duncan hadn't thought about his old friend for an age. *Friends, then enemies, and perhaps friends again. I wonder where he is now?* Maybe in one of the rebel gangs plaguing the north. Wouldn't it be ironic if Carter had been with the ambush of the royal army as it marched on Northhaven. *You saved my life in the sky mines, Carter. It'd be a shame if I had to kill you now. Stay lost. Stay an escaped slave until the Imperium's blood lust is sated and it leaves the Lanca, and then crawl out of the forests and the wilds to live under an assumed name. I owe you that much, at least.* And Carter's father dead of course. *For kidnapping Cassandra and gunning me down.* But Duncan would leave that particular piece of revenge to Paetro, if he could. Paetro Barca needed it. For his dead daughter and his honour. His sanity. Only a blood-price would do.

Paetro rolled his eyes. 'Firing single-shot rifles, was it? Black powder with pebbles for ammunition? I said, war, not chasing after partridges in the woods.'

'You said I was showing promise at last after our last bout?'

'You're fast enough on your toes, Duncan of Weyland. The kind of speed and endurance that only comes with youth. But you lack the instincts built by decades of soldiering. To obey orders without question. To shoot first rather than hesitate, wondering if the foe you must kill is deserving of death. That's why our house hires from the legions where it can. Old soldiers with tested instincts.'

Killer instincts. Duncan had won his freedom as a slave by saving lives. Helrena's and Lady Cassandra's. Could he prosper by taking them so easily? Did Duncan need a foe to prove himself an enemy by shooting first before he felt justified in killing them? *If I had simply shot Jacob Carnehan on sight at our last encounter, would we be here today?* Cassandra wouldn't have been taken as a prisoner during the slave revolt. Helrena might have stayed in Vandia and never fought to join the punishment fleet. *And maybe she wouldn't be planning to marry Prince Gyal.* Well, the world was full of might-have-beens.

*

The Cold Court. This high, chill place had been where the ancient Rodalian monarchs received petitioners and conducted the business of their realm. The flat top of one of the high mountains that rose above the canyon bluffs where Hadra-Hareer had been carved and burrowed out of the stone. A single, simple granite throne carved too, along with stone benches for the courtiers and citizens of the mountain country. Jacob shivered in the freezing, driving wind, knowing that it could grow far worse. *The Valley of the Hell-winds. Well-named.* Even with a thick coat, Jacob felt the chill more than any of the Rodalians waiting here, courtiers, soldiers, priests and the newly elected Speaker of the Winds. Nima Tash's perfect, porcelain skin seemed to glow in the light up here while his face felt as though it should be turning blue. Sariel waited with Jacob. The strange old sorcerer appeared as untroubled by the wind chill as Nima. Jacob had heard all about the history of this place from the locals who worked at the monastery. Millennia before, Rodal had been governed by kings and queens, little different from Weyland's rulers. Here the mountain monarchs had sat in session until a king called Hackchen led two hundred warriors to defend the narrow Chalhand pass into Rodal from the greatest clan horde ever to be assembled. Hackchen was unmarried and without heirs, so before he left Hadra-Hareer, he extracted an oath from his council that his advisers would rule with the consent of the people, and that the great families and houses of Rodal would never again squabble over the vacant throne. Hackchen had died a hero's death, buried below mounds of his nomad foes, and the council had honoured his wishes and kept to their oath. They still sang songs of Hackchen's exploits and bravery in the high villages and towns. Hackchen the Last. Hackchen the Greatest. That the Speaker of the Winds had chosen to meet the Vandian invaders here rather than inside the city's warmth carried a deep symbolism that would be totally lost on the Imperium's lackeys.

Baron Machus appeared red-faced from the climb up the winding stone staircase, his retinue of cloaked and armoured legionaries disarmed of their pistols and short-swords. That the baron was willing to enter the enemy's den cloaked only in the flag of truce spoke either of courage or a foolhardy disregard for his own safety. *Or perhaps it's arrogance?* The Vandians never seemed to lack for that.

'Legend has it that anyone visiting the Cold Court with murder in their heart is picked up by the spirits and dashed on the rocks during the climb up here,' Sariel whispered to Jacob.

'I reckon they've made an exception for this Vandian, then,' said Jacob. 'Because if I'm any judge of character, there's nothing much but murder in his heart.'

The baron and his retinue advanced before the throne and halted. One of the imperial officers stepped forward and raised his voice to announce the presence of his master. 'Baron Machus, Legate Commander of the Celestial Caste and emissary of His Most Noble Highness Prince Gyal, anointed son of the most holy Emperor Jaelis.'

Jacob noted that none of the Rodalian officials returned the courtesy of introducing the Speaker of the Winds. *The silence of contempt.*

'What the hell kind of place is this?' demanded the baron, discarding any pretence of diplomacy. His brutish fist swept across the flat wind-swept bluff they stood on. 'I thought you people burrowed into the stone, rodents huddling together for warmth. Is it too crowded in the passages below? Or are you just trying to keep your pathetically small number of soldiers out of my sight?'

'This is the formal seat of the Speaker of the Winds,' said Nima Tash, slapping her throne carved from the bare black rock. 'And this our court. It reminds us what Rodal is and what its people must be to survive on top of the Walls of the World. If you wish comfort, return to Arcadia. Or better yet, go back to your distant homeland.'

'Keep your closed sewer of a city hidden from me, then,' laughed Baron Machus. 'I have not arrived to be amused by what passes for the sights here.'

'Why have you come to Rodal, Vandian?' demanded Nima.

'To offer you a simple choice,' said Baron Machus. 'We require you to surrender all rebel Weylanders within your nation's borders as well as the Vandian citizen the criminal dogs took as prisoner . . . light of the Imperium and daughter of Princess Helrena, the most glorious Lady Cassandra Skar. If you fail to meet these terms by nightfall tomorrow, your nation will burn.'

'Rodal is stone,' said Nima. 'It does not burn.'

'The people clinging to this windy, misbegotten country of yours will light up just fine,' said the baron.

Nima's eyes narrowed. 'We shall see.'

'Yes,' grunted the baron, 'I can see that you're the daughter of the Rodalian with the big mouth we hanged.'

'You think to provoke me into rash violence with your insults? You do not face the daughter of a murdered politician here. You stand before the newly elected Speaker of the Winds.'

'Well-named,' leered the baron. 'Given that wind is all I've enjoyed since arriving in this shit-hole. Most of it's been a freezing gale, but up here it's all the hot kind.'

'Then you shall have something else.' Nima clapped her hands and a retainer came forward to present the baron with a wooden walnut case.

'What is this?' said the baron, examining the box. He opened the lid to reveal two ivory-handled daggers laid out on a bed of red silk.

'It is traditional to present a visiting herald from a foe with gifts,' said Nima. 'These knives belonged to my father. One is for you as the empire's emissary; one is for the master who holds the hound's leash. Prince Gyal of Vandia, I believe.'

Machus snorted in amusement. The unattractive noise sounded like a swine rooting about a trough. 'You think to buy us off with a brace of blades? Are you a fool?'

'No, Vandian. They are my answer to you. I do not require a day to consider your Imperium's terms. Those you spoke of are under the protection of salt and roof within Hadra-Hareer. The same protection you broke when you hung the previous Speaker of the Winds. The tradition of hospitality is the only reason you will leave Hadra-Hareer alive today, rather than having your severed head returned inside a sack. The knives are also our tradition, a different one. The *Blood Steel*. I present you with my father's blades and my curse. I will recover them from you and your master's corpse in due course.'

'Then you are a fool after all,' said Baron Machus, closing the case shut with an angry snap. 'You think the Imperium lacks for provinces with high peaks? We've fought plenty of mountain tribes before. Your little cracks and crevices aren't nearly deep enough to hide your people from our legions. I'll bring your two knives back and stick them up your arse, though. I'll do that for you.'

'You are welcome to try. I'll be waiting,' said Nima.

'I—,' the baron stopped. He had noticed Sariel among the Rodalians standing behind the throne. With the sorcerer's golden skin and long leather coat etched with hundreds of illustrations, Jacob was surprised it had taken so long. 'That one!' said the baron, pointing to the elderly bard. 'He is a notorious outlaw wanted within the Imperium.'

'This man too is under the protection of salt and roof here,' said Nima.

'Under which name do you impugn me as a criminal?' demanded Sariel, stepping forward.

'Sariel Skel-bane,' said the baron. 'Although I've seen a good few many more aliases on the posters bearing your likeness.'

'Killing skels isn't a crime, it's a duty. And I have to say I feel much the same about Vandians. But you must be a wealthy man, my celestial caste friend. So many slaves to die and work for you. Why should a rich baron of the Imperium bother about the paltry reward on Sariel Skel-bane's head?'

'Killing outlaws is my duty,' growled the baron. 'And my pleasure.'

Sariel tapped his staff against the rock. 'I suggest you find simpler ones. You'll live longer to enjoy them.'

'Old man, old man. You don't look so much. I wonder what all the fuss is about. I suppose even our hoodsmen can get it wrong.'

'Grit in the Imperium's gullet,' smiled Sariel. 'But who's to digest me?'

The baron's hand dipped down towards the belt by his side, but his fingers were reminded by their empty touch that he and his retinue had been disarmed.

Nima rose up from her stone seat. 'You will not have the Weylanders or any of our nation's guests. Visit again, Vandian, befoul our air, and you and your allies will discover only blood here.'

'And this is really the message you want me to relay to His Highness Prince Gyal . . . a son of the all-mighty emperor? Do you have any idea of what you are facing across the border in Weyland?'

'Just brutes with expensive, elaborate machines. Rodal has known many enemies over the ages. You are just one more. It's never the steel that counts, only the soldiers who come bearing it.'

'You're savages in need of an education.' The baron spat on the rock in front of the throne and stalked away with his retinue.

'That must have felt good,' said Jacob.

'I feel only sadness,' said Nima. 'I have not just given them my Blood Steel. I have given them the nation's.'

'You give to them only what they would have arrived to take anyway,' said Sariel.

'I sleep no easier for knowing the truth of that,' said Nima, grimly. The speakers and soldiers and priests parted for the Speaker of the Winds as she departed the court. Unlike the Vandians, she did not follow down the exposed steps leading to the canyon floor below. Nima headed for a door hidden in the cracks of the heights behind them, steel painted as black as rock and as thick as the vault of a bank. An interior stairwell down to the hidden depths of Hadra-Hareer.

'Quicksilver has his war after all,' said Sariel 'How do you feel about it, Your Grace?'

'Cold,' said Jacob, honestly.

'I hope you are as effective a general as you believe yourself to be.'

'You should know. You joined with my mind inside the sky mines.'

Sariel grunted. 'The man who can beat the Imperium and destroy King Marcus is the man who would have stayed in the Burn. United the shattered lands and ruled them. Not won all those victories and murdered all those kings, only to toss them aside and flee and hide himself behind a pastor's cant and scripture.'

'I am who I am.'

'But will it be enough?'

'Reckon it better be. I'm finished with hiding and running. I've got just one last king to strangle before I'll call matters done.'

'King Marcus and Emperor Jaelis, they are only a rash on the skin. The true sickness runs far deeper,' said Sariel. 'You saw the stealer I fought in the shadow of the stratovolcano, you sensed its kin beating on the doors of this world when we travelled using the gate of stones. There is a reason that my face is on wanted posters in every Vandian garrison, and it has little to do with a little mischievous tweaking of the emperor's nose decades ago. The battle you would wage is only a tiny shadow of the real war. There are schemes and plots across Pellas that are almost beyond your comprehension.'

'No point in a simple man worrying about them, then,' said Jacob.

'One enemy at a time, one bullet at a time. That's the only philosophy I've ever needed.' *And look where it's got you,* Mary's voice whispered.

'Your son will be of assistance to me, however,' added Sariel.

Jacob nodded. 'Take Carter. Far away from Rodal.'

'He'll hear of what you do here,' said Sariel. 'Even if he doesn't have to see it.'

'Might be all of Pellas will hear,' said Jacob. *But only if I arrange the slaughter right. If I fail, I'll just be a forgotten footnote in a long, sad history.*

FOUR

THE SORCERER'S JOURNEY

Carter's new quarters weren't that different from his cell and incarceration. He wasn't sure if that was because the Rodalians treated their prisoners in a civilized manner, or they housed the capital's citizens like prisoners. Two rooms instead of one now, the cold hard carved rock of the wall softened by a few rugs and tapestries. Everything lit during the day by a strange soft light. The illumination caught by mirror arrays inside chimney stacks that protruded from the surface of the wind blown canyons and mountain slopes. And, of course, his old accommodation had lacked one important thing – the most important thing of all. Willow. She had come to Carter and he had known she wanted to be reassured, even as she had grabbed him and kissed him and they had fallen to the bed and made love in this strange place. After all, she had said, she couldn't get any more pregnant than she already was. But Carter didn't care about that, beyond the hurt Willow had already taken getting to this point. A forced marriage he couldn't protect her from. Carter still felt guilty about that. Sometimes it seemed that guilt was all he had to offer Willow Landor. *I'm not good for much else, these days. But at least we're free. I'm free.* Even if that was free to face Willow's unhappiness about how little time he would spend in Hadra-Hareer. *Freedom always comes with a price attached, it seems.* Freedom as a slave of the empire had been paid in blood. Freedom in Rodal came with Willow's tears. Carter truly hated to be the cause of any more suffering for her. They rested together in bed, warm under the woollen blankets and looking at the ceiling. There weren't many answers there, Carter realized.

'I can come with you and Sariel,' said Willow at last, but the madness of the notion must have occurred to her even as she spoke it.

'You're in no condition to travel,' protested Carter.

'Plenty of travellers give birth in their caravans.'

'They're born to it. Every day of their life they travel surrounded and protected by their clan,' said Carter. 'Won't be much trading where I'm going with Sariel by the sounds of it. And we'll be travelling light and fast.'

'Sariel can convert the stone circles into portals that touch the far-called side of Pellas,' said Willow. 'Surely he can protect one woman, even if that woman is carrying a child in her belly?'

'The steppes are dangerous,' said Carter. He slapped the chamber's heavy stone walls. 'Without this in the hordes' way . . .'

'Is that meant to reassure me? The steppes are where you're heading. When I was trapped in Arcadia I thought I'd lost you forever. Now, just as soon as you're free of your jail cell, you're straight back putting your neck on the block again.'

'It's not as though I want to leave you here,' said Carter. 'Hadra-Hareer is safer than Weyland.'

'The Vandians will travel to Rodal. Hunting for rebels and everyone who took part in the slave revolt.'

'They might,' said Carter. 'But there are some things I trust in.'

'Rodal's caverns and thick rock walls?'

'My father,' said Carter.

'He scares me now, Carter,' said Willow. 'He's nothing like the pastor I grew up with.'

'I know. That's why I trust my father to keep you safe. He travelled across the world to rescue us. He survived that journey against all the odds.'

'Your father doesn't want justice for the nation,' said Willow. 'He's just fixing to kill anyone who had anything to do with your mother's murder.'

'I can hardly fault him for that.' *I'll see them dead myself for killing her.*

Willow grabbed Carter by the arms. 'You live for life, not revenge.

I don't care what the risks are out on the plains. All I'm asking is to brave them alongside you.'

'I don't think it's an accident the way the rebellion played out,' said Carter. 'It's as though my father planned for Midsburg to fall, just so the army would end up under his command. I think he's been saving Rodal like a stone in his back pocket to sling against Vandia.'

'You know how many people we lost in Midsburg? Half the army and city dead and those who survived in chains. And you think the pastor *planned* that?'

'I know it sounds crazy, but yes. I think he planned that.'

'Then I have even more reason to leave with you,' said Willow. 'I can't stay here and play the part of your father's conscience. And that's what he wants from me.'

'You've got someone else to think about,' said Carter, placing a hand gently against her belly.

'How can you say that? This baby won't be yours. It'll be that evil bastard Wallingbeck's. Let me travel alongside you and Sariel, maybe the journey will—'

Carter reached out to reassure Willow. 'That's no way to think. When your baby comes into the world, they won't be an *it*, only a little *he* or *she*. And they're not going to care then that Benner Landor and his wife drugged you and kidnapped you and forced an unwanted marriage on you. The baby won't care about King Marcus or Vandia and whatever Sariel has got planned. Vandia, the civil war, it'll mean nothing. The child will just love you and you'll need to love them.'

'I need you to live,' pleaded Willow. 'How can I go on without you? Don't make me face this without you.'

'I'm sure as hell not planning to die for Sariel,' said Carter. 'I'm coming back. For you and the baby both. He'll have a father and it won't be some southern nobleman paid to give Benner Landor's daughter a courtier's title.'

'My child needs that father *now*. I had a terrible premonition last night,' said Willow. 'Nothing good is going to come from you following that rascal of a sorcerer away from Rodal.'

And I've been touched by little but bad dreams of late. But Carter didn't want to load any extra worries on Willow's shoulders. 'I cut a deal with the old dog in Midsburg,' said Carter. 'I told Sariel that when you

109

and my father were rescued from Arcadia's hospitality and safely out of the usurper's clutches, I'd help him in return. I owe the old coot.'

'Sariel rescued your father from King Marcus' dungeons, but he never saved me. I did that all by myself. Isn't there war enough in Weyland? You don't have to travel on a wild goose chase with Sariel to find blood.'

'Sariel needs me to help track down his friends: to heal them like I did him in the sky mines.'

Willow shuddered as though someone had walked over the soil of her grave. 'You unlocked his soul and released a storm into the world.'

'Something happened to me when I fell inside the stratovolcano during my botched escape attempt,' said Carter. 'I know it sounds crazy, but my mind filled with the entire world's dreams. When Sariel appeared at my deathbed and healed me; those dreams, my memories, they flooded out from my mind and went into his.' *Where they belonged.* And Sariel had been changed by those echoes of the past. From a half-mad bard recounting insane tales and making fanciful boasts, into something far darker. Willow hadn't known Sariel before the awakening to realize the difference. *If Willow had,* Carter suspected, *she would never let me leave Hadra-Hareer with the peculiar wizard.*

'We could become travellers,' said Willow. 'We have more than enough money to buy a sturdy wagon and a train of healthy horses. We can put Weyland behind us ... leave the entire League. We could travel south into the Great Gaskald forests. Follow the forests into Tresterer and join one of the free caravans heading east. My false husband and my wretched father would never find us.'

Carter cringed at the thought of what she'd endured down south. 'Don't call Wallingbeck your husband. Owen annulled the marriage.'

'And my father's barely my father anymore. Only Leyla Holten's husband and cat's paw. But the Landors and their rich friends have ended up in control of Weyland all the same. There's no future for us in the Lanca.'

'The royalists might have boots in the north, but they don't control the land yet. This is not like you,' said Carter. 'You're always the optimistic one, hoping for the best and finding it in other people too. We survived as slaves in the sky mines. We did the impossible and escaped. We'll survive the rebellion against the usurper, too.'

Willow rubbed her extended belly. 'Carrying the viscount's baby turned me into a realist, Carter. I watched Midsburg burn and the assembly's army smashed and scattered like straw falling to wildfire. Our army's living in the wilds like a gang of marauders and we are now all exiles. We're barely welcome in Rodal, even with the new Speaker of the Winds supporting Prince Owen and the north. How can we possibly win against the combined forces of Vandia and King Marcus?'

'I don't know,' said Carter. *I really don't.* 'But it's a fight we have to win.'

'The plan was to get the assembly to vote the usurper off his stolen throne, to ratify Prince Owen's claim to it. That hope dissolved along with parliament. We tried fighting . . . and look where that's got us. Civil war and defeat in all but name. Even taking Lady Cassandra as a hostage failed. Kerge and Sheplar lost her to raiders and Vandia's arrived to punish the slave revolt just the same. If we don't flee the league, we'll end up dead or back as slaves inside the sky mines. King Marcus has won. The Imperium has won. I don't care what your father has planned; nobody can survive against such terrible odds. We've slipped, Carter. We need to lift ourselves out of the dirt and flee while we still can.'

A voice sounded behind them. *Sariel.* 'You are in Rodal, now. The Walls of the World. Nobody trips over a mountain. Only small pebbles cause you to slip. Pass all the pebbles in your path and you will find you have crossed the mountain.'

Willow's glanced irritably at the interloper, as though here was the author of all their misfortunes. 'You! What are you doing here?'

Sariel stared knowingly at Willow. 'Father Carnehan told me his son was due to discuss our journey with you, Miss Landor. I have come calling because you deserve to know the truth and the stakes of that journey.'

'It's arrant foolishness,' said Willow. 'Weyland is burning to the ground in civil war and that's not enough for you? You have to venture off in search of mad fancies out on the steppes where the savages will skin you alive just for not having blue skin?'

'I am sorry,' sighed Sariel. 'I have endured for so very long. Seen so many things. Miss Landor, there are always wars in Pellas. Revolutions and rebellions and invasions. Men and women squabbling over thrones and councils and who is to sit on them. What seems to you to be so important is merely the wind rustling the leaves to me. Part of the natural order of things.'

'This is our *lives*,' said Willow. 'I want to have one. With Carter. You offered to take us to the other end of Pellas once. Somewhere safe and far from this madness. Will you not make that offer again if I ask? If I *beg* you?'

'I made that offer when I thought the rest of my kind lost,' said Sariel. 'Following my travels across Pellas, I now have reason to believe they are very much alive. I require Carter's assistance to quicken what has been forgotten inside them.'

'Why me?' asked Carter. 'Why now? I know you've kept your word to me. My father's free of King Marcus' chains and Willow is safe. I'll return the courtesy and hold up my end of the bargain. But before I take one step away from Hadra-Hareer, I need to hear the truth.'

'There is a wider war raging across Pellas than the one being fought inside Weyland,' said Sariel. 'Although, I grant you, the civil war is a very small part of the larger battle. Do you really want to know who the true foe is? You glimpsed our enemy briefly during the last battle in Vandia. A stealer. Their kind is at work across Pellas, scheming to eradicate humanity. They have tried many different methods and many times across the millennia. Plagues and wars and unrest are their tools. Stealers love nothing so much as power. It attracts them like insects swarming honey spilt across the grass. As you might imagine, they find the Imperium a very comfortable nest. All the resources and might they need to advance their schemes.'

'And you and your people oppose them?' said Carter.

'We do. Like the enemy, my kind possesses many names in Pellas. In Weyland, we are often referred to as the *ethreaal*.'

'That's ridiculous,' said Willow. 'Stealers and ethreaal. Those are names from the scriptures. You expect me to believe you are—'

'My people are neither saints nor angels,' said Sariel. He rubbed his back with one hand, the wound where his wings had been ripped from his spine. 'And outside of what passes for prayers, I have never communed with your God or any other deities. Although I was once able to fly. The ethreaal and stealers have always wandered at the world's margins, mistaken for shadow and light. If we have been written into your holy texts, it is solely because our struggle concerns humanity's very survival.'

'Why would the stealers want us dead?' asked Carter.

'Why do bacteria want to make you sick? Because that is the purpose of disease. The point of their existence.'

Willow shook her head, 'And what evidence do you have to convince us of any of these tall tales?'

'Now your eyes have been opened to the truth, you will begin to find evidence all around you,' said Sariel. 'You may start by looking west across the Lancean Ocean. The Burn is the stealers' handiwork. They sowed seeds of hatred in the west across many centuries, stoking resentment and turning tribe against tribe. Helped provide tools of devastation to the kingdoms across the water, pouring as much fuel as was needed to spark the war-to-end-all-wars. The Burn was a failure that helped convince the stealers that more powerful means needed to be sought to extinguish mankind.'

'A failure?' said Willow. 'Blood is still being spilled in the Burn! The war's raged for centuries.'

'Precisely,' said Sariel. 'Even in the blackened wasteland of the west, humanity still lingers to fight on. Plagues and famines and endless warfare and yet still people cling grimly on to life across the ocean. The stealers set fire to the house, only to watch beetles crawl out of the ashes, using blackened, dead wood to feed and survive.'

Carter felt anger at the old man's insinuation. 'We are not insects.'

'To the stealers that is precisely what you are. Worse, perhaps. A plague without end. They regard themselves as your cure.'

'And are we any more than ants to you?' said Willow. 'The way you talk about us.'

'There once was a colony of red ants that lived in the lush green grasslands of Hirundo,' said Sariel, by way of an explanation. 'These ants were regularly preyed on by wasps. The wasps flew down on to the worker ants and paralyzed victims before flying back to their nest to devour the helpless ants. The ants begged their queen for help and so she sent a vast force of soldiers to protect the workers. But the wasps attacked again and paralyzed the column of soldier ants, carrying them away to the nest for supper too. The workers despaired, fearing even to leave the ant hill to gather food. They grew hungry and weak and desperate. Quarrelling with each other and sensing the end of their age. Then one day a female barn swallow took up residence in the woods nearby, and by the next morning, every wasp had simply disappeared. It was a miracle! The worker ants rejoiced. Some ants said they should crown this barn swallow their new queen. Others said the bird was the Supreme Goddess of Red Ants in disguise and required worship. To settle the mystery of the miracle, the ants set out for the barn swallow's tree. When they reached the bottom of the tree trunk, they yelled upwards, offering thanks and bribes and devotions and begging to know what the barn swallow truly was. Do you know what answer the bird gave to the crimson sea of creatures below?'

Carter shook his head.

'The barn swallow spat out a half-digested wasp into the grass and called down, "Not hungry in the slightest anymore." My people oppose the stealers,' said Sariel. 'That fact alone should be enough for you.'

'You're not telling us the complete truth,' accused Willow.

'Oh, but everything you hear from my lips is only a perspective, never completely the truth,' said Sariel. 'And thanks to your fine young gentleman here, my mind is now filled with a world of competing perspectives. Memories have been returning to me ever since I departed Vandia. My kind's place in the world and the enemy's. I was one of a group of seven sent to thwart the stealers. The party was the last hope of my kind, the final toss of the dice. In many ways, the war we wage against the stealers is already lost. Unfortunately, my party was ambushed by the enemy when we emerged through a portal. I survived, greatly reduced and humbled. Much like the stealers, we ethreaal are very hard to destroy completely. But we can be shattered and wiped of purpose and history. Such was my state when first we met in your library guild hold outside Northhaven, Carter Carnehan. Confused. Lost. Clinging to the broken shards of my purpose on Pellas.'

'My dreams, the nightmares,' said Carter. 'They always belonged to you.'

'Yes,' said Sariel. 'What you discovered below the stratovolcano was an ancient centre of my people. Concealed by magma and poison gas where unwelcome visitors are unlikely to venture. The refuge sensed my touch upon you and realized that I was wandering across Pellas broken. The refuge took you in and altered your body . . . used your mind as a vessel to store what I needed to remember myself again. The refuge was fairly direct in its work. Some might say brutal. But then it is a simple machine with little experience of the subtleties of humanity. Then it released you, trusting that we might meet again. You are more than a simple creature of Pellas, now, Carter Carnehan. You have been remade as a key. And I require you to unlock the other survivors of my expedition. Restore them back to themselves. We need to complete our work before the stealers settle their schemes.'

'What work?' asked Carter.

'We carried with us something we called the great weapon,' said Sariel. 'It is the only thing that will stop the stealers and their evil. I need to gather my people to use it.'

'Why do I get the feeling that there is little great about this weapon?' said Willow.

'The stealers will not be stopped by blade and bullet. If we fail, then none of what happens in Rodal or Weyland or even Vandia will matter much. There will be no more histories to record the passions of your age. Instead, your people will be extinct and Pellas will know endless cold and darkness.' Sariel reached out kindly towards Willow, although Carter noticed she shivered at his touch. 'That is why I can no longer simply open a gate to some far-called nation millions of miles from Weyland and squirrel you and Carter safely away at the far-called ends of Pellas. It would please me to see you both out of harm's way. But it would be an utter waste of time. Darkness is descending. There are not leagues enough in the world to out-distance our final conflict. Only two choices remain. Fight and win. Or lose and perish.'

'So that's it, then?' said Willow. 'You're going to take Carter and disappear through one of your cursed gates?'

'Not quite. We need to avoid using the standing stones except in dire emergency or to travel distances that are impractical by other means. And for good reason. Every time I activate a portal, the enemy knows exactly where I have travelled and destroys the gate to put it beyond use. I may as well light a signal fire telling the stealers where to hunt for me. It is no coincidence that the Vandian expeditionary force arrived to help King Marcus after I used a portal inside Weyland to return here. I have arranged for the female skyguard officer who flew you to Hadra-Hareer to be freed. She will fly us into the steppes and when the fuel runs out, we will walk the rest of the way.'

'Vandia came seeking revenge for the slave revolt,' said Carter. 'Not you.'

'The Imperium is complex enough to have more than one motive for what it does. Emperor Jaelis is heavily under the influence of the stealers,' said Sariel. 'He suffers from a sickness of the mind similar to dementia. That is often a sign that the stealers are swaying the emperor's decisions more directly than offering simple advice. Jaelis's mind is being eaten away like a rotten apple. An unpleasant end, it must be said, to a particularly unpleasant and violent brute.'

A sudden worry struck Carter. He rubbed his throbbing forehead. 'And what about my mind?' *Am I going mad?*

'You are only suffering from tension-induced hypochondria, Lord Carnehan,' said Sariel. 'Most of a human mind lies still and vacant. Empty corridors. Yours is merely being used to store a few crates that belong to my people.'

'I thought I was going insane on the sky mines!' snapped Carter.

'Oh, but that's because you were,' smiled Sariel. 'When we met in Vandia and you passed me all that was mine, I was very careful to erect a more appropriate wall between the trove of knowledge inside your mind and what you might call your soul. That which makes you, *you*. You will not go mad now. And neither will you become a senile, half-crazed paranoid like Emperor Jaelis.'

'I'm having your dreams again,' said Carter. 'Memories that aren't mine. Things I can't even credit as possible.'

'A little leakage is only to be expected. But nothing like you experienced before, am I correct? As I said, you have been remade as a key . . . the key to all of our survival. And a rusty key could very well snap in the lock. Hence such enhancements as I made to your mind. Your safety is of paramount importance to me.' Sariel smiled at Willow. 'You may trust that, Miss Landor, even if you trust little else of what I say.' Carter heard what the old man whispered to Willow before he departed the chamber. 'Seek out the deepest quarters in Hadra-Hareer. Quicksilver means to break a king and an empire both on those crags outside.'

'I'm not sure who's the craziest here,' said Willow, taking Carter's hand and squeezing it as hard as though she was dangling from one of Rodal's crags. 'Your father, that devil, you for following him, or me for allowing myself to be abandoned here.'

'You're resting here,' said Carter. 'And I'll return.'

'Make sure you do,' said Willow. 'Because without you . . .'

Carter and Willow held each other, clinging tight, attempting to make the moment last forever. Carter felt Willow's warmth seeping into his. Another memory for him to travel with. A memory that even the god-like stealers and ethreaal and their strange ancient conflict couldn't impinge on. 'That's why I'm coming back.'

'I don't trust Sariel,' said Willow. 'I know he helped save us from the sky mines and kept your father alive on their voyage to Vandia, but I don't trust him. Not his mad grand conflict or his intentions or his tall tales. He's using you and the rest of us. We're the ants in his story; you know that, don't you? And a hungry swallow can peck apart an ant hill as easily as a wasps' nest.'

Carter tried to summon a reassuring smile. He worried it might have come out as a grimace. *We're caught between rival storms with no choice but to ride them out.* He prayed with every iota of his being that Rodal and the Walls of the World proved strong enough to keep Willow safe.

Alexamir Arinnbold did not question Temmell's need for a copy of the Rodalian's holy ledger of the winds. He was a wizard. Sorcerers, like gods and goddesses, often asked for the strangest of gifts, Alexamir understood that from his people's legends. Had Borty the Bladehearted demanded a precise accounting from Isal of the Plains when the god rode down from heaven on a chariot drawn by twelve flaming steeds? *So, you'll make me king, will you? But first, why exactly do you need the cloak of the Demon Scarbo? If there's no good reason for you to have it, you can stick your kingship up your arse and whistle for your cloak. I won't be stealing it.* Alexamir snorted. It was enough that Temmell had promised to make the gift of Cassandra's healing permanent.

Alexamir was being carried deep into Rodal in one of Temmell's wooden pigeons, a small two-man flying wing flown by the clans' most proficient pilot, an old warrior called Zald Mirok. Zald was calm and unflappable, a great horseman in his day, so it was said. But that day had passed long ago. Zald might not be able to ride for two days and nights and win a battle at the other end, but his experience and cold nerve made him the top pilot among the nomads. Admittedly, that was a very small pool to begin with. Temmell's chosen men had been trained by the aerial equivalent of sell-swords; thin, distrusting pilots from the countries east of Hellin who had, they'd claimed, served on the great aerial carriers which crisscrossed the skies, never landing, always moving. Not skyguards like those they must face among the rice-eaters. But mercenaries who had flown the shuttle planes trading between grass and sky. And the mercenaries had been right to be distrustful. After the initial cadre of nomads' training was completed, the foreigners had been stabbed to death in their beds on Temmell's orders, their bodies fed to the camps' swine. They wouldn't be complaining of training blue-arsed savages in the art of the sky-saddle in any tavern within a thousand miles of the Lanca; not unless they were carousing those taverns in hell.

At first, Alexamir had been insulted that he wasn't trusted to fly himself into Rodal. But when he heard the proposed route, he was silently glad that honour had been denied him on the wizard's orders. It had been easy flying at first, a straight route over the steppes, landing at marked hills where wagons waited with wooden kegs of fuel. After the plains lay behind them, Zald had carried them into Rodal zig-zagging wildly through the Mask Heights. So-called because the rice-eaters who clung to those peaks survived with tanks of air inside their mountainside huts, never seen without strange leather breathing apparatus. It was the least populated part of the mountains. The peaks bore the additional advantage of rising so high that the mountains broke every storm, redirecting them north or south on to the lower ranges. The Mask Heights were, literally, above the weather. So high that raiders from the north couldn't hope to scale them on foot. What need, then, to set Rodal's skyguard to patrol the Mask Heights? *A decision they will soon come to regret.*

Alexamir and Zald drifted in at night, their wooden pigeon painted as black as a bat, following the mountain streams down to where they merged into a mighty flow feeding the Yarl River further south-east. Zald landed them in a mudflat between the river and an alpine forest. Then the two interlopers had dragged the wooden pigeon into a small glade, little more than a good-sized circle of wet meadow, covering it with the same green netting which concealed the clans' aircraft on the steppes. Alexamir gazed into a rock pool alongside the river, watching a strange Rodalian face gaze back at him, features twisted and soft, the skin leeched pale of his proud blue tone. His own face, but as he might have looked if he had been born a miserable rice-eater rather than a free rider. *The glamour is so strong; I look like a rice-eater even to myself!* No wonder Zald had complained how uncomfortable he felt flying his enchanted brother into Rodal, oblivious to the high honour of bearing the Prince of Thieves within his craft. Alexamir was torn between hoping that the infiltration spell would last long enough for his adventures inside the capital, worry that the glamour might misfire leaving him looking like this forever, and fervent prayers that it would wear off before he returned to the steppes – lest one of his people stick a dagger in his side or confused him for a thrall for the taking. He left Zald in the forest setting snares for rabbits, surrounded by silvery white birch, as cold and ugly as raven-picked bones. Some of the trees were left bent at odd angles from the last storm. Forests here had that trick, Temmell had warned him. Roots able to flex and reorient without losing their trunks to a gale. *Sneaky trees. Whole forests of ugly sneaky trees.* He hoped the trees weren't an omen for his coming theft. The existence of the clans' new wooden pigeons was a secret so priceless that the risk of the plane's discovery spoke volumes for the value of Alexamir's booty. Temmell had tutored Alexamir in the mores and manners of the Rodalians. Long, hard and gruelling had been the thief's training, and the sorcerer's final advice – for Alexamir to keep his mouth shut as much as possible – was hardly a vote of confidence in his ability to pass as one of the mountain people. *The gods must favour me, surely? Otherwise, they would not have given me the Golden Fox. But they broke her after their gift. Was that to humble me? Or prove me worthy by taking on this task for Temmell? On my success lies the future of the clans, or so he says. No rider is ever given a horse he cannot master. What better task for the most talented thief to* live for a thousand years? And where stealth will not serve, I have a dagger hungry for my enemies' hearts.

He hiked for two days through the lower slopes of the Mask Heights, sweating inside an itchy Rodalian shirt and dark bear-fur-lined coat. He kept his hood down, even during the drizzling rain. Temmell's glamour over Alexamir was superficial. It had altered his face but not changed his nomad blood, able to sleep naked in a winter meadow and never once freeze. Swaddled in these heavy clothes he felt like a corpse ready for burial, wrapped in leather armour and a funeral shroud made of his tent. *But then, the enchantment has also left me my strength. How much worse if I had been turned into a weakling rice-eater, tired after an hour's sprint, barely able to lift a boulder without cracking my spine. No, better that this sorcery lies skin deep.* The clothes were old but well repaired. Cleaned of the blood from whatever unlucky Rodalian had once worn them. He had an air-mask hanging on the back of his neck as part of his disguise, but at this altitude it was thankfully unnecessary. Alexamir followed the directions Temmell had made him memorize, avoiding the sparse settlements in this part of the country. Navigating south-east by the cold clear waters until he reached the Yarl River itself. There he marched with the current until he reached a small river port where merchants arrived from the east on billowing sails, carrying goods to be portered down ramps and slung over the side of mules and mountain ponies. The settlement itself was no more than thirty buildings, surrounded by a wooden palisade that had seen better days. Strange-looking holes had been cut into the fortification. Not arrow-loops, but to channel the wind without collapsing. A barrier good for keeping out wolves and bears, but not human attackers. This far inside the centre of the country, there would be few nomads raiding in search of saddle wives. Too far a journey back to the steppes with an ungrateful struggling peasant girl in tow. A sentry on a watch tower waved at Alexamir as he passed through the village's open gates and he returned the greeting. *If you could see me in my true skin, you would scream until your lungs burst.* Every house in the village was a low, thick-stoned affair, all windows hidden out of sight from outside and opening on to a central courtyard. Not out of fear of men, but protection from the fierce storms. *Dreary grey stone. Nothing like the brightly coloured warm tents of the Nijumeti.* The beasts in the merchant caravans stared lazily at Alexamir as he passed them, the air-masks they needed at higher altitudes swinging lazily under their necks. *I wonder if I look like a rider or a rice-eater to them – if the glamour tricks animals as well as Rodalians?* He glanced about the docks, looking for the giant hunting hounds that often followed after Rodalian patrols. A canine encounter was the last thing he needed right now. Their large dogs were as canny as people, and he didn't need his disguise questioned by any madly barking hound. But no hounds were in sight along the wooden piers. Just trading boats, piers and a few river fishing coracles.

Alexamir found a flat-bottomed river cog as empty of passengers as could be hoped for and booked passage to Hadra-Hareer. The boat bore a name, as proudly as any horse or a flying wing: the *Arrow Jang*. Merely the act of passing over his copper coins to its master, a man called Shan, felt alien to Alexamir. How much more honourable would it have been to creep in at night and cut the boat's anchor lines, stealing the craft and taking her downstream? Sadly for the nomad's honour, blending in was what was required. Stepping on to the soil of the rice-eater's capital as just one more visitor. And to be fair, the boat currently appeared to need a crew of twenty to work it and keep the unruly wooden contraption on course and well-mastered. Glorious to steal but hard for a single man to sail, even one as supremely talented as Alexamir. *But I could have done it. Temmell's chosen men taught me to fly their wooden pigeons. How much harder can pointing an over-sized raft down a river be?* Let the foreigners handle the boat then, this was not fit work for such a magnificent hero as Alexamir. It felt strange as he sat on the planking of the cog's deck, watching the crew work the single square-rigged sail. They were sailing with the thrust of the river. In truth, there wasn't much for its crew to do on the downriver portion of the voyage apart from teasing him. Alexamir tried not to flinch each time the boat rolled and yawed in the rapids, but the crew sensed this experience was new to him and laughed at the traveller. *But these fools are themselves fooled, for they tease Norbu the goat herder — who does not even exist — not the greatest among the Nijumeti.*

'This would be your first time down from the heights, lad?' grinned the skipper. Captain Shan was a snub-nosed riverman with a grey beard that made Alexamir itch just to look at it.

'It is,' said Alexamir. His cover story as well as the truth of the matter. When he spoke, his voice sounded as sing-song and as clipped as any rice-eater. The foreign accent still a surprise every time he opened his mouth to spill a cunning lie. 'My brother's lived in Hadra-Hareer for a year and he sent word that he has arranged a good apprenticeship for me.'

'You won't like the city, Norbu,' said Shan, confidently. 'Too many people, too little space. No clean gusts like those of the High Mask. Lad like you should sign up on one of the boats. Get trained in river-craft. With your muscles, you'd porter cargo and trim sails with ease.'

'Family is family,' said Alexamir.

'True enough,' said Shan. 'You can't pick them. But you need to be careful where you're heading. The spirits may well be blowing bad fortune over the capital's walls soon enough.'

Alexamir flinched. *Does he suspect why I am here?* 'Bad fortune?'

'The war, lad. The civil war in Weyland. Have you not heard of the war to the south up in the cloud scrapers?'

'Oh, that. I have heard of fighting in Weyland. Two men who want to be king and only one throne to be shared between them.'

'You're not a complete bumpkin, then. As good a summary of our neighbour's sad affairs as ever I've heard.'

'But their land is far from here.'

'Aye, but not quite far-called enough,' said the riverboat skipper, lighting a thin pipe. 'For centuries our nations stood together. Yet as soon as those ungrateful Weyland devils found the means to scrape together their own skyguard, our kites were banished from their air, as unwelcome as plague in a child's cot. And now the new Speaker of the Winds is making common cause with one of the factions in the Weylanders' blood feud. What good will come of that?'

'I'll tell you what good,' called one the sailors. 'The chance to avenge Palden Tash's death.'

'A disgrace, I'll grant you,' said the skipper. 'And a dark dishonour, to trade the protection of salt and roof for foul murder instead. But when you step between the duelling daggers of another family's blood feud and shout for peace, you shouldn't be surprised if one of the blades slips and accidentally ends up decorating your own gut.'

'Blood follows blood,' said Alexamir.

'May it never be yours,' said the skipper, 'or mine. You mark my words, lad, you may yet be grateful for the chance to sail back to the Mask's foothills, trade warm chambers inside Hadra-Hareer for a mat in a high village house on the cloud scrapers.'

'You find trouble swirling in every current,' complained the sailor.

'And is that not a captain's job? May our new Speaker of the Winds yet find the wisdom to understand the same in time.'

'If I was the Speaker,' said the sailor, 'I would send our skyguard down to the King of Weyland's palace and burn it to ashes for murdering Palden Tash. Let a fire-pot or two fall on this Bad Marcus' fat head to remind him of the cost of treachery.'

'Then let us say a prayer of thanks to the kind winds of Langaltso that you are my foolish nephew and not from any family grand enough to be put before the council and voted in as speaker. I want my skyguard in the clear air above Rodal. Protecting us, as is their sworn duty.'

The *Arrow Jang* followed the Yarl's fast swirling waters for days, little for Alexamir to do but listen to the quarrelsome crew arguing good-naturedly between themselves while he tried to avoid new passengers taken on at each river port they docked at. There were trapped furs to be traded and fresh vegetables to be bought. At least the vegetables made a change. The staple diet on board was a white fish caught in the river by the crew, which Alexamir had to pretend to enjoy, even when it was served in a spicy sauce of minced fish mixed with red peppers and onions. Fish-heads would grin mockingly at Alexamir from the corner of his wooden bowl, sharp-toothed and crafty, nothing like good wholesome lamb or solid oxen meat. Ready to catch in his throat with small bones too numerous to be removed. It was well known that the only people who happily ate fish were the coastal clans west of the steppes. Beach-clingers and dirty trident wielders. Sneaky cowards who would flee out to sea on their tiny vessels sooner than face a man on horseback. That was what regularly eating fish did to you. Still, Alexamir did his best. Or at least, his alter-ego Norbu did his best. *We should call the Rodalians fish-eaters rather than rice-eaters. This is only for you, Golden Fox. The gods will protect me from fish-eaters' cowardice, surely, while I am honouring my people during the raid.*

As the *Arrow Jang* sailed east, Alexamir began to notice the regions they went through growing more populated. They passed high towns clinging to mountains, the choice of river ports to halt at growing more frequent. At one of the river towns a wandering penitent priest joined the vessel, causing Captain Shan to complain about how he was expected to give free passage to every shave-headed monk who took it in his heart to stroll down from a temple. The scrawny orange-robed priest gave no name apart from describing himself as an acolyte of Dro'alung. Alexamir was secretly glad the monk had joined their voyage. Now he did the praying for the crew and passengers, rather than voyagers conducting their own. He'd kneel at the front of the vessel, his hand thumping his traveller's stave into the decking. It had a little metal wind-vane on top, four spinning silver blades – beaten into the shape of the heads of a monkey, dragon, yak and goat. Professional praying on Alexamir's behalf was superior to his amateur efforts and the rest of the crew obviously felt the same way. Temmell possessed a book naming over six hundred Rodalian spirits of the wind, and if there was any one thing that was going to give Alexamir away as a proud horseman rather than a mealy-mouthed rice-eater, it was misremembering some air-blown god of these mad people. Luckily, every region's mountain tribes held their own pantheon, calling common spirits by local names largely alien to their neighbours. Alexamir spent as much time as possible on deck. He and his fellow passengers such as the priest shared an open chamber below that ran squeezed next to the cargo chamber. It was windowless and dank, any light coming from small wooden grilles in the deck – old bug-infested sacking for beds on the hard wood. The sailors' accommodation wasn't any better; just on the other side of the *Arrow* with a few hammocks for sleeping quarters. Only the captain had a cabin worthy of the name at the vessel's stern. *It does not matter. I do not need comfort. I can ride ten thousand miles sleeping on horseback and only dismounting to water the grass.*

'You're an unusual fellow, Norbu,' said the skipper, one afternoon.

Alexamir's hand touched the back of his coat where his dagger rested. *Still there.* 'I am?'

'Many a man in the High Mask dies on the same mountain they were born on without even leaving it. You've travelled through the

Low Mask already, and now down the bubbling length of half the Yarl River. You must have been far-called in a previous life.'

'It's a good trade that calls me.'

'And what trade would that be?'

'A vent-man,' said Alexamir, recalling the careful lies that the old sorcerer had made him memorize.

Captain Shan shivered. 'A big fellow like you, crawling up an air shaft with a hammer and chisel? I know it pays well and is in the gift of the little guilds, but that's nothing but a fool's trade. Can't spend your coin if you're lying broken under a rock slide.'

'Man can fall off a mountain any day of the week.'

'But if you tumble off a trading cog, chances are you'll reach the shore. Every man and woman on the Arrow knows how to swim. Easier to teach a fellow that, than how to pull their bones back after a fall down an air shaft.'

'Perhaps I shall bounce.' Alexamir had been warned against boasting, but this was just a little one, unlikely to give him away.

'You're not a careful man, Norbu. Brave but not careful. You sure there's not a village girl up in the scrapers crafting a little leather breathing mask for what's warming her belly?'

'Do I look like such a man, Captain?'

'Hard to tell,' said Shan, winking. 'But there's many a maid happy to see the *Arrow* come into port . . . and not just for the goods in our cargo hold. A Yarl trader can have only one wife, yet keep many comforts.'

One wife? Alexamir tried to keep a look of pity off his face for the old trader. Why, a hero like Alexamir would be embarrassed by anything less than three true wives and twelve saddle wives. More than that would be greedy. And expensive to feed. But heroes did not trouble themselves with petty ledger-keeping when it came to their households or their appetites. That was for thralls to worry about. 'There is a woman. I plan to return to her.'

'Yes, but will you return to your love carrying a fat purse of coins, or hobbling on two walking sticks and bearing a shattered spine?'

'Hopefully I will take the path that returns a man bearing treasure.'

'I shall pray you are not disappointed,' said Shan.

If you could see through this enchantment, Captain you'd be praying for your crew to put a harbour hook through my skull. The river skipper walked off, realizing that this was yet another afternoon where Norbu wasn't going to be convinced to sign up as crew.

It was a day colder than those that had preceded it when the *Arrow* came sailing towards a dam-like structure built across the canyon, a vast dark wooden structure rather than stone, reaching as high as the mesa top. A wide opening in the structure arched over the Yarl River, enough space for seventy cogs to sail abreast below the dam. *A wind temple.* Alexamir had heard of these giant oddities, but his raiding along the Rodalian borders had never carried him deep enough into the country to witness one before. It was no solid mass of timber such as a dam beavers might build across a river, but a wall rising high above them riddled with thousands of hatches and ports, a complex mess of pulley systems linked to the temple squatting atop the wall. *So, this is how the rice-eaters call their spirits?* It seemed a tame breed of demon who would answer a priest signalling by fluttering heavy wooden shutters. At least the witch riders of his people chewed herbs which set the mind spinning wild and the soul soaring free. What were these monks doing . . . merely banging doors and making a clatter? Alexamir grunted to himself in amusement. *Perhaps that is how they tame the storms of the mountains? They make so much racket that their spirits cannot sleep, and then the demons descend upon Rodal in angry fury to shut the stupid monks up.*

The *Arrow* docked at a pier to the structure's side, the shadow of the temple and dam plunging the cog into twilight. Their holy passenger left to speak with the group of orange-robed priests waiting to greet him. He returned to the cog and conducted a hushed discussion with Shan before departing the boat for good. The priest had reached his destination, and whatever bill of passage he'd incurred, it had been paid with information.

Shan came striding past and saw Alexamir staring at him curiously. 'The spirits are rising in the west. A mighty gale is coming down upon us.'

'The monk told you this?'

'Dro'alung is a messenger, a calling wind,' said the skipper. Alexamir wasn't sure if Shan meant the priest or the spirits the monk

126

served. Either way, the nomad didn't fancy experiencing sailing down the Yarl River on the wrong end of a fierce blow.

'Don't look so damned miserable, Norbu,' said the boat's master. 'I know you don't get real weather up in the scrapers, but down here you'll see a thing or two. Nothing we haven't dealt with before. The priests on the temple will know which spirits to call with their chimes and doors. They will pray us spirits to calm the wild winds; dismiss any which are evil. Meanwhile us mere mortals will sail for a wind harbour.'

Alexamir nodded as though this course of action was already well known to him. Somewhere up in that temple was a fragment of the holy log-book he was being sent to copy. He could only imagine the priests' reaction if they knew he was arriving to steal away the source of their power. Why, they'd stream down the slopes of the valley like a mob of orange-robed crows, waving their staves towards the sky while cursing him as a filthy invader. That was a pleasant thought. Leaving Rodal with his prize and Temmell's healing of the Golden Fox guaranteed. *No other thief could do what I must do. Steal their priests' magic and steal it so well they will not even know I have it!* His chest swelled with pride at the thought that this duty had been entrusted to him alone. *Temmell chose wisely. No other rider could do this.*

Alexamir sniffed the air on deck. He didn't need to be a true Rodalian to smell the approach of a mighty storm, still hidden beyond the horizon, but the weight of its distant anger was making his skin itch. Stillness fell over the shore, birds disappearing for sheltering cracks and crevices in the mountains, the creak of insects in the dry grass fading away. The river flattening and eerily quiet; even the fish diving deep and their air bubbles vanishing. He wasn't the only one on board who sensed what was coming. The ship's captain began shouting irritated orders to the crew, hurrying them about their business. The *Arrow* put the river behind them shortly after, entering a port where they followed a narrow wooden-lined canal through two locks and along the channel into a cavern cut into the sheer mountain wall. One of the well-built wind harbours the skipper had talked about. The canal curved through tunnels, their passage twisting multiple times to break any storms raging outside. The *Arrow* ended up inside an artificial gallery, a stone harbour surrounded by chambers excavated for rest and refuge. This close to the capital the *Arrow* shared dock with ten similar vessels. Not just a harbour for river traffic, but a haven for overland travellers as well. From the cog's deck, Alexamir could see the chambers currently accommodated hundreds of merchants, travellers, pilgrims, trappers and tradesmen. It was a rich tapestry of humanity, lit by a hundred spears of light from mirrored passages snaking up to the mountain slopes. Not just Rodalians in the crowd, but many foreigners too, traveller caravans that had been tracking along the riverbank on horse and wheel. People away from their birthplace; no homes to take shelter inside and hunker down while the local spirits slaked their anger. Alexamir regarded the travellers with fascination. Caravans did not dare to cross the steppes, for they would soon find their goods stolen and their endless ranging traded for life as a Nijumeti camp thrall. But these wayfarers traded everywhere outside of the steppes. As much a nomad as any clan rider might call himself. Never stopping or setting down roots. Transients who traversed millions of miles across the turn of their lives. Never once revisiting the same league of land. Alexamir understood them about as well as he understood the rice-eaters. *So timid. They do not travel in force, like a horde. Never brave enough to claim the grass they roam. Everywhere they blow they are strangers and visitors, fearing those who hold the soil as they drift across the land. No warrior's pride or honour in such a life. Freer, though, than these Rodalian rodents who meekly cling to rocks and make their shelters inside caves.*

Wardens pushed through the crowds thronging the wind harbour, shouting the time remaining of their confinement. Holy men connected to the temple outside, swaddled in orange robes. Six hours left. Alexamir left the Arrow and stretched his legs, moving through the exotic crowd, just another stranger among many. His disguise held well enough. Nobody paid him a second glance. The air-mask hanging from the back of his neck marked him out as a simple mountain lad, unworthy of conversation unless there was a crooked card game running to pick his pocket, or a stall owner trying to offload spoiled food. Just a hulking Rodalian yokel down from the scrapers. No sounds from the storm beating outside carried into the wind harbour. *Too far under the mountain.* What he could hear was a babble of different languages and strange accents speaking common Trade

Tongue, or Radio, as it was called within the League. Curious smells from unfamiliar food cooking on the stalls' griddles. After a while, the confusion of nationalities and races began to wear on the simple thief from the steppes and he returned to the *Arrow*. At the bottom of the gangplank connecting cog to stone harbour quay, Alexamir discovered a group of six men arguing with the ship's master. Pale foreign faces in grey military-style uniforms, hard-looking men not from Rodal. They put Alexamir in mind of the Hellenise smugglers which the Krul of Kruls suffered to trade arms and machine parts with the clans, but their angry accents were less pleasing to the ear and none of the devils possessed the flame-hair that oft marked out a bootlegger. They carried pistols, sabres and rifles as though the weapons were an extension of their bodies. *Warriors. Battle-hardened men.* Alexamir checked his dagger was still with him. He could earn his way into the good graces of the Arrow's master with a few slit throats if matters turned ugly here. As Alexamir got closer, he read the signs from the soldiers. *No, we are safe.* None of these foreign fighters appeared prepared to draw weapons. They were deep inside a foreign land and were well aware of what fate awaited them should they offer serious violence to any locals. The same sad fate that might befall Alexamir if Temmell's spell faded early.

'I do not like the idea of giving passage to armed bandits,' said Shan. 'Leave your weapons under bond here with the harbour wardens and I will carry you to Hadra-Hareer.'

'These here weapons,' said a stocky, short soldier at the front of the company, 'are the tools of our trade. You wouldn't ask a mason to leave his hammer and chisel behind? You wouldn't ask a doctor to leave his vials and herbs and scalpel with the harbour master?'

Alexamir couldn't help but stare at the soldier. He sported an ugly crimson scar down his face, as though someone had tried to split it in half with an axe and only just failed. *That might make him a poor excuse of a warrior to take the wound, or a fearsome warrior to have survived it.*

Shan raised his hands in exasperation. 'It is your trade that concerns me. Where fighting men travel, they bring a fight with them.'

'We left the fight behind in Weyland,' said the ugly warrior. 'If we wanted more of it, we'd have stayed. Trust me. There's plenty of war left south of your mountains.'

So, these are Weylanders? Alexamir's gaze travelled over their thread-bare clothes. Dirty and worn, much like the soldiers' pinched faces. But their rifle barrels were well-oiled and in good condition. That spoke well. And they were disciplined, too. Letting the short ugly one have his say without arguing amongst themselves.

'And there it should stay,' said Shan.

'If it makes you rest easier, we'll surrender our weapons for the voyage's duration. You can keep them nice and snug in a locked chest in your hold or your cabin. Whatever pleases. Just so long as we get 'em back at Hadra-Hareer.'

'Very well,' said Shan. 'But you will give me no trouble. If you brawl with the other passengers or cheat my crew at dice, you will be tossed out at the very next port. You can make the rest of your way on boot leather.'

'Don't you be worrying, Captain,' said the ugly one. 'We've all had enough of mule train saddle sores to last us the rest of our lives. This is a hard land to cross and a little river breeze will be just the thing to keep us settled until we reach Hadra-Hareer.'

'And what will you do then?'

'We'll take fresh orders from Prince Owen's generals. Don't doubt we'll be sent back south to harry Bad Marcus and the usurper's forces.'

Shan shook his head sadly. 'This is no good. You will bring trouble on our heads.'

The stocky one grinned, making his split face even uglier. 'We'll keep our killing on the right side of the border, don't you worry about that, Captain.'

Shan looked as though he might change his mind, but then he waved them up the gangplank. 'Pile your arms against the mast. All of them. Not a fruit knife left swinging on your belt.'

At the ugly one's command, the soldiers swung the rifles down from shoulder straps and unbelted their pistols and sabres.

'You keep an eye on these Weylanders for me, Norbu,' said the cog's skipper to Alexamir while the soldiers marched up into the *Arrow*, making a gift of their weapons in the sail's shadow. 'I do not trust them.'

'Yet you trust their coin enough to give them passage to Hadra-Hareer,' noted Alexamir.

The boat's master shrugged. 'I am not so rich that I can afford to turn away good copper. You will discover there are far too many filthy foreigners inside the capital. Weylanders just like these, looking to carry on their kin-war from within our borders. What are six more soldiers to add to their numbers? Our borders were wisely shut to their ilk not so long ago. But our new Speaker opens them and offers exile to this boy-prince who would supplant his uncle-king. Ever since, our roads have been choked by rag-tag fighters travelling to swear fealty to their Weyland prince and sharpen their swords in our shadow.' Shan snorted. 'What would it serve to turn such vagabonds away from the *Arrow*? They would just follow the river down to the capital on foot. Better I earn their coin than the mule train merchants.'

It seemed a self-serving argument to Alexamir, but he said nothing. He needed to stay on the good side of the cog's master until they reached Hadra-Hareer. Let Shan bluster and argue with his crew, they seemed ready enough for the quarrel.

The *Arrow* left the wind harbour before evening descended. Outside, there was little sign any storm had just come through. The buildings in the small port town stood intact. The waters of the Yarl River had kept within its banks. No trees had fallen, although many were leaning towards the east, flexible roots bowed as if in supplication to the Rodalian spirits of the wind. The alpine forests would right themselves soon enough. The *Arrow* continued her voyage towards Hadra-Hareer. It was easy enough to keep a watch on the foreign soldiers for the vessel's master. They held back from stealing and brawling, true to their word. The stocky repellent-looking soldier who had done the speaking for the party in the wind harbour knew what Alexamir was doing and started to seek 'Norbu' out to converse with him. Nocks was the laconic soldier's name. Alexamir came to suspect there was more to the soldier's attention than Nocks just demonstrating he knew the nomad had been set to spy on him. One afternoon, lounging on the deck, the nomad's suspicions were confirmed.

Nocks' guileful eyes halted knowingly on Alexamir while he leant over the *Arrow*'s side, taking in the breeze from the Yarl's fast-flowing waters. 'So, you think I'm fixing to slit the crew's throats, steal the captain's ship maybe?'

'Are you?' asked Alexamir.

'I'm not the sailing type. A boat can take you places, but it's the destination which interests me, not the voyage. You understand what I'm talking about, don't you?'

There was an undercurrent in the soldier's words which put Alexamir deeply at unease. As though the stubby soldier was staring into Alexamir and seeing right through the sorcerer's enchantment.

'You've got a right strong face,' continued Nocks. 'Puts me in mind of somebody else I knew once.'

Alexamir had to prevent himself grinding his teeth. *What do you know, Weylander?* 'Have you visited the scrapers?'

'That I ain't. No, this fellow was a proper brute of a man I served with in the Burn when I was fighting with the free companies. You heard of the Burn, haven't you? Far-called across the waters of the Lancean Ocean. Could have done with that air-mask of yours then, just to hide the stink of the place. Centuries of blood and fire and a war that's still smouldering. A thousand petty kingdoms and princes at each other's throats and the fight going on for so long nobody can much remember why. Always work for a soldier in the Burn. More mercenaries than farmers when your staple crop is battle.'

'Who would wish to cross the ocean?' said Alexamir. He suppressed a shiver. *Saltwater, nothing a horse or rider can drink, endless water to the horizon and beyond.* Honest nomads and heroic thieves such as Alexamir travelled over land, never sea. *Bad enough the fresh waters of this cursed Yarl.*

'Nobody in their right mind. Nobody with a choice in the matter. A man doesn't always have one, though. Take that friend I was talking about. He's a Nijumeti clansman. Got himself into some serious trouble with what passes for nobility up in the steppes. Had to flee into exile across the waters, and that tells you just how serious the bad blood was. Nijumeti, they hate the sea like it's plague. Brave as gods of war on the land, but put one of them on a clipper and they just curl and sob like babies until they make land again.'

Alexamir didn't like where this conversation was heading, not in the slightest. 'What was your friend's name?'

Nocks smiled slyly. 'Why, he'd be Artdan Arinnbold.'

That cannot be. My father! He died on a hunting expedition with the Krul of Kruls, gored to death by a hill lion. Alexamir gazed at the ugly

132

Weylander, desperately trying to conceal his shock. 'What was the bad blood?'

Nocks casually shrugged. 'Woman, I think. Or maybe it was a gambling debt that ended in murder. Everyone in the free companies has a sad story. You get tired of hearing 'em after the first year, even your own.'

Alexamir thought of his mother, living in the Great Krul's palace. Supposedly taken in as an honour debt to a dead saddle-brother. Alexamir raised almost as one of the Krul's sons, always favoured among the riders. *Was that an honour debt or an act of thievery? Was that an honour debt or the guilt of black treachery twisting in the Great Krul's heart?* His mother taken as a prize while his father narrowly escaped a cowardly ambush and fled? Was everything Alexamir thought he'd known of his life as a rider a lie? 'And this nomad's fate . . . ?'

'Hell if I know, now. I got myself a chance to come home to Weyland and serve in the royal army. Didn't appeal much to Artdan. Soft living, he called it. Cursed me for a silk-a-bed. He stayed fighting as a sell-sword in the Burn. Maybe he's still out there. Could be he's dead. Free companies always offer good fighting. Never offered much by the way of guarantees. If anyone could survive out there, it'd be that ol' killer, though. You learnt the art of fighting marching in Artdan's shadow. He could put a quarrel from a great-bow straight through an armoured foe's helm at four hundred yards, draw two swords and slice a horse in half with the man in the saddle split from helm to belt. Surely wish that big wolf was fighting by my side the last few months, though. Could have used him at Midsburg, bullets as thick as flies down there.'

Alexamir nearly choked on his words as they came out. 'A hard man to kill.' *Everything a lie. The Krul I serve. Out here, risking my neck for his wizard. No,* a voice deep down called to him. *Risking your neck for the Golden Fox. Not for the Great Krul.*

'Just like me,' grunted Nocks, running his finger down the red cable splitting his face. 'Man who did this to me is going to regret it one day.'

'Not a recent wound,' said Alexamir, masking his distress with empty words. *The Krul of Kruls. Curse the man to hell.* And how did he get to be the horde's master? By killing every clan chief who stood in his way, making alliances and intimidating the rest. It wasn't just the wizard's counsel that had served Kani Yargul so well. He was the ultimate thief. Ruthless and brutal. Stealing what he wanted and putting those in the dirt who stood in his way. Was Alexamir's mother among his prizes? Kani Yargul's saddle-brother another among his tally of cruel victories?

'Didn't pick it up in the civil war,' said Nocks. 'But it smarts every day. Some nights I can't get to sleep for my little memento throbbing like I just took the wound fresh.'

'A sabre slash?' *Perhaps his story is a coincidence? No, it can't be. A rider with the same name and similar enough in face to me for this Weylander to see the resemblance. My father is not dead. I was lied to. Deceived.*

Nocks shook his head. 'No. I did it myself. With a pistol. It misfired and took my face off rather than blowing my brains out, which was what I was aiming for at the time.'

Alexamir stared at the soldier as if he was insane. *Is he raving or speaking the truth?*

'*Why?*' Nocks convulsed into a barking laugh as filthy as a sewer. 'That's the question, ain't it? There were a bunch of forest savages coming to crucify me against a tree, build a fire around my boots and roast poor ol' Nocks for supper. Creatures so twisted they hardly count as human anymore. The bullet was a mercy.'

'But you said a man did this to you?'

'It was the man who tossed me a single bullet as the Lord's own clemency, right before he left me for dead. But I don't reckon ol' Nocks can die. Not unless I choose to. Perhaps not even then.' Nocks hooted loudly, amused by his self-proclaimed invincibility. 'That's what those forest cannibals thought, anyhow. Staked me out to die, like a haunch of beef that needed ageing. After I survived for five days nailed to that tree, the savages started to worship me, before they sent me on my way riding a timber-wolf the size of a plough horse. Nocks, holy Nocks, blessed by the stealers for his fine ways with a blade and a gun.' He fell into a fit of dirty laughter again.

Alexamir was half-convinced that this Weylander had become demented during his trials. *Battle-crazed.* To be possessed by the gods during a confrontation was to be blessed, being sent the red rage a sign of their favour. But it became a curse if the spirits did not immediately flee after the fight. Staying inside a rider, worming into his soul and heart, tipping him into killing furies over spilt drinks or accidental jostles around the camp fire. Perhaps this Weylander who claimed to have fought with a father Alexamir long believed dead, this Nocks, was truly insane.

Can this devil be a test, sent by the gods to make me doubt my task? If so, they will fail. I will succeed for Lady Cassandra's sake. Temmell will give me her healing in return for a handful of stolen pages. Let Kani Yargul be cursed and trampled under Atamva's hooves. Does my father truly still live? Truly? 'How long did it take you to cross the ocean and reach the other shore?'

'Six months crossing by trading ship with stopovers at the Rottnest Isles and Furinn Point. Picking worms out of biscuits with my dagger when I wasn't so seasick I couldn't eat 'em anyway. Never much had a liking for the Lancean Ocean. Storms and sea-serpents and pirates. You show me a sailor and I'll show you a dunce with a sail too stupid to make a living any other way.'

Alexamir's people called it the Endless Ocean. Six months sailing over the cursed salted wastes. It might as well be endless. And if Alexamir made the journey and survived it, what would he find in the war-torn countries on the other side of the sea? An old warrior who barely remembered his young son? A boy who served the same Krul who had attempted to have Artdan Arinnbold murdered, who had stolen his wife. *What if I came to him with the tale of how I slit Kani Yargul's treacherous throat? What if I came to him bearing the joyous news that his exile was at last over. That he could return home to the clans?* But how would Alexamir do that? He was an exceptional thief, not a mighty sorcerer like Temmell. If he managed to slip past the Krul of Krul's guards and kill the leader, what then? Kani Yargul had united the clans. Promised them fabulous victories over the filthy foreigners who kept the Nijumeti contained inside the steppes as though the grasslands were the riders' cage. What would Alexamir have to offer hundreds of angry clan elders and warriors who presently stood so high within the horde? Their leader's untimely death in a now ancient blood feud, repayment for bad dealing over a stolen wife? Alexamir would be earning his own death with Kani Yargul's blood. *But perhaps that is a price worth paying?*

'Sure is odd,' said Nocks. 'You being the spit of Artdan. Wide and wagon-heavy for a Rodalian, too. Course, if that old wolf had come raiding down this way and left a bun warming the oven of some village girl, you'd have a blue tint to your skin, wouldn't you, *Norbu?*'

Yes, it was as though the unsightly soldier saw straight through Temmell's enchantment. Alexamir tapped the air-mask hanging around his neck. 'Nomads never raid the Mask Heights.'

'True enough,' leered Nocks. 'Nijumeti maraud for the sheer devil-ment of it, and 'tain't much fun scaling slopes so high you need to keep your hut stocked with air tanks to live there.'

They sailed on for another three days and nights, carried fast by the current. It took until the fourth day for the voyage to turn ugly. Alexamir was leaning against the vessel's side, watching the crew work around him. Ahead of them another bluff-bowed and wide-beamed fishing boat drifted in the stream, her planking carved from red alpine wood, a crew of four casting a net while managing her single white main-sail. A day hadn't passed without Alexamir passing a dozen similar shallow-drafts plying their trade in the Yarl. Identical craft worked out of every river village. As he looked closer, this boat seemed to be having difficulties. Her crew struggled wildly with their netting; one of the sailors abruptly pulled off his feet and catapulted across the small deck. Out in the currents, the fishing boat suddenly started to spin madly as though she had been captured by a whirlpool.

This unexpected sight hadn't escaped the attention of a rigger up in the *Arrow*'s sails; his yells rousing crewmen across the deck, halting them mid-task. 'Tusoteth! *Tusoteth!*'

Alexamir grabbed a sailor running past. 'What is he calling?'

The riverman pushed past Alexamir as though the passenger before him didn't exist, not bothering to answer, sprinting towards the hold. The look of pure panic on his face spoke volumes, however. *Are we to fight the river's wild, mischievous currents now?* It was as though Rodal wished to end Alexamir's incursion into the mountains before he stole the spirits' power. *First it sends winds to chase me. Now this. Whatever this is.* 'Atamva protect me,' muttered Alexamir. 'Show these devilish spirits why you never allow them to trouble the grasslands. Show them why you are the most powerful of all among the gods.'

Nocks appeared on the bow, his eyes blinking as though he had just been roused from a slumber. 'What's going on here?'

'Trouble,' said Alexamir. 'There is a fishing boat ahead in difficulty on the river. But our crew—' He indicated the mad flurry of action all around them. 'They understand well enough whatever woe it is we face.'

'Ain't no blow coming,' said Nocks, raising a finger to test the air. 'And we're not running for a wind harbour.'

Sailors emerged from below decks clutching swords, boat hooks and harpoons. *And you don't need steel to fight this land's wind devils.*

'Damned if there ain't a dance being thrown and nobody invited me,' said Nocks. The soldier cast around for the grey-uniformed fighters he travelled with. He found the Weylanders among the press of running crew and startled passengers and barked orders at them. 'Grab me my rifle and sabre and get your own too. Lively at it!'

'But the skipper said—'

'Shan may be a captain, but hell if he's commissioned in the Army of the Perryfax. These water-rats are as jumpy as spit on a hot skillet and Nocks needs the feel of steel in his fist.'

Out on the Yarl, Alexamir noticed the fishing boat's rotations slowing. For a moment he thought their panic was to be short-lived, but then he caught sight of exactly what had halted the vessel's mad spin. Pushing out of the currents came a long grey tentacle, dripping wet and covered with razored suckers. It rose forty feet above the fishing vessel, growing like a mighty tree given sorcerous life from a seed. As quickly as it rose it plunged down, smashing into the fishing boat's centre and sending an explosion of timber into the air. The flat-bottomed ship split in two, both halves of the vessel caught by the current and dragged into the path of the *Arrow*. Half her crew spilled into the river and madly swam for shore. These were fast wide waters in the Yarl and it was hard enough for competent swimmers to make it to land at the best of times. *These aren't the best of times.* A hill of wet flesh appeared in front of the fishermen, a great barbed beak rising from the water to snap them up. It was as though they had simply been dragged into a cave by a riptide – but this cave happened to be attached to a gut and a fierce appetite. None of the *Arrow*'s crew made any attempt to appease the creature; to hope that its appetite might be satisfied with the fishing vessel and leave the larger trading cog alone. The thud of crossbow bolts and curved short-bow arrows sounded across the decking, sailors aiming directly into the now sinking bulk of flesh. It absorbed their volley and wore it like hairs across its slimy, slipping mass. The single tentacle spun around in a rude gesture of defiance, whipping into the fishing boat's retreating remains, snapping what was left of her sail and clearing the remaining fishermen into the water. They vainly attempted to swim towards the hollering sailors on board the *Arrow*, but the fishermen hadn't made ten strokes before they vanished from the water, yanked below the surface by the monster. They disappeared with the speed of lead weights dropped into the current. It only took seconds for the last fisherman to pass from sight before the vast tree of flesh started ascending again. It rose on the *Arrow's* starboard side. The limb climbed high and curved trembling above the cog, water streaming from its long ridge of barbed suckers. Then, as though there were eyes on the cursed thing, the tentacle heaved down to curl around two sailors on the main deck, standing their ground and firing arrow after arrow into the limb. The knot of flesh closed around the men, lifting them struggling into the air, banging against the mast, waving the half-dead crewmen tauntingly at the remaining sailors and passengers. *Atamva preserve me. This thing is a demon, a river demon. It cares nothing for me or the book I travel to steal. It merely means to make us its meal. Rice-eater, rider and Weylander alike.*

Alexamir leapt on to a barrel and threw himself on to the broken rigging, using the rope to carry him past the far side of the evil limb. He rode the line's momentum as a pendulum, and at the end of the swing dropped down on to the tentacle's wet back, driving his sharp Rodalian dagger deep into the flesh. It felt like the rare rubber Temmell traded for with the Hellenise smugglers, but gushed thick oily blood while Alexamir rode gravity down towards the deck, giving the beast a long scar on the way down to remember well. *You think I am afraid of you just because I travel on the water? You think to catch a hero of my ilk trembling like a foal with a fever merely because you attack me on a deep, fast river? You do not know this Nijumeti.* It kept hold of the two sailors, this tussle-tooth, despite the wound he had given it, before flipping the sailors sideways and casting them howling overboard into the Yarl to add to its supper. *I will have my prize and you will have my dagger and the Golden Fox will have her legs back.* The now empty tentacle came switching around in search of Alexamir and he ducked below it, carving out its flesh with a flash of steel. *The damn knife is sharp, but too shallow to sever the limb.* His hand was soaked in dark oily gore. He might as well have been pulling a calf out of a steer. But it was death he was about this day, not life. Perhaps his. *I shall slice you a thousand times and not think it too much. The river will run black with your blood.*

Off to the side the skipper and one of his cousins came running towards the vessel's side, hauling something long, sharp and barbed. They were followed by four Weyland soldiers, grey-coats clutching their rifles close and shooting as they ran, putting bullets into the massive tentacle. It had experienced more than enough of the cog's inhabitants, this tussle-tooth, and by whatever senses the limb commanded, it curled out contemptuously like a battering ram of wet flesh, knocking over the rice-eaters and Weylanders alike, sending them barrelling across the wet planking. Then it darted back towards Alexamir. He tried to vault over the tentacle, but the monstrous limb shifted angle at the last moment, slamming the wind out of his gut as it closed around him, pulling him off the decking. His dagger tumbled away across the deck, lost from fingers spasming in the bone-crushing pressure of the beast's embrace. At last Alexamir was glad for the stupid, itching, over-hot clothes he had been made to wear, the fabric of his disguise tearing as the spiny suckers flowed around his body. The tentacle whipped him in an insane circuit around the air, as tight around his waist as being trapped beneath a rockfall. *Trying to disorient me before my drowning?* And drowned is what Alexamir would be if he fell into the Yarl. He could barely dog-paddle through a stream, let alone survive the wicked torrent below. He looked down dizzily and saw the hill of flesh rising out of the water again, a sharp evil beak opening and closing. On either side of the beak, he faced two beady eyes, far too small for such a river monster staring in loathing at him. They belonged to a bird of prey rather than this boat-cracking leviathan. Alexamir's arms flailed free and he tried to prise apart the tentacle's grip with his hand, but his gore-slicked fingers slipped off the greasy limb. He banged on its flesh fit to collapse the edge of

139

a mountain, but the creature merely spun him faster in the air. He spat at Tussle-tooth and showed it his finest scornful grin, but this only served to make the monster begin lowering him towards its chattering maw.

'Norbu!'

That ugly dog Nocks, running across the *Arrow*'s deck, below and to Alexamir's side. He lugged the large spear-like thing previously borne by the cog's master and crewman. Nocks hurled the black shaft towards Alexamir and the nomad caught it in his right hand. The Weylander was a squat little ball of muscle to have made the throw. *Heavy. Too thick for a decent spear.* Polished wood with a barbed metal tip, and something else. A fuse spitting flames at the back-end. Alexamir realized what this device was that the captain and his cousin had been manhandling towards the river's edge. *A black-powder harpoon.*

'Sword!' choked Alexamir, just loud enough for the Weyland soldier to hear in-between the tentacle flailing him about.

Having hurled the harpoon, a sabre was an easy enough weapon for Nocks to pull out of its scabbard and pitch towards 'Norbu'. His sword arced through the air, the blade's knotted hilt nearly slipping out of Alexamir's blood-covered fingers, but he held it fast enough to slide his fist below the curved hilt's basket. He reached back with his other hand and cast the harpoon down as strong as any lightning bolt tossed by a storm-god, burying barb and sinking the harpoon straight into the monster's left eye. For a second the tentacle mauling Alexamir froze and left him hanging in the air above the water, its grip easing just enough for him to breathe again.

'There is your breakfast, Tussle-tooth,' laughed Alexamir, fixing the remaining baleful eye with his warrior's grimace. The tentacle curved violently out, obviously aiming to beat Alexamir against the mast and smash him like an egg. 'And here comes your second serving.' Alexamir slashed down with the sabre. He was the Prince of Thieves and while he might resemble some pasty-faced rice-eating lout of a goat herder, the blood of the Arinnbolds burned through his veins as his gift. The sharp Weyland cavalry sabre blade struck the tentacle and curved straight through the filthy thick flesh, just as a Nijumeti would decapitate a rival from horseback. What was left of the bleeding stump fell away just as the harpoon exploded. Alexamir didn't see the black powder harpoon detonate, but he felt the heat of the blast as he tumbled down through the air towards the deck below, followed by a wet rain of flesh coming down across the *Arrow*. As he struck the planking he rolled into a trained saddle-tumble, and when he came to his feet, he saw the remains of a hill of flesh sinking below the waters. *Eat well, fish. Enjoy my gift today and remember well the name of Alexamir Arinnbold.*

'It is very rare to encounter a Tusoteth this far west,' spat the skipper, his chest heaving and face ruddy from exertion. The cog's master limped to the vessel's side and watched the dead beast follow the fishing boat to hell. The side of his face was black as coals from the bruising kiss of the monster's tentacle. 'They live in the deep marsh waters of Hellin, but sometimes their young swing upstream and enter the river, growing close to adult size. Always hungry and full of fury, with only fish to feed on rather than cattle and waders.'

'Ain't nearly rare enough for me,' spat Nocks. Alexamir handed the Weylander back his sabre, and the ugly soldier wiped the dark blood off on the torn sail before pushing it back in its scabbard. Incredibly, the two sailors from the *Arrow* who had been thrown into the water were visible on the northern bank of the Yarl. Wet, bedraggled but alive. They had survived their dunking and the attentions of the creature. *You are kind to them, Atamva. But then, those two are crazy enough to make their living upon the water, and you oft protect the insane.*

'The *Arrow Jang* owes you a debt,' said Shan to Alexamir and the group of Weylanders. 'But I will still require you to stow your guns and swords inside my chest for the remainder of the voyage.'

'We pay in lead and you pay in thanks,' said Nocks. 'A soldier can grow mighty poor fighting like that.'

'Then it is lucky for us all that you fight for the honour of your foreign prince and his parliament.' He laid a hand on Alexamir's shoulder. 'And you are a true scraper, Norbu, as hard and tough and strong as the high mountains which gave you life. You would not have to face such wicked creatures on most of our voyages.'

'And in the capital, I'll never face such evils,' said Alexamir. *And if you knew what I truly was, you'd feed me to the next brother of Tussle-tooth to swim across your bow.*

The remainder of the voyage passed uneventfully enough, river traffic growing more frequent as their passage along the Yarl carried them through canyons and valleys towards Rodal's capital. Wind harbours and villages dotted the waterside, many travellers and pilgrims and traders following the roads along both riverbanks. Wagons and caravans. Trains of merchants with ponies and yaks laden with bundles of cargo. Water from the river flowed into irrigation systems, feeding flooded paddy fields and carried off towards the slopes by wooden aqueducts. It seemed a remarkable folly to Alexamir, staying fixed somewhere long enough to grow crops, rather than freely following the steppes' rich grasses with cattle and clan. *The spirits that inhabit Rodal are cruel. They deny the rice-eaters such a bounty. They keep their people pinned to the same ground so they always know where to find victims to torment.* Each stop drew Alexamir closer to his prize. Skyguard fighters occasionally skimmed down from their patrols and buzzed the canyons, bored pilots in the Rodalians' wooden pigeons turning victory rolls for the amusement of the *Arrow*'s passengers and crew. *They would not be so pleased if they knew Temmell has given the clans the magic of their wings. These rice-eaters are due for a rude surprise when the horde rides again.*

Two weeks after they had been attacked by the marsh creature, the *Arrow* came within sight of Hadra-Hareer, twin mountains rising high above the steep red-walled canyons that enveloped the Yarl River on both sides. White-walled buildings clung to the mountains, scarcely visible through a cloud mist clinging to the peaks, and Alexamir watched triangular flying wings swooping into hangar tunnels up there. *The crows have built their nest on high.* Similar structures to the mountain city's clung to the canyon walls the *Arrow* sailed past. Alexamir noted what he saw with a professional raider's eye. White stone oblongs dotted with uniformly narrow windows, able to be sealed by shutters against attackers and storms with equal ease. Narrow enough to pass rifle barrels and crossbows while keeping out any invader wider than a snake. Seventy feet off the ground, inaccessible to attackers who didn't carry tall siege ladders or the taste for scaling heights by hand under heavy fire. The buildings clung on to the side of the canyon where the twin mountains towered. On the opposite bank he counted only a few sentry towers rising from the mesa top, the occasional wind harbour and hundreds of narrow entrances into the canyons, some arched like caves, others open gorges with lofty walls but barely wide enough for a laden pony to pass. He shivered at the thought of what it would be like for the horde to assault this dry, hard, grassless place. Trying to gallop through a maze of twisting canyon trails where one shepherd on high with a pile of rocks could make corpses of an entire clan. Then assaulting buildings high on the canyon walls. *And what would we find if we broke through? Dark passages leading into their foul tomb of a city. Temmell chose me well for this piece of thievery. Only Alexamir has the courage to enter Hadra-Hareer by guile and the skill to copy the spells the wizard needs.*

The *Arrow* slid into a network of wooden piers, anchoring with trading cogs bobbing off either side. Hundreds of labourers moved across the piers, loading and unloading vessels, working pulleys on gantries filled with workers. There was a rare noise here. Loud with yelled orders and the calls of sailors, porters and riverside traders. A series of ferries pulled on ropes added to the crowds, carrying travellers and merchant caravans in from the opposite riverbank. Further down the canyon there was an airstrip where a plane looked like it was being prepared for launch. It was a lot bigger than the two-person flying wings of the Rodalian skyguard. Foreign, then. Unlike the *Arrow's* previous layovers, no harbour town or crescent of warehouses and riverside buildings waited for them beyond the vessel. The piers serviced a single entrance carved into the canyon's walls, but what an entrance. Stone steps rose up to pass below an arch that must have been at least a hundred feet wide and fifty feet tall, hundreds of people passing between forty sturdy crenellated columns that helped hold up the distant ceiling. A portcullis sat suspended high above the throng of Rodalians, spikes as sharp as spears and as welcoming as the teeth of a lion's mouth, this gullet protected by a further fortune in metal in the form of two vault-like gates on rollers that could be drawn together, sealing the capital's ground entrance off with all the finality of a rock-slide. A long line of statues gazed down on Alexamir, carved in the canyon wall above the gate, hideous crouching gargoyles with wincing faces from a nightmare. *The rice-eaters should know it takes more than stone sentries to scare the Prince of Thieves. I will need to teach them.*

Alexamir rested his hands on the side of the ship and took in the scene. All of life was here outside the city entrance. Traders and merchants. Pilgrims and fishermen. Porters and hawkers. The day's labours and even a little romance. Just down below the ship there was a small passenger carriage waiting on the port road enacting what looked like the concluding moments of a tender farewell. A young man and a woman saying goodbye to each other. The woman was pregnant, although Alexamir could only just tell, as she wore a thick green hooded cloak against the cold. The man left her in tears and mounted the carriage, joining a bored-looking female in a leather military-style aviator's uniform and an old man with a thick white beard. Alexamir couldn't see the cloaked woman's face, but the aviator looked handsome enough. The young man's second wife, perhaps? A trader of the air re-joining his aerial clan, leaving a pregnant girl behind? It was hard to tell. All Alexamir had seen of the great merchant carriers that crossed the skies were the plundered ruins of the aircraft that had run out of fuel trying to cross the steppes. Just before the carriage rattled away, its twin yaks pulling it towards the narrow airfield, Alexamir saw that the old man had noticed the nomad's voyeuristic intrusion into his family affair, staring up at the ship and 'Norbu' with a puzzled gaze. *Is there something about that old fellow's face that looks familiar?* He dismissed the thought. *I know nobody in this city.* Alexamir couldn't help but grin. This old dog was probably the elder who had insisted the boy re-join the clan and leave his foreign dalliance behind. *The same reason the crew of the* Arrow Jang *think I'm really travelling here – a dishonoured girl left behind in my village and a disgraced Norbu off to seek his fortune.* When he looked again the cloaked girl was lost among the crowd and the carriage gone. Behind him, the cog's skipper was busy supervising the emptying of his cargo hold and Alexamir gave the master a hasty wave as he swayed down the gangplank across to the harbour-side, eager to enter the capital city at last. His boots had just swapped the wood of the pier for the muddy ground of the canyon when the squat Weyland soldier, Nocks, caught up with him. The soldier had taken his time, collecting his belongings from the ship's hold, but then there was a queue of passengers jostling for their baggage and eager to leave for the capital.

'I know what you are, Norbu,' said Nocks.

'You should do, you threw me the steel to sever the monster's tentacle. I'm the man who saved your hide on the river.'

'Damned if I threw that blade to any Rodalian. I could melt me a thousand shepherds down and I still couldn't pour them mountain boys into a decent battle. I've seen Rodalians fight and I've seen Niju-meti use their skills. You fight like a drunken madman, all fury and no fear. You're kin of Artdan, all right. A steppes-raised rider. You even sound like Artdan. I don't know what skin dyes you're using to fool these river-rats, but it don't fool old Nocks. I cut you, I reckon you'll bleed as blue as the sky.'

'Look down,' said Alexamir. The Weylander's gaze drifted down to the dagger pressed against the uniform covering his gut. 'If you breathe a word to the rice-eaters on the gate, I'll carve out your heart and let the Yarl carry your corpse all the way to Hellin.'

'Ain't no need to be unfriendly,' said Nocks, as though he was genuinely taken aback by the presence of Alexamir's blade. 'I know you're here for mischief. If all I wanted was an end to your fun, I could have had a friendly word with Shan back on the *Arrow*. Mentioned my suspicions and how he could test the colour of your blood to prove it. As it happens, I'm about a little mischief in Hadra-Hareer myself.'

'You are here with the Weylanders to swear fealty to your exiled prince.'

'Well, *they* are. But me? Hell, it's far easier for a soldier to change the colour of his uniform than it is for a blue-skinned raider to masquerade as some high-altitude hayseed. Ol' Nocks, he's got a little side-business to attend to, and it surely isn't for the pretender's benefit. It might be that if our mischief were to coincide, our chances for success could double up, too.'

It is bad luck to kill a man who helped save your life. Although perhaps it is Norbu's life that was saved, not Alexamir's. In which case killing this foreign devil would still be smiled upon by the gods. 'Are you a thief, Weylander?'

'In a manner of speaking. I'm here for a bit of rustling. The female kind, if you catch my meaning.'

'I should slide this dagger in your side and let the river take you.'

'Bad form after I tossed you a sword. Couldn't let any kin of Artdan's end up munched inside a marsh monster's ugly gob. The big man would never forgive me.'

Atamva sent this foreign fighter as a messenger . . . warning me of my father's betrayal at the hands of his saddle-brother, my father's survival against all odds. Perhaps Nocks has been sent to help me inside Hadra-Hareer, too? The scarred Weylander seemed an unlikely sort of ally, but he had already proved his worth in the battle on the cog. 'I am the mightiest of Nijumeti. You would be counted lucky to fight beside me.'

'Heard that one before. In the Burn, as I remember. So what is Artdan to you? An uncle? A father?'

'Someone whose honour needs to be revenged.'

Nocks snorted. 'I'll go with father. That just makes you another dirt-crazy nomad. Ain't a Nijumeti alive who doesn't ride with more feuds than a hound carries fleas.'

'Artdan Arinnbold's betrayal carries a price. It will be paid.' *But not by me . . . by Kani Yargul.* 'Atamva brought you before me for a reason. The gods demand vengeance.'

'Maybe they do at that,' chuckled Nocks. 'I reckon you and me are going to have some fun in Hadra-Hareer, that we are.'

It was uncanny, Duncan considered, how closely the Rodalian landscape below matched the scale model he had glimpsed during Prince Gyal's briefing. One of many advantages of the Vandians being able to fly over the area . . . capturing images of the coming battlefield and rendering it across a tactician's tabletop. Before Duncan, the twin mountains of Hadra and Hareer loomed like titans in the distance, the girdle of grey stone buildings clinging to both crags masked by thin white clouds. Hadra was the lower of the peaks at nine thousand feet, while Hareer climbed to over ten thousand feet. Most of Rodal's capital city lay underground, excavated below the canyon bluff where the twin peaks rose. But even the layout of these hidden underground chambers had been mapped by the ground-penetrating sensors of the Imperium's fleet. The flight route taken by Vandia's massed squadron of three hundred helos had also been carefully charted in advance. Bypassing the Rodalian cities of Baknam and Zimar and their skyguard and attendant ground defences, flying so low that pines and sequoia along the ridges almost brushed the legionaries' boots, legs swinging lazily from their flying machines' open hatches. Duncan's helo had been named the *Airhorne* by the two female pilots seated at the front of the craft, its name painted in elaborate crimson calligraphy below the canopy; almost too graceful for the ugly armoured fuselage. Most of the soldiers seated in Duncan and Paetro's helo were sharpshooters and scouts. They sat on helmets, protecting their family jewels from any shepherds and farmers on the slopes below with birding rifles, locals who might care to hazard a shot into their ranks. Oddly, hugging the ground inside a helo made the flight seem far more dizzying to Duncan than if they had been arrowing in at some great height. Paetro, of course, appeared unbothered by the whole experience. *But then, he fought with the legion for decades. How many times has he sat in one of these steel cans, waiting to descend on a surprised enemy?*

Vandia's helo force was a mixture of attack craft and troop transports, the latter heavily armoured two-rotor affairs. The former flew replete with rocket pods, angling in and out under a single blurring blade, their sleek lines disrupted by weapon turrets. With lower fuselages rendered mottled blue and grey to blend into the clouds, the crafts' upper portions glowered in a matte-black scattered with legion insignia, the kill sigils of previous campaigns. A colourful assortment of fierce teeth, eyes, talons and bestial muzzles had been hand-painted across the fore of each metal-nosed aircraft. *Beetles and Hornets.* That was how the soldiers referred to their helos. *Beetles*, the armoured transport aircraft; *Hornets*, their deadly gunships. And the helos weren't the only force in the sky this morning. Above them powered *The Caller*, a steel whale tracking a shoal of minnows to her destination. The ship resembled a cathedral tower ripped from its base, tipped on its side and sent thundering through the heavens. Rodal possessed nothing like Vandia's helos, able to stop in the air and hover like deadly hummingbirds ... but when it came to the Imperium's monstrous capital ships, the locals might as well be bare-arsed barbarians staring in wonder up at the city-sized merchant carriers traversing the heavens. Air rippled around the stones, distorted by the lifting field. This low down in gravity's clutches, the anti-gravity stones studding *The Caller*'s hull pulsed with an ethereal blue light. Like many of the aerial warships that projected the empire's power, *The Caller*'s bow had been shaped as a dragon's maw, the lights from twin bridge domes serving as her eyes, re-making the flaming engines at her stern as a flying beast's fiery trail. Eight pivoting cylindrical engine pods on port and starboard supplemented the anti-gravity stones' lift, helping *The Caller* turn, hover and swoop.

Duncan yawned, but not from any lack of excitement; anticipation and fear coursed through his veins. They had set out well before dusk to time the Imperial force's arrival at Hadra-Hareer with first light, hundreds of helos' blades rotating into a synchronized roar and lifting up into the darkness from the empire's new camps outside Northhaven. 'We're meant to be overwhelming Hadra-Hareer with a show of might, so why is it that we're flying in with the smallest capital ship in the expeditionary force?'

'The rest of the fleet are designed to haul legions and slaves and trade goods,' said Paetro. '*The Caller* is an imperial battery ship. The only thing she's carrying are bombs, rockets, missiles and frames packed with shells for her batteries. She may be half the beam of Princess Helrena's flagship, but she's all lithe muscle, is our little maiden.'

Duncan poked his head out of the hatch and located *The Caller*'s dark hull, relying on the strap snaking up to the helo cabin's roof to stop him tumbling out. It was freezing outside. The cold of their altitude combined with the driving wind. *I doubt if it's any warmer down below. No wonder the Rodalian merchants always arrived in North-haven wrapped in thick fur coats.* The weapon-pocked belly of the beast burned through the chill air far above their helo. Small compared to Princess Helrena's flagship was still a relative matter when it came to the vessels turned out by the Imperium's war foundries. A turret with three cannons piercing a domed mount tracked slowly around on her keel. Duncan could just make out the sailors' heads under its transparent spotters' canopy, finding only rocky scrub-covered peaks on either side to target. *They won't waste their shells.* It wasn't going to be much of a contest between the Rodalian skyguard and the Vandian invaders. Duncan had grown up watching the tiny triangles of Rodal's single-pilot flying wings turning in the sky above the borderlands. In the days when Weyland's northern neighbour had been considered a welcome ally, rather than defying King Marcus, harbouring rebels and traitors while peevishly clinging to their claimed neutrality. Wooden flying wing frames and silk cloth fuselages wouldn't slow slugs from the heavy electric rifles mounted on either side of Duncan's helo.

Rodalian wing-guns might prove adequate for scattering nomad horsemen and tracing lines of bullets across a pirate carrier's fighters, but these helos' cockpits, engines and fuel tanks were protected by tough composite armour. As for *The Caller*, attacking her with the midget Rodalian flying wings would be like seagulls trying to mob a frigate into surrendering.

'Have you visited this country before, lad?' asked Paetro.

'My father took us out hunting in the foothills once,' said Duncan. 'But we never ventured too deeply into Rodal's mountains.' He recalled their trip with a grimace. It had been after his mother died, and far from proving a rare moment of relaxation for Benner Landor, the hunting expedition had been mounted to court visiting foundry owners from the south, an attempt to win fuel contracts from their manufactories. Willow had stayed at home and Duncan's sister hadn't missed much. 'Most of our house's trade travels into the Lanca proper,' added Duncan. 'South, not north. Rodal's a poor country by comparison. Insular.' *Nothing much comes out of those mountains but trouble.* That was what Benner Landor used to say. Not much gratitude from the old man, given that nomad raiding parties rarely made it alive through the mountains to trouble the burghers of Northhaven.

'These Rodalians mounted a skyguard for centuries, though,' said Paetro. 'When Weyland did not.'

'King Marcus' skyguard may be newly minted, but Weyland already flies aircraft twenty times the size of a Rodalian flying wing. The winds are worshipped as holy spirits up here. The pilots of the Rodalian skyguard are closer to priests. The craftsmen that fashion their flying wings live in temples like monks, too. Every warplane is crafted by hand. No assemblies or mills or manufactories.'

'Well, we'll look to give Rodal's pilots something worthy of a prayer after we turn up,' growled Paetro. 'Make them wish that they had handed over the rebels and the little highness, both, when they were asked politely, like.'

How I wish Cassandra was back with us. The Rodalians better have her safe in a well-protected cell. Cassandra's safety aside, Duncan was more than glad that Baron Machus had been sent back humiliated and empty handed. He'd snatched Adella out from under Duncan's protection in the sky mines as though the young Weylander was nothing.

As a slave at the time, of course, that was precisely what Duncan had been. *Nothing.* Worse yet, the duplicitous brute of a baron had gone on to betray Princess Helrena, coming perilously close to arranging her murder and Cassandra's kidnap by a clan of assassins employed by the venomous Circae. *Turning on his own cousin to feather his nest. Is there anything worse than a dog that turns kin-slayer?* Duncan shared that experience with the princess, too. His sister Willow had proved herself all too capable of trying to have him murdered.

'You didn't have to come with us today,' said Paetro, breaking Duncan's dark thoughts.

'It was my job to protect Lady Cassandra too,' said Duncan. *And didn't we both fail in our duty.*

'Princess Helrena is on a different path, now,' said Paetro, reminding Duncan of her union with Prince Gyal. 'One that leads all the way to the imperial throne.'

'I'm not doing this for the princess,' said Duncan. *And if I repeat that enough, maybe I'll even end up believing it myself.* 'Well, I am. But for duty. For the house. For Lady Cassandra.'

'Good. Stick to the plan of battle and may we both live to reclaim our honour,' said Paetro. 'We're not looking to storm Hadra-Hareer this morning, only cut the capital off from the rest of the country. I wouldn't fancy fighting my way through their tunnels and caves in close quarters. Too many advantages for the defenders.'

Duncan nodded in agreement. A siege with surrender at the end of it suited him just fine. He had seen all he wanted to of confined, claustrophobic shafts in the sky mines' excavations. If the young Weylander never had to squeeze through another lamp-lit slurry tunnel, he would die a happy man.

'Final briefing,' announced Paetro to the forty lightly armoured soldiers packing the troop transport's hold. These were house troops, part of the contingent loyal to Helrena Skar. In Weyland, the force inside the transport helo would have been called a company. The Vandians referred to it as a *stick*. Ten sticks to a maniple, five maniples to a cohort and up to fifty cohorts to a legion. Duncan had the impression that like Paetro, these guardsmen had previously served with the Imperium's legions. Duncan had come to know a good few of them since departing Vandis for the shores of his old home. There were

Charia and Arria Wyon, female twins and veteran sharp-shooters, as willowy and deadly as the single-shot long-barrelled rifles they carried. Both soldiers spare with their words. For entertainment, they carried a set of gem-tipped engraving tools with them, and for a couple of coins, they would happily carve animals, lucky icons and miniature vistas into the barrels, cylinders and blades of their compatriots' weapons. Then there was Little Aldro, a seven-foot brute of a man with ashen skin and corded muscles that seemed oddly lumpen, from some province of the empire whose population were a good few twists of the spiral removed from the common pattern. There was snow-haired Kenem Posda, who seemed too old to still serve as a house guardsman, yet moved with a lithe agility of a soldier half his age that set the knives and equipment packs hanging off his leather belt jangling. He possessed tight, knowing eyes that could burn right through you.

Paetro unrolled a Vandian assault map across the helo's metal floor, spreading a sheaf of aerial reconnaissance images beside it. 'We're setting down here on the Yarl Heights. Our primary task is to cover the sappers assigned to the capital's northern edge. The sappers' helos will be landing opposite us, directly above Hadra-Hareer's Trade Gate. It's one of only two ground-level entrances into the capital. We'll be aiming into the buildings along the North Rim ravine. Sharpshooters are to target any defender attempting to cut down our sappers, either literally or figuratively, as they rappel into position and lay their charges.'

'The locals will be shooting at us from windows little larger than loop-holes,' noted Charia Wyon. 'While we only have boulders for cover.'

'That's why you and your sister are here and not warming the guardroom at the Castle of Snakes,' said Paetro. 'You're the best shots we have. Give the defenders something else to worry about.'

'So, the gates get blown. Won't we need those tunnels to storm the city?' asked Little Aldro.

'Not until the locals are good and hungry. These hares have only two passages of size into their warren,' said Paetro. 'The mountain barbarians think that's going to protect Hadra-Hareer, but instead we'll make a stone coffin of their capital. After that? Well, they need to bring in food from their rice fields and valleys to eat. Most of it rides down the Yarl River by barge, a scattering more comes in by mule train through the mountain trails to the north and along the airfields and roads in the southern valley. Once we command the heights on both sides of the capital, we'll cut off their supply lines and starve the locals out. They've made their home in rocks; let's see how they manage eating 'em.'

'What about the city built high into the side of the two mountains, sir?' asked Kenem Posda, tapping one of the black and white images. 'I mark gun fortifications here that will overlook our position on the ravine. These dark slits are launch tunnels for skyguard hangars?'

'Aye,' said Paetro. 'That's why *The Caller* is flying with us. She's going to turn that city hanging off the two mountains into landslides and rubble. Their ramparts and cannons up in the peaks are designed to hold off a bunch of horse-riding savages who regularly try to invade from the north, a few anti-aircraft guns to see off any aerial pirates who come calling. *The Caller* will introduce these barbarians to the novelty of three-thousand-pound armour-piercing shells ringing in their ears.'

'And the enemy skyguard, sir?'

'Nothing we haven't faced before. Weyland's friendly monarch told us all about what the Rodalians are sporting. Fixed wing corn-oil smokers, plywood construction and unarmoured. Single rear-mounted rotor on a flying wing, nine-stroke engine. Outside of the trade winds, they top out at about 120 miles per hour. Largest kite they can launch is a two-seater with a pilot and a spotter/bombardier who tosses grenades over the side by hand. Radios up this way have battery arrays that fill a long guild hold, so the locals don't fly with communications onboard.'

'No radios?' said Kenem Posda in disbelief. 'But how do the barbarians take their orders once they're in the air?'

'Semaphore flags,' said Paetro.

Howls of laughter rose from the soldiers, and despite himself, Duncan felt a flush of shame on behalf of Weyland's simple mountain neighbours. *We're no better in Weyland.* The sooner he got back to true civilization inside the Imperium and put his humble origins well behind him, the better. Let King Marcus and the rebel assembly's fighters snipe at each other out in the prefectures. Like two bald men fighting over a comb, as far as Duncan was concerned. *It'll be over, soon. The starving Rodalian townspeople will hand Lady Cassandra back, over their leaders' dead bodies if it comes to it. This mad campaign will be finished with, and I'll be back home. My real home. Vandia. Not some backward corner at the far-called end of the world.*

Paetro slapped Duncan's shoulder. 'You're the local knowledge. Anything I've missed?'

'The Rodalian skyguard are meant to be experts at riding mountain winds.'

'You mean they've got weather scryers more accurate than usual?' asked one of the guardsmen.

'It's a religious thing. Each wind has a name and they make offerings to them in their temples.' Even as Duncan said the words, he realized how ridiculous he sounded. There were splutters of laughter from among the cohort.

'They're full of wind!' someone hooted.

'Stow that,' barked Paetro. 'You've been at this long enough to know how it goes. A barbarian spear can slice through a soldier's neck just as easily as a bullet from an electric rifle. The first barbarian you underestimate is the one who'll stick a dagger up your arse and ask you how it feels.'

'This will be the last action of the campaign?' asked Little Aldro. His voice sounded like a deep rumbling landslide as it slid through his chest.

'I reckon it will,' said Paetro. He rolled up the map which showed their part in the planned action. 'If these Rodalian fools had bit down on their pride and swallowed their traditions of hospitality, we'd have the little highness back and Baron Machus's feathers wouldn't have been ruffled.'

'Don't need ruffling, they need trimming,' said Kenem Posda.

'Yesterday's enemy is today's ally,' said Paetro. 'You know how that goes, too, back in the empire. Right now Prince Gyal and the baron's troops are flying with us, not against us. We get this done, we go back home. Alive's better than dead. Any arguments with that?'

None from me. The soldiers grunted and shook their heads. An intense wave of heat slapped across Duncan's face, his ears suddenly ringing from a sound so overwhelming it was beyond noise. For a second he thought that *The Caller* had exploded, some terrible accident in the vessel's ammunition chambers; but the cloud of flame expanding from her hull cleared to reveal the three main guns on her twenty-inch battery recoiling back into their turret mounting, shards of oily smoke marking the passage of monstrous shells and answered by a distant plume of mountainside and masonry from the capital's second mountain, Hareer. They were firing from miles out, but distance mattered for nought when it came to the Imperium's might. Duncan tried to imagine the scene of panic in Hadra-Hareer right now. Whole sections of the mountain excavated by *The Caller*. Buildings clinging to the slopes disintegrated, others sliding into the abyss, townspeople tumbling into the clear blue sky as though an ant nest had been kicked over; deeper chambers inside the mountain proper collapsing, Rodalians buried alive, choking in dust and smoke. Nothing could stand before Vandia. Rodal was going to fall every bit as easily, quickly and efficiently as the resounding death blow struck against the Weyland rebels' capital at Midsburg. *They should have learnt*, grimaced Duncan. *Prince Gyal hung the Speaker of the Winds just for speaking out against Vandia's presence. Wasn't that lesson enough? And how many are going to die now, for the sake of their leaders' pride?* Stupid Rodalians. Unlucky Rodalians.

'*The Caller* likes the sound of her own voice,' said Paetro.

'Don't reckon the locals will ever grow too fond of it,' growled Kenem Posda, clutching his rifle between his legs as though the weapon was a favoured walking stick. 'Even though old Kenem is.'

Duncan's stout, shave-headed Vandian friend pointed out of the open hatch towards the slopes of Hareer. Tiny dark triangles arrowing out of the hangars built into the mountain, escaping while the launch tunnels were still intact. 'And we've encouraged some birds to fly their nest in the caves.'

Duncan could see tiny puffs of smoke from the city ramparts girdling both mountains, cannon fire, but it seemed their low, fast helo squadron was still too far away to feel the effects of the capital's counter-salvo. Not even the sound of Rodalian shells whistling between the aircraft. 'Their skyguard are climbing for height,' noted Duncan.

'They know what they're about, at any rate,' said Paetro. 'That's the one advantage a fixed wing flier has over a helo. Go high. Swoop down and aim for our rotors. This might get interesting yet.'

'I was so hoping for simple,' rumbled Aldro.

'Nothing simpler than death, big lad.'

Again *The Caller* opened up with her main turrets, the sky split by thunder, the dragon-mouthed vessel's hull left trembling in anticipation as the first mountain, Hadra, took a turn at receiving the Imperium's displeasure. Away in the distance the summit blew a fume of rubble and rock into the bright, clear air.

Kenem Posda leaned out of the hatch and spat into the air. Outside, there was a change of pitch as the gunship escort abandoned the troop transports. 'Off with our Hornets. That's it, my beauties, you sting those barbarian pilots a good one, long before they ever reach poor old Kenem's bones.'

All around Duncan the gunships peeled off, arrowing up for altitude. Helos could make three times the speed of any Rodalian flying wing and then stop dead in the air, hovering still while their guns tracked a passing enemy flier. This was nothing that the mountain people had flown against before. Tradition and mysticism and hand-crafted fighters against the advanced science and battle-hardened veterans of Vandia. *I wouldn't want to be a Rodalian right now.* Duncan wasn't entirely sure he wanted to be himself right now. *Paetro was right, I could have stayed behind.* And have Princess Helrena mark him as craven. *I have to do this. Bringing Cassandra back to Helrena is the only way I'm going to prove my worth to her.* But what would such success really be worth to Helrena, with a dynastic marriage to arrange. *It's my duty. Cassandra has to be alive and unharmed. She has to.*

Between the speed of the approaching helo squadron and the approach of the attackers, it seemed only seconds before Duncan had his chance. *We're climbing for height, too. No need to scrape our bellies on the trees now that we've been spotted, I suppose.* Their helo began to twist violently to the left and right, and around the sky Duncan heard the rattle of guns. The dogfight had begun. *The Caller* arced off to the east, her massive engine's thrum diminishing with distance. Duncan realized what she was doing. *Not spooked by the attackers.* In reality, the battery ship's crew knew she was as good as impervious to the tiny

Rodalian flying wings swinging down on her like gnats bothering a bull. *She's opening a clear line of fire on Hadra-Hareer that doesn't have us caught between the city and her cannons.* A sudden pull to the left had Duncan clutching white-knuckled to his crew strap. He caught a glimpse of a skyguard flying wing flashing past – one of their troop transports left spinning wildly in the air as it attempted to descend for an emergency landing, a single rotor left humming as its rear blades hung broken and useless, stalled on a dark smoking engine mount. Every few seconds the panicked, white-faced legionaries in the troop cabin swung into view, clutching on to their safety straps. They were fully armoured soldiers of the legion, not guardsmen. And they were probably dead for all the metal they wore. *That could be me. That could be me.*

Some of the guardsmen in Duncan's cabin raised their rifles and aimed them out of the open hatch, but Paetro yelled at them to hold their fire. 'Save your damned ammunition until you see one of those corn-oil smokers roll past us close enough to spit on. You'll need every cartridge when you land. Let our hornets do their job without risking stray fire from the beetles as well.'

A gunship came tilting past their open hatch as though it had heard Paetro, a black dragon painted across its hull, the fierce head ending on a gun turret under the pilot station, malevolent eyes swivelling on the turret as bullets roared into the sky. Tracer rounds were interspersed between the plane-killing ordinances, hot white flashes that left its volley scratched against the air like a molten spear, bright afterimages flickering across the back of Duncan's retina as he blinked his eyelids. He never saw if the hunting helo had claimed a kill. Duncan tried not to vomit as they continued to execute wild manoeuvres, tiny glimpses of the wider fight snatched through the open hatch. *I wasn't half as fearful during the siege of Midsburg.* Then he had ridden in battle on a monstrously large tank, practically a castle on tracks. *Of course, I could jump off and take cover at any point. But up here? I'm merely a witness until we land.* Duncan jumped up off his seat as a clang rang off the side of his helo, a hammer blow against their hull. One of the shells in the air had struck the helo, leaving a dent in the side where their armour had done its job. A stray. *One of ours or one of theirs?* It only would have mattered if it had been fired closer and reached penetration velocity. *So this is war, then?* Fleeting across the landscape with random death flying in every direction; none of it with a care for a man's soul. If he was good or evil. If he had hopes or a family. The worthless and the worthy claimed by the same blind hand. He could still hear the clamour of *The Caller*'s colossal guns; imagine the city clinging to the twin mountains crumbling under her stern rebuke. There was no tiredness left within Duncan, now. Driven away by his last plunge through the air. All around him the house's guardsmen prayed, muttering, some to the Imperium Cosmocrator, the official cult of imperial worship, many more to whatever local deities the soldiers worshipped in their home nations. Gods and divinities he had never heard of. Duncan tried to remember the common prayers of the Saints, but all he could conjure up was Pastor Carnehan's hard, cold face as he put a bullet in Duncan's heart back in Vandia. *Forget him. Leave him to Paetro.* It made Duncan feel slightly easier that even battle-hardened veterans appeared to share his terror. *Sitting ducks up here until we land and take our fate in our own hands.* They were close enough to Hadra-Hareer now to feel the thump of shells from the capital's ramparts exploding in the air around them, the helo shaking, angry pops as distant shrapnel shards bounced off their fuselage. *The battle is coming. Coming to me.*

The door at the front of the troop cabin swung open. Paetro stood up and swayed himself across to a view of the cockpit. One of the two pilots turned around, her head hidden by a bulbous green helmet with a dark crystal visor for eyes, a metal-stamped face-mask shaped as an eagle staring impassively at the officer. 'Setting down on the peaks in two minutes. Be obliged, Barca, if you and your steel-shirts clear the *Airhorne* before some local kite drops in and empties its wing guns on us.'

'Barbarians aren't giving you trouble, are they Sabiana?'

'More canny and accurate than our lying bastard briefing, I'll say that for them. If they weren't out there flying on those midget toys, we might be in for a real fight.'

'We'll be out of your bird faster than a tax collector's smile. Time to earn your pay, my beauties,' grinned Paetro, hanging on to the cargo lashing. 'We're the tip of the spear, today. Time for a lungful of fresh mountain air.'

'Almost a shame to spoil it with gun smoke,' said Kenem Posda.

'That should be an honest smell for working dogs like us.'

'Mayhaps that's why Prince Gyal and Baron Machus are asleep back in the camp,' said the guardsman.

'The celestial caste sent a few of the emperor's Twelfth Legion with us for company, instead. What more do you want? An invite to a ball at the Diamond Palace?'

'We know our place,' rumbled Little Aldro. 'I'll dance with these mountain barbarians instead.'

'Aye, and make sure they drop to the floor first.'

Duncan saw they were slowing down, the helo blades' pitch changing as the engines worked harder to hover without forward velocity, and then the cabin's deck swung side to side, hovering half a foot off the hard stone of the mesa top. He unclipped himself with the others, jumping out of the hatch furthest from the canyon edge. Duncan was hit by a fierce cold gale – hard to tell if was the rotors' roaring down-draft or one of the legendary winds of Rodal. He sprinted after the others across a bluff split by fissures and littered with boulders and outcrops, following the sound of mountaineering equipment jangling against their backpacks. Ahead of him smoked the rubble-strewn stumps of a pair of watchtowers, which, until minutes ago, had guarded one of the many traders' trails snaking through the canyon. It looked like the squadron's hornets had been in here and done their job, clearing the escarpment of all opposition that would have given the Vandian guardsmen trouble. The defenders on the other side of the canyon were still in situ, however. Cannon bursts from ramparts clinging to the nearest peak, Hadra, thumped off the dark grey rock, showers of stone and flames erupting out around their position. Duncan followed Paetro, diving behind a boulder big enough to shelter three crouching invaders. As Duncan swivelled around he witnessed the rest of the *Airhorne*'s contingent running low, taking position behind every outcrop and granite shelf large enough to deflect shrapnel. Their helo was already lifting away, showing them the aircraft's camouflaged belly as its pilots pirouetted the craft in mid-air and swung west; chased by the mountain city's cannons, but well clear of the gunships' crossfire and *The Caller*'s monstrous batteries.

If Paetro's raiders were flustered by their reception, they hid the signs well. The marksmen calmly extended the barrels of their rifles, slotting range extensions into place that would have been too unwieldy to hold inside a cramped helo cabin. They followed this with the addition of optical sights, long telescope-like affairs that clipped into place across the weapon's stock. The guardsmen might have been chimney sweeps calmly assembling brushes inside a patron's salon for all the worry flicking across their faces: total concentration on their rifles. *We've done it. We're in position.* Duncan's pounding heart slowed. He reached back to touch his gun, the words *Gratch Foundry* stamped into its steel, and drew a measure of confidence from his shoulder-slung weapon. Like Paetro, Duncan lugged a semi-automatic gas-piston carbine rather than a sharpshooter's long gun – the perfect helo legionary's weapon. Light, accurate and fast-firing. It might not have been one of the legion's weighty electric guns, able to spit a hail storm of bullets, but comparing it to any rifle Rodal or Weyland could manufacture would have been like comparing a well-honed steel knife to a sharp oak stick. A drum magazine on top carried sixty rounds while a rotating bolt minimized its recoil. One of these in the hands of a Vandian legionary was worth a company of Weyland troops. He'd have to thank the workers of the Gratch Weapons Foundry when he returned to the Imperium.

Mandus Talia was the other soldier sharing Duncan and Pactro's cover. He was the stick's radio operator, a heavy aerial-topped slab of a backpack lashed on to his spine as though it was an extension of his body, which it might as well have been. Talia always appeared too high-strung to Duncan for a life of soldiering, although Paetro swore the man was an artist who could conjure a connection to an artillery unit even while buried inside a cave. *There are probably a few of those around here. That level of talent might come in useful.* Accompanied by a fizzing and popping, Talia cupped the black mouthpiece hanging from a curled rubber cable against his mouth. The man teased the radio into life, ready to relay any orders. No dispatch riders risking life and limb, being shot at on horseback. Commanders able to send orders across the battlefield and see them obeyed almost instantly. *As good as magic, here. The black kind that leaves the empire's enemies floundering to keep up with Vandia's legions.* Duncan squatted on top of the Yarl Heights, a view south over the Yarl Valley. Across the gaping canyon,

Duncan could see the Trade Gate. In reality not one gate but many. A series of grey, steel-doored openings atop a stone staircase, carved into the North Rim's canyon wall and leading deep into the city under the twin mountains. He wasn't quite far forward enough to watch the Yarl River's fast-moving green waters winding through the canyon bed, but he could spy what was left of the wooden jetty that had met the river in front of the Trade Gate. Black splintered wood, a trio of hornets pulling out of the canyon where they had raked the gate with rockets and turret guns. Little puffs of rifle smoke came from arrow slits where Rodalian defenders were shooting at the aircraft; firing from buildings carved out of the rock, hanging on to the top of the canyon on either side of the Trade Gate.

Little Aldro came running up on Duncan's right, a sharpshooters' rifle cradled in his arms. 'There's a crevice sitting between them two keeps. Narrow enough to jump across. It widens out into a pony trail below. I found a staircase leading down to the trail in what's left of the tower.'

'Any merchant stupid enough to drive their caravan through a battle deserves a grenade dropped down on their mules,' said Paetro.

'The barbarians inside the city will be desperate enough when their gates come tumbling down and we close their burrow,' said Aldro. 'Desperate enough to pay traders with silver weight-for-weight for potatoes. You'll see traders coming here then. Sure as scavengers after a slaughter.'

'The Rodalians prefer rice,' said Duncan.

Paetro nodded. 'So let's give them a fine serving of lead sauce to wash it down with. Take position, big lad. The miners' helo will be settling above the city gate any minute. Mark the defenders' rifle slits well. Our hornets are buzzing in and out down there to draw fire against their armoured skin instead of our miners' soft arses. Raise *The Caller*, Mandus. Let them know the Trade Gate is in our sights and we're ready to cover our lads as they toss lines down.'

'I'll try,' said Mandus, sounding as though he'd just been asked to pick up one of the mountains. *The Caller* had disappeared behind the rise of the twin mountains, but Duncan could still hear her main batteries. At this distance, it sounded like thunder. *A thunderstorm would feel like a blessing compared to what the Rodalians on the mountain are experiencing right now.* Skyguard flying wings crisscrossed the air, engaged in aerial combat against the helo squadron. No skyguard had spotted the interlopers on the Yarl Heights yet. Hopefully, the single stick of Vandian guardsmen would stay of negligible interest set against *The Caller*'s deadly threat. If that situation changed, Duncan might yet find himself sheltering behind boulders as diving flying wings tore chunks out of the heights.

All along the ridge the helo's hand-picked guardsmen had taken up position, sheltering behind ledges and boulders, their sharp-shooting rifles extended at full length, barrels resting on folding legs. A couple of guardsmen had set up on their rear, including Kenem Posda, making sure they weren't surprised by Rodalians already on the heights.

'Wind's fierce,' called Charia Wyon from behind a rise of rock.

'I'll spot for you,' offered Duncan, having to raise his voice above the howling mountain winds.

'They train you for observation while you were Princess Helrena's bodyguard?'

Duncan glanced at Paetro before he ducked down to where the soldier crouched. 'Don't think there's much I haven't been trained in, of late.'

'Wise enough. Never know how the house's enemies are going to come at us. Moment you think you do, that's the moment you die.' She set up a tiny wind gauge on a tripod in front of her, three rotating silk sails on a metal sphere with a dial to take readings. The sails were fair flying around with the gale. Charia Wyon passed Duncan a telescope. 'Feel how you're shivering with the cold? That'll make the air denser for shooting. Combined with this gale . . . hell of a day for fighting.'

Duncan extended the leather-lined telescope and stared through its lens. There was a cross-hair reticule at the other end of the scope and it had its own leg mountings to fold out and keep it steady on the ground.

'I'll fire a ranging shot,' said Charia. 'Aiming for the gargoyle head far left above the Trade Gate. Watch the round's vapour trail and tell me if I'm high or low on my slant range.'

'Won't the Rodalians hear you . . . see your muzzle flash?'

Charia shook her head. 'They can't hear our shots at this range and those tin cans mounted at the end of our guns work to suppress flash and smoke. I could be firing at the barbarians all day and they'd only know I was here when one of them drops.'

Duncan found the gargoyle using the telescope, the last of a line of creatures on the ledge above the gate. It protruded from the side of the canyon wall – a fat leering demon's face: bulbous nose; a strange-looking jowled beard around a hare lip; two distended arms, one clutching a dagger, the other a tome of some sort. *No doubt one of the evil spirits of the wind that Hadra-Hareer needs protection from. They should have carved those things as Vandians. That's who they need to fear more.* 'I have it.'

Charia worked the bolt on the back of her rifle, rested its butt against her shoulder and let loose with a murderous crack. A shower of stone rained down on the gargoyle's slab-like eyebrows, a slight haze of distortion in the air where the shell had passed.

'High.'

Charia adjusted the sight mounted above her weapon. 'Again.'

A second shot split the air. This time the gargoyle's forehead broke into pieces. 'Haircut.'

'I was aiming for laughing boy's tongue,' growled Charia. She adjusted the sight again, checked the dial on the wind gauge and pulled the bolt to chamber another round into the weapon. 'Again.'

Her third shot was the charm. It struck the lip and the whole gargoyle crumpled apart from the violence of the impact, shards of stone tumbling down on to the deserted staircase below the city entrance. 'Right down its gullet.'

Charia rolled over and loaded a fresh round into her long rifle's breech. 'I've never shot into a blow like this before. It's madness. Gyal should have dropped a maniple of cannon-cockers up here, not sharpshooters.'

Duncan grimaced. *Yes, but an artillery shell wouldn't discriminate among defenders and the Imperium's miners.*

'Well,' sighed Charia, 'there's nobody else here but us. Find me some barbarians whose future I can cut short.'

On the other side of the canyon floor their three hornets had withdrawn. Then Duncan caught sight of a troop helo dipping in above the North Rim, hovering a foot above the surface as soldiers hurled themselves out of the helo's cabin. Almost as quickly as it had appeared, the helo pulled away, leaving the force of miners on the lip of the canyon's ledge, scattered directly above the Trade Gate. Each soldier wore a backpack heavy with charges. Probably enough to send the whole company to their deaths if one caught a stray bullet and exploded. The miners moved above the edge, ready to begin their descent; lines unfurled down, secured against the mesa top. Cracks exploded around Duncan as the sharpshooters opened fire, a wood-splintering sound, each bullet sent towards one of the buildings clinging to the North Rim's canyon wall.

Duncan pointed the telescope toward the city and scanned for defenders at the windows. Windows on the canyon were thin slits with grooves for internal storm shutters to lower inside its walls. Perfect loopholes for defending Hadra-Hareer, as well as keeping its inhabitants warm from freezing cold gales. He could only just make out the occasional rifle barrel jutting out of a loophole, searching for the helos that had been attacking the capital moments ago. There were balconies, wall-walks and terraces on some of the buildings, but these were closed off and just as empty of citizens as the docks and piers below the Trade Gate. *Is this how Rodal fights? They hide inside their stone burrows at the first sign of danger while they send up their skyguard to die for them?* Duncan was disappointed, despite himself. What had happened to the famous Walls of the League? Defended by the plucky mountain people against every nomad horde who had ever tried to fight their way across the peaks and invade Weyland? *Hell if I should complain, given I'm the invader now.* Over on the opposite canyon the miners sailed down their lines unopposed. No defenders rushing out on to the ledges to cut lines or shoot at the Vandians. It would only take a couple more minutes for the miners to drill holes for their charges and set fuses, then Hadra-Hareer would be a lot more sealed off and 'safe' from the rest of the world than the Rodalians ever wanted. *This is too easy.* The thought floated into Duncan's head, unbidden. As easy as the fall of the rebel capital at Midsburg. But the rebels had at least put up some semblance of an opposition, even if it had quickly crumbled under the combined might of the Imperium and their local ally King Marcus.

A yell from Kenem Posda was followed by a report of weapon fire bouncing off the boulders in front of the guardsmen. *Someone has flanked us.* Duncan turned around. Wafts of gun smoke hung in the cold air from a slope of grey rock to the rear of one of the destroyed towers. Defenders from the tower who had survived, or a patrol from the keep out in the canyon trails? He raised his carbine and squeezed off a handful of shots at the ledge where the Rodalians had taken position, a ratcheting sound from his ammunition drum as it turned, accompanying a painful thump of the butt against his shoulder. Kenem Posda and the other rear guards added their rifles to his fusillade. Duncan couldn't see the defenders, but a return flurry of shots sounded their defiance. Hollow, dull little thuds. *Pistol shots*, Duncan realized. Somewhere along the line of Paetro's harsh training routine, Duncan had become an authority on the weapons he had to protect his charge against. *When did that happen?*

'They're dug in there as tight as ticks,' shouted Paetro. 'We need to close with them.'

He waved the flat of his palm to the right, sending Kenem Posda and the other guardsmen half-squatting, half-running towards the rise behind them. Paetro and Duncan opened fire with their carbines, keeping the mountain soldiers' heads down, then moved to the left as Kenem and his comrade returned the favour. Bullets fleeted off the stone as Duncan sprinted, flecks of rock leaping off the boulders as he avoided their foe's fire. He nearly slipped on a pile of loose pebbles while sprinting forward, recovering his balance to slide behind a sharp oblong rock shelf.

'Cover,' ordered Paetro, and Duncan just had time to raise his carbine and thump three more shots off against the cliffs where the Rodalians were hiding. He still couldn't see their enemy, only the fume of gun smoke drifting across the rocks. From the corner of his eyes, he saw Kenem Posda advancing at speed, but no sign of the other guardsman. Had the soldier fallen? Duncan cursed this fight. *Just the same as the rebel ambush when we marched into Northhaven.* How come everyone always seemed able to see Duncan Landor well enough to shoot at him, but his enemies were only ever ghosts, barely visible from gun flash and powder trace? That didn't seem like any kind of battlefield to him. *It's hardly fair.*

'Get to the shelter of what's left of the keep,' ordered Paetro. Duncan could hardly hear the hoary old soldier's commands. Had the rifle shots left him deafened? No, it was the wind building up around them. The howl slipping into a roar.

Duncan nodded. A flurry of shots from their right, half-heard in the gale, Kenem grabbing the Rodalians' attention.

'Move!'

Duncan followed the veteran, dodging right and left as he tried to stay as low as possible while maintaining momentum, the ricochet of rounds against rock indication enough the Rodalians still had him well-marked. Paetro leapt over a round ridge of broken stone wall jutting out, Duncan fast behind him. The keep wall had been two feet-thick of solid rock; Duncan crossed it like it was hardly there. He landed on a paved interior still warm to the touch from the bombardment that had ruined it, the surface littered with fist-sized shards of half melted stone. There was the splintered wooden hatch Little Aldro had reported, exposing a spiral staircase to the caravan trails below. Perhaps this had been a customs post once, helping halt the smugglers' trade with the capital? That explained why the Rodalians were trying to sting him with pistols rather than rifles. These weren't soldiers they faced, but whatever the local equivalent of the North-haven district police was. Shots rang off what was left of the keep's splintered buttress. *But gut-shot by a revenue officer is still gut-shot and every bit as dead.*

Paetro crouched behind the keep's wall and opened a side pouch on his knapsack, removing a pair of ugly-looking stick grenades . . . a spiked cylindrical iron weight atop a wooden handle. He tossed one to Duncan, jerked a thumb towards the slope where the Rodalians had taken cover and raised three fingers. *Two. One.* Duncan yanked the pull-cord out from the bottom of the handle, knelt up and hurled the heavy thing spinning towards the slope, crossing the path of Paetro's grenade mid-air. Duncan ducked down and let the intense heat of the two explosions arc over the keep's remains. He risked a glance over the ruined keep wall and saw a screen of smoke half-hiding the rockfall that had resulted. No more pistol shots. But were the defenders dead or had they moved away before—? Someone called behind the keep. It was Charia, vaulting over the boulders with her rifle.

165

'They're dead and buried,' barked Paetro. 'You're clear. Mark your targets again.'

Charia stopped short of the wall and held up her wind gauge. Two of the sails were missing and the third was ripped to shreds. 'It was gusting at well over a hundred miles an hour through the canyon when my gauge was torn apart. Might as well be shooting underwater for all the range I have.'

Paetro looked dumbfounded. 'But the winds weren't more than thirty when we arrived?'

Duncan thought of the empty terraces on the city opposite. Deserted now. *What do they know that we don't?*

Kenem Posda crossed warily over to them, keeping his carbine pointed in the direction of the slope sealed by their grenades. 'Do you hear that noise? What the hell is it? It sounds like a train.'

There *was* something pounding in the distance. Duncan tried to listen. A thump-thump-thump. Like a train. Or perhaps a distant anvil being worked by the gods' own hammer.

'It can't be cannon fire?' said Charia. 'There isn't artillery large enough to make that noise.'

'I think that's wind,' said Duncan. 'Pounding against the mountains.'

'Cannon fire,' said Paetro. He pointed towards the twin mountains. 'That's what's wrong. There's no more fire from the city up there. Hadra-Hareer's silent. They've withdrawn their batteries from the slopes.'

Duncan turned. *The Caller* emerged from behind the peaks of Hadra, but she was flying at a strange angle, struggling, her main engines burning so bright she might have been a foundry furnace, engine pods along her hull at full-burn as they attempted to augment the lift of the vessel's anti-gravity stones. Suddenly one of the engine pods tore away, flying high into the air as though an invisible entity was pulling legs off a spider and *The Caller* was the victim in question. The Imperium's massive battery ship was quickly being reduced to the status of a leaf in a hurricane, even as she was still being buzzed by the skyguard's flying wings. The enemy fighters rode the whipping gusts, an angry mob of birds emptying their wing guns into the hull of *The Caller*, carrion crows pecking at a dying corpse. It was as though the

Rodalian pilots were joined with the wind, harnessing the hurricane's flow, using it to rotate and turn at velocities far beyond the power of their simple engines, ripping apart the helos left twisting helplessly in the air. Anything the unnatural hurricane wasn't killing in the sky the Rodalian pilots picked from the air as their prey. Rodal's flying wings pressed their attack even as the wind gripped *The Caller* and rolled her sideways in the air, engine pods snapping off like seeds in a gale before the battery ship's bulk struck Hadra's jagged slopes. She was rent by explosions and flashes of light that left Duncan half-blinded for a second. As the smoke was snatched by the cyclone, Duncan saw their vessel had been torn in two. The dragon-nosed bridge spun helplessly detached, spilling crew and sailors into the sky while the half with the engine continued to be wracked by detonations. Shells that should have been destined for her massive turret guns fed the main engine's explosions. She had become a giant steel firework, spinning in the air, useless and deadly only to herself.

Screams sounded from the Yarl Heights' ledge, drawing Duncan's eyes away from the insane sight of a Vandian warship torn apart by nature. Sharpshooters sprinted back towards the perceived safety of the slopes, fleeing the yawning canyon gap. They were pursued by a wall of dust and rubble and rock whipping out of the valley, a hurricane's worth of natural shrapnel burning at their skin, tearing at their uniforms.

'They've summoned their mountain spirits,' moaned Kenem Posda. 'Curse me for a fool for mocking you, Duncan of Weyland. For mocking the barbarians' damn demons of the wind.'

'Over here!' yelled Duncan. He could no longer hear the sprinting guardsmen's screams, the unholy thumping from the mountain range overwhelming mere mortal howls.

'Arria!' yelled the female sharpshooter, entreating her sister to run faster. 'Arria!'

Arria Wyon emerged from the cloud of boiling rubble, her thin body shielded by Little Aldro's massive bulk, both trying to put enough distance between themselves and the gale to survive. They had taken perhaps five steps when they were pulled into the sky as though they had discovered the secret of levitation. Clutched by the wind they turned and spiralled, feet treading the air without effect until a side current caught them and they left Duncan's sight as fast as rockets fired from a helo.

Duncan and Kenem pulled Charia back into the shattered keep, the woman wailing in agony and rage for her lost sister.

'Down here,' barked Paetro. He yanked out the wooden door's remains, exposing the staircase to the trails. The four of them almost fell down its stone steps, following corkscrew turns, seeking any burrow to escape the Rodalian spirits' terrible vengeance crashing above them. Halfway down the stairs they came to an opening. It led into a chamber carved out of the canyon stone. Duncan sparked a wall-mounted oil lamp into life. It was a low-roofed oblong storage room, crates and rope-secured bundles piled against one wall. Half stumbling, the four of them pushed into the store, pursued by an eerie whistling rising and falling in the staircase. The trail below had been connected to the mesa top by the keep's destruction, dust from below flowing up past them. Duncan and the others made a wall across the doorway by shifting the stores, leaving enough of a gap that they wouldn't suffocate in their makeshift shelter. Duncan was as good company as the others while they rode out the storm, sitting morosely in the gloom for hours. Kenem muttered every few minutes. 'Never seen anything like that. Never.' Charia hardly speaking, just sobbing intermittently while clutching her long rifle tight as though planning revenge against the winds. Paetro sat cross-legged, scratching at his bald scalp, as grim and silent as a slab of granite. *As grim as only total failure can be*. They had come here to take a city and free Lady Cassandra, and instead lost almost quarter of their army in a single morning.

FIVE

A WAR FOR THE LAND MASTER

Willow was tired and not just from her pregnancy. She knew the job she had accepted from Jacob – acting as coordinator between the exiles and their Rodalian hosts in the matter of Weyland's refugees – was a sop to distract Willow from her worries over Carter and keep her out of old man Carnehan's hair. *But the duties are real enough.* More people arriving every week. Stories of starvation and war and bandits on the road. As exhausting to hear the refugees' tales as the almost endless work of feeding and housing them. Even more so given she seemed to be continually hungry, drowsy and flushed hot. Attending Hadra-Hareer's council chamber inside the Golden Well with Prince Owen, Jacob Carnehan, Nima Tash and a handful of trusted Rodalian and rebel advisers, soldiers and politicians, was an extra interruption she didn't need today. Two high-ranking military officers Willow hadn't recognized were introduced as Skyguard Marshal Samden Stol and Land Master Namdak Galasang. They both regarded Willow with suspicion when Nima informed the chamber who she was. Samden Stol appeared as ancient, thin and light as the winds his skyguard pilots rode, although he covered up his age – quite literally – with a large black bear-fur trimmed flying coat. Namdak Galasang needed no coat to make him appear bulkier. Younger than the commander of the Rodalian Skyguard by about half the old officer's years, Galasang could have been a menhir carved out of the mountainside, a golem's life-spark breathed into the substantial frame that filled his brown uniform. *I wonder if he became general of their ground forces by simply beating every other contender to death with his fists? He looks mean enough.* And his fists large enough for the job.

One man was notable for his absence. But finally Jacob Carnehan arrived, flanked by two grey-uniformed soldiers who joined the Rodalian council guards at the chamber's entrance.

Nima Tash regarded the pastor with impatience. 'You are late.'

'I've been inspecting the Guild of Radiomen's hold on Hadra's slopes,' said Jacob. 'It's intact, thank the Lord . . . we're going to need to keep it open to signal the wind temples. Pray up another storm to break a storm. Sending skyguard pilots out as courier crows is too slow. Risky, as well. Maybe taking a bullet in a dogfight with the Vandians.'

'It is your presence here that called these Vandian invaders down on us,' accused Skyguard Marshal Stol.

'Granting Prince Owen political asylum in Rodal was my decision,' said Nima Tash.

'And that decision made clouded by grief over your father's death.'

'My father's *murder*. A family has its honour, but so must a nation. The Imperium murdered our leader; butchered its way across the territory of our ally, Weyland. Then it flew to our capital to pillage Rodal like a band of brigands, intending to assassinate guests under our protection.'

'A wise man finds a lost yak and returns it *before* he's branded as a rustler.'

Willow could suffer his argument in silence no more. 'The Lanca tolerates no slavery inside its borders. These are human beings you talk of, not stray cattle.'

Stol shook his head wearily. 'Have you run out of refugees to molly-coddle? Why are you even here, girl?'

'Because she is one of our honoured guests,' said Nima. 'And because she can speak of these Vandians and their schemes better than any Rodalian. Willow Landor was a slave of the Imperium. Taken from Northhaven and forced to work within its mines. She should be dead, but she is alive. The winds of fate have blessed her.'

Willow rubbed her swollen belly. *I don't feel particularly blessed.*

'Then this is *your* war,' said Stol.

She stared angrily at the old man, so confident of his certainties. 'No, it's a tide looking to drown me. And the tide is coming in for everyone here.'

'How are our Weylander guests after the attack?' asked Nima.

'Scared,' said Willow. *Terrified would be a better word.* 'They thought they had escaped the war back home.'

'We have not yet seen war,' growled Land Master Namdak Galasang. 'The Vandians are arrogant. They flew in expecting an easy victory. We gave them a well-deserved slap and they recoiled in shock. I think they are not much used to it. They will come at Hadra-Hareer again.'

'On that much we agree,' said Stol. 'My scouts report ground forces massing along the Weyland border. These Vandians have armoured fighting vehicles as large as steel keeps on tracks. And the regiments of our so-called *allies* in Weyland swell their numbers.'

'King Marcus' regiments,' said Owen.

'The distinction is lost upon me. You claim to be the rightful heir to Weyland . . . will these soldiers obey you and return to barracks? No. They wish to remove your head with a sabre and brandish it on a traitor's spike outside your royal palace. You speak of a disputed throne across the border. It matters nothing to me which of my neighbour's prefectures the hostile regiments hail from. Only that their rifles and lances remain pointed at my homeland.'

'The Weylanders here fought bravely side by side with us during the attack,' said Nima.

'And thousands more Weylanders are now fleeing into our mountains,' said Stol. 'Women, children and farmers. Will they be as brave under fire?'

Nima Tash sighed and looked at Jacob. 'This is true. Since we repulsed the attack on the capital, King Marcus and his Vandian butchers have redoubled their ravages against the north. Many loyal to your parliament's cause are escaping burnt farms and towns and escaping into Rodal.'

'The bloody nose the enemy got here encouraged a lot of Weylanders to take their rifles down from above their fireplaces. Send a few bullets flying towards Bad Marcus' over-extended supply lines. That's a fine thing by my reckoning.'

'But there are so many refugees,' said Nima. 'How are we to cope?'

'You think that's an accident?' said Jacob. 'Every hungry mouth Marcus and Vandia drive out of Lowharl, Gareshire and Havenharl and across into Rodal places an extra strain on your famine stores. When you're planning a siege, this is just the song your band plays to warm up the dance.'

Nima stood up and paced the table's length. 'I do not find such music to my taste. I ask again. How is Rodal to cope?'

'It doesn't have to,' said Jacob. 'Send the soldiers from every parliamentarian regiment that is still half-constituted up to Hadra-Hareer. Fighters we can use. Fighters we can afford to feed. Everyone else, you ship east along the rivers and into Hellin.'

Prince Owen practically leapt out of his chair. 'Hellin! Bogs and swamps and fever will claim half our people before they see out a week.'

'It is true,' warned Nima. 'There are legends of the Nijumeti hordes who tried to invade Hellin. Once a decade thousands of ancient desiccated corpses rise out of the quicksand as a warning to the nomads' descendants, before being swallowed and drowned anew.'

'If Hellin's not to the refugees' taste, our folks can sail south down the Broadaxe into Tresterer,' said Jacob. 'Tresterer's a member of the Lanca. They won't honour the league's pact of defence and come to our aid. Let Tresterer feed our Weylanders on their own soil. It'll make their king in Navon feel less guilty about being a fat, useless coward.'

'I cannot allow this,' said Prince Owen. 'How many of my people will survive such a journey?'

'More than will survive if they stay in the north. And allowing doesn't come into it.'

'They are Weylanders! They support our cause.'

'I'd say that the ones laying low in Havenharl's wilds, bushwhacking southern supply trains . . . they're our supporters. The ones taking orders from the couriers we slip south, they're our supporters. The ones tossing burning torches on to thatch where the Army of the Boles' looters are billeted, they're our supporters. But the ones retreating into Rodal? They're just scared civilians looking to save their own skins.'

'We have to help them,' pleaded Willow. The thought of her old friends and neighbours dying on the road and in the wilderness, harried by her father's and brother's troops made her feel sick to the core.

'And how would you do that?' asked Jacob. 'Shepherd them inside Hadra-Hareer? Have them starve fifty to a requisitioned room while Bad Marcus and the Vandians shell the capital's slopes? Dirty and thirsty, dying of dysentery until even rat meat is a delicacy they'd gladly murder their neighbour over. Sieges are no place for civilians. I'd take my chances chasing hares and wood pigeons in the wilds every time. There's nothing here for our people but a hard, bloody pounding.'

'And the same for my people,' growled Skyguard Marshal Stol.

'Difference is, it's your land. You're the Walls of the World. Rodal: nobody ever forced you to cling to these mountains. You've been here millennia, growing harder and meaner every generation. Slaughtering nomads and raiders and everyone who ever tried to invade. I'm just asking you to slaughter one more.'

'Where we are now; we hardly have a choice,' said Nima.

'No,' said Jacob. Willow thought she detected a hint of genuine sorrow in the pastor's voice. 'When wolves gather and attack, there never is. Fight or get eaten. That's your choice.'

Or withdraw. Willow shifted uncomfortably in the hard wooden seat. *How much better to be a traveller. Never stopping. Following the passage of the sun across Pellas.* Able to leave every squabble and feud of those tied to the soil; avoid the fight by simply setting a fresh direction and never looking back. *Lord, I wish that was me and Carter, now.*

'Yes, we are the Walls of the World. It is the burden hardest to bear when the wolves are coming,' said Nima. 'Marshal, Land Master, you have the city's defences.'

The two officers stood and bowed towards her. 'We serve,' said Namdak Galasang.

'The skyguard flies with the spirits and our duty,' responded the old officer, his voice tired but firm.

'See to the city's grain stores,' Nima ordered the city officials. 'Ensure the reservoirs below the Lake of Clouds run full and clean. And clear every rockfall across the Yarl Trails. If there is to be a siege, we will need every narrow, minor mule-track open to smuggle fresh supplies in.'

The discussion switched to how the Land Master's forces should be used to defend against ground attacks, fighting in coordination with the skyguard. What armies King Marcus and his Vandian allies had mustered to throw against Rodal's capital. The lessons the rebel troops had learnt from the fall of Midsburg. Willow found herself almost drifting asleep. *I'm eating, sleeping . . . living for two. And what world is my child is going to be born into?*

When the council meeting ended, Willow pinned Jacob Carnehan down before he could disappear. 'Have you heard anything from Carter or Sariel yet?'

'No, I haven't.'

'Shouldn't their pilot have returned by now and reported their safe delivery to the hinterlands of Arak-natikh?'

'Maybe so,' said Jacob. 'But you don't need to worry.'

He said it with such conviction that Willow almost believed him. That was another change in Jacob Carnehan. Not an ounce of un-certainty or doubt in anything he said or did. *But I have enough for us both.* 'How can you say that?'

'I travelled across half the world alongside Sariel. Faced things I can hardly describe. It'll take more than a misplaced transport aircraft to sink that old devil. I trust him with Carter's life. And they're as well off where they are as here, with the Vandians knocking on the door.'

Please let that be true. That one thing. 'You told me once that I was to act as your conscience. You can't just abandon our people fleeing the civil war in Weyland.'

Jacob shook his head. 'The best way to help them is to divert the usurper and his Vandian friends' forces. Every royalist soldier laying siege to Hadra-Hareer is a soldier too busy to hang and shoot north-ern deserters.'

'What are you becoming?'

'What I need to be, Willow. To win.'

'We're not winning here,' said Willow, trying not to sob. 'Think of everything we've already lost.'

'Oh, I do,' said Jacob. 'I go to sleep and every night I'm standing by the soil of Mary's grave in Northhaven, surrounded by the bodies of half the town; parishioners I knew and loved, all planted in the ground by the murdering slavers. And when I'm not there, I'm back on the dark soil of that hell-sent imperial stratovolcano, crunching through the bones of every slave who died as a prisoner.'

'We should have never taken refuge in the mountains.' *We should have fled and kept on going.*

'This isn't a refuge,' growled Jacob, seizing Willow by the arms. 'This is an anvil. This is where Bad Marcus and the Imperium will be beaten with a hammer, smashed again and again until they break.'

'How are you different from Bad Marcus?' *How am I different from any other Landor?*

'I intend to stand over the usurper's grave,' said Jacob. 'That's all the difference in the world.'

'You don't need a conscience,' said Willow, freeing herself from his grasp. 'You need a soul.'

Jacob called out to her, but she ignored him. Willow made to leave the council chamber, almost escaping it, when Prince Owen intercepted her on the way out. 'You look like you need a rest, Willow.'

'I won't find one yet. I need to see to our people inside the Shades Chamber,' said Willow. 'That's where the new arrivals are being lodged. I might not be able to help everyone fleeing the war, but I can help the ones we've already taken in.'

'I'll come with you,' said Prince Owen. He glanced with hostility towards Jacob. The prince's cane and limp were his reminder of the brutal manner in which Carter's father had assumed control of the army after the rout at Midsburg. 'You should not be working such long hours, not in your—' he indicated her belly.

Willow couldn't help but cling to her duty's numerous distractions. *A chance to forget the winds of war buffeting against our mountainous haven. To forget the shame of what my family has done, is still doing, back home. I would have gone crazy, dragging my weight around the city with nothing to do but worry and pray Carter's still alive. Praying every night, he's not being roasted on a nomad's spit or buried in the ground and used for spear practice.*

'I need to do something to help,' said Willow. 'I really do. Come, then. The people are always glad to see you. It helps lift their spirits.'

'For the life of me, I don't know why,' said Owen. 'I half-expect to be met with thrown rocks every time I walk Hadra-Hareer's wells and chambers. And not just from the locals. Our people. I lost the north the war in Weyland. I lost them their parliament, their homes and in many cases their family's freedom. Sometimes I think it might have been better if I'd never escaped from Vandia. If I had stayed a slave inside the sky mines.'

'No,' said Willow. 'You fought for us in Weyland, just like you helped keep us alive on the mining station. You think if you'd perished inside the Imperium things would be better in Weyland? Tell that to all the betrayed citizens sold into slavery just to keep Bad Marcus in Vandian gold. Tell that to everyone working as serfs in the fields and factories owned by Marcus' friends. Your brothers died in the mines. Did their deaths make Weyland a better land? Your family was murdered by Marcus when he stole your father's throne. Did their burial improve Weyland one whit? There's only a single grave that will make us better. Your uncle's . . .'

'You sound like old man Carnehan when you speak like that. Filled with hatred and revenge.'

Willow shivered at the thought. 'He's not wrong about everything.'

'Even if we did the impossible, even if the north wins, what I would be king of? Half a land. A nation rent asunder. Things can never go back to the way they were. Too much blood has been spilled. Families set against families. Brother against sister. Friend against friend. These hatreds will last generations. I fear they will outlast us all.'

You might be speaking about my family. How can I forgive Duncan and my father for their crimes? And if I can't forgive my own brother and father, how can anyone else? 'It won't be easy.'

'That much is true. I understand that you have moved your lodgings to the Shades Chamber?'

Willow nodded. 'It's where I'm expected to find room for the people still coming in on the Pilgrim's Way. I need to understand how everyone is rubbing along with the Rodalians and each other.'

'That place's atmosphere is not what I would describe as particularly conducive to a woman carrying a baby.'

'There are worse areas.' *But there are better ones, too.* The Golden Well was one of the Rodalian capital's wealthiest quarters, and from what Willow saw in the corridors beyond the council chamber, it looked set to grow wealthier still. Workers passed her pulling handcarts filled with metal stripped from the storm-crashed Vandian warship, hauling salvage to blacksmiths to be melted down into bars and trading coins. A fortune in steel and aluminium and other metals. Soon there would be nothing left of the destroyed vessel. Traders passing along Rodal's caravan routes would find prices for their ingots greatly depressed for many years, she suspected.

Willow and Owen reached the circular atrium of the well itself, carved out of the mountain's core. Unlike the buildings clinging to Hareer's peak, the well was buried deep enough inside the rock to have shrugged off every Vandian shell during their raid against the capital. Ninety storeys of delicate pale-stoned buildings, balconies and terraces circled the open space, mirror stacks glowing with light from outside. The void Willow stood over was crisscrossed by hundreds of wooden gantries and stone bridges, filled with humanity's hum, the splash of waterfalls and rain-filled aqueducts. A cloud of butterflies left the vines and trailing flowers hanging in front of Willow and fluttered down the open passage toward the council chamber. Unlike Northhaven's butterflies, these insects were granite grey and marbled with thin lines of bright crimson, emerald and purple. Where they settled on the rock walls they looked like a living mosaic. Every well inside the capital had four lifts at the cardinal points of the compass, as well as dozens of staircases for those that wished to walk up or down a few storeys. Willow and Owen were closest to the Golden Well's southern lift. They strolled around the balconied level until they reached the gate and its keepers, joining a crowd of locals milling around for the lift's arrival.

They waited ten minutes, then the lift's wrought-iron doors were pulled back by the keepers to reveal a wooden-panelled room as large a church hall. The crowd shuffled forward to join a couple of hundred Rodalians inside. The gates shut and the lift descended, stopping at every level. It might have been quicker to use one of the well's spiral staircases, but Willow had tried that once, finding herself out of breath after descending a mere six storeys. Even without the baby's extra weight, she suspected the descents and climbs of Rodal's subterranean streets might prove too much for her feet. At the bottom of the well, Willow and Owen entered the passage leading across to the

Drain. Long enough to warrant the cost of a trip in a yak-pulled open wagon, at least as far as Willow was concerned. Although it was a tunnel, the passage always put Willow in mind of the largest bridges crossing Arcadia's canals – the same mix of ramshackle homes, stores, trades and taverns lining the route. Similar smells and hawkers' cries, even if these dwellings were carved into mountain stone.

'Do you ever think I'm the wrong man?' asked the prince, rocking on the taxi wagon's open bench, six passengers squeezed on either side of them. 'Perhaps it would be better if Carnehan wore the crown like the warlord from the Burn my uncle claims he once was. Father Carnehan will put the torch to our land if it means beating Bad Marcus. He'd happily sacrifice every citizen in the country to kill the usurper and still call it a victory. Perhaps that's what the war demands.'

Willow watched a child at the end of the bench, arguing with her brother until her mother cuffed the child's head. 'He's only leading the assembly's army, not the country. The peace will need something different. It will need someone who cares for more than crushing Bad Marcus.'

'Everything seemed simpler when we were the empire's slaves. We had our quotas. We knew what we needed to do to survive. To be fed. We understood that attempting to escape meant death and collective executions. But now? Over the border, half our own countrymen would hang us as soon as look at us. *This* is where my cause has led us.'

Willow could see Prince Owen was still deeply worried about Anna Kurtain. Anna had only just survived the fall of Midsburg and many of her wounds would never heal. *You gave Owen the strength to survive in the mines, Anna. He needs you now, as much as I need Carter for any of this to make sense. To bear what we must do to survive.* 'You're a good man, Owen.'

'May I yet be good enough,' said the prince, 'to meet these times.'

The wagon halted inside the Drain. An aptly-named maze of caverns. Always damp and running with water from the lake filling the mesa top above this section of the capital. She rarely saw a local without a warm jacket here. They passed on foot through its chambers and entered the passage to the Shades Chamber, a second wagon ride down a merchant-lined tunnel, emerging at the chamber's lowest level. Another well, but the floor of this one was filled with labourers. Many emerged from low, long side chambers where mushroom rice was cultivated. Willow had little appetite for it, herself. Too chewy and smoky for her taste. The remainder of the people were builders. They were extending the capital from this well, tunnelling out.

She stared up for a second, the rise of levels narrowing up to a distant termination point. The light here restricted for the crop chambers. She suddenly felt dizzy. Prince Owen reached out to steady Willow and she returned her gaze to the ground. To recover, she watched the workers on the far side of the chamber, excavating a new well inside the canyon deeps below the South Rim. This project had been grinding on for the best part of a century and many of the Weylanders given refuge inside Rodal laboured inside the excavations and mines. Paying for their keep with the only coin they had... their labour. Out on the farms of Havenharl, willing travellers thanked hosts for food and board by chopping wood and helping plough fields. Here, the same tradition went hand-in-hand with a pickaxe and shovel. There were women and older children directing rubble-filled mine carts into the tunnels, scattered across the rails alongside the male Weylanders. *We're a proud people, even beaten and hiding from the southern army. Nobody wants to feel they're accepting charity by sheltering here.* Willow and Owen's appearance was quickly followed by a gathering crowd. Weylanders wanting to know of missing relatives and friends; requests to move lodgings closer to their kin; people pressing for news of the war beyond the border; word of whether Hadra-Hareer would be attacked again; requests for extra rations and a doctor's attentions; worries and pleas and concerns and offers to take up arms and fight. Willow tried to comfort the crowd. She tried to reassure and help them... not feel overwhelmed by the cacophony of cries and demands.

Too busy to notice the grin of triumph on the squat, scar-faced man hidden hanging at the back of the mob of refugees. But then, Nocks needed not to be noticed to quietly trail the quarry back to her quarters. *Willowy Willow. You and me are going to have a proper reunion real soon.*

*

Duncan watched Paetro tossing a smoke grenade into the centre of the clearing, crimson smoke billowing into the air. He had lost count of how many days the four survivors from the abortive attack on Hadra-Hareer had trekked through the cold, dry alpine woodland along the canyon-tops, their numbers swelled to an unlucky thirteen now by fellow stragglers – house guardsmen, legionaries and a crashed helo pilot. Hiding within forests where trees still slowly reached back for the sky after feeling the hurricane's wrath. Forests that bowed like slaves before the wind and only rose after its wild majesty had passed. Avoiding locals who would happily toss any invader caught alive off the nearest cliff; surviving on dwindling pack rations while singularly failing to trap local game. Now they'd spotted a pair of transport helos low in the air as opposed to regular flights of Rodalian flying wings hunting Vandians, the cover of the trees that had helped them survive the mountain clans' revenge was suddenly a hindrance to their rescue.

See the smoke, willed Duncan, the two Vandian craft flying out of sight, the sound of their rotors' drone dwindling. Slowly the hum grew fainter. Duncan's heart sank. But then the noise changed pitch. *Is it coming back?* The drone transformed into a circling twin-rotored helo, making a lazy circuit in the air as it checked out the soldiers screaming and leaping in the clearing below. Satisfied these were friendlies, the hovering helo came down, a storm of needle-thin leaves whipping around Duncan's boots. They retreated to the clearing's edge; barely large enough to accommodate the helo without its rotors clipping the tree-line. Its wheels jounced on the ground and a hatch pulled back revealing two soldiers, one leaning against a heavy mounted electric rifle in case this was an ambush, the other soldier happily familiar. Duncan had never been so glad to see Mandus Talia's face, the radioman seemingly diminished without a heavy communications pack strapped to his back. His normally dour features cracked into a smile. Whether from seeing his comrades alive or joy at his own survival, Duncan couldn't say. They ran for the helo, Mandus pulling Duncan inside as the other soldiers practically threw themselves into the safety of the rescuers' aircraft.

'I told them you were alive!' exclaimed Mandus. 'I sprinted like a madman towards that ruined keep you disappeared into, but I was caught by the hurricane. Met a rock in the air which dented my skull.

When I woke, I was stretched out up high in the branches of a tree. Still had a working radio, though, to call in our beetles to lift me out.'

'You always did have the luck of a devil,' said Paetro. 'It's damnable good to see your ugly mug alive. Anyone else from the company? What was the butcher's bill from the raid?'

Mandus sadly shook his head. His hands and face carried hundreds of thin barely healed cuts; the gale had sandblasted the soldier and left him looking as if he'd spent a week as the guest of an imperial torturer. 'The company is gone, everyone dead. That demon wind ripped us apart. *The Caller* was destroyed, lost almost every helo in the first wave and many of the troops riding with them. Our squadrons' second wave watched the forward birds falling out of the air and a few helos turned back in time. Add a few soldiers on the ground who managed to find cracks and crevices to crawl into and wait out the hurricane. Only five in twenty of those who set out for Hadra-Hareer made it back to tell of it.'

'I've been through my share of bad battles before,' said Paetro. 'Never a rout, though. That's a first for me.'

Maybe a first for Vandia, too, thought Duncan. 'Prince Gyal's final parting victory has been blown away.'

'He isn't happy,' said Mandus. 'Spitting blood is what I hear.'

'Just not his own,' said Duncan.

'It's the Imperium's honour, though, lad,' said Paetro. 'There'll be enough blame for this fiasco for *everyone* to share.'

Duncan resisted the urge to smile. Prince Gyal was the commander of the punishment fleet. His head was the one on the executioner's block. How he had fought to grab that prize from Helrena. Treated her little better than a common legionary, excluding her from all military counsels. *You wanted the glory, my prince. Now you are going to take it, every last drop of it, and won't the taste be bitter in your mouth.*

'There's going to be a second assault,' coughed Mandus. 'Different tactics. A ground attack.'

'Ground attack? We *were* on the ground and look at us now. Isn't that the definition of madness?' complained Duncan. 'Repeating the same action and expecting a different result?'

Paetro grunted. 'I doubt that the prince wants to return to Vandia and explain to the emperor how the slave revolt's dishonour was

181

followed up by the drubbing of his punishment fleet. Gyal doesn't have much of a choice in the matter now. Either Hadra-Hareer falls or he does. So it's back to the camp at Northhaven and polish our swords for a second try.'

'Not us, sir,' said Mandus. 'We've got another mission. Our helo's under orders to rendezvous with Princess Helrena.'

Duncan remembered his last glimpse of *The Caller*, the mighty battery ship twisting in the storm and bursting apart on the peaks, cracked with the ease of an egg. 'Gyal won't have a marriage if Helrena's ordered to fly against Hadra-Hareer.' *There'll be no house left to marry into.*

'The raid's failure is Gyal's problem. The princess doesn't give a fig about Hadra-Hareer anymore,' said Mandus. 'Not after this morning's news. We received a fix on Lady Cassandra's position from some local traders with a taste for imperial gold. Lady Cassandra isn't a prisoner inside Hadra-Hareer. She's free, north of Rodal!'

How can that be? 'There's nothing north of Rodal but steppes and nomads on horseback,' said Duncan. 'A grass sea thick with clans of spear-throwing Nijumeti warriors.'

Mandus shrugged. 'Sounds as if Lady Cassandra is riding with them.'

'There's Vandian blood for you,' said Paetro, pride filling every word. 'The little highness used the chaos of the civil war to escape that dog Carnehan and slip away north. We trained her well, lad. Best we bring her back home quick before she ends up crowning herself Queen of the Wilds out there.'

Duncan reeled from the unexpected news. *Cassandra is free and safe? Then Prince Gyal can't use Cassandra's rescue as leverage over Helrena. She can cut the fool loose and claim the imperial throne for herself.* No wonder Mandus's demeanour seemed unusually sunny. *Our part in this pointless foreign adventure is over. We can return to Vandia with Cassandra and our victory against the rebels. Leave the rest of the mess to Gyal. This is perfect! Cassandra will be safe. Helrena will be free from Gyal's machinations. Free to choose me!*

Similar thoughts had obviously occurred to Paetro. 'Back to civilization. I won't be sorry to put your home behind me, Duncan.'

Duncan felt conflicted. Any residual homesickness he had felt in

Vandia had well and truly gone. *All the fighting and the scheming and the disappointments.* And now it was over. Just like that. A derailed train couldn't have shaken him more. They would recover Helrena's only child and return her home. In all likelihood, this was the last time Duncan would ever walk the land where he had been born.

'My home's Vandia now as much as it is yours,' said Duncan. *No, there isn't much of my homeland I will miss.* Maybe Leyla's delicate attentions and adoration. The rest of it could go to hell. *My murderous sister and grasping father. The warring assembly and grasping King Marcus. Northhaven and our backward, primitive nation at the far-called end of the caravan routes. The Imperium isn't wrong when they label us as barbarians. But Weyland's barbarity won't be my embarrassment any longer.* That happy day couldn't arrive soon enough.

Alexamir and Nocks moved cautiously up the mountain slope, holding a heavy wooden crate resting between a pair of splints – Alexamir at the rear, the Weylander at the front. Alexamir's eyes swept the slope. Hundreds of workers wrapped in warm cloaks against the wind; locals carrying sacks, crates and wooden boxes for their booty. *At least we don't look out of place here.* With a fortune in scrap waiting to be torn, hammered and cut off the crashed Vandian warship, plenty of rice-eaters scurried outside the city. Entry on to the peak was now strictly regulated with passes from the office of the Land Master; lest the entire city empty itself, abandon defence construction for prospecting the sudden fortune in metal torn out of the sky. In acquiring their papers, Nocks had proved his worth. Or perhaps it would be more accurate to say, the spies helping King Marcus inside Hadra-Hareer had proved their worth. Providing safe accommodation, food, money and something more valuable than all of those . . . the details and layout of the monks' temple. Alexamir had recently visited the temple as a pilgrim to see it for himself, but the spies' information showed *other* ways of getting access to its rooms. Many of the agents served with the Hellenise embassy. Slippery double-dealers seeking to befriend the victor of the struggle for Weyland's throne. *And if the victor looks set to change, their help will evaporate like the morning dew.* Maybe it was paranoia, but Alexamir suspected the Hellenise were spying on him, too. Trying to learn what he and Nocks had entered

Hadra-Hareer to do. Like any good thief, Alexamir's hackles prickled when secret watchers were about. But he had yet to catch them at it. Just a feeling of unease. For the moment, the Hellenise aided Nocks, and Nocks aided Alexamir. That was all that counted. The gods had provided and Alexamir accepted it as his due. Night would be falling soon. *Darkness is always a thief's friend.*

'Look at that beauty,' said Nocks, wistfully, glancing towards the massive downed air machine. Much of its metallic fuselage had been cut away and taken inside the city. It did not resemble the crashed merchant carriers of Alexamir's acquaintance – mostly wood, canvas and card-like struts burnt up after a crash. This Vandian craft was a black powder cannon compared to a sharpened stick. *But still the Rodalians' spirits struck her from the sky.* Alexamir banished his doubts. *But the spirits that protect this city have not yet faced the Prince of Thieves.*

'Have you ever seen so much metal sitting in one place,' Nocks continued. 'Just begging to be carried away?'

The Weylander isn't wrong. Such a fortune in metals wouldn't have lasted a day out on the steppes if she had, *Atamva willing*, been brought down inside his homeland. Cassandra would have been saddened to see this sight, though. Her people's mighty warship wrecked and stripped, covered by rice-eaters like carrion crows over a corpse. 'The treasure I seek is worth more,' said Alexamir as they climbed, the nomad trying not to stumble with the weight of the crate.

'To your Krul of Kruls, perhaps,' said Nocks.

'I was speaking of the Golden Fox.' Alexamir hadn't told the scar-faced soldier that the woman he ventured here for was a Vandian princess. As far as Nocks was concerned, she was just a sick loved one. Alexamir was willing to trust the foreign fighter as far as their raids here coincided, but little more. *For every good reason there is to tell the truth, there is a better reason to lie.*

'You can buy ladies cheaper by the hour,' grunted Nocks.

'Hearts bought with silver are filled with poison.'

'Wasn't their hearts I was talking of renting. Old Nocks, he's forgotten all them curious wrinkles of your Nijumeti code. You're as mule-headed as your pa. Well, if it's sweeter for the theft of it, you'll get your chance of a taste of that with me too.'

'Before I help you, I will steal a copy of the Deb-rlung'rta.' They climbed further away from the wreckage.

'Just another old temple book? Damned if I ever understood you people.'

'The power to call the rice-eaters' spirits . . . who would not desire it?'

'A fresh hurricane starts blowing up, I suggest heading for the nearest wind harbour before praying for storm's end,' grunted Nocks, amused at his own humour. 'And if you want a healing for your true, true love, then I reckon buying medicines from a Rodalian doctor will see you a sight further than your shaman's promises.'

'If you had met our clan's sorcerer, you would not speak with such disrespect. He is a powerful man.'

'Well, it's your game as much it is mine, "Norbu".'

How Alexamir would be glad to have Norbu disappear from the face of the world forever. The rice-eater from the Mask Heights had started as a tale, a fiction of his clan's sorcerer, and would end as one too. '*This* game is a deadly one.'

'You're preaching to the choir. I fought at Midsburg,' said Nocks. 'Them Vandians broke the city like an egg against an iron anvil. I reckon when the Imperium knows what to make of their bad luck here, they'll be back with a vengeance. You and me better both be gone by then. After they start raising siege works around Hadra-Hareer, one Weylander and a half-caste Rodalian at the end of a gun sight will look much the same as the next.'

And when Temmell's enchantment over my features fade, there will be a Nijumet inside the city for the rice-eaters to hang as a spy. No, as far as Alexamir was concerned, any siege should start *after* he had escaped the rice-eaters' capital. Not trapping him inside. Following that happy event, the Golden Fox's people could damage Hadra-Hareer as much as made them happy. Lady Cassandra had claimed her empire would come looking for her. And here her people were. *Atamva, hear me, let them travel no further north. Do not take the Golden Fox from me before I can prove myself to her. This is my time. This is my prize.* In truth, the sight of the ruined ship on the slopes filled him with dread. Alexamir hadn't witnessed the raid's fighting first-hand. The city bells sounding an attack had barely finished ringing when the warning of a storm followed. But the wealth of the crash below spoke of how little a dirt-poor nomad like him had to offer the Golden Fox compared to her homeland's riches. *How does Lady Cassandra see me? A fool? A savage? A diversion? This is my one and only chance to prove to her what the Prince of Thieves is capable of. To dazzle her with my cunning and claim her heart. The gods would never have carried me so far if they meant for me to fail, surely?*

Nocks stopped and they lowered the crate to the rock for the Weylander to examine his map. Ahead of them, between a ring of boulders, a brick stack as tall as a man's height jutted out from the slope. One of thousands of similar chimneys dotting the twin mountains and canyon tops. 'Reckon this is the right vent.'

There was an irony in the fact Norbu had been bound for Hadra-Hareer to repair and maintain the city's air vents, and here was Alexamir about to attempt the same dangerous trade. *You enjoy your jokes, Atamva. I shall make you roar with amusement by stealing your rivals' power. Just see me safely through their dirty squeeze holes.* Alexamir rummaged inside the crate. Below the tools needed for breaking apart the Vandian ship were rods and keys designed to remove the iron grates blocking his way.

'You get stuck down there, don't be counting on me to get you out. Best you starve yourself thin enough to climb free.'

'I will shake their mountain apart with my bare hands sooner than fail here,' said Alexamir. *This Weylander is frightened of shadows in a shaft. No wonder Nocks departed the lands over the sea and left the battles for my father to enjoy. This is what happens to a people who only have a solitary god to protect them. It's a miracle Nocks ever summoned up the courage to raid Hadra-Hareer for this saddle-wife he speaks of with such lust.* 'Keep your watch until I return.'

'Don't tarry too long, boy,' urged Nocks. 'These slopes are going to get mighty empty of wreckers when the stars come out. The passes in our pockets will get examined real hard if we're the last team back inside.'

'You worry too much, old man,' said Alexamir. *And what I am about to steal will not be found by any guards' search. Not unless they can read minds.* He strapped the tools around his waist, belted a rucksack of equipment around his chest and climbed into the stack, working his way to the vent's entrance. There, he knelt, brushed debris off the iron grille. When it was clear, he moved sideways to the narrow ledge before using his keys to open the gate's lock. His keys fitted as well as the Hellenise agents had promised.

'If it was me,' opined Nocks from above, 'I'd just go in the temple's front way and kill a few monks until they brought me out this holy relic you're fixing on stealing.'

'Atamva favours the hard ride,' said Alexamir. And the Weylander was unaware the monks must never know their ancient enemy possessed the Deb-rlung'rta's contents. Scattering the corpses of guards and monks around the temple would give even the dimmest Rodalian pause for thought. *The hard ride, indeed.* Alexamir uncoiled the ropes he had brought with him. He found a rusty iron pin in the shaft's wall and secured his line, then began to scramble down.

'Like a ferret after the hares,' said Nocks from above. Alexamir didn't reply. *Who knows how far the echoes will travel or where they might end up.* He carried a couple of torch wands tucked behind his belt. Raising the covers, he activated the sunstones embedded along their length. Expensive, but a tar-soaked wooden torch would quickly be blown out by the flow of air down below.

Alexamir continued his descent, out of sight and sound of his untrustworthy partner. He tried not to shiver as he penetrated the chill darkness. Nobody born to the open hills and endless steppes of the north felt comfortable in a city's confines, let alone these mountain tombs carved out by the rice-eaters. For Alexamir, shimmying down the Rodalians' shafts and ventilation chimneys was uncomfortable, excruciating work. *Dangerous if I had been trained for the trade.* Even more dangerous if the nomad hadn't committed to memory every trap set to murder unwanted visitors. The little guild that maintained Hadra-Hareer's air passages had the art of more than clearing cave-ins and rock falls. They took a pride in their hidden razor lines, pressure plates activating poisoned darts, fire blasts, sand drownings, skull-crushing stone pendulums and switch-stone plunges down into staked pits. Of course, the people who had sold this information on to the Hellenise spies might have been lying or omitted a few traps, trusting the thief at the other end of the transaction would come to a bad end. *But they reckoned without Alexamir Arinnbold. The Prince of*

Thieves could avoid and disarm every trap without their help. This way is faster, but I will not rely on the dogs' map. I rely on my wits and my skill. This is how the gods tested him. Tested his resolve and his passion for the Golden Fox.

While the passage started out glacial from the cold mountain air outside, it soon grew warmer with air carried from the subterranean city. Climbing down this shaft was much like descending into a well, only enough torchlight to see the walls by his side, never what lay below or above. The mirrored shafts that carried daylight into Hadra-Hareer ran on a parallel labyrinth too narrow for a man to enter. The nomad kept on descending. Slow work when a single slip would prove fatal. The head of his line had a carabiner clip he carefully attached to iron pins driven into the shaft by the tunnel's builders. Alexamir's line had been woven around a cord. A hard yank on the cord's handle opened the clip and sent the rope tumbling down towards him to fix to the next pin. *Climbing back up these shafts will be harder work.* He would need to whirl the rope around like a lasso, catching the open clip around every pin above him. Climbing, and then repeating the manoeuvre. *If only that cowardly Weylander the gods sent me was courageous enough to venture down here with me. Climbing in pairs is easier. Any fool knows this.* He reached a second grille with only darkness and more shaft below the metal barrier. Two horizontal air passages fed off the shaft. Alexamir's prize lay somewhere below, but he had no intention of opening this particular gate with his tools. Doing so would open a hidden door in the well; a door leading to a ramp loaded with a very large and heavy granite ball designed to leave his body smeared across the chimney's distant floor. He gathered up his climbing gear and selected the passage with a stone carving of a three-eyed gargoyle above its entrance, falling to his hands and knees to crawl through the inlet. *The other tunnel has only traps to offer the Prince of Thieves.*

He followed the maze of claustrophobic horizontal tunnels for half an hour, needlessly complex, avoiding the trapped tunnels and dead ends, opening each gate and grille he encountered. Every now and then he came across another shaft to descend, unfurling his lines and climbing gear. Then more cramped horizontal passages. Alexamir experienced a moment's hesitation when a circular chamber with six tunnels failed to materialize, but he resolved to push on. As uncomfortable as crawling through these tight passages was for one who lived for the open skies, crawling backwards would be worse. He found a junction with two passages where both marker gargoyles had crumbled away. *I thought this lay behind me? Left then, I think.* He crawled ahead and, after ten minutes of leaden progress, finally arrived inside the six-tunnel junction. Enough space inside to stand and stretch his cramped bones and muscles.

Alexamir lifted a torch out to examine the features of the wind spirits carved above each tunnel. As he did so, he heard a challenge echo out of the fourth passage. Low and distant, but clearly discernible.

'Who is there?' called the voice.

A vent-man! Atamva preserve me. Alexamir said nothing, hoping the worker would think him a rat scurrying about the vents.

'I know every sound inside here,' echoed the voice again. 'Give me no answer and you'll hear mine fast enough.' There was a low click in the distance. The sound of a pistol being cocked. Alexamir touched the knife on his belt. He would have brought his sword along, but it hardly fitted his false tale of a couple of wreckers out stripping the Vandian ship.

Alexamir found the inlet he wanted and scrambled into the narrow passage, hoping to put enough distance between him and the vent-man to throw the worker. *Keep on heading for their temple. Perhaps the vent-man will lose my trail.* Alexamir made as many tight turns as he could inside, scaling the horizontal chimneys by hand without rope-work to slow him down. *I have climbed the heights of Rodal to raid this forsaken land. What are a few chimneys to a man such as me?* The nomad covered up all but one of his torches, keeping the illumination so low he could barely see where he was going himself, relying solely on his memory and questing fingers to guide him. *Is that a glow behind me?* He turned into a horizontal passage so narrow he could barely squeeze through. *I don't think this is marked on the map?* Alexamir had memorized an area of the passages so narrow only the youngest, smallest vent-men could enter. *But it is far from here, surely?* Unless Alexamir was lost, disoriented by the chase. *No, my memory is as strong as sword steel. I can navigate the steppes at night and locate the same blade of grass I made camp on the previous year.* His tunnel grew narrower still. The only way Alexamir would pass through here was by staying until he starved himself thin, just like the Weylander had suggested. *I have to turn back.* He reversed course, crawling and backing up until he came to a junction whose space he could use to turn around. This was the fourth junction he had passed. *Yes, I know where I am.* But so did the vent-man. He spotted a dim glow from a torch identical to those he carried. Alexamir turned into the safety of the passage, out of the way of a pistol shot.

'It's Norbu,' called Alexamir. 'One of the new apprentices.'

A laugh from the darkness. 'There's thirty apprentices currently on the rolls and not one of them with that name, thief.'

Alexamir cursed.

'Tell me then "apprentice", how large is the bounty our guild pays for every dead intruder dragged out of the shafts?'

'Two nights in your wife's bed,' laughed Alexamir. 'Or three with your hag of a mother biting the pillow.'

'So, perhaps not a thief, but a beggarly bard with a talent for jokes? Were you chased up here from a bedroom by some maid's jealous husband? In either event, the money your corpse will earn me remains the same.'

Alexamir groaned. The nomad crawled as fast as he could down the tunnel. This tunnel felt damp below his hands and he could hear the drip-drop of water ahead. There would be another shaft ahead, if his remembrance of the map was correct. *And here it is. Just where it should be.* The nomad remembered the shameful time he had fought an older boy from the clan, wrestling with him in the rapids of a river. How the lout had held young Alexamir's head under the water with his superior strength. How alien and strange the battle had seemed, water streaming around them, threatening to drag him under and pull him away. His aunt had smacked him around the head when she'd heard how badly he had lost. 'He is the son of a fish netter!' Nonna swore at him. 'He knows how to swim and knows that you do not. He goaded you into wrestling by the riverbank so he could throw you in. Always choose your own field of battle, or you choose only your defeat. You must first fight using your brain before you fight using your hands.'

This is my foe's field, but I am no boy now.

A crack sounded, followed by a ricochet of a round on the wall behind him. *Missed!* Alexamir gave the vent-man no further banter to use to help direct his fire. The nomad secured his line to the well's highest iron pin. A second, louder shot exploded behind him. The vent-man hadn't aimed into the correct side-passage yet, but that third killing shot was coming, Alexamir could feel it. He swung his hands on to the lip of the well and tentatively entered the shaft, just narrow enough to place his back against the wall and walk its walls down without the time-consuming business of line and clip. Alexamir hadn't scaled more than a tenth of the deep well's drop when the vent-man's fierce victory whoop sounded above him. The nomad grabbed the end of the climbing line dangling before him, but the clip and line method of descent was even slower than spine-walking it. The rice-eater leaned over the well's mouth and aimed his pistol down towards a target a blind man wouldn't fail to hit.

'You've made me work for this one,' the vent-man called triumphantly. Alexamir sensed the gun's sight focusing on the top of his skull. 'Sing me a song as you fall!'

SIX

THE VANDIAN MISSION

Cassandra sat in a chair, the wooden table in front of her covered by a pile of Temmell's books. Histories, for the most part. The particular tome in front of her was the first volume in a series titled *The Rise of Empire*, penned by a long-dead scholar called Cinneide Tarson. Vandia's achievements weren't mentioned once, however. This book was all about the empire north of the steppes, Persdad. That it had risen at all seemed to be attributed by Cinneide to the nomads of the steppes, who had burnt their path through the nations preceding Persdad, hastening its formation much like the scars on a wound, sealing the Nijumeti into the territory they currently roamed. Cassandra had passed the ruins of city-states sacked by the riders out on the grasslands. Little more than boulder-strewn hills now, shadows in the ground marking once-mighty citadels. *At least the history texts are of some interest.*

Temmell possessed a great many tomes, but much of the golden-skinned sorcerer's library was of a wholly practical nature. Books on botany and anatomy, flight and engineering, metallurgy and chemistry, a variety of atlases; albeit of the crude, inaccurate variety that would have disgraced any Guild of Librarians' hold, let alone the Imperial Ordnance Survey Service's charts. Everything the trickster once needed to make a living as a travelling peddler and medicine man. Temmell had certainly landed on his feet among the nomads, the clans duped into believing the self-proclaimed sorcerer's claims about his powers and talents. *Except there's the glamour that makes Alexamir appear Rodalian. A powerfully strange sort of hypnotism. How does Temmell manage that? And there is my broken spine.* The bizarre nature of Cassandra's healing. Ten sparse minutes of glorious mobility every morning, fully healed, sauntering and then sprinting before she collapsed pole-axed towards the grass. Her legs useless again, as dead as if both limbs had been amputated following her flying wing crash. *Everything I was taught about surgery and anatomy by Doctor Horvak says my temporary recovery should be impossible. I am either healed or I am wounded. Not flipped between the two states like a tossed coin each morning.*

Temmell administered no new drugs to Cassandra, although he preferred keeping her inside his quarters in the centre of the camouflaged aircraft works. That, Cassandra suspected, had more to do with the sorcerer's desire to keep a beady eye on her while Alexamir risked his life on her behalf. Nothing to do with repeated medical treatments. Alexamir's Aunt Nonna accepted this new arrangement with reluctant grace. Nonna wasn't in a position to countermand the sorcerer's hospitality. Instead, she insisted on visiting with food every morning, afternoon and evening, as though the servants in the Great Krul's service were incapable of cooking. Still, Cassandra was always happy to see the old woman. She reminded her that Alexamir was in the world. Risking his neck in Rodal so the untrustworthy sorcerer would complete her treatment. And how Cassandra prayed Temmell would, that he *could*. How cruel would it be if Alexamir returned with the stolen secrets of the Rodalian monks only for Temmell to shrug and admit that her healing was only a temporary treatment and that is all it could ever be. *If ten minutes healed a day is to be my lot, how could I go on?*

After an hour of perusing books, Casandra saw Nonna appear at the door. She smelt her before she heard her. Nonna came bearing a cold pie called a kurnak inside her small pottery dish – filled with chewy goat meat, berries, mushrooms and a little honey.

Cassandra hadn't realized she was hungry until the old aunt entered the sorcerer's lair. 'Any word of Alexamir?'

'What word do you think to receive, girl?' sniffed Nonna. 'All the metal we have stolen rests in our blades, not iron towers which foreign fools use to call the invisible radio spirits. Alexamir Arinnbold carried no cage of homing crows with him, and even if the fool had, I dare say he would have cooked them all up over his campfire by now.'

'I hoped the pilot Zald might have returned with Alexamir or word of his success . . .'

'Pah, the mighty Zald Mirok? If I know that old hound, he is snoring loudly in the shade of his wooden pigeon, an empty bottle by his side and dreaming of the days when he rode a swift horse like a real warrior. Two fools together, on a fool's errand for a cunning foreign galoot. Never in my day.'

He's no fool. 'Alexamir will survive. He has to.'

'Alexamir is a capable thief,' said Nonna. 'But that devil Temmell needs a fool as much as he needs a thief. He knows my nephew's soul well. Always trying to prove himself in front of the Great Krul.'

'Don't all clansmen ride to prove their strength?'

'Not all riders have their mother warming the Great Krul's tent. Not all riders were raised as much a son of the Great Krul as his own blood. Alexamir is the same as my dead dolt of a brother. He would ride through hell for Kani Yargul. If Temmell has his way, I dare say my nephew will not lack for opportunities to show his hooves to hell's minions.'

'You should not speak ill of the dead. Insulting your ancestors brings bad fortune.'

'A fie for my ancestors,' snorted Nonna. 'And a double fie for Alexamir's father. My brother has been feasting like a hero beside Atamva and the hosts of the fallen while those who survive him work their fingers to the bone scrubbing clothes in the stream, gathering firewood, skinning goats and burning their fingers over hot clay cauldrons.' She thrust her gnarled fingers under Cassandra's nose. 'Look at my hands. They belonged to a warrior princess once, fit for any man who dared consider himself Nijumeti and attempted to steal me. I could once fire a bow riding backwards while skinning a hare, dismount with a somersault and slice the necks of three rival clansmen, and then curse the morning's work as only half-done.'

'A pity there is no man in the tent now.'

'There was never any man worthy of me. It is the curse of all those born to beauty and great cunning. Kani Yargul tried to steal me twice and I kicked him in the balls both times and cursed him for a weak-livered courtier. If he had tried a third time, I would have sliced his jewels off and made them into a bolas to chase off all the other wolves who came yapping after me.'

Cassandra believed it. Age had slowed Nonna a little, but Cassandra could tell from the way that the old woman moved that she had been blade-trained every bit as thoroughly as any Vandian noblewoman. *And where has it got her? For that matter, what did it bring me? A prisoner of my own flesh, dependent on an ambitious madman's dreams and dark sorceries.*

Nonna leapt up at the sound of an explosion in the distance, scattering her food as she practically sniffed the air. 'What in the name of Seven Horses was that?'

A fuel explosion? 'It came from inside the aircraft works.'

'These twice-plagued wooden pigeons,' said Nonna. 'They are not our way. Such craft belong to rice-eaters and outsiders who sorely tempt holy vengeance by trespassing across the heavens.' She disappeared outside to investigate, leaving Cassandra staring at her pie-filled plate and wondering. Nonna returned with two of Temmell's men, big riders with curved swords strapped to their backs.

'You are sent for,' said one of the warriors.

'If it's expertise in extinguishing aircraft fires you need, I suggest you seek out Sheplar Lesh,' said Cassandra.

'Come,' repeated the second man. He pushed Nonna back as she attempted to leave with them. 'Not you, woman. You are not sent for.'

'You send for my blade,' snapped the old woman. 'You lay your dirty hand on me again and you'll be holding the reins with the arm I didn't slice to the grass.'

The two warriors grabbed Cassandra and carried her outside Temmell's quarters. Cassandra's mare waited there, tied to the building, and she shrugged off the riders' thick hands as she mounted the saddle. *How quickly I've grown accustomed to using my arms to pull me up and throw my dead useless legs across the nag.* Nonna emerged from the entrance, looking irritated and worried in equal measure.

'Stay here, Nonna,' said Cassandra. 'I'll be back soon enough.'

'Sharp eyes, Golden Fox,' muttered the aunt. 'With a sharper blade for what you ride across.'

A pall of thick dark smoke rose from somewhere on the steppes, perhaps inside the concealed manufactory itself? *Is it Alexamir? If the ancestors love me, please, let him not have returned home only to crash.* The two men leapt into the saddles of their own horses and led her through the maze of half-stripped carriers, construction huts and mounds of salvage. Towards a sight she never thought she would see again. Just outside the camouflage netting thrown over the primitive aircraft works. Three grounded helos, another two hovering in the air, heavily armed gunships of Vandian design. And back behind the rolling hills and the small river, her heart quickened at the sight of a capital ship of the Imperium, soil still smoking from where her engine pods had scoured the grass upon landing. *That ship, she looks like . . .* it was at that moment she noticed a group of house guardsmen being led towards the works by Temmell. Cassandra could hardly believe her eyes. *After all this time. Mother, Paetro, Duncan!* They had come for her, found her. *But how?* Then she noticed the trader and smuggler, Brean Luagh, happily strutting at the front of the Vandian party. *So, Brean found something more valuable than aircraft fuel and metal engine parts to sell.* Her soul felt ripped apart. *Will they take me away with them? How can I go now? What about Alexamir, still risking his life for me? How can I never see him again? Know if he lives or dies?* Cassandra felt as though she was two people inside one body, and only one could leave to return to the Imperium.

'As you asked,' said Temmell, halting in front of Cassandra's horse. He raised his hand at her. 'Your daughter.'

'Do you think I asked?' said Princess Helrena. She indicated the pall of smoke coming from a crashed carrier, the giant half-stripped aircraft further damaged by incendiary shells if Cassandra was any judge. 'If I had kept on "asking" there would not be a barbarian left alive within a hundred miles of here.'

'The Nijumeti are a civilized if simple people,' smiled Temmell, ingratiatingly. 'Despite some indications to the contrary. Have we not given roof and salt to your daughter? Treated Lady Cassandra as though she was one of our own clanswomen?'

'If you maltreated my daughter, the range of my "asking" would have extended to every blade of grass in this dry, flat land of yours,' threatened Princess Helrena. She beckoned Cassandra. 'Are you not going to dismount? Give me a proper welcome?'

'She cannot,' said Brean Luagh.

Cassandra's mother turned and shot the trader a dark glare. 'What do you mean, she *cannot*?'

Brean advanced towards Cassandra's horse and raised his arms to her. 'Come, lady. Let me help you down.'

Cassandra dismounted into his arms and let him bear her towards the shocked visitors. *You fool, Brean Luagh. You didn't tell them about my injuries. Of course they flew here for me, not knowing.* But then, how could any foreign-born smuggler from Hellin hope to understand what her impairment meant inside the Imperium?

Princess Helrena was practically shaking, the sight of her missing daughter being presented in this ignoble manner. 'How badly are you injured?'

Cassandra shook her head and shrugged, fearing to speak the answer. 'My spine was crushed. The aircraft I escaped my captors in came down hard on the steppes during combat.'

Paetro stared worriedly up at her. At his failed responsibility. Guilt and shame tugged at the corners of his mouth. 'Send for the surgeon from the ship. Get him down here at once.'

Soldiers rushed back to a helo to radio for the man. Cassandra vaguely recognized the doctor when he appeared from a newly settled fourth transporter. An old silver-bearded man attached to the house's medical staff, a couple of orderlies behind him, bearing heavy black bags containing the instruments of his trade. *I know you. You're the one who gave me the vaccine for Red Fever the last time the sickness swept through Vandis.* They lay her on the soil like a bedroll. The surgeon rolled up the simple cotton and leather clothing from her back and examined her body. First with warm hands, then with a variety of cold medical instruments. At the last, the surgeon brought out a heavy device with two handholds jutting at its side like iron ears, gripping it tightly with both hands. He pushed the cold metal against her spine and took an x-ray image of her back, skeletal bones and flesh imaged in spectral green on the glass plate at the machine's rear. He examined the image slowly, then discussed it with his two assistants before walking across to Cassandra's mother. Princess Helrena had a hushed conversation with the doctor, her temper obviously not improved by their news. Then she finally returned to speak with her daughter.

'You have fractured three vertebras and your spinal cord has been severed in at least two places. Even the imperial surgeons cannot heal you. You will never walk again.'

'But I can,' insisted Cassandra. She glanced urgently at Temmell. 'Tell my mother. Tell her of my healing each morning.'

'That is but a potion for the pain,' said the sorcerer.

'There is no potion,' spat Cassandra. 'I can walk, unassisted. I can even sprint. For at least ten minutes each morning, before I return to this paralyzed state.'

'You fly,' said Temmell, sadly. 'You soar. Caught up in the visions of our healing herbs.'

'Are you so desperate to avoid upholding your honour?' Helrena glanced in the direction of the surgeon again, but he just sadly shook his head. *You lying dog, Temmell!*

'What honour?' said Duncan, confused, to Helrena. 'We've found her at last. She's safe! We can take Lady Cassandra home.' Cassandra almost felt sorry for her old protector. *He doesn't know. Poor Duncan. You have spent so much time among us, but you still don't understand what it is to be born celestial caste. What it is to hold the Imperium against the rest of the world.*

'Lady Cassandra has no home among us,' said Helrena. 'Her life is finished.'

'But we can take her back,' persisted Duncan. 'There must be a doctor inside the Imperium able to help her. They saved me when I was half-dead on the battlefield! They healed Paetro too.'

'Even the Imperial Medical College has limits to its medicine,' said Helrena. She stared angrily at Brean Luagh. 'Put her back on the horse. Let her pretend to be a person again among these barbarians.'

'Sweet mercy,' said the trader as he reluctantly carried Cassandra to her mare, 'you cannot be serious? I brought you here to your own blood. You're going to abandon her now to the Nijumeti?'

Cassandra pulled herself back into the saddle, hardly daring to look at her mother's face for the shame she felt. The Vandians stood in a line in front of her, their faces hard and disapproving for the most part. A few with disappointment or remorse at her obvious humiliation. Temmell came over and held her horse's reins. *As though I'm rejected goods at the fair. And he's right. That's all I am.*

'I have no blood here,' said Helrena. 'My blood would understand what is necessary to bring honour to her house. How this must end.'

'No!' begged Duncan.

'Please be quiet, Duncan of Weyland,' whispered Cassandra. 'My mother is right. I may not carry a dagger by my side, but there have been blades within reach. I could have stolen one and ended my suffering.'

'This is madness,' said Duncan. 'You can talk, you can eat, you can use your hands and your mind.'

'And the first challenge issued against my house, against me?' said Cassandra. 'Would you and Paetro push my wheelchair around for me during the duel? You stood inside the arena and watched my mother fight. Would you turn my existence into a freak-show and see our house harried to extinction by its enemies?'

Duncan lurched back, rendered mute by the horror of how quickly her rescue had turned into heartbreak for them both.

'What about my money?' demanded Brean Luagh, facing the Vandians. 'The reward for finding the lady, for returning her to you?'

'The house always honours its debts,' said Helrena, coldly. She raised a hand towards her retinue and a soldier stepped forward carrying a heavy leather satchel. The princess took it from her guardsman and lifted its flap, showing the Hellenise smuggler the gold trading coins piled inside. She passed it across to the smuggler. 'As agreed, this is yours.' She raised a finger in Temmell's direction. 'You are this tribe's leader, despite the lack of blue tint on your skin?'

'The Krul of Kruls is currently away with a hunting party,' said Temmell. 'Else he would be here to meet with you. Your arrival is certainly worthy of attention. I am his ... adviser.'

'And how would you advise your absent barbarian chieftain to deal with a trader who gave away the location of your camp and brought dangerous far-called foreigners into your land?'

Temmell's intense gaze turned in the smuggler's direction. 'That the time to hunt has not yet ended.'

Helrena nodded curtly. 'I believe that is wise advice.'

'I am coming back with you,' Brean spluttered at the Vandian visitors.

Helrena patted the side of the smuggler's coin-filled satchel. 'Sadly, you can no longer afford the fare . . . triple the weight of this. My counsel would be to toss your gold in the grass as you flee. Hope that your hunters knife each other over the spoils. You will not find it particularly easy to run with a pack as heavy as that.'

'Please!' Brean glanced madly around, but seeing no mercy among either the Vandians or the nomads, he stumbled away towards the long grass beyond the makeshift aircraft works. Still clutching his reward. *Your death sentence.* Brean was a fool, but perhaps he had tried to help Cassandra. *No, he just tried to make himself rich. As far as he was concerned, you were a stray head of cattle and he was the rustler.*

'Not *too* much of a head start,' observed Helrena.

'He could run for a week and the clans would still ride him down,' said Temmell.

Princess Helrena grunted, then strode away towards the four helos. She gave the aircraft a taut wave and their main blades began to spin into lift mode, balance bars quivering with each engine roaring into life.

Cassandra called after her. 'Please, at least say goodbye!' *She'll come back. My mother won't leave me like this.* 'Help give me the strength . . .'

But Lady Cassandra's mother didn't even break step. *She would have shown more emotion over a corpse she was able to mourn than to me.*

Duncan reached Cassandra's nag, her old master-of-arms, Paetro, trudging behind with the weight of the world on his shoulders. *It's my world and he, at least, knows it's over.* 'Helrena will change her mind. I'll make her, Cassandra, I swear to you.'

'Duncan, she's the head of house and she has spoken. I'll never see my mother again.' *Or Vandia. This is my life, here now. With Alexamir.*

'She will!' insisted Duncan, gazing desperately at the departing princess.

'You'll end up banished if you keep speaking for me,' said Cassandra. 'Make him see sense, Paetro.'

The stocky bodyguard tugged Duncan away from her horse. 'The little highness is speaking the truth, lad. We have to leave here now. Or we'll be the ones trying to out-pace barbarian hunting lances alongside that young Hellenise chancer.'

'I'm sorry, Paetro,' said Cassandra. *Sorry you had to discover me like this.*

'Don't be sorry, little highness. I trained you as well as any of us. Stay on that horse with a sword in your hand and you'll end up the Queen of the Steppes, you see if you don't.'

'I tried to find my honour; at least at the start, I did.' *But in the end I wanted to live too much. For Alexamir's sake, if not my own.*

'Vandia's far-called and beyond the horizon,' said Paetro, gazing out across the endless prairie and the low hills. Tears wet his eyes as well as Cassandra's. 'That's a big sky. Everywhere is different. You live well for me. Hold to the barbarians' customs here and live well.'

'I'm not abandoning you,' sobbed Duncan.

Cassandra nodded to Paetro and her old bodyguard dragged the Weylander back struggling towards the helo, assisted by a couple of burly guardsmen from the landing force. They forced Duncan inside a transporter and held him there, Paetro standing by its open hatch. He raised his hand in a weary farewell and the hatch door closed. One by one, the four helos lifted up, turning in the air and heading for the massive metal warship squatting on the other side of the river. Cassandra didn't see her mother in the cockpit or the observation ports. Not even one final glance.

Cassandra turned her attention to Temmell. 'You lied to them. They might have taken me if they thought there was even a hope I could use my legs again . . .'

'But you didn't want to leave, did you? Not truly.'

'You lied to them!'

'I merely denied the truth. Which among them would believe my enchantment over your flesh?' asked the sorcerer. 'Not even your own family. They hold to their power and I hold to mine.'

'You need to keep me trapped here, don't you? A convenient piece of bait to dangle in front of Alexamir.'

'Perhaps I value our little evening conversations more than you think,' smiled the sorcerer. 'Someone whose interests stretch further than how many cattle your kin have stolen during the week . . .'

'What do you really want, Temmell?'

'Always just a little bit more than I already have,' said the odd golden-skinned man. He rubbed his forehead with the back of his hand, sounding vexed. 'There was more, once. But what was it? Would that I could pick it out of my throbbing soup of a mind. No matter. I shall start by regaining lost face. Your people dare come here and rake my new skyguard with their rockets and cannons? To treat with me as though I am one of their filthy slaves? They will pay sorely for their arrogance!'

Cassandra snorted in derision. 'I would settle for being glad your land has nothing the Imperium's legions desire.' *Certainly not me, anymore.*

Temmell's sly eyes watched the giant Vandian warship. He said nothing more until the vessel rose into the air, swivelling on pillars of fire from her engine pods, anti-gravity stones studding her hull flaring into life and pushing her into the sky. 'As I said, they have their power. I have *mine*.'

They left me. Abandoned me. It was one thing to learn the Code of Caste from birth. To watch badly wounded duellists swaying in the arena sand and call for the Knife of Honour from the emperor's stand, to open their bowels with the blade. Quite another to experience the code's cruel logic first-hand. *Of course my mother abandoned me. I should never have hoped otherwise.* 'I am finished,' she whispered.

'Not yet,' said Temmell. He had fine hearing. 'All that training, all that dedication. Every day. Duty every single hour. A living blade polished to perfection. No existence but service to the house and empire. No amusements. Never a second of freedom to live your life as you might choose. You pick up a single blemish and what do they do? They discard the knife on the ground. Toss it into the dirt without a second thought. No longer wanted. Doesn't that make you angry?'

'Yes,' growled Cassandra. She was shocked how easily her grief boiled into fury. A fiery sea of magma that even a stratovolcano's crater could not contain. 'I'm not broken. I'm *not*.' *To hell with the house and the Imperium. How dare they stand here with pity and shame in their eyes, judging me. I survived. I'm free and alive, and even without my legs, I'm more than they could ever make me. And I will make myself more yet.*

'You are only what you believe. A better lesson than dusty words in old texts, don't you think?' said Temmell. 'Everything passes and so little of it matters. Not what you thought once was of consequence, certainly. The world turns with the tedious inevitability of the wheels on a trader's wagon. And it all fades. What you love and cherish. Your life, my life, all our little certainties. They all fly away in the end.'

'Then what do we live for?'

'Oh, I'd suggest making fine mischief,' said Temmell. 'And best suiting ourselves.'

Cassandra gazed down at her stupid useless legs. She loathed them almost as much as she did this lying trickster. 'I should never have let Alexamir risk himself for me.'

'Tell yourself that you had no choice in the matter,' suggested Temmell.

'If Alexamir is killed or hurt in Rodal, I shall crawl every inch of this land to track you down. I'll pull the feathers out of your concealed wings as though I was plucking a plump chicken and finish by slitting your throat to see what colour blood your abomination of a heart pumps.'

'You deserve to walk again,' laughed Temmell. 'Your imperial friend spoke the truth. You deserve to be Queen of the Steppes. Perhaps more than Kani Yargul deserves to be Krul of Kruls.'

'May we all get what we *deserve.*'

'I do believe you have unlocked the first door of your cage,' said Temmell. 'If Alexamir survives his little task for me, I shall be sure to open the last gate for you. I will let you loose on the world again. I don't think Pellas will thank me for the deed, but then when has it ever? Gratitude is a sickness suffered by dogs.' Temmell shook his head and stood up straight, as though waking from a slumber. 'I will find myself, out here, one day. Fires to put out. Yes, and a few more to start. Go back to the tent of Alexamir's aunt. Drink your troubles away on her milky firewater. Forget your old life. It was worthless and this is as fine a place to be reborn as anywhere.'

Cassandra tugged on the reins and set her nag trotting towards old Nonna and her cooling supper. She kept one eye on the horizon, but no longer watching for Vandian rescue aircraft. *Alexamir. Return alive for me. You must.*

There was a chuckle from the lip of the well above and Alexamir, his desperate spine-walking along the shaft temporarily halted, imagined the vent-man sighting on his skull and conjuring up all the things the bounty on an intruder's corpse would pay for. *I just have one more gift to add.* The nomad's left foot hit empty space where a side-tunnel had been carved into the well's wall. *Exactly where the map said it would.*

'You want a song?' Alexamir called up. 'Here it is!'

He released the tension of his body stretched out across the shaft, using the sudden momentum to swing himself forward on the climbing line, carried across towards the side-tunnel. As his bulk came down on his climbing line, the first pin in the well's mouth above took his full weight. The booby-trapped iron pin cracked forward on its hidden lever mechanism. A cloud of arrows released from the ceiling of the passage above the well. Many of the projectiles whistled down through the shaft, shooting into the narrow space so recently vacated by Alexamir. But enough of the volley met the vent-man's back. He went from leaning over the well to tumbling down into it. Alexamir hit the side-passage, rolled, and turned just in time to see the vent-man's corpse plummeting past, his back feathered with arrow shafts. A second later the rice-eater's pistol and mess of climbing gear came cracking past, jouncing off the well's sides and heading after their owner. Alexamir poked his head out, watching the dim light from the worker's torch painting the sides of the well, the illumination growing smaller and smaller, before vanishing to a distant termination. So deep he didn't even hear the impact of landing. With any luck, the vent-man's death would be written off as forgetfulness, tying his line's clip to one of the traps set to murder intruders. Alexamir leaned out, grabbed the end of his line still attached to the iron pin and triggered the clip release, catching the line as it tumbled.

'Thank you, Aunt,' whispered Alexamir. *First fight using your brain.* His escape had been as narrow as Hadra-Hareer's labyrinth of air vents. He had barely reached the snared shaft with enough time to climb into the side-tunnel. *A second slower and it would be me at the bottom of the shaft, riddled with bullets. Truly, Atamva, you favour the bold.* He gobbed down the shaft. Many thought the Nijumeti tradition of spitting on defeated foes was an insult, but it was not. *You have to wet the souls of the fallen so they will not burn when they pass the Three Fiery Rivers circling hell. As long as they fought bravely. The cowards cry to keep from burning. Any fool knows this.*

Thankfully, the remainder of his claustrophobic voyage through the hidden depths of the rice-eaters' tomb was made without encountering any other locals. The air grew closer, warmer, the scent of Rodalians on it, and he knew he was getting close to the temple of the monks. He had timed his arrival for long after the last townspeople should have departed the temple complex. *And hopefully, many of the monks will be resting or in prayer.*

Alexamir's prior visit to the Temple of the Winds – posing as one of hundreds of pilgrims and worshippers – had been more than enough to convince him that an indirect approach through the temple's ventilation shafts was the best way to gain his prize. Chamber after chamber, echoing and cavernous, filled with the chants of priests and the clack-clack-clack of prayer wheels being turned, dozens of heavy wooden doors and portals that would be locked and guarded after the temple shut to the public. Actually stealing the Rodalians' holy text, he mused, would have been a far easier task than having to memorize the monks' holy of holies and escape without the crime being detected. So much easier to take the book by guile and brute force, kill as many as needed, and leave a trail of rice-eaters' bodies all the way through the passes of Hadra-Hareer.

Luckily for Temmell Longgate, the gods had provided him with Alexamir Arinnbold's services. His map through the airshafts led him directly to the Chamber of Lights, the temple's inner sanctum. He removed the iron grille high in the ceiling and secured his climbing line to the pin closest to the opening. One last check before he descended. No monks here. This part of the temple was locked away at the rear of the connected rooms – one way in, one way out. During the day, pilgrims had to queue for hours before they were ushered through this place in near silence in small groups; only the monks muttering prayers and giving thanks as they accompanied the penitent worshippers. *Sadly for the rice-eaters, my prayers are as false as my skin.*

The floor of the chamber lay seventy feet below him. There was no light from outside the mountain now, the mirrored chutes lining the wall and ceiling protruding dull and dark. Four wooden wheels studded with glow-stones hung from the ceiling, alternating with yellow and orange stones, one of the wheels near enough to Alexamir for him to touch and swing from – if he had been minded. Instead, he quickly shimmied down the line, coming down fast enough to catch friction burns from the rope. The chamber's walls had been painted with proud frescoes of scenes from the monks' teachings. The nearest was a flying wing wrestling with the currents of an unfriendly wind high above a mountain range, a grim look of determination on the pilot's face below his aviator's goggles. Friendly spirits hurtled up from the slopes below, encouraged to his aid by a monk with a staff standing small on the ground. *They boast of being able to summon the wind to their aid, but where are their spirits now? Locked outside, while I am the wolf prowling inside their lamb pen. So many monks, yet none of them quite holy enough to be taken into the confidence of their spirits. The winds love to whisper. But they did not whisper warnings of me.*

Across the floor lay six brick-walled pools surrounding a seventh, far larger one, in the centre of the chamber. The six round pools were set as petals circling the head of the largest well. Each had a winch-like contraption resting above the water's surface. And each pool, lapping with laboriously blessed holy water, contained a holy book at the bottom of the well. Precious copper plates etched with their holy teachings. This arrangement, Alexamir had been told, was because the power of the texts was such that should they be left out of the water for more than an hour, the books summoned terrible forces that would melt the pages – claiming the souls of those that minded the texts and dissolving even the sturdy metal-leafed pages. Only cooling inside blessed water preserved their texts from this fate. Alexamir moved towards the central reservoir, halting as he heard a sound. A voice, laughing, had carried along the corridor outside the Chamber of Lights. But it was from far away. And it was the greatest of the seven lights that he had come to filch, here in the centre. *The Deb-rlung'rta.* He strained to hear any rice-eater near enough to realize the winch was in use, but the temple gave him only silence, so he set to his task. A wooden handle on a drum brought up the cable chains bearing the cage from below. The smear of orange that was the copper-plated book came up near-silently. Somebody had taken a lot of trouble to grease the chains this well. Alexamir approved. *I suppose the monks do not want their devotions and holy silence interrupted by squealing iron.* The cage broke the surface of the pool and swayed there, dripping water. There were no locks on the rectangular cage holding the text inside and Alexamir felt a sudden nag of apprehension. *Will I burst into flames when I touch it – is that why it is unlocked? Will their spirits whistle down the air shafts above, pull me away and break my bones inside their dark tunnels?* He said a quick prayer to Atamva and every god of the grass who owed him a favour and turned the cage towards him, lifting off its roof. The tome inside was large and weighty. The book would have easily filled a rider's main saddlebag all by itself if theft had been the nomad's intention . . . and given the horse good reason to curse its owner. He hauled the Deb-rlung'rta out – like carrying a hefty boulder – and bore it over to a stone pew overlooking the pool, where its reading was obviously intended. He wasn't sure what was to happen when he opened the pages. The slippery sorcerer had merely suggested the enchantment of disguise over Alexamir would allow him to gaze at the pages and retain their holy secrets, but when he stared at the first page, he had his doubts. It was just a mess of squiggles, as if someone had taken a dagger's tip to the copper plate in boredom and scored meaningless shapes there. *Does the sorcerer know I cannot read anything other than maps?* Well, tough on him if he didn't. Alexamir had broken into the Temple of the Winds in the heart of the enemies' fastness and capital. *If the foreign fool's magic doesn't work as promised, he will still honour the healing of the Golden Fox or be known among all the clans as the greatest oath-breaker to disappoint a hero since Jonovich the Liar sold the Krul's own sword to a demon.* The next page was the same incomprehensible litter of what were undoubtedly letters. It was when Alexamir reached the third page that someone stabbed a thin dagger of ice into his forehead, the cold shock of the attack almost sending him reeling back from the stone pew. He grasped tightly on to the pew, the vision of the holy book swimming in and out of view. Then things grew clear. Gloriously clear. It was as though someone had lowered an enchanted crystal visor over his eyes, everything glowing with intense diamond-sharp clarity. Alexamir swayed there for a few seconds more getting used to the new senses he had been gifted. The Deb-rlung'rta was a child's toy compared to the thousands of motes of dust dancing in the light of the glow-stone wheels, the frescoes' stories on every wall vivid and bright even in the gloom. He ran a finger over the stone pew, marble lines like the tributaries of rivers on a map that only he could understand. This was the opposite of being drunk. Not slumbering but fully awake. He had broken into the Chamber of so-called Lights, but *he* was the lantern now, casting the light of his brilliance with every gaze. Contentedly, he turned the heavy pages of the Rodalians' book of the winds, each curve, curl, arch and bow of the characters a thing of beauty, still unintelligible, but gently so, as pleasing as the stars of the constellations as they crawled through the night sky. Pages clacked over, as though he was playing a game of encircling stones against himself. He again heard the sound of the voice drifting down the corridor outside the chamber. This time he marked it properly: a male's voice, elderly, speaking loudly to overcome his loss of hearing. Sitting around two hundred feet away, and from the shifts of the echo, inside the outer temple rooms. There was a second voice too, speaking at a correct volume; so younger, an initiate monk being lectured about his tardiness, no doubt. Each page of the Deb-rlung'rta dropped like a felled tree, quickly perused and appreciated before the next metal sheet turned. It didn't take more than five minutes to reach the end of the text – well before the hour expired that would call evil spirits upon him. He fetched the weighty metal book back to the cage, shut the cage door, and lowered it back to its blessing inside the pool of holy water. As Alexamir gripped the bottom of the climbing line and made to climb back towards the ceiling, he was deeply tempted to wander the walls and examine the images of the temple walls, too. *Why didn't I notice these the first time I visited?* But the sorcerer was not paying him for all the monks' tales of wisdom, only their holy of holies, and this he now carried, folded inside him, invisible and unseen, like the knowledge of navigating by the stars, or reading a map. Alexamir scaled the rope, pulled up the climbing line, resealed the grille with the steel tool designed for the task, and then he crawled out towards the surface, the clarity of the universe slowly fading to a dull, throbbing disappointment with each foot he crept.

Duncan watched Helrena arguing furiously with Prince Gyal. Duncan stood sentry silently, brooding, with Paetro beside him. The only other witness to the argument was Apolleon, the chief of the hoodsmen. The master of the Imperium's secret police had recently arrived from Vandia on a fast cruiser called the *Dark Moon*. His presence further unsettled Duncan. *Nothing good is ever augured by that man's arrival.* Duncan wasn't even sure if Apolleon *was* fully human. *I caught a glimpse of your true self, Apolleon.* Back in the Castle of Snakes when their laboratory had been attacked. Another body flickering between the shadows, leaping to the castle's defence, evil and spider-like. Or perhaps what Duncan had glimpsed was just a side-effect of the chemicals spilled when Circae's assassins came to kidnap Lady Cassandra. He wiped a tear away from his eye, trying to forget how forlorn and small Cassandra had looked on top of her mare as their helo lifted away. *I failed you, Cassandra. I allowed you to be abducted by Jacob Carnehan. I allowed you to be kept as a prisoner. And when we finally tracked you down, I watched your own people discard you like a broken tool in the grass.* Duncan couldn't even look at himself in a mirror anymore when he shaved. *What have I become?* 'A true son of the Imperium,' whispered a voice that might have been his conscience.

'You must remain with the expeditionary force,' commanded Prince Gyal as he stalked up and down the chamber. Princess Helrena bit back an obviously hostile retort. Once the sight of such tension between Helrena and Gyal would have filled Duncan's heart with satisfaction. Now, it only reminded him how everything he had hoped to pass lay as ashes in his mouth.

'My daughter is dead to me,' said Helrena. 'There is nothing to stay here for.'

Prince Gyal's face contorted with anger. '*Nothing!* I lost a quarter of the expeditionary force to these cursed mountain tribes.'

'You lost them to bad weather, my prince,' sneered Helrena. 'There is a reason why tribes in the north excavate their towns deep within mountains and rocks, why their forests bleed sap and dislocate trunks so trees may regrow after a storm has passed. There is a reason why the barbarians in this part of the world know Rodal as the Walls of the World and only dirt-poor madmen abide there. Nobody wants it. Nobody values it. Why should we?'

Gyal jabbed a finger towards Helrena. 'Those who led the slave revolt still shelter inside that cursed canyon warren.'

'A pitiful handful. While recaptured slaves fill our ships' holds with their natural condition restored, alongside many thousands of their kin as company to help pay for the revolt. You smashed the rebels at Midsburg. You won your victory there. You extracted Vandia's retribution. You took slaves. It is I who has lost everything. This war has finished for me; this punishment expedition is at an end.'

'I will have my revenge!'

'Against what? The rocks and the gales? Who is there left to punish? Rock-dwelling barbarians and their goats and yaks? You can't sentence them to any worse fate than life in that mountainous storm-lashed freak of a land they consider home. Forget Rodal and set course for Vandia. Do you think our enemies back home are so content as to bide their time? To wait for the punishment fleet to root out every escaped slave and barbarian villager who ever gave a runaway sky-miner shelter? You tarry here for too long and you'll return to find a triumph being hosted in honour of a newly crowned emperor. An emperor jealous of pristine victories not his own; assassins' blades hired to seek out too-successful field commanders back with the legions.'

'I shall be emperor,' snarled Gyal. 'With you by my side as empress.'

'Remain distracted in Rodal and I will be kneeling by your side in Execution Square as a fine example of what fate awaits over-ambitious rivals,' warned Helrena. 'Victories are like farts. Only your own smells sweet. If you want to stay and pull wings off bugs up in the freezing mountains, do so. You will expend blood and treasure and leave a few sacked rice paddies behind you to show for your wounded pride.'

'If an emperor is not proud, if a Vandian is not proud, then he is nothing.' Gyal's hand angrily cut the air. 'It is done. Decided. If Hadra-Hareer won't fall to air-power, it will fall to siege. The legions will seize every wind-harbour the barbarians use as protection from the storms; make them *our* shelters. I shall throw our forces like a noose around their mountains. No food or supplies will enter Hadra-Hareer. The barbarians will send their starving children out from behind their walls and *beg* me to take them as slaves merely so they may live another day.'

'You do not have the forces to mount such a siege,' said Helrena. 'And more to the point, neither of us has the time for a protracted blockade.'

'King Marcus will provide barbarian regiments to swell our ranks,' said Gyal. 'And I have sent for the skels. My gold calls thousands more fighters to our flag – mercenaries and local free companies and pirates-for-hire. I will muster the forces to make an end of this campaign to my satisfaction.'

'Think with your mind, not your wounded pride. I intend to travel home and attend the court . . . ensure that the emperor receives the right reports from our campaign.' She stared across at the secret police's master. 'I am sure that there are many who will be only too glad to spin a different tale.'

Apolleon nodded thoughtfully. 'That is not a bad idea. No, not bad at all. Fill the slave markets with prisoners. Let the celestial caste have a taste of the booty that will return with the punishment fleet. Whet their appetites. You can enter mourning for Lady Cassandra. Circae and her allies will be unable to act against you, not without their manoeuvres being perceived as the height of bad taste. Buy extra time to claim the Diamond Throne.'

'And how fares the health of the noble Emperor Jaelis?' asked Gyal.

Apolleon grinned. 'Less and less noble every week. Where the emperor's mind fails, his body now follows. Princess Helrena is correct. The time to act is approaching.'

'When the emperor dies, Apolleon, I will need the backing of your hoodsmen,' said Helrena. 'During the scramble for the throne the threat of the secret police will help dissuade our foes from courting the army. None of us can afford a military conflict inside the Imperium. Announcing your support early would be advantageous to us.'

'If in bad form, given Emperor Jaelis still warms the throne,' said Apolleon. 'You must be patient. I will not be returning to the court for a little while yet. I haven't been dispatched to this far-called backwater to check on your progress . . . I come hunting for the outlaw Sariel Skel-bane.'

'Him again?' spat Helrena. 'Your obsession with capturing that old vagrant helped seal our defeat during the slave revolt. Is his distraction to cost me the throne now, too?'

'There are matters beyond your concern,' said Apolleon. 'And this is one of them. You need merely accept that Sariel Skel-bane's long overdue execution is necessary to a great many things. Including *your* future.'

'It's my future that interests me, not ancient history. I need your support in the capital, in Vandis,' demanded Helrena. 'Not settling old grudges against some elderly bandit who made the hoodsmen appear incompetent during the first flush of his youth.'

'Those "grudges" you speak of are mine to settle.'

Helrena appeared disgusted by the reply. 'So now I have *two* thick-headed pride-swelled allies to worry about? May my ancestors send me women as allies rather than men.'

'We are on the right course, Princess,' reassured Apolleon. 'The art of politics is the art of the unexpected. And what could be more un-expected than two arch-enemies returning from campaign as firm allies? After the union of the disparate factions supporting your houses, you will possess an almost unstoppable momentum towards the throne. All the more powerful given your rivals will be taken completely by surprise. Unprepared for the marriage and the realignment of power it entails. An adroit stratagem.'

'Yes. It's almost as if we don't need you,' said Helrena.

'You will discover how much you require the hoodsmen's support after I return to Vandia,' said Apolleon. 'I might have suggested this fascinating new strategy myself, except I imagined it ending with one of your daggers slipped into the other's spine.'

'Let love bloom in self-interest's soil,' said Prince Gyal.

'I would not expect to remain Circae's favoured pet when she learns of this news,' Apolleon warned the prince. 'I believe the old woman's hatred of her ex-daughter-in-law is a touch greater than her regard for you.'

'It will not matter,' said Gyal. 'Helrena and I shall seize the throne together. A new emperor and empress, a new age for the Imperium. Circae will have to accept the news with good grace. Who would dare to oppose an empress?'

Apolleon's wily eyes crinkled. 'You might be surprised.'

'She will accept it or learn how easy it is for an old woman who has lived her life to pass away with the night.'

'Circae's support would be useful,' said Apolleon. 'Who knows, perhaps your union will soften her heart?'

'Granite doesn't soften,' growled Helrena. 'It only calcifies.'

'Go to Vandia then,' said Prince Gyal. He pointed angrily at Hel-rena, sounding for all the world like a petulant child. 'Leave the war for me to prosecute. I will win it and bathe in the escaped slaves' blood before I return.'

'And I always imagined the mark of an emperor was how much blood he spared rather than shed,' said Helrena.

Gyal muttered and stalked away. Duncan watched Prince Gyal and the secret police's master depart the chamber together before he approached Helrena. *Good riddance to both of them. With any luck, Apolleon will lose himself in the wilderness chasing shadows, while Gyal's skull will be crushed by loose boulders inside the Valley of the Hell-winds.*

'Tell me that you are really returning to Vandia to seize the throne for yourself?' said Duncan. 'That you didn't mean any of what you just said?'

'You forget your place,' snapped Helrena. 'It is true that this alliance wasn't something I arrived at willingly, but Apolleon is right about one thing. The momentum from the union will carry me all the way to the Diamond Throne.'

'You can rule alone,' argued Duncan.

'I could *fail* alone,' said Helrena. 'You think the leadership of the Imperium is a prize waiting lonely to be claimed? There is not a merchant, citizen or soldier in the Imperium who would not risk everything they possess for the throne if they thought they had just a chance at seizing it. With Gyal's supporters added to my own, *my* chance is there. Without Gyal's forces? I'm just another head of house jostling hungrily among the pack. Taking control is merely the start of the game. Long after the throne is claimed, new allies will be needed to hold the empire and solidify support. Time to gather endorsements and win over old opponents through patronage and appointments.'

'I haven't forgotten my place,' said Duncan. 'It's by your side.'

Helrena shook her head. 'Once. No longer. I must leave the bulk of my guardsmen fighting with Gyal's forces or risk being accused of abandoning my post. My return to Vandia has to be interpreted as a mother's mourning, not the dereliction of her duty.'

'Cassandra's not dead!' shouted Duncan.

'She *is* dead,' roared Helrena. 'Rotting flesh and a lost soul struggling to recover her honour through a clean death. She's no longer a Vandian. No longer celestial caste. How can she be anything other than dead?'

'I don't understand you,' said Duncan. *How can you even think like that?*

'Then understand that Vandia is strength,' said Helrena. 'The day the empire is not is the day it falls.' She looked at Paetro. 'You will be posted here with Duncan of Weyland. Assist the prince in burning rocks until his doltish pride is sated.'

Paetro bowed, sadly. 'As you say, Princess.'

'No!' begged Duncan.

'You are banished from the Castle of Snakes, Duncan Landor,' said Helrena. 'You will stay here until the day I find your nature more agreeable. Serve with the punishment fleet. After the fall of Hadra-Hareer, remain with the empire's embassy in Weyland. Put your local knowledge to good use for Vandia.'

'Please...'

But Helrena was already striding down a corridor away from the room.

'How can she act so coldly towards Cassandra, her own daughter?' *To me.*

'The princess feels pain,' said Paetro. 'As much as you or I. More... she's the little highness's mother. But Helrena's too much of a celestial caste to show it. No weakness, lad. Not in front of us. Especially not in front of Prince Gyal or Apolleon.'

Duncan shook his head in frustration. 'This is wrong. All of it... wrong. Helrena's marriage to that serpent Gyal. Abandoning Cassandra. Leaving us behind.'

'It's how the Vandians think, lad. How could we remain at Princess Helrena's side? Reminding her of the little highness every time she saw us.'

I thought I was free of my past. But here I am, as trapped inside Weyland as I was in the sky mines before I won my freedom. How the saints must be laughing at the irony. 'Our duty is to protect Helrena. How can we manage that from Weyland?'

'No, our first duty was to protect the little highness. And in that we failed. This campaign is our penance.'

Not for me. 'If I'm stuck in Weyland, then I'm returning for Lady Cassandra after Hadra-Hareer falls and Gyal buggers off back home. When the campaign finishes, I'll track Cassandra down in the steppes and carry her to Northhaven. At least she can live her life in some comfort inside Hawkland Park.'

'The princess didn't order that,' warned Paetro.

'She didn't forbid it, either,' said Duncan.

'It's not the Vandian way.'

'So it seems. But I'm only a lower-caste citizen,' said Duncan. 'An ex-slave on the make. It's my bloody way. Let Vandia believe what it will about weakness and honour, the empire seems to be too far-called to care. Here I'm Duncan Landor, heir to a great northern house. In Weyland, *I'm* the prince.'

Paetro sighed. 'Then I'll travel with you.'

'I'm the one banished to this backwater, not you.'

'I was born inside a tribute nation, lad, not the empire. I may have come to understand the Vandian code, but it wasn't the milk I was raised on. Leaving the little highness like a wounded bird in the grass for the first prowling cat to discover sits mightily hard on me, too. Besides, someone has to keep you alive when you run into those blue-skinned brutes again.'

'You're a good friend, Paetro Barca.'

'Remind me again if we survive Gyal's little war. A prince's pride and vanity aren't going to be much armour against mountain gales and cannon shells aimed our way from Hadra-Hareer's ramparts.'

Duncan shrugged. *It's a siege. How dangerous can it be?* He had a feeling he was going to find out.

SEVEN

VISITORS FOR WILLOW

Willow welcomed Anna Kurtain into her lodgings with a sense of relief. *Whatever problems Anna has, they're small beans compared to the complaints and worries of the refugees fleeing Weyland.*

'Ever since I was wounded by that assassin inside Midsburg,' said Anna, 'Owen's treated me like I'm a porcelain heirloom. Far too valuable to put in harm's way.'

'He's just worried about you,' said Willow. She had a feeling that almost losing Anna had awakened the prince's true feelings for his long-term companion. *And about time, too.* Of course, it wasn't just Anna's wounds that had nearly taken the woman away from the prince. Jacob Carnehan had kidnapped Anna and used the threat of making sure Owen never saw her again to force the prince to abandon the rebels' doomed last-ditch stand at Midsburg.

Anna shook her head, angrily. 'It's insulting is what it is. I was the one who kept Owen alive in the sky mines, and after that, when we escaped to Weyland. Without me, Owen's true identity would have been betrayed a dozen times over to the Vandians.'

'I understand all about being treated with kid gloves,' said Willow, rubbing her heavy, relentless belly.

'In fairness, you aren't in much condition to go trekking with your Northhaven boy,' said Anna.

'Sometimes I wish I'd been born barren,' said Willow. 'Then Viscount Wallingbeck would have divorced me quickly enough, however much money my family promised to lavish over his estate. I'd be worthless to the viscount. Worthless as a game piece to the all-mighty House of Landor as well.'

'Don't say that. That's nothing to wish for. You have to believe that things happened as they did for a reason,' said Anna. 'Owen survived Bad Marcus' assassination of his family. Then he survived as a slave in Vandia. Finally, he escaped and helped us all return home. What's the odds of all those survivals lumped together? Owen's fated to cast the usurper off his throne. He has to be.'

Willow wished that was true but couldn't for the life of her see how it'd transpire now. 'And what about you and how things have gone down?'

'I've given a lot of thought to that,' said Anna. 'Back where I used to live near the Lakes, my brother and I were meant to be travelling south with our grandmother. She was going to take the springs at Tresterer and wanted us along with her to see a little of the world. Paid for our hotel rooms and our fares with the Guild of Rails and everything. But the evening before we were due to travel, she slipped in a puddle in the street and broke her leg. The trip had to be put off. Four days later, our town was hit by skel slavers and my brother and me were grabbed up. If it hadn't rained the night before . . . if my grandmother had gone a different way through town . . . if a shopkeeper had just mopped up that puddle. We would have been safely out of the way hundreds of mile from the raid.'

'And then you wouldn't have been taken to the sky mines to save Prince Owen's life,' said Willow. She could tell from the pain in Anna's voice how much the woman missed her brother. Willow and the other escaped slaves had at least been able to reassure Anna he was still alive, though. She had encountered the young man inside the great aerial carrier the skels used to launch their slave raids – his clockmaker's training keeping him alive as an engineer repairing the city-sized aircraft's machinery.

'That's about the size of it.'

'Well, if fate's got a place for me, I have to believe it's by Carter's side,' said Willow. It was strange now, looking back on events. Being the heir to a great house meant that Willow should never have lacked for suitors. But in reality, growing up in Northhaven where everyone knew who you were and who your father was, it had been a curse of eternal loneliness. As though there had been a glass wall laid around Willow which nobody had dared to scale for fear of the wrath of the mighty Landors. Carter was one of the few people who hadn't seemed bothered by her status, although it had taken the horror of surviving the sky mines to bring them both together. And now the Vandians and their empire and their revenge had driven the two of them apart, at least physically. She tried not to think of how much she missed Carter. What danger he might be in out in the wilds. Willow thought she heard a noise from the back of her rooms, but she dismissed it. There were always gurgling water pipes and rustling air vents inside the city. 'But Carter's off with Sariel, chasing the vagrant's ale-addled ancient fancies and I'm trapped here. As big as a whale and near as beached as one, too.'

'He's a strange one, that Sariel,' agreed Anna. 'But he's got powers. Without the old wanderer and Carter's father, we would never have escaped Vandia alive.'

'And where else would we be, I wonder?'

'I've got as much reason to distrust Father Carnehan as any, the way he's used me. But as my father used to say about our local assembly-man, he may be a son-of-a-bitch, but he's *our* son-of-a-bitch. We're going to need a few like Jacob Carnehan in Hadra-Hareer in the days to come.'

'You think we'll survive here, Anna?'

'This city is a hell of a place to attack,' shrugged the prince's bodyguard. 'The Vandians' first assault broke apart like a glass bottle hurled off the mountain peaks. But you know as well as I do how the Imperium thinks.'

'They won't give up, will they?'

'Main reason they're here is to punish us for humiliating them in the slave revolt. Once the local town bully loses his reputation, it's one short step from victimizer to victimized.'

'Vandia's not exactly local, though,' said Willow.

'That's one thing working in our favour. This war's got to have the longest supply line in history.'

'You sound like Father Carnehan.'

Anna's eyes narrowed. 'I sound like *General* Carnehan. He knows war, I'll give him that. A lot more than he knows about holy texts and gods and saints.'

Maybe God's kept him alive. Or maybe it's the Devil's stealers who've preserved the man? Willow shook her head and trembled. It still seemed a madness, the difference between the man she had known from childhood and the man she now watched stalking through Hadra-Hareer's passages. The man of peace who shunned all violence. Who had given gentle sermons and chiding admonishments whenever his congregation erred from mercy and peace. The Jacob Carnehan Willow knew had been broken and something terrible had slipped out of the shell that had been left. Perhaps the monster had always been inside. The saints know, since the civil war had started, she had seen monsters crawl out of too many. *Is there one inside me, too?* 'I wanted us to run,' said Willow. 'I asked Carter to leave with me.'

'How far can you flee?' asked Anna. 'Further than the range of a Vandian warship? Further than their slavers' planes? There's always evil in the world. If not the Imperium's, then someone else's. For too much of my life, I was kept caged by evil. I don't reckon I've got much running left in me. You can't run to freedom. You just have to plant your feet and take it.'

'By force,' sighed Willow.

'You could try reason, good intentions and fine words,' said Anna. 'But when the brutes coming at you have got a whip in one hand and a pistol in the other, you won't be debating for long.'

'I wish there was another way.'

'You find it, Willow, be sure to let me know. What—?' Too late, Anna Kurtain heard the movement behind her and snatched at her pistol holster, but the large Rodalian who seemed to appear from nowhere seized her from behind, covering her face with a rag stinking of chloroform.

How's this thief broken in? Willow took a step back, nearly tumbling over a chair. Anna possessed a lithe strength . . . the fitness of youth honed by years of hard labour inside the sky mines; but taken by surprise it was of little use. The prince's bodyguard struggled in her attacker's massive muscled arms, her boots kicking against the air until she trembled to stillness and was unceremoniously dropped over a rug. The assault had only taken seconds. *Thief? Robber? One of the factions that want Rodal to stay out of Weyland's war? I don't have any weapons inside the room.* Willow threw the chair in front of her and backed away, her eyes casting desperately around for any heavy object she could grasp and wield as a mace. As she looked she realized too late that another attacker had circled behind her. *No!* The second assailant seized her arms and pressed a blade against her soft throat. She groaned as she recognized a too-familiar stench. Aged beer and sweat and malice. Willow moaned again as a spiteful voice sounded hot against her ear, confirming her assailant's identity. *Nocks.* Her step-mother's brutal terrier. *What's he doing inside Rodal? He should be across the border serving with my father's regiment.*

The large Rodalian who had broken into her apartment advanced on her. Willow lashed a foot at him, but he stopped short before her boot could connect. Nocks tightened his grip.

'Don't you mind the big lad, Willowy Willow,' rasped Nocks. 'Norbu's something of an expert on raiding cities and carrying away saddle-wives.'

Willow had scarce seen a Rodalian as large or wide as this man. *And why is Nocks talking about saddle-wives? That's a steppes tradition, nothing to do with the mountains?*

'You did not tell me that the woman you sought was with child,' said the brute named as Norbu. 'It is always bad luck to claim a saddle-wife carrying another's son.'

'Oh, this one is nothing but bad luck any way you cut it,' laughed Nocks.

'I'll scream and you won't dare use that knife,' hissed Willow, hoping the evil manservant could still be controlled by fear of her father.

The squat brute snorted in amusement. 'Ain't that the beauty of having your room buried under so many tonnes of stone. You work your lungs all you like, Willow Landor. It's just you, me and the big lad down here.'

'Leave her and let's carry away the other girl,' urged Norbu. 'Take the dark-skinned one instead. She is a beauty worthy of any man's tent – she fought fast and well, too. This Willow's belly will slow your escape down.'

'I'm stealing to order,' said Nocks, clenching Willow roughly as she tried to struggle free. 'Much like yourself, son. This little firebrand is the wife of a nobleman down south . . . and he's the one who baked the bun in her oven. The man wants her back with the bun too, and more importantly, so does the woman I serve.'

'My step-mother can go to hell,' Willow spat.

Norbu did not seem happy with Willow's state, but he lifted his rag still wet with the sickly-sweet stench of chloroform. 'Then I shall use the sleeping cloth and let us be done with this.'

'All in good time,' snickered Nocks. 'I scratched your back out on the slopes and this is where you scratch mine . . . a man should beat down on his steak a little before he consumes it. You made the mistress look like a fool, Willowy Willow. Betraying the marriage she kindly arranged for you and running off with the pretender and his rebel army. So I'm taking you back to Lady Leyla and the viscount. He wants his child out of your belly before the mistress gives you a proper chastisement as payment for your double-dealing. Made her promise to give me first crack of that whip.'

'My sham of a marriage has already been annulled by Prince Owen.'

'You want to talk shams, how about setting a boy-pretender against a man-king? Takes an army to make a man king, and the horse you so unwisely backed don't have one anymore. Just a handful of bandits and bushwhackers running around the north, slowly being hunted down. That and a few deserters holed up in the rocks around Rodal. Prince Owen says he's divorced you? After I roll you across the border inside a smuggler's barrel, you'll find out whose law holds sway. In this card game, I'm betting a king against a prince.'

'Jacob Carnehan will kill you for this!' *And if he doesn't, I will.*

'I surely do hope he comes after us to try. The big general in the city. But no. I reckon the ol' badger's picked his tunnel to die in, and the Vandians will fly here soon enough to finish the job they started. You and me will be long gone before the city's sacked, though. You always did like your reading back in Hawkland Park. You can read about the fall of Hadra-Hareer in the newspapers when you're returned to your husband's loving household.'

Willow tried to shove herself back, surprise the brute into loosening his grip, but the ugly goblin stood as hard as stone. 'To hell with Wallingbeck, too.'

'You've been a grave disappointment to all of us, girl,' chuckled Nocks. 'Time you began setting matters right.'

The giant Rodalian advanced on Willow and pushed the warm wet cloth down hard across her nose, pinching her nostrils. She tried to choke and cough her way past the cloying fumes, find fresh air as her eyes watered and stung, but she met only darkness.

It seemed like Carter had been crossing the steppes for months, although the reality of the matter was that he could count his journey in weeks. Of course, if it had just been *his* journey alone, he might have borne it better. But not only was Carter travelling with Sariel – fallen back through habit into wild boasts and implausible stories – but he'd also been saddled with the argumentative presence of their pilot, Beula Fetterman. She should have flown her two passengers into the steppes and held back enough fuel in the plane's tank to return to Rodal's border fortresses. Instead, she had continued to point the aircraft into the grasslands until its engines were sucking on fumes and vapours, until they had landed and been forced to abandon the plane on the endless prairie; far outside the range of recovery by anyone other than a train of wagons filled with aviation fuel. Fetterman blamed a faulty fuel gauge for the error, but wasn't that the point of a supposedly trained pilot . . . someone to double-check the work of the ground crew before passengers entrusted their lives to her aerial craft? Now, not only did Carter have to put up with Fetterman's complaints and caustic remarks, but she'd failed to report their safe landing to the authorities in Rodal. Carter could only imagine what Willow was thinking now in Hadra-Hareer, failing to receive the report of their safe arrival. *She'll be worried sick. And she's got enough to worry about with the war on her doorstep and a baby on the way.* Carter felt guilty about leaving the woman he loved, even though putting her in the way of the hostile nomads would have been insanity. Her absence made him feel guilty about being here, trekking after Sariel, instead of trapped in Hadra-Hareer, hemmed in by Rodalian mountain ranges. A near-powerless witness to the final stages of the war they had lost across the border. Here, the ground was soft. The grass was thick and green. The sky and the clouds ran on forever, wider than any human could hold on to. Out here, one boot in front of the other, he was getting closer to something. Or at least, he felt he was. *But maybe what I'm doing is running away. From Willow and another man's child. From the fight in Weyland and what my father's turning into. Damn it, even when I joined the rebel army it's felt like I was running away half the time. I escaped the sky mines and I've been fleeing ever since.*

Fetterman marched ahead of them as if she knew the way. Like Carter and Sariel, she was weighed down with a heavy backpack. Food and supplies. Warm blankets against the incongruously cold nights. Every now and then she glanced surreptitiously behind her to place Carter and Sariel in her wake. *If any one of us here understands where we are going, it's Sariel.*

'Tell the aviator to set her compass nor'east,' said Sariel.

Carter couldn't blame the old trickster for not wanting to converse with Fetterman. *Try being locked up in a cell with her for weeks in Hadra-Hareer.* She glanced crossly back at him. Carter whistled and made a gesture towards the given compass point.

'How long will we be marching like this?' she called out.

Carter raised his voice. 'Quicker for you if you'd headed back to the mountains.'

'And wouldn't you like to see me murdered!' shouted Fetterman. 'A lone target for the Nijumeti raiders.'

'I'd feel right sorry for the first nomad that came across her,' muttered Carter. 'Especially if they tried to seize her for a saddle-wife.'

'She reminds me of my seventh wife,' said Sariel. 'Who flaunted her beauty but hid her scolding tongue until we had circled the maypole together in front of a priest. What was her name, again? Ah, yes. Shalne Ardeni.'

'How did matters end between you and her?'

'I tricked Shalne into divorcing me for a marriage to the Sultan of Utorcore,' said Sariel. 'The sultan was a merciless tyrant, and the unexpected disturbance served by his new bride saved many hundreds of thousands of innocents from war and prosecution by his army. Their union is why I shall never journey to Utorcore again.'

'I sure wish we could come across one of those circles of standing stones and shortcut *this* journey,' said Carter.

'Such risks must be saved for voyages far longer than this one,' noted Sariel. Worryingly, it sounded like the crafty old fox had something in mind beyond merely crossing the steppes.

'The stealers would track us down?'

'Soon enough their allies would,' said Sariel. 'We are well within range of the Vandians operating out of Weyland.'

Carter grunted. 'I remember.' On their first night camping in the steppes, shivering in the cold with no fire to act as a signal to the nomads, they had seen a Vandian patrol ship scorching through the night, passing high and distant. What it was doing this far north, Carter couldn't say. *No damn good, that much is certain.* 'You think they were scouting for slaves for their skels to raid?'

'It is possible.'

'I never came across any Nijumeti inside the sky mines,' said Carter. 'I got the impression the Vandians wanted their slaves with a certain level of book-learning.'

'For the sky mines, perhaps,' said Sariel. 'Having barbarians accidentally blowing up the emperor's precious mines because they think a fuse is black magic is hardly profitable. But there are slaves from many nations and races throughout the empire. Vandians prefer not to break their backs by tilling the soil, labouring in mills or busying themselves with the drudgery of keeping a home.'

'So what do the locals do instead?'

'Feel superior to the slaves. You might say that is one of the slave force's main draws as far as the Imperium's celestial caste is concerned.'

Carter was puzzled. 'But don't the castes at the bottom of the heap get bored with idleness?'

'Some work. But it is difficult to find a job when the next worker wears chains and is made to toil for free. Many jobs that are available pay so little that they would make almost no difference to you or your family's life. The pointlessness of not taking labour may rot away your soul, but accepting it often makes you feel like a dupe when you see your friends and neighbours living just the same as you without its burdens. For the idle masses, there are the constant distractions of the arena and games and feasts. There are also players and a variety of diversions on the public kino screens. Lotteries. Competitions.

Gambling – both legal and illegal. Sin and crime are regulated close to legality inside Vandia. Luckily for the rulers there is always a healthy pool of slave fighters to die in the arenas, too.'

'How can the lower castes afford to survive if unemployment is their lot?'

'Think of the Imperium as a pyramid,' said Sariel. 'At the very top is the celestial caste controlling the great houses, enjoying the wealth and power of gods made mortal. Scheming against each other occupies most of their time. Then there are the educated middle castes: scientists, soldiers, manufactory masters, engineers, secret police, surgeons and the like. Advancing through the many graduations of caste or just avoiding slipping into the lower castes for themselves and their children is enough to keep them busy. Then there is the great teeming mass of the lower castes, penned up in the rabble towers; fed and watered by the Gratis Imperium, the benevolent grace of the Emperor Jaelis. Vandia's citizenry are made slaves through living dependent on their masters' whims. Be caught speaking out against the wrong person or in favour of the wrong cause and watch your family starve on punishment rations. Below the lower castes, there are many millions of captured slaves or tribute workers sent by the Imperium's subjected neighbours, as well as mercenaries attracted by the legions' pay. In reality, the difference between a slave and a lower-caste citizen is an accident of birth. Everyone perfectly balanced on top of everyone else. The hostility and envy of the rest of the world against the Imperium acts as glue. There is always the bone of hope, false hope, but hope nevertheless, to dangle in front of the masses. Even a slave may be freed and made a citizen should they please their master or mistress sufficiently.'

Carter shook his head. 'It sounds . . . insane.'

'Speaking honestly, it is certainly an unnatural state of affairs,' shrugged Sariel. 'A state only preserved by the immense wealth of ores bled from their stratovolcano. The riches of the world, traded for the world's science, power and industry; remade as the steel bones of the whole terrible structure. But the Imperium is a pyramid, and a pyramid is the most stable of constructions. All the weight of it pushing down and squeezing into itself.'

'Into *people*.'

'People made Vandia,' said Sariel, sadly. 'You can't hang what they chose to make on me or mine. You can't even blame the stealers. They didn't build Vandia. The stealers found a rotten fruit and burrowed into it. That's what maggots are for.'

'And what are you for, Sariel, truly?'

'Free wine and the forbearance of great princes. Long life. Good counsel and open borders and intelligent conversation.'

'I'd like the real answer one day.'

'One day I might just give it to you,' said Sariel. 'In the interim, you'll need to settle for helping me frustrate the ambitions of the maggots before they gnaw away the last of the fruit.'

Ahead of them, Beula Fetterman stopped by the brow of a low foothill. She dropped down to one knee and pointed at the sky behind them. *An aircraft*. A dark triangle drifted across the sky. As the plane grew closer Carter could hear the engine's drone. Distant at first, a mosquito hum, then louder as it continued its flight many miles to their west.

'That looks small,' said Carter. 'A two-person flying wing.'

'Can't be Rodalian,' said Fetterman, sounding confused. 'We're beyond fuel range of the mountains.'

A pity you didn't realize that earlier, thought Carter, but he kept his criticism to himself. It didn't take much to make the pilot explode, leaving a dour, lingering mood over the party for hours.

'Doesn't look up to much from this distance,' said Carter, watching the plane dip and wobble through the air. *Even the wrecks flown by the skel slavers are faster and more durable than that. It's certainly not Vandian.* 'How the heck did it fly this far out?'

'Perhaps someone is refuelling it locally,' said Sariel, darkly.

'Don't be a fool,' snorted Fetterman. 'Who is there to do that in the grasslands? The only things the steppes hold are savages on horseback and a painful death. The Nijumeti would sooner pour oil over you and roast you over a fire-pit than sell fuel to you, even if they had stolen a few fuel barrels from a caravan. No, that plane is launched from a merchant carrier . . . it's a ground-to-air trading shuttle.'

'Then why can we not see the carrier?' asked Sariel, pointing to the clear sky. 'And why, with so little trade, would a merchant carrier bother to launch a landing plane over the steppes?'

Fetterman's features creased dismissively. 'They're picking up fresh water from one of the rivers. It's easy to run low on water when you try to cross the length of the Arak-natikh.'

'So it is,' said Sariel, but his doubtful tone of voice left much hanging in the wind. The aircraft passed out of sight fast enough, leaving the three travellers to march on for the rest of the day. That night they found a small copse of trees, a thin orchard, in the lee of one of the low hills and made their camp inside for its windbreak. Carter was careful to dig out a small, deep fire pit to conceal the light of their camp, and when it was done, he fashioned a stake out of a fallen branch and cooked the meat of a hare they had trapped the day before. It didn't take much to cook the stringy meat, which was good, as he kept the fire low to ensure a weak, wispy smoke.

Fetterman gnawed on her share of the meal. 'Do you know where you're going, old man?'

'I know where I've been,' said Sariel, 'which tends to equate to more or less the same thing.'

The aviator grunted unhappily. 'Saints preserve me. Just give me an honest answer. How much longer until we reach where we need to be?'

'I'd imagine a week more,' said Sariel. 'But then, I understand the clans embrace a free, roaming lifestyle. It is probably why they are known as *nomads*. A moving target is always hard to hit.'

'And why did Prince Owen order me to fly you here?'

'Because General Carnchan asked him to,' said Sariel.

'But what are *we* doing here?' she barked, increasingly frustrated.

'Oh, eating a rabbit supper for the large part. Enjoying the bracing night and a wide vista of stars.'

Carter sure did enjoy seeing someone else driven to irritation by the wandering vagrant's manners. *Makes a change from me.*

'Why are you seeking out the nomads?'

'Because they're here.'

'You are not answering me. You're cracked. What makes you think the Nijumeti won't just scalp you and stake you out on the grass over the first ant hill they find?'

'The clans tend to respect those touched by madness,' said Sariel.

'I recommend the condition. Leaving your sanity behind is one of the most liberating experiences.'

'Damn you, how is this journey to aid the rebellion?'

'When you have a sickness,' said Sariel, slowly, as though talking to a child, 'it behoves you to treat the root cause of the disease rather than just rub salve on the wounds.'

'You're talking in riddles.'

Sariel examined the hare meat on the end of his stake. 'A philosopher is someone who can fatten a plump riddle out of the thinnest of answers.'

'Philosophy will not win an inch of ground in our war!' spat Fetterman.

'That depends on which war,' said Sariel, before adding pointedly, 'and perhaps which side you are on.'

The aviator stood up angrily from the comfort of the fire and grabbed up her rifle from the grass. 'I'll take first watch. May the night's cold freeze some sense into your addled brain before sunrise.' She stalked out of the trees.

'Miss Fetterman might be more bearable company with the answers to some of those questions,' said Carter.

'And my seventh wife might have made the Sultan of Utorcore very happy,' said Sariel, throwing his canvas groundsheet over the damp ground to make his bed. He lay down, coughed and drew the wool blanket around him. 'But I'm still not inclined to go back to discover the truth of the matter.'

When sleep found Carter, it was a shallow, worry-filled affair. Not for himself or what might go wrong on their journey, but for his family's fate back in Rodal. If the Vandians felt free enough to spend time scouting the steppes for more victims, what did that say about their control over Rodal? *Maybe Willow and my father are already dead or prisoners in some cramped, stinking cage awaiting shipment to the slave markets of the Imperium?* Carter drifted uneasily into slumber, the hardness of the ground and bite of the cold air flowing through the trees holding off a restful sleep. He tried not to focus too hard on how long he remained in that anxious state, just the thought of it enough to hold a deep sleep away. At last, an unhappy grey unconsciousness claimed Carter. How long he was out he could not say.

It was a strange gurgling noise that awoke him. His eyes fluttered open. Carter struggled to make sense of what he could see from the fire pit's embers and moonlight falling through the fine canopy, dawn's first gleaming hanging close. *Is that?* A silhouette stood over Sariel's sleeping blanket. A female form ... Beula Fetterman, and as she moved away from the blanket on the ground, Carter saw the dagger plunged into the old trickster's chest, so deep only the hilt was left visible. All weariness vanished. Carter kicked off his blanket and lunged for the rifle by his side, but he was too slow. The aviator had her own rifle raised straight toward him.

'Not another inch towards the gun,' ordered Fetterman. 'I want you alive long enough to dig this doddering fool's grave.'

She's gone insane. Cold stung Carter's face. 'Just because Sariel wouldn't tell you where we're heading to or why we're going there?'

'No,' she sneered. 'Just because we are far enough away from the border that your bodies won't be found by anyone from the Lanca.'

'We're your *mission.*'

'Yes, you are. In a manner of speaking, but never the pretender's mission. I take my orders from the royalist army. They sent me to Rodal to bring Lady Cassandra back to King Marcus. He wanted the return of the Vandian emperor's granddaughter as a gift to keep the Imperium happy. Lean over slowly, just enough to pick up your rifle by the tip of its barrel and toss it over here in front of me.'

Carter groaned but did as she ordered. There was a crack as the gun landed, striking a stone in the grass. *Another traitor.* 'How can you do this?'

She never took her eyes off Carter as she kicked the rifle away to her side. 'Oh, but I'm late for what I was ordered to do. You're lucky the emperor's granddaughter is still missing. I should have already killed you, Carnehan. If the Rodalians hadn't arrested us and thrown us in the poky together, you'd have met with an "accident" a long time ago. Plunging a knife through this old fool's heart and cutting his throat in his sleep? That's a bonus and my pleasure.'

'If you shoot me, you'll never find out why we were sent here.'

'I don't care,' laughed Fetterman. 'Trying to hire mercenaries from the clans to fight alongside you? Some secret treaty the pretender hopes to cut with these Nijumeti savages? Finding Lady Cassandra to use her as a hostage again? Whatever you're travelling for dies tonight with you two idiots.'

'They'll hang you in Hadra-Hareer for this.'

'No, they won't,' said Fetterman. She swivelled and kicked Sariel's corpse. 'I'll tell them you ordered me to fly over the steppes until I ran out of fuel. Then you and the old devil set off into the north on your fools' errand, leaving me to hike back to the nearest border fortress. Who would be surprised if they never lay eyes on the pair of you again? And the truth of the matter is that before long there'll be nobody left in Rodal to even care. King Marcus has crushed the rebellion. His foreign allies will finish off the last of you left cowering inside Rodal, along with anyone unwise enough to stand by the pretender's cause. Your father, your girl, the pretender and his court of traitors in exile. Everyone will be dead.'

'You've got it all figured out.'

Fetterman jabbed her rifle at Carter. 'Well, I know who here's digging the grave big enough for two. Lift the spade out of your pack and get on with the job.'

Poor Sariel's murdered. Of all the stupid ways to go. The boastful old vagrant had survived a journey around half the world to save Carter and the other slaves taken by the Imperium. Saved Jacob Carnehan's hide more than once. Only to be murdered in his sleep by an aviator turned spy, slain in the wilds by a royalist fanatic. Even the ageing rascal would have been hard-pressed to spin a tale of fame and distinction from this sorry fiasco. But outside the pages of cheap novels, wasn't this how all outlaws ended their life? Not in a blaze of glory in some heroic last stand, surrounded by the piled bodies of their enemies. But shot in the back in a tavern. Jumped in an alley when drunk. Or the swift painful slice of a dagger across a sleeping throat. Carter crossed sadly to his pack and drew out the spade, a small army trenching tool that needed to be folded out to its full length. Its blade was muddy. He hadn't had time to clean it after digging their fire pit.

Carter dug its blade into the chill hard ground, breaking the soil. 'You never struck me as the religious type.'

'This isn't for your soul, pastor's boy. It's for mine. I don't want vultures circling your bodies and warning every clansmen in the vicinity there are strangers in the steppes. I'd like a nice uneventful trek back to Rodal. Not a pursuit with me needing to ambush Nijumeti scouts every night.'

'Wouldn't want to put you to any bother,' muttered Carter.

'You won't.'

Despite the cold, the work of digging the grave left Carter sweating. A good way to catch a fever. Maybe even sick enough to die. *But not before this turncoat puts a bullet in my heart.* All too soon Carter's work was done. The hole was dug. He felt the warmth of the rising sun outside the trees. *My last day in the world.* 'You going to leave a marker on our grave?'

'What for? This is a big land. It will be centuries until someone wanders across your bones. And besides, I don't think you'd like what I'd write anyway.' Beula Fetterman raised her rifle and Carter waited to die.

As councils were wont to run, Jacob could tell this meeting was going to be fat with difficult discussions. They were gathered to mull over the news that the Rodalian town of Zimar had been seized by the massed forces of Vandia and Marcus' royalists. Now they faced ground forces heading up the Pilgrim's Way, seizing wind harbours along the key trade route as they advanced. Leapfrogging slowly towards the capital, village by village, mountain by mountain. He could smell the fear in the meeting chamber. *And fear and panic are worth a dozen legions to our enemy. Marcus and his allies will dig in properly around the capital. A siege. Look to starve us out. I don't know where this imperial princeling Gyal learned the trade of war, but he's not a complete idiot.* The mountains' killing winds weren't going to be summoned to such devastating effect a second time.

Nima Tash arrived in the chamber with a grim face, sitting with the head of the army to her left and the chief of the skyguard to her right. 'We are to wait for Prince Owen?'

I've had enough of his defeatism; whining complaints born of privilege. 'We are not,' said Jacob.

'Let us make a start of this. We have just received worrying intelligence from our scout wing,' announced Skyguard Marshal Samden Stol. 'They have discovered mercenary carriers in the air, circling the territory captured by the royalists and their allies. Flying high above

Zimar, at the very edge of their operating ceiling. Many of the aircraft are skel carriers.'

At last. 'Seems like they want every dog they've got thrown into this fight.'

'You sound happy about this?' said Nima Tash.

Jacob could hardly deny it. 'I'm always happy when my enemy does something I expect, Madam Speaker. It makes my life easier.'

'Harder to locate the joy in such news for me,' grumbled the head of the Rodalian army. Land Master Namdak Galasang pushed his slab-like hands across the table as though he planned to topple a mountain on the Imperium's legions. 'With the skels' arrival, the invaders' aerial forces have an advantage of speed, armament *and* numbers. We have always relied on command of the skies to keep Rodal safe from those that would breach the peace of the Lanca.'

'It is true,' said Samden Stol. 'Our army's ranks are adequate to defeat bandits and hunt down nomad raiders, but the Walls of the World face north towards the Nijumeti horde. Our fortresses and garrisons are fixed the wrong way for this war.'

'We have what we have,' said Nima. 'We must fight with that.'

'There have been many reports filtering in from the north,' said the land master. 'Unusual activity. The clans have not been fighting each other with much enthusiasm of late. This new Krul of Kruls has imposed an order of a sort on the Nijumeti. You know what that means . . .'

'That the border fortresses will be earning their substantial upkeep again soon enough,' sighed Nima.

'We cannot strip our garrisons up there and march a relief force down through the valleys of the Mask Heights. Every soldier and pilot will be needed at Chalhand and Dalranga when a full horde is formed and led against us.'

Jacob stared at the politician. 'How likely are the nomads to open up a second front?'

'They are true opportunists like all bandits,' said Nima. 'They see a weakly defended caravan and they ride down on it.'

And currently we're looking like the caravan with its escort too light on swords. This wasn't news Jacob needed. Sadly, it wasn't likely to be the last bad account he'd receive this day. 'Has the plane flying Carter and Sariel up north returned to your border fortresses?'

'There has been no report of it landing yet,' said the sky marshal.

Overdue, then. Overdue in a land overrun by savages with bad intentions. Could he trust Sariel to keep Carter safe? Could he trust anybody other than himself anymore?

'But the scout wing did report one additional detail that will no doubt be of some personal interest to you,' continued Samden Stol. His tired old eyes fixed on Jacob. 'One of the carriers above Zimar is well known to us.'

'Known to you?'

'A notorious pirate who plagues the trade routes of the Lancean Ocean. The *Plunderbird*.'

Jacob grunted. 'So, what do you want me to say?'

'That the pirate captain of the *Plunderbird* is your brother!'

'The commander of that carrier is a *privateer*,' said Jacob. 'Black Barnaby sells his forces to whoever pays the best and can write a letter of marque for licensed pillage. Barnaby may be my blood, but Prince Gyal can pay his crew enough imperial gold to make every fighter on the carrier consider Gyal their best and truest brother.'

Nima spoke sadly. 'This will strike against the morale of our defenders. Look, they will say, even General Carnehan's own family fights against us.'

'And how many families in Weyland have been split down the middle by the civil war?' said Jacob. 'You do know who Owen's uncle is?'

'Don't you feel anything?' demanded the Speaker of the Winds.

'I buried a wife and a town full of friends because of the people advancing on this city,' growled Jacob. 'I buried a good few more fighting to rescue Carter and Northhaven's young. Since Bad Marcus dissolved the national assembly and launched his damn coup, all I've been doing is watching good people being put down in the soil. You want to know *what* I feel? That up to now there have been too many graves dug for exactly the wrong kind of folks.'

'My people aren't here to die for yours,' said Nima.

'Then you had better decide what you will die for,' said Jacob.

'Because when Vandia and the southern army tighten the noose around your necks, they'll deserve an answer to that.'

Off to their side the large doors of the chamber drew open, sentries standing aside, and Prince Owen stalked inside the chamber. Jacob noted the strange look on his face. *Something else to worry about, I reckon.*

'What is it?' asked Jacob.

Prince Owen took his seat as though the weight of city rested on his shoulders. The nobleman could hardly meet Jacob's gaze. After a long pause he spoke. 'Willow Landor has been snatched from Hadra-Hareer. She was ambushed inside her rooms last night. Anna Kurtain was with Willow at the time and tried to fight off their attackers, but they overpowered her.'

Jacob drew his breath in slowly, so as not to show what he felt. What he wanted to scream and shout. He managed a single word, hissed out like a dagger being drawn. 'Who?'

'Agents of my uncle, presumably. This was no random robbery. Nothing of value was taken from Willow's lodgings. Anna was left unconscious but alive. Only Willow was kidnapped. The usurper would be a fool if his spies hadn't been sent to enter the city disguised as refugees. And whatever else my uncle is, the man is no fool.'

No, that would be me. For listening to you. For allowing thousands of Weylanders inside the city to eat our food and prove a burden on our supplies. 'Did Miss Kurtain see who the raiders were, how many?'

'Two men, she thinks. One of them a large Rodalian. They left something odd behind.'

'What?'

Owen slid a pistol across to Jacob, old and blood-stained. 'This was abandoned on the table in Willow's lodgings, no rounds in the cylinder, only a single bullet found upright next to the gun.'

'Is it a threat?' asked Nima Tash. 'That if we try to chase the raiders down they will put a bullet in Willow?'

'No,' said Jacob, a fury rose inside him. *The gun I left for Nix so he could finish his life. One bullet inside the chamber to put an end to his miserable existence.* 'It's a message for me.'

Owen looked confused. 'What does it mean?'

'That if you want a job done right you really need to rely on yourself.' *I should have killed Nix. After he murdered Wiggins I should have just throttled his thick neck until his eyes bulged. That's what I get for allowing Nix to blow his own brains out. Justice should never be served poetic. Just direct and fast.*

'We will send a pursuit from the city after her,' announced Namdak Galasang.

Jacob tried to bite down on his frustration. *Too late. Far too late.* 'And fight our way straight through the siege lines? The chances are she's already in the Vandians' hands or a prisoner with the royalist army by now.'

'I promised Willow safe protection here,' said Owen. 'She saved my life inside the sky mines. We cannot simply do nothing.'

And I promised my son I would keep Willow out of harm's way here. Bad Marcus has made liars of us both. The king wants to twist a dagger in my gut every way he can. 'Have the radio guild send word to your towns to be on the lookout for Miss Landor and her abductors. One of them is likely to be a short, ugly Weylander of around fifty years. A scar down the middle of his face. He goes by the name of Nix or Nocks. I'm sure he uses many other names, too. If he hasn't already run into the southern army's siege lines inside Rodal, he'll be heading to Weyland by the fastest, most direct route possible.'

'Will this Nix murder Willow?' asked Owen.

'Nix kills people like other men light up their pipe. He's the dirtiest of the usurper's pit-dogs. But no, Willow's not dead yet. Not with her annulled marriage made to an ally of Bad Marcus. I reckon Viscount Wallingbeck wants to collect on his heir. But after that . . .' *Dear Lord, don't let them use Willow against me. Don't let them build a gallows for her next to a siege tower, just to give me another worry to think about besides beating them. Willow doesn't deserve it. Carter doesn't deserve to go through what we did after his mother's death.*

'This is my fault,' said Owen.

No, I reckon this is mine, and more my fault than I can let you know. 'We'll fix the blame after we fix Nix and his raiders. And give Gyal and the usurper something to worry about besides the cost to the Imperium of paying for mercenaries.'

'And how are we to do that?'

'I have a plan,' said Jacob.

He had got the Speaker of the Wind's attention. 'How do you suggest our defence proceeds?'

How I always intended it to proceed. Jacob leaned forward. 'By doing the one thing Bad Marcus and the Imperium's killers will never expect us to do.'

EIGHT

CASSANDRA'S GIFT

The first inkling Cassandra had that something of import would happen this morning was when Nonna started sniffing the chill air inside the tent as though noxious vapours had invaded their home.

'You have already emptied the chamber pot from last night,' said Cassandra. They were both sitting around a circular folding wooden table inside the tent. 'I saw you do it.'

'Am I so old that I forget to buckle my dagger around my waist, girl?' said Nonna.

'Of course not.'

'One day I shall reach an age when Kalu the Apportioner reminds me it's time for me to join my ancestors. Should I fight him, he will send his servants to steal my memories one by one until I'm left a husk.' Nonna picked up the hare she was skinning. 'But that unhappy day has not yet arrived.'

'May it be many years hence,' said Cassandra. 'So, what is it that you scent?'

'Nothing under canvas,' said the old nomad. 'There is a little witch rider in all of the clan's women . . . I smell news carried on the morning wind.'

Cassandra did not know what to say to that. 'Something is always happening somewhere.'

'I do not mean which warrior has stolen another's goat or which

237

wife has been creeping into a tent not her husband's. It is not mere tittle-tattle that I smell.'

'Wars ending and starting? Thrones being filled and thrones being lost?'

'I said news, not the inevitable ambitions of the high-born,' said Nonna, banging the separated hare meat against a stone to tenderize it. She tossed its fur to Cassandra to add to the other two taken. 'We shall see if I am right.'

Cassandra was glad of the near endless stream of daily tasks Nonna could conjure. It gave Cassandra a distraction from the memory of her mother stalking away, never looking back once as her rescuers lifted off, abandoning Cassandra. When she wasn't brooding on an exile's lot, she fretted over Alexamir's fate. Begging every ancestor and god she had heard of for intervention in the nomad's mission.

When someone did come calling on their tent, Cassandra was surprised to see it wasn't the trickster Temmell or one of his lackeys. It was Kani Yargul. The war leader of the horde ducked under the tent's opening, pushing back the flaps as though this was his home.

'And what brings the illustrious Krul of Kruls to my abode?' asked Nonna, hardly looking at the grass king. 'If you have any complaints about my sister's humours then you need not carry them here.'

Yargul grunted. 'My tent is tranquil. As, I hope, is your younger sister.' He glanced over at Cassandra, his eyes narrowing. 'I wish to ensure our clan guest is well; Alexamir's strange little Golden Fox.'

'And why would she not be?'

'To be cast off by your own people is no easy thing to bear.'

Cassandra picked up a skinning blade from the table. She had a feeling that the clan's leader had arrived out of curiosity, to see what sort of strange foreigner Alexamir had chosen to risk his life for. If Yargul was angry over the scornful manner in which the Vandians had arrived here while he was out hunting, he concealed it well. 'You are worried that I will take my life to end my exile?'

'You are a woman and a foreigner. Is this your fate?'

'And you are a fool,' growled Nonna. 'This girl is young and loves life. It is for Kalu the Apportioner to judge her time, to drag her spirit away spitting and fighting every step of the way.'

Yargul noted Cassandra flinching at the aunt's words. He tapped the sword dangling from his belt. 'Perhaps you believe I should have this old woman's head for her insolence?'

I would rather you didn't. Despite her acerbic nature, Nonna was the closest thing she had to a friend here without Alexamir. Cassandra chose her words carefully. 'In Vandia the emperor ordered an entire embassy's staff handed to his torturers for the offence of a single ambassador releasing wind in his presence.'

Yargul roared with laughter. 'We are Nijumeti, girl. We speak plainly and fart even louder. A good release of arse-breeze only means you have been well-dined. If your emperor kills people for farting, he might as well kill them for breathing in his presence.'

'It was meant to instil respect,' said Cassandra.

'No, it was meant to instil *fear*. Respect is earned by rising from your throne and beating the ears of your real opponents until they bleed, not jumping at shadows. A Krul is followed because his riders know the direction he takes the clan is true.'

'And a Krul of Kruls?'

'Riders will follow as long as the direction he leads the clans makes them wealthy, well fed and victorious.'

'That seems a precariously strapped saddle,' said Cassandra.

'I have been given many strong children,' said Yargul. 'Yet none of them will become Krul on the day I fall. They have enjoyed the curse of an easy life.'

Cassandra took a needle to the fur in front of her. 'The same could be said for me.'

'Temmell tells me Vandian nobles train their young hard and long in combat so that your empire will prevail. We do the same with our heirs. But to be born to a great family is not the same as to be born with greatness. That is a hunger you must find inside your own gut. The sharpest steel is always beaten the hardest and longest.'

'This is true of you?' asked Cassandra.

'As I stand here it is. Have you never heard my nickname among the riders?'

Cassandra shook her head.

'It is the *Anvil*,' interjected Nonna. 'But I have another name for you, Kani Yargul. One you would be less pleased with. *Little Tongs*.'

The nomad king slapped his massive muscled thighs and laughed.

'Pah! Woman, you are still sour milk that I claimed your sister over you for the Krul of Krul's tent. I shall tell you where my name comes from, Golden Fox. Only days after my birth the plague we call Red Grass Fever burnt me and left my frame feeble and sickly. Failing to master a wild horse on both my sixth and seventh birthdays, my clan cast me out, leaving me to my end in the hills. Clan Stanim's blacksmith, Makar, discovered me while he was out hunting, a walking skeleton sucking on roots and close to death. Old Makar's two apprentices had recently died from the fever and so he said that as the fever had deprived him of his helpers, the cursed sickness now owed him at least one replacement.

'He claimed me for his new apprentice. Every day he made me strike iron. My arms began as reeds, so puny they could barely lift a set of tongs. But Makar hammered me with a smith's labours, as I learnt to hammer and fold metal into sabres. "The sharpest steel is always beaten the hardest and longest," he would tell me. "What the fever has started, I will finish." And so I hammered until I could lift the largest of his tools. Then I hammered until I could drive an anvil punch through plate armour. My arms slowly grew from reeds to oak. When this was done he made me pick up his anvil and carry it after the forge's fire had dwindled. First for minutes, then for hours, finally for days. I sweated and cursed him, but he just laughed at me. Then the breath in my chest swelled from a thin breeze into a storm. My legs turned from twigs into trunks.'

Cassandra stared at the Krul. She could see none of the boy in the man, now. Not as described. He was perhaps only a decade younger than her grandfather, Emperor Jaelis. But while Cassandra's grandfather held to the throne like a half-eaten spectre, imagining conspiracies and plots all around him, this leader joyfully rode at the front of a stampeding horde, swinging a sword and casting spears through his enemies' hearts. 'Is Makar still inside the camp?'

'Makar is with the clan's fallen,' said Yargul. 'The dagger of too many years sliced away his thread upon this world. On the night he left with Kalu the Apportioner, I told him I intended to honour his trade. Makar reached out to me from his deathbed and said, "You were never born to be a smith. You were born to be an anvil." And in this prophecy, he was correct.'

'So it seems.'

'You are a costly guest,' said the Great Krul. 'Your people come for you and think to give orders to mine as though Nijumeti are their thralls. Then they abandon you here and fly away in their mighty metal warship.'

'So they did,' said Cassandra, trying to hide the hurt in her voice.

'I understand what it is to be exiled from your own blood and saddle,' said Yargul not unkindly. He picked up the skinning knife and drove it into the table's wood. 'Never forget that the sharpest steel is always beaten the hardest and longest.'

'Makar's two dead apprentices were his sons,' said Nonna after the nomad ruler departed the tent, his blade still quivering in the wood. 'If the sickness had been a warrior, Makar would have tracked it across the world and strangled it in its sleep. He made Kani Yargul his son to defy the fates and spit upon their rule.'

'And in the same way, Alexamir is the Great Krul's son?'

'A widow-son,' said Nonna. 'If my nephew proves worthy of the title.'

He is, thought Cassandra. She had no doubts on that matter.

'Makar made many deadly swords for the clan before his end,' said Nonna. 'I sometimes wonder if Kani Yargul isn't the sharpest of them all.'

'You do not sound entirely happy about it.'

'I once chased glory as hard and long as any man,' said Nonna. 'Victories I found. But little contentment. We ride to live. We ride to die. Alexamir is all I have to show for my life.'

And I, thought Cassandra. *And I*. She groaned and there was an audible click from her spine as Temmell's spell worked its daily miracle upon her.

'Go then,' scowled Nonna. 'Enjoy your brief healing, before your legs wither to twigs as thin as our Krul of Krul's once tottered with. If you find one of the smiths, borrow his anvil and stagger about the grass with it like a fool. Perhaps your legs will grow as strong and fast as the fleetest of stallions.'

'I will be back soon.'

'Yes, soon enough,' warned Nonna. 'I don't wish to scour the camp to find you collapsed on the soil like a bag of grain for my old bones to lug back to the tent.'

Beula Fetterman's rifle exploded and Carter staggered back with shock, but it wasn't the jolt of being shot. *No pain. She's missed me.* Carter realized that he had closed his eyes. He blinked them open to discover the aviator rearing forward. She screamed like a banshee, the cry strangled to a halt in her throat when she tumbled down into the freshly dug grave. As she fell, Carter noticed the dagger buried in her spine, her own blade, then his eyes fixed on Sariel swaying behind the grave, as pale as a ghost, but still, incredibly, alive. Fetterman twitched in the dirt before falling still. Fetterman had traded places with Carter. *The grave wasn't for me after all.*

'She cut your throat?' Carter stuttered. 'I heard it. The knife was stuck through your damn heart!'

Sariel rubbed his back, where the stubs of his wings were, before his wings had been dismembered by the stealers' torture. 'And how many hearts do you think a creature that soars through the vaults of heaven needs beating inside his miraculous chest to lift their weight off the ground?'

Carter remembered one of his father's more unlikely stories, a story Carter had dismissed as a tall tale. About how Sariel's arm had been ripped off during Jacob Carnehan's journey across Pellas and how the old trickster had joined the limb back to his body. Healed himself with much the same ease as a child moulding a clay figure in the mud.

'Sweet saints! Just how hard to kill are you?'

'All things must die in time. So let us agree like fine gentlemen of the road that it is easier for knaves outside my race to reduce my body, deprive me of my memory and purpose, than to seek a more permanent solution to my existence.'

Yes, exactly how you were when you came calling on the library hold. Carter felt a shiver of fear rise inside him. A supernatural dread about just who – *what* – he was really travelling with here. Willow's apocryphal words echoed in his mind. *We're the ants in his story; you know that, don't you?* 'You're here because I healed you.'

'And now I must return the favour and save us all,' said Sariel. He gazed down sadly on the aviator's corpse. 'But not this one, not this well-gorged gudgeon.'

A suspicion nagged at Carter. 'You knew she wasn't what she seemed.'

'She was far too careful and skilled a pilot to allow her plane to run out of fuel. She wanted to accompany us, just as she wished the three of us far from Rodal. I could not believe her motive for joining our band was a worthy one. She had a sour soul. Did you not smell it? Like rancid milk.'

'You might have said something to me ... a warning at least.'

'A good spy is trained to notice changes of behaviour. Heavens forbid that you might have started being polite to her, attempting to mask your true feelings.'

'You goaded Fetterman into acting.'

'It was natural for the marrowless malcontent to decide to murder us when she realized she would only be discovering the nature of our mission upon reaching our destination.'

'And what if she had started by slitting *my* throat?'

'I am a light sleeper, Lord Carnehan. Have no concern; I am certain I could have stopped her before she murdered you.' Sariel clutched his chest where the dagger had been driven into his body. His shirt soaked wet with what passed for the sorcerer's blood. 'I, however, am wounded.'

You should be dead. Carter ran to his pack to search for the roll of bandages and a copper flask of pure medical grade alcohol he had brought with him. 'How deep is it?'

'Leave your baggage be. I do not need Weylander potions and salves to heal,' said Sariel. He reached down to the ground and drew Carter's sabre out of its scabbard, taking the blade and resting it in the coals of the fire pit until the steel glowed white hot. 'Seal my wound with fire and trust my body to heal the internal defilement of my person.' Sariel removed his long leather coat, covered with the artwork of hundreds of stories and tales, before unbuttoning a green silk shirt. Both had been expensively ornate at one point in their existence; but, much like the bard himself, they had grown worn and weathered by an age on the road. The old man knelt in front of Carter as though his young travelling companion was an axe man and

Sariel the victim preparing for an execution. Carter gazed down at the wound on Sariel's chest. It was like nothing he had seen before. Sariel's wound bubbled with blood, but not red blood... yellow and as thick as cream, as though a milk pail had been pierced with a chisel.

Carter tried not to flinch from the strangeness of the injury. He picked up one of the pegs of kindling waiting to be tossed into the fire pit and held the wood out to Sariel. 'Grip this between your teeth or you'll bite your tongue off.'

Sariel shook his head. 'Am I a stallion that needs a bit for his tack? Pain is in the mind and I am the master of mine. Seal my wound, Lord Carnehan, and be done with it.'

Carter took the sword. The hilt had been bound in leather to make its grip sure enough to swing from horseback, but he still felt the intense heat creeping down the blade. 'You are certain...?'

'Be done.'

Carter lowered the sword and pressed the flat of the blade on the wound and there was a hiss of burning flesh. Sariel grimaced but didn't groan, let alone scream. Oddly, no stench came from the flesh, as there should have been from a normal man's wound. Carter drew the blade away. Below, a rise of angry, scarred flesh was left across Sariel's skin, but no more bleeding.

'That's a damnable useful trick,' said Carter.

'It is no trick! The knack of fire healing was imparted to me by—'

'Atamva!' cried a voice behind them.

Carter wheeled around. A line of twenty Nijumeti warriors stood in a semicircle around the clearing, their chests bare and blue, a display of large muscles as hard as stone. Unnervingly, the savages had appeared as silently and unseen as a morning mist. Carter still held the sword in his hand, but his rifle lay on the ground where he had tossed it over to Fetterman. Those they faced had their bows raised towards Carter, each sinuous weapon curved like an 'M', left hand clutching the wood's decorative leather covering, right hand holding a notched arrow steady. *I'll be a pin-cushion if I even try to rush them.* Carter reluctantly lowered his blade towards the leaf-strewn soil.

'What do we have here?' said one Nijumet stepping forward. He was older than the other nomads and he carried no bow. *Their leader?*

'Thieves fallen out amongst themselves? One a corpse in the grave, one a pup and the last an ancient weirdling who bleeds butter-cream?'

'I am no thief,' said Carter.

'No insult, here. You steal our air and pollute our land by your very presence,' said the nomad. 'At least have the spirit to raid our cattle as well.'

'We need no more thralls,' barked one of the bowmen standing behind the patrol leader. 'Kill the boy and let me burn the weirdling to ashes. That will be an end to his sorcerous tricks.'

'If you know enough to burn me,' said Sariel, 'you also know that you will be leaving an unquiet spirit for Annayla the Moon Goddess to dispatch to seek vengeance.'

There was a murmur of discontent among the nomads that a foreign invader should know of their clan's ways.

'He *is* a weirdling,' said the leader. 'You remember what Temmell had instructed for such as he.'

'We have too many foreign devils inside our land now,' said the bowman. Carter wasn't sure if the warrior was agreeing with the leader or arguing with him. Everything these people said sounded like a boast or the start of a quarrel. 'Too many that arrive unwanted from the sky. Too many who trespass by land. Too many thralls as slaves these days. Bad enough that we must suffer those filthy traders from Hellin.'

'Temmell has spoken for the Krul of Kruls,' barked the leader. 'Which would you disobey first?'

'Am I a fool? So be it, then.'

The nomad leader drew his knife and jabbed its razored point towards Carter and Sariel. 'You are to meet your death. Both of you!'

'What are you so happy about?' demanded Duncan, ducking back as a shot cracked off the rock he sheltered behind.

'Happy? This is bread and butter to me, lad,' said Pactro.

Duncan risked a quick glance down the slope. It was hard to tell where the shot had originated from on the other side of the valley. *It looks like there are defenders in the village, inside the wind-harbour and among the rocks of valley walls.* 'I prefer to take my breakfast with a smaller helping of gunpowder.'

'Well, maybe we wouldn't be first to the table every time if Prince Gyal hadn't taken against you,' accused old Kenem Posda.

'Watch your tongue,' barked Paetro.

'You don't have to defend me,' said Duncan. 'Kenem's right. This isn't a coincidence. Every time there's a fresh assault, we're ordered to act as the tip of the spear. Prince Gyal's trying to get me killed. It makes me wish he'd just do things the Vandian way and arrange for some assassins to stick a knife in my back inside the camp one dark night.' *I don't even know why Gyal is jealous of me. I've been exiled to the end of the world. He's the one who will be going back to Helrena, not me.*

Kenem Posda spat against the rock; the kind of sound that made it clear that he could easily regard Duncan's assassination as the best way out of serving on a permanent suicide squad, too.

'This *is* the Vandian way,' said Charia Wyon, assembling her long-rifle inside the cover of the small cave they had found. It was a confined space. They hadn't been left much room, not with forty legionaries and house troops taking shelter inside. 'Someone slips a dagger in your spine, Princess Helrena will be asking why and who. If these mountain barbarians do the job for Gyal instead, there's no questions asked. No starting a new reign together with a little seed of mistrust at the centre of the Diamond Court.'

Except maybe, why did I have to exile Duncan and get him killed? But Duncan knew that he was flattering himself. *Once Helrena is sitting on the imperial throne, I'll just be some forgotten far-called ex-lover of hers. Maybe me being dead would make things easier for her too. But then, who else is there to rescue Cassandra from the clans apart from faithful Duncan Landor?*

'Well, neither of those two has been crowned yet,' grumbled Kenem.

'Saying no to a woman is a dangerous thing at the best of times,' said Charia. 'Saying no to an imperial princess of the celestial caste, doubly so. What the hell would you have done, Kenem Posda?'

'Chance would be a fine thing at my age.'

Paetro risked a peek over the rocks, another shot ricocheting off the granite. 'At least Gyal is trying to get us killed the right way, now.'

'This is the right way?' said Duncan, disturbed.

'Pushing up the Pilgrim's Way with land forces, securing the route to

246

Hadra-Hareer village by village, wind-harbour by wind-harbour, only leap-frogging on helos when Rodal's cursed mountain storms aren't raging. Concentrating superior forces against our backward enemy. Slow, steady, nothing flashy. It's what we should have done from the start. If we had, we never would have lost *The Caller*. Wouldn't have lost a quarter of our forces in the assault on Hadra-Hareer.'

'We were promised a quick, easy war by Gyal,' said Kenem.

'Isn't that the promise of every campaign?' said Paetro. 'How many easy wars have you experienced, old man? Use the fingers on your left hand and come back to me when you reach your thumb.'

Duncan said nothing, but he had a sneaking suspicion that it wasn't a coincidence their revised battle plan had arrived along with the cunning head of the Imperium's secret police. It was heartening to see that Apolleon was good for something other than his obsession with hunting down Sariel Skel-bane.

'Gyal's idiot strategy saw my sister killed,' said Charia. 'I swear, I see him out on the battlefield and . . .' She patted her long-barrelled sniper's rifle meaningfully.

'Stow the mutinous squawking,' ordered Paetro. 'A battlefield has ears to hear more than the squeal of a legionary's dying.'

'You never stood by while some careless glory-hound of an officer accidentally stepped in front of a barbarian's spear?' asked the female legionary. 'Maybe even help them along a little? You've served in a different legion, then.'

'Celestial caste prefer to be murdered by their own,' warned Paetro. 'They're funny that way. Talking treason is going to see you disappeared by the hoodsmen long before a spear strikes you down.'

'My oath is to Helrena's house, not Gyal's,' said Charia, but she let the matter drop.

'What's this damn village called again?' asked Kenem.

'Ganyid Thang,' said Duncan. 'It means Happy Valley in Rodalian.'

'Be happy when we've taken it,' said Kenem. 'Until then, I don't think there's a whole lot of joy coming anybody's way.'

Paetro shook his head. 'It's not blowing a hurricane outside. We've got an honest fight. What more does it take to make you happy, old man?'

'Twenty years and twenty pounds lighter. Then I might have some fun.'

One of the signal runners, a young soldier called Carbo, came sprinting into cover, his face flushed and bright in the cold air. Trained radiomen had been in short supply since the failed attack on the capital. They were sharing their radio pack with a dozen sticks, the radio officer off in another cave right now, leaving Duncan relying on runners and riders like Carbo. *Just the same as the benighted Weyland army.*

'Any news of our local allies? The king's men?' Paetro didn't bother keeping the contempt out of his voice and Duncan couldn't blame him. *Compared to the might of the legions, Weylanders are only shopkeepers playing soldier.*

'There's a force stuck behind us three miles away, the Seventh Merlanda Volunteer Infantry Regiment, pinned down,' said Carbo. 'Ten companies of foot.'

Duncan bit his teeth. *Dickinson's Drunks*, after their commander Colonel Dickinson, an ageing aristocrat who ran what was advertised as the largest brewery in the south. That was nearly a thousand men under arms. And they needed to be marching down the valley towards Ganyid Thang if Duncan and his friends were going to survive this. 'I thought we had cleared the path of defenders?'

'Looks like the barbarians we fought to get through here were a decoy,' said the runner. 'Their real force was hiding deeper back in the mountains. They let us pass then ambushed the Weylanders in our van.'

'They didn't want to tackle the heavy armour we brought up with us,' said Kenem.

'No, they're still playing hit and run, just like back in Weyland,' said Duncan. 'And they're striking us where we're weakest.' Duncan didn't need a gask's talents to see Jacob Carnehan's hand was behind this plan. Even without the Imperium's armoured vehicles and mobile bombards, a single electric rifle in the hands of a legionary could lay down the fire of a dozen Rodalians. Of course, the Rodalians had let the superior Vandian force pass through before cutting them off and ambushing Weyland's royalist army.

'The mountain barbarians are learning,' growled Paetro. 'They've lost half the villages, towns and harbours along the Pilgrim's Way, but they're learning how to give us a fight worthy of the name on the ground, too.'

'We learn to fight like them, they learn to fight like us,' said Duncan.

'And victory goes to the side who learns fastest,' noted Kenem Posda.

'It's not a victory that Prince Gyal wants here,' said Charia, 'it's a spectacular throne-grabbing triumph.'

Paetro patted Carbo on the shoulder. 'So what's the orders, lad? Do we turn back to help dig the king's men out of their mud, or . . . ?'

'Baron Machus has ordered us to press our claim, sir. The Weylanders will have to look after their own.'

Kenem scowled at Duncan and muttered something he couldn't quite hear. *I'm sure it wasn't complimentary.*

'And will the good baron be gracing us with his presence during the assault?' asked Paetro.

'The armoured legion will hold to the south until the valley floor has been swept for mines.'

'Of course,' said Paetro. 'We wouldn't want buried powder barrels taking the shine off one of the baron's precious tanks.'

And without the armours' cannons in support, I'm far likelier to be put under the dirt here. Machus was so much Prince Gyal's lapdog, it was a wonder the baron didn't bark when he saw the emperor-in-waiting approaching. Duncan briefly wondered if the baron knew that he and Adella had been planning to elope back in Weyland. Maybe it wasn't only a jealous prince that Duncan had to contend with on the Rodalian front. Not that the brute Machus should even care. He had carried half his house's harem with him to Weyland, not wishing to be deprived of female company during the campaign. *And from what I've heard, the baron's been adding to it from the locals every week we've been fighting, as well.*

'We should remain free of the barbarian's corn-smokers, though,' said Carbo. 'Radioman reports a squadron of enemy kites flying in to strafe the regiment has just been engaged in the air.'

'Good. At least we won't be seeing them here today.'

'Armour in reserve, boots to the front and clear skies. Puts me in mind of the siege of Uschen with Captain Aivas,' said Kenem.

Paetro nodded. 'Let's make sure we get through this day with as few casualties.'

Cassandra's father. 'Aivas was a good officer?' asked Duncan.

'Aye, that he was. A little too good for the slippery times we live in, as it proved.' Paetro moved out from under cover and whistled loudly. A couple of minutes later a legionary called Balbus came scrambling down the slopes of the valley behind them, chased by a flurry of shots from the Rodalian sharpshooters in the village. Balbus was short and whippet-thin. He had signed up from some distant mountainous protectorate of the Imperium, and like the rest of his people, was a few twists of the spiral removed from his comrades – as distinguished by his seven-fingered hands. To give him his due, the man scurried up Rodal's heights with all the agility of a mountain goat.

'I was wondering where you'd got to, Fingers,' said Charia.

'Balbus counting guns,' said the legionary in a thick accent, tapping a folding brass telescope on a sling. The soldier always seemed curiously shy and reticent to Duncan, even more so in the presence of female legionaries such as Charia. Balbus knelt down in the cave and sketched in the soil what he had observed. He drew their valley as a 'U' shape. Duncan and the others had their shelter on the left-hand slope of the dale's left-hand arm, the baron and the rest of the Vandian force hanging back in the bend's right-hand stretch. Then he sketched the village of Ganyid Thang as a series of squares and the cavernous mouth of the wind-harbour carved out of the valley wall behind the settlement. 'Guns concentrated here and here,' he said, drawing a circle on either side of Ganyid Thang and its wind-harbour. 'Not villagers. Mountain army. Fine shots. This is what Balbus sees.'

'More guns inside the village's flanks or more guns along the mountain peaks?' asked Paetro.

'More up high,' said Balbus. 'In valley slopes and mountains behind.'

'They've laid out a nice straight path for us to attack down,' said Paetro. 'Right through the centre of the village and into their wind-harbour, which is what we've come to secure anyway.'

'Do you think they're planning a second ambush?' asked Duncan. 'They could have half the Rodalian army hiding in those mountains over there and we wouldn't know it.'

'Might be,' said Paetro. 'So what's up above us, Balbus? Any sign of barbarians keeping their heads down and biding their time on our side of the valley?'

'No,' said the legionary, simply.

'You're sure?' asked Duncan.

'Certain.'

'Balbus's instincts in the peaks are a match for any rice-eater,' said Paetro. 'His word's gold as far as I'm concerned.'

'They'd want to ambush us from both sides of the valley to be sure,' said Duncan.

'Yes. They're not fools. So what are we not seeing then, lad?'

'Just what could get us killed.'

'Aye, that much is certain.' Paetro turned to the soldiers crouching in the cave. 'We'll infiltrate our way across the valley floor and skirt along Ganyid Thang's left flank. Fight our way through that side of the village. Unless their scouts are blind, they'll know we've got sixty tanks idling their engines around the corner. They'll presume we're heading down there to offer infantry support to our armour, which by rights should be rolling through the houses on the village's right flank. Maybe the mountain tribes will hold back on whatever their dirty scheme is until the baron decides to join the feast, too.'

Duncan nodded. It was as good a plan of attack as they could execute given the circumstances. The Rodalians couldn't know that the baron intended to keep on holding his big guns in reserve, trusting Duncan would catch a bullet and rid Prince Gyal of a troublesome rival.

'Charia, up into the slopes above us with you. Take the four long-gunsmen and cover our advance. Work your way through the tribe's sharpshooters, officers and marksmen first. Balbus, you and young Carbo follow her and keep your telescope trained where the rest of us will be forging ahead. Any sign of nasty surprises, Carbo, you sprint down and find me. I want good warning. Not left with my pants hanging around my ankles.'

Paetro's sharpshooters did as they had been ordered, spreading out into the slopes above the cave. When they had taken up position, Duncan, Paetro and the rest of the legionaries broke cover and started moving through the valley. They stayed low and advanced fast through stands of dark green needled evergreens, paddy fields and long burial mounds which, from their size and extent, contained some once-highly elevated Rodalian nobles. Bullets whistled past from the white buildings on the valley's opposite side. Each puff of smoke was answered by Charia's squad behind them. Duelling marksmen, with the core of the company used for bait to draw the enemy out. Duncan's blood coursed so fast he could hear his heart thumping. Ganyid Thang nestled on the far slopes, a series of around fifty smaller buildings in front of ten larger, fortress-sized buildings to the rear, and higher still the dark entrance into the wind-harbour. The village's constructions were blocky and thick-walled, narrow slits for windows. Built for protection against the fierce storms, but bastions that served equally as well for defence in warfare. *They wouldn't last long against the Imperium's metal castles on caterpillar tracks, though*. But thanks to Duncan's presence here, the monstrously large vehicles would stay well out of the fight. *Don't look back. Don't slow to see who might have been cut down behind you.* Little geysers of dirt erupted around his boots as he drew closer to the village, yells from the legionaries behind him, and then he was in the lee of one of the white-plastered walls, his lungs burning from the exertion. *This is a stiff fight.* The enemy was all around. Up on the roofs. Behind window slits. In the rocky slopes behind the village. But to locate them properly you'd have to hang like a rube out in the open, watching for flashes of smoke and fire, catching a bullet for your troubles.

A bullet twanged off a wall, spraying brick fragments over his shoulder. Duncan thought he saw movement from a roof ahead and sprayed a volley from his rifle, the rifle butt slamming painfully against his shoulder. He hadn't sighted, and beyond taking chunks out of roof masonry, he suspected he'd just expended four bullets for nothing. *It's like fighting an invisible enemy. So how come they still seem able to see me?*

Paetro slipped beside Duncan. 'This doesn't seem right, lad.'

'Nobody standing up to take a shot in the clear? While magically still being able to take pot-shots at me. Never did seem right.'

'Welcome to street fighting,' said Paetro. 'No, this village. It's as if they're not fighting to hold it.'

Duncan glanced nervously around, checking each shuttered window slit for a rifle barrel jutting out. 'You're sure of that?'

'Concentrate on slowing your breath. It'll clear your mind and steady your aim.' Paetro glanced around the corner, finding nothing that seemed to please him. 'We'll keep on skirting the village. Head for the slope back there. I want to see how well defended their wind-harbour is.' Paetro turned back to the men running low behind him and flashed them a series of directions using the legion's sign language.

They passed rapidly through Ganyid Thang's fringes, attracting the occasional shot from the mountains or the village. Paetro appeared to treat the fire with contempt. As if nothing could hurt him. Duncan wondered how much of that was an old soldier's act. *I wonder how long I'd need to serve with the house before I could pull it off as deftly.*

Ganyid Thang's wind-harbour was much the same as the others Duncan had visited. A tunnel mouth carved into the mountain slopes, perhaps fifty feet across and twenty high. It might have been a stone works save for the fact that the walls inside had been brick-sealed and the gargoyle-like faces of a host of wind spirits leered down from around the entrance. A pistol shot barked in their direction and Duncan caught sight of a shadowy form pulling back into the cover of the wind-harbour.

'Stay back,' ordered Paetro. Duncan saw the old soldier had the wooden handle of a grenade grasped in his hand; the ugly spiked metal can on top packed with powder and shrapnel barbs. He yanked the pin out of the bottom of the grenade's wooden grip and then sent it spinning towards the entrance. A thunderous explosion followed, a shower of hot rock fragments and metal before its echoes faded angrily within the entrance tunnel. There was no more sign of opposition from inside. But there was something else. The grenade's blast had blown away dirt and wiry grass from in front of the wind-harbour, leaving uncovered what had been shallowly buried. Duncan pointed out the freshly disturbed soil to the side of the cavern . . . a half-exposed twine fuse. 'That's why they left a lightly defended path through the centre of the village.'

'What kind of war is it when the barbarians try to bury you under their own rocks?' complained Paetro.

'If the Rodalians deprive us of all the wind-harbours from here to Hadra-Hareer, they'll slow our advance; make us vulnerable to Rodal's storms.'

'It's a ruthless commander who burns his own grain stores to stop his enemies eating them.'

Duncan knew exactly who Paetro meant. *Jacob Carnehan again, curse the man.* 'I'll find the master fuse and cut it.'

'Be careful,' said Paetro. 'I wager they've mined more than the wind-harbour. The last settlement Mad Machus took, the baron circled his tanks around the wind-harbour and fed it shells until the townspeople sheltering inside surrendered.' Paetro pointed to the heights behind the wind-harbour. 'What do you think the barbarians are hoping he repeats the tactic?'

'A landslide, as well?'

'Aye. When the barbarians realize their plan to crush us inside their wind-harbour has failed, they'll boil down from those slopes, lad.'

'If they've got the numbers,' said Duncan. 'Maybe entombing the legion was all of their plan?'

'We'll find out the hard way, I reckon.'

Duncan sprinted from the cover of the street to the entrance, Paetro sending a volley up into the slopes above, but, as rapidly as Duncan dashed, he didn't hear any answering fire. *Yes, they want us to fight our way inside there.*

Duncan drew to a halt inside the entrance. The Rodalian who had shot at him lay still and silent twenty feet down the tunnel on his front, killed outright by the grenade's explosion. Every wind-harbour seized before had cost a considerable butcher's bill paid in Vandian and royalist blood. Desperate hand-to-hand fighting as the tunnels and chambers inside were cleared of defenders. Many wind-harbours possessed secret access passages, tunnels and chimneys to carry down air or light by mirrors. Labyrinths where Vandians and King Marcus' soldiers could crawl in by the squad and never be seen again. This chamber, Duncan suspected, would prove empty. *Or have they left more of a suicide detail than a single soldier to put up token resistance and draw us inside?* Duncan carefully explored the wind-harbour's opening. Up ahead was the first of many twists and turns to break the storm's force. *So where would I set a master fuse?* He discovered a sentry alcove in the wall, where a guard could keep out of the worst of a storm while staying on post to help stragglers and new arrivals pass inside. Its stone cavity was lined with wood, and some of the planks looked like they had recently been removed and replaced. Duncan slipped a steel dagger out of his belt and levered at the timber until it broke. Behind the facade lay a space newly carved inside the rock-face. It contained a tiny wooden drum not much bigger than a biscuit tin. The canister sat connected to a nest of oil-soaked twine fuses and Duncan well recognized the container from years in the local territorial guard. Fuse paste packed into the casket, an incendiary core burning down the middle. The lid was painted red, the colour indicating the time taken to burn out and ignite. Duncan ripped the fuse lines from the drum and tossed the now useless device out into the tunnel. Then he checked the sentry post opposite, finding the alcove empty of further surprises. *The Rodalians' turn for a shock. When the charges they've set in this place fail to explode.*

As Duncan returned to Paetro's position he found Kenem Posda had caught up with them, 'It's done. They'd left a fuse drum burning inside. I've ripped it out.'

'Bad day for them,' said Paetro. 'They're not going to bury us or the baron's tanks today.'

'So, that's why they're so light on swords in the village,' said Kenem. 'Sneaky buggers.'

'They might still bring down a landslide on us,' said Duncan. 'Out of spite. The detonator for that will be up there in their hands.'

'Pull back to the village's western edge. That should be clear enough of rockfalls if it comes to it. We'll make our stand there. See how far the barbarians' taste for destroying their own property stretches today.'

'What about our orders . . . pressing our claim?' said Kenem.

'That's how I'm choosing to do it,' said Paetro. 'If the baron wants to complain, he can drive into the village on his big shiny steel bombard to do it in person. Maybe I'll forget to mention my suspicions about how many powder barrels they have hidden up on the peaks.'

'Now you sound like Charia,' said Duncan.

'She was right about one thing. There's a difference between rolling a grenade inside an idiot's tent and finding a barbarian's done the job for you.'

'What's the difference?'

'On a good day, a firing squad,' said Paetro.

They fell back to the low, single-storey buildings in the far corner of the village, legionaries retreating with them as they ran. Paetro's troops seized a block of four connected buildings on the edge of Ganyid Thang; a high, stone-walled structure with a series of low stone dry-pools to remove moisture from rice. This was a farm, large enough to support three families tending the valley's fields. There was a clear sweep of fire into the pass on two sides, easily reinforced by legionaries coming down from the opposite slope. And now the narrow shuttered windows would be working for the Vandians as they defended it. *No sign of the farmers who lived here, though.* Someone had taken the trouble to evacuate the locals before the attack. And not inside the wind-harbour, where the populace usually fled.

They remained hunkered down inside for half an hour, exchanging the occasional shot with Rodalian marksmen from nearby rooftops, as well as chasing off enemy warriors easing around adjacent buildings. From up on the roof Duncan heard a shouted warning not to shoot, and a minute later Carbo appeared, his face crimson and dirt-streaked from his sprint across the valley.

'What is it, then?' barked Paetro.

'Mountain soldiers, maybe seven hundred of them, moving down the east slope in three companies.'

'No doubt vexed we've tickled their trap and have yet to set it off.'

'Charia and her long-gunsmen are asking to come across and make nests inside the village.'

'You run back and order Charia to keep shifting position across the west slope, pick off the barbarians. Then you find whichever cave the radioman's hiding in and inform our illustrious leader that the enemy are attempting to set off a landslide above the wind-harbour and bury the legion's armoured brigade. My recommendation is that the baron swings around the village, holds well outside while he mounts a heavy bombardment against the rice-eaters.'

'Will he heed that?' asked Duncan.

'Who knows?' said Paetro. 'I'm just the tip of the spear.' He turned to the legionaries kneeling behind window slits around the room. 'And what does a spear do?'

'Impale!' came the shout.

'And after I've passed word to the baron?' asked Carbo.

'Stay with Charia,' said Paetro. 'And observe. When you get back to the house in Vandia, tell them how we fought here.'

'Permission to return.'

'No, lad. A runner passes the word. That's your job. You just make sure you tell them.'

'And what do I tell Charia about this?'

'Tell her she's about to be promoted.'

Duncan watched the young runner slip reluctantly away from the building. 'You don't think Baron Machus is going to ride to the rescue today?'

'I'd say the baron has his orders, wouldn't you?'

Duncan felt the bitter anger rise at Prince Gyal's scheming. 'Leave me here, then, damn you. I'll draw fire and cover everyone else's retreat back to the cave.'

'We're all damned, Duncan of Weyland. Damned, the moment we left our nations to accept the legion's coin. Didn't know enough of anything else worth a damn but to sign up with the house when we finished our twenty years.'

'Kenem,' Duncan pressed. 'You know why we're really here. Talk some sense into this thick-headed bull.'

Kenem Posda patted the thick farm walls. 'Too many years on me to go haring hither and thither. Too many hard fights behind me to have any savage with a taste for rice saying I finally turned tail from one. This place will do.'

'Yes,' said Paetro. 'This place will do.'

'There are fifty of us and seven hundred of them! We won't last an hour.'

Paetro called to the soldiers. 'One hour of fighting or eternity without a name? If anyone here doesn't want to make that trade, then you have my permission to join the marksmen in the high slopes.'

Hoots of derision echoed around the farm. Not a soldier moved away from the window slits. 'We're not here for Machus or Gyal,' said Paetro. 'Perhaps not even for Princess Helrena. We never were. You understand?'

At last, Duncan thought he did. *We're here for each other.*

And that was when the furious screams from hundreds of Rodalians charging down the slope broke across the farm.

Cassandra hobbled out into the sunlight, her legs awakening beneath her, stiff and leaden. She knew she just had time enough to head out for the stream, reach it to wash her feet, then return to the tent before Temmell's healing spell dissipated. The yellow sun had begun its journey in the east. She could hear the song of buttonquails running around the long grass on the stream's far, sandy-soiled bank. Following the sound of birds, she arrived. Nobody else was here. Those who had drawn water for a tent's first meal had already done so. Washing of clothes would happen later when the rays of the hot sun would steam garments dry quickly and efficiently. She removed her boots and dipped her bare feet in the stream, enjoying the feel of the chill water running across her toes. As Cassandra sat she heard a cry rise in the camp. She stood to look. Somebody was riding in on a horse from the direction of Temmell's makeshift air-works, children running after the horse and cheering. Then she saw who it was. Zald Mirok. The old nomad who had left with Alexamir to fly into Rodal on the raid. *He's alone!* Her heart sank. *For the love of the ancestors, where's Alexamir?* Two had flown out and only one had flown back? She jumped up, pulling her boots back on without even drying her feet, almost tripping as she sprinted back, dodging tents inside the camp. When Cassandra reached where Mirok had been riding, she couldn't see the warrior or hear the children yelling. *He's dismounted. Where—?*

She passed through the camp, trying to locate the pilot again, but without luck. She would need to return to the tent soon, or risk falling out here, hamstrung. As Cassandra desperately cast her eyes about a voice sounded behind her. A voice she had prayed a thousand times to hear again.

'Have you no greeting for me?'

She whirled about. *Alexamir!* Cassandra opened her mouth but could only manage a surprised croak. She ran to him and tried again. 'Thank the ancestors, you're alive!'

'Why thank them?' laughed Alexamir. He picked her up and whirled her through the air, putting her down again and leaving her dizzy. 'Thank instead my gods for making Alexamir Arinnbold the greatest of all thieves. Rodal's dark buried city tried to make a corpse of me, but their guards and their traps were no match for my cunning.'

'You've copied the book.'

'I stole its contents and I took a few other prizes, besides,' said Alexamir.

Something is wrong, though. I can hear it in his words. 'What prizes would they be, to trouble your victory?'

'Atamva sent me a mercenary who once fought in the Burn. An ally to help me break into the city and steal away from it, too. He gave me the gift of the truth.'

Why does he scowl so? 'It was not a happy truth?'

'A blood truth for a blood feud,' said Alexamir.

Is this why he's come back, to fight before he has a chance to live? 'Tell me!'

'Later,' said Alexamir. 'The thought of you kept me warm sleeping on cold grass, it kept me cool in the scalding air sitting behind Zald Mirok in his shaking wooden pigeon.'

'And now you have me, not just the memory of me.' Cassandra suddenly stopped. 'My legs. I haven't fallen to the ground yet!'

'You are healed,' said Alexamir.

Cassandra had to think twice on what Alexamir had just said. 'But Temmell hasn't laid hands on me.'

'He has what he wants,' said Alexamir. 'Temmell was the first person to greet us after we landed. He's already picked the memories of his holy book out of my mind like a hungry goatherd spearing river eels from a stream.'

'But how am I whole again?' *Can we trust Temmell? What if my healing is temporary and he comes with a second suicide mission for Alexamir?*

'Temmell laughed when I demanded my price,' explained Alexamir. 'He said that the trick wasn't in healing you, but in stopping his cure from taking hold permanently. That is why he had you carried to his sorcerer's den so frequently. Not to renew the healing, but keep his enchantment from healing you for good.'

Cassandra felt a quick flash of anger. 'You mean I could have left the camp and if I had stayed out of Temmell's clutches, my legs would have been restored to me?'

Alexamir nodded. 'All sorcerers are tricksters. Temmell has what

259

he wants. I have what I want. But what of you, my Golden Fox? Do you have what you want?'

She hugged him tight. 'I do.'

'Temmell told me about the camp's uninvited visitors. Your mother and her soldiers . . . what they did to you.'

'They did nothing to me,' said Cassandra. Now she knew Alexamir had survived she could say the words and mean them. 'Nothing but give me the gift of my freedom.'

'Your broken spine is cured now. If you went back to them you would have your birthright, would you not?'

'Yes,' said Cassandra. 'I would have it all given back to me. And I would be a prisoner to the name I was born with, the imperial blood that flows through my veins.'

'I will keep my word if you wish it. Return you to your empire.'

'That is not a word I wish to hear.'

'Well then,' beamed Alexamir. 'Temmell has his stolen rice-eater spells, but I have stolen something far more precious which the sly wizard will never have.'

'It's not stolen when it's offered to you,' said Cassandra.

'See how it is,' joked Alexamir, 'you have not even had your hand stained dark by a witch's marriage-henna and already you seek to curtail my amusement.'

'If it keeps you happy, I'll tell everyone I meet how the Prince of Thieves courageously raided Rodal not once but twice to abduct me.'

'And you must not stint on the part of the tale where I set fire to the rice-eaters' town the second time.'

'Perish the thought.' Cassandra was about to tell Alexamir how happy his return would make his aunt when an unusually large party of Nijumeti came bearing down towards them through the centre of the camp. Two lines of warriors marched with what looked like captives in their centre, followed on both sides and behind by a small crowd of jeering and hooting nomads. Cassandra moved aside with Alexamir to let the party pass. As they did, she realized with a jolt that the faces of the two prisoners trudging forward in the centre were familiar ones.

'I know them!' exclaimed Cassandra. It was Carter Carnehan and Sariel Skel-bane, two of her abductors from the imperium.

'As do I,' said Alexamir, sounding almost as shocked as her by his realization. 'I saw that pair leaving the rice-eaters' capital when I arrived. I thought them traders of the air.'

'They are not,' said Cassandra. 'They're Weylanders – two of the escaped slaves who held me hostage on the other side of the mountains. The younger one is Carter Carnehan, son of the preacher who first captured me. The white-bearded devil is Sariel Skel-bane, an outlaw with a long list of crimes against the Imperium. By all accounts, Vandia's secret police, the hoodsmen, have been pursuing him since before I was born.'

'A famous thief, then? A pity such deeds will not help them here,' said Alexamir.

Cassandra and Alexamir pushed their way through the jostling crowd of nomads, slowing by one of the warriors marching behind the pair of Weylanders.

'How did you come across these foreigners?' asked Alexamir.

'One of our wooden pigeons training new pilots passed over them. They marched across the steppes as boldly if they were Nijumet-born. Our fliers raised a hunting party on their return,' said the fighter. 'Be wary of the old one. He is a weirdling. He pulls knives out of his heart as you might remove thorns from your skin, and then heals himself with a hot blade.'

'Then it will be the Test of Fire,' said Alexamir.

The soldier nodded with a sharp flash of teeth.

'What test is that?' asked Cassandra.

'It is the trial ordered by Temmell's command,' said Alexamir. 'When sorcerers are uncovered crossing our territory, their magic must be tested by the clan. They will be tied to stakes and set on flames. If the sorceries they possess mean the horde well, these two will survive. If it means us ill, the burning fire will cleanse them to ashes and ashes they will remain.'

Cassandra winced. *A very convenient way for Temmell to handle potential rivals to his position.* These two were her enemies, but she knew the Weylanders had treated her far better than any Vandian would have done a similar prisoner-of-war. *And now they will burn for it.*

NINE

A SKYGUARD FOR THE NOMADS

Carter had grown used enough to the prod of swords, jabbing spear butts and slaps from his Nijumeti guards, but the sight of dry kindling and straw being piled around the pair of stakes outside made his heart grow cold.

'Are they cannibals fixing to roast us?' Carter whispered to Sariel, his pale knuckles gripping the bamboo bars of their cage.

'Not unless these rough-hewn maltworms have picked up a new bad habit,' said Sariel.

Carter imagined what it would be like to be strapped to that stake, feel flames licking around his legs and skin blistering before the fire really took hold. *Not a good death.* But then, he had stopped believing that such a contradictory thing existed long ago. 'I thought you said the man we sought was a friend of yours?'

'A friend once, yes, but more than that, Lord Carnehan,' said Sariel. 'He was the leader of our group sent to frustrate the stealers' ambitions. You might say he was the greatest of us.'

'I had rather hoped that our reward for finding your sorcerer might be more than a torch put to my toes.'

'Temmell will be much as you found me when first we met,' said Sariel. 'He has rebuilt himself and forgotten much. We must trust that curiosity brings Temmell Longgate to us, if only to witness our end.'

'And then . . . ?'

'That words and reason may stay our execution. You need to lay your hands on him. You are the key that will unlock him.'

Carter stared at the bonfire tinder, trying to tread down the feeling of terror. 'I can only do that if I'm not made into a hog-roast. If words are not enough . . . ?'

'I will goad the nomads using superior insults until they set me aflame first,' said Sariel. 'They'll make you watch my fate as punishment.'

'That'll make me feel better, will it?'

'That stake out there is an amateur's attempt – do they think to bring an end to the miraculous Sariel with twigs and straw, with a mere tepid tickling? When the stealers ambushed my party the devils used flame-squirts and napalm to render me to ashes, then scattered my remains across Pellas. It took me centuries to heal! My blackened corpse will start moving, healing itself. It will be proof of my sorcery and the Nijumeti will be far too terrified to turn on you.'

They'll be terrified! 'What if they light a torch on me first to punish you?'

'You have a melancholy turn of mind, Lord Carnehan.'

'Water rations,' announced a voice. 'We don't need you so thirsty you will faint during your trial.'

Carter quickly glanced up. *That voice?* It was Sheplar and Kerge standing outside his cage. *They're alive!* They both wore Nijumeti leather slave collars around their necks. A sign that nobody but their master could kill or claim them without a blood price being extracted.

'It is as I told you,' said the Rodalian aviator. 'A dark leather coat with many tales drawn across it. Who else could it be?'

'And Carter Carnehan,' said Kerge. 'I wish we were reunited under happier circumstances, manling.'

Carter shook the cage's bars in excitement. 'Sweet saints, but it's good to see you two! Can you get us out of here?'

Sheplar glanced around between the tents. Dozens of warriors lounged in front of open cooking fires, drinking and laughing. Not so drunk yet that they would miss a pair of camp thralls trying to force open the cage's door. 'You must be patient.'

'I shall try to convince the mistress of my tent to intervene,' said Kerge. 'We have both been taken by the horde for thralls. My owner is a powerful seer, a witch rider. She loathes Temmell and will do anything she can to frustrate his plans. If he says you are to burn, she will wish to set you free. At the very least, you may be put to work as slaves here alongside us.'

'I never thought I'd be glad to be a slave again,' said Carter. 'But it's a whole lot better than being ashes.'

'We will not be thralls for long,' said Sheplar. 'We are planning to escape and warn Rodal about the horde.'

'They've already heard about the clans uniting under some grass king called Kani Yargul,' said Carter. 'Your leaders in Hadra-Hareer seemed as worried about the horde as they are of Weyland's civil war spilling over into Rodal. The border fortresses are preparing to repulse riders.'

'It is not horsemen they will face,' said Sheplar. 'The Nijumeti have built themselves a skyguard.'

'What? They can't have!' said Carter. Then he remembered that mysterious aircraft they had seen out above the plains. *Not a merchant shuttle after all.*

'I assure you it is true. It is why I am alive. Rodalians make poor stable-thralls and tent slaves, but as someone who understands a flying wing . . . the horde's sorcerer, Temmell, keeps me labouring inside their new air-works.'

A pair of warriors came strutting past and Kerge lifted the water bucket while Sheplar took a wooden ladle and passed water between the bars, as if this was their purpose here.

'Temmell Longgate *is* still in the steppes,' said Sariel, glowing with satisfaction as the warriors left their earshot.

'You dishonourable old vagrant,' swore Sheplar, shaking his ladle at the trickster. 'What do you know of Temmell? Is this another of your deranged schemes to see your friends perish for you?'

'It is not for the pigeon to understand where the eagle intends to fly,' said Sariel.

'It is not the pigeon trapped inside the cage here, old fool,' hissed Sheplar. 'I have been fashioning a flying wing of my own out of junk the nomads think too ruined to be used. Under Temmell's direction, riders have dragged the wreckage of every crashed carrier they can find back here. They no longer strip wrecks for sword metal. Kani

Yargul adds scavenged materials to supplies smuggled in from the despicable Hellenise. Through Temmell's devilry, a primitive skyguard has been raised.'

'But surely the Nijumeti won't be a match in the air for your fighters?' asked Carter.

'With surprise on their side? It is not only flying wings that are being fashioned out on the steppes. Temmell is building engine-less gliders for the Great Krul. Craft large enough to carry horses and riders.'

Gliders? Carter cursed. *So it is to be a full invasion of Rodal by the horde.* Bad enough Carter's father and Willow faced the combined might of Vandia and Bad Marcus' southern armies. *How can they survive a nomad invasion, as well?* The Walls of the World had always stood firm against the nomads. But a wall that could simply be flown over was no longer much of a fortification.

'Take the element of surprise away from the clans, and Rodal has a fighting chance. Gliders are slow and unwieldy. Easy prey to a wing gun,' said Sheplar. He stared sadly at Carter and Sariel. 'But the flying wing I am constructing has only two seats. For myself and Kerge. I have not enough parts to build larger. If I did, I would have made space to carry the young bumo away with us, too.'

Bumo? The aviator meant the emperor's granddaughter. 'Lady Cassandra is a slave here, too?'

'Not so much a slave, manling,' explained Kerge. 'She is to be the saddle-wife of a local rogue.'

'You need not concern yourself with the girl,' said Sheplar. 'Her use as a hostage is at an end. The bumo's back was broken when her flying wing crashed here. The Vandians have already come calling in force for her, only to reject the girl as a cripple. She is not a thrall here. She is an exile.'

Carter almost felt sorry for the young noblewoman. Then he remembered how half his friends had died in her family's sky mines working, and a good many others slain escaping the Imperium's clutches. 'Hard customs, which too many of us tasted. Maybe it's only justice that she's had a little of it back.'

'Perhaps,' said Sheplar. 'Still, I would take her if I could. She was under our protection. But I have no time. If Rodal is not warned of Kani Yargul's new skyguard . . .'

'You don't need to hammer together a carrier,' said Carter. 'Not for us *or* Lady Cassandra. When your bird is sturdy enough to fly away from here, you two both hightail it. Warn Rodal. Whatever happens to us, happens to us.'

'Have you forgotten our task?' asked Sariel.

'It's my family in Hadra-Hareer I need to remember,' said Carter. 'I agreed to follow you. I never agreed to let Willow and my father die back in the mountains.'

Sariel pointed at Sheplar and Kerge. 'You must bring Temmell here to view the test of fire.'

'Does the master take orders from the slave?' Sheplar looked cross.

'Then beg him not to come, and let him arrive to spite you,' said Sariel. 'I care not how it is arranged. Fail and the fire that starts here will end with the light of the world extinguished.'

'Your light, perhaps.' Sheplar sounded like that might be just punishment, as well. 'If there is a god of boastful braggarts, then he will count the loss hard.'

'Talk sense to this flying fool,' Sariel demanded of Carter.

'We will do what we can,' whispered Kerge, the gask tugging Sheplar back. Any longer at the cage and the two thralls would be joining the execution.

Carter watched his two friends disappear. *Dear God, I know I haven't done much by your teachings recently, but help those two get us out of this. There's got to be some good in what I've been doing somewhere.*

'If I burn first and you survive,' said Sariel, as serious as Carter had ever heard him speak, 'you will need to pass me my memories back as well as healing Temmell. Exactly as you did in the sky mines.'

'Your memories don't haunt me like they used to,' said Carter. 'Are you sure they're still there?'

'The mind is a marvellous thing, Lord Carnehan,' said Sariel. 'That you do not feel their weight is only a testimony to my skill as a healer. You have a very sound dam constructed inside your mind to hold them. But a key you were made and a key you remain.'

'You healed me,' sighed Carter. 'If it comes to it, I'll do the same for you.'

'Good, then a bargain has been struck,' said Sariel. He stood alongside Carter and gripped the cage's bars, gazing at the twin stakes beyond. 'There's nothing I hate so much as dying.'

Hell, I wish I could feel as certain as you about my chances of resurrection.

Every Rodalian charge came accompanied by hideous blood-curdling screams, answered from inside the farm buildings by the chattering roar of modern Imperium rifles. Many of the barbarians clutched single-shot breech-loading weapons, or long, spindly six-shot rifles with revolver-style rotating cylinders; but what the Rodalians lacked in firepower they made up for in massed numbers. Squads of three or four warriors charging in from multiple directions with bayonets glinting, leaving the cover of the village streets and testing the defenders' positions for weaknesses. Bullets thudded against the walls of Duncan's makeshift fortress, shutters torn off their narrow slit-like windows by grenade blasts. When enemy grenadiers came sprinting towards the farm buildings, they swung spherical wooden grenades like bolas above their heads, spinning the munitions so fast you'd think their short burning fuses would be extinguished. Duncan ducked as a fiery blast blew in through the window slit he protected. The thick wall shook from the impact but didn't breach. Nothing of this engagement was as Duncan had imagined it should be. His view of the battle restricted to a four-inch-wide slit of the street, enemy warriors sprinting past, less than a second to trigger a return shot from his rifle. Missing or hitting. Impossible to tell with the thunderclap of rifle fire from legionaries by his side. People falling outside. Legionaries dragged down bleeding from the rooftop into the safety of the room, twisting and turning in agony across the floor as bandages were applied. Curses and screams and dying on all sides. The clatter of empty magazines tossed behind on to tiles, the click of fresh ammunition clips slapped into place. Bolts on the side of the rifles banging back, hundreds of spent ammunition casings rattling hot across the floor. Casings and blood to slip on when you tried to turn and shift your tense, cramped muscles. The company had piled up every piece of furniture they could find against the thick wooden door, now so splintered by the enemy fusillade that it was a wonder the door still held in place. The burnt odour of cordite mingled with smoke from the weapons discharge, filling Duncan's nostrils with nothing but the acrid smell of burning.

Paetro dashed down the simple wooden staircase leading to the roof. 'Sappers attempting to blow the corner!'

Duncan surrendered his window slit to a wounded legionary and sprung across to the stairs, metal casings rolling under the soles of his boots, a handful of defenders pushing behind him to answer Paetro's call. *If one building goes down here we'll lose them all. A regiment's worth of Rodalians will be clambering over the rubble and looking to stick us with the cutlery on the end of their rifles.*

'We're out of grenades,' shouted Paetro.

Duncan ducked behind the low wall of the flat roof terrace. Legionaries on either side exchanged shots with warriors on the opposite rooftops. Paetro and Kenem Posda were just down from him. They were shooting on single shot rather than automatic bursts to conserve ammunition. Duncan saw what Paetro had spotted. Perhaps forty enemy soldiers moving along the street to the right. A group of six attackers manhandled what looked like a wooden battering ram. But rather than a simple blunt steel-reinforced head, the ram's sides were fixed with kegs of powder. *They jam that anywhere along our walls and we're going to have rubble for a flank.*

Duncan raised his rifle and sighted on the figures in the street, pumping three or four shots into the advancing warriors. Rifles crackled beside the young Weylander. Fire returned towards him, cracking masonry away, fleeting in from the other rooftops and the street he'd just targeted. The squad carrying the explosive battering ram arrowed into the lee of the closest buildings, almost out of the field of fire of Duncan's rifle. The ram's escort shot from the hip as they advanced, one bullet taking the legionary to Duncan's left straight in the forehead. The Vandian soldier tumbled over the wall and down into the street below, falling across a pair of dead Rodalians, another corpse to be buried.

'Too close,' snarled Paetro.

Duncan turned as furious yells resounded across two other streets, fresh waves of warriors charging through the village in force, obviously timed to give the defenders something to worry about other than that battering ram.

The salvo of the rooftop sharpshooters turned into a hail of bullets as the charging soldiers opened up on the farm building in concert, dust and masonry crackling around Duncan. Before he could duck down there was a massive explosion. Duncan glanced down to try to find where the battering ram had blasted its way into the farm building, but then he saw the column of smoke rose streets away. Where the road had been boiling over with charging Rodalians, now it was a cratered mess filled with fire, smoke and confusion. As Duncan stared dumbfounded there was a scream overhead, an aircraft passing low at speed. Not a helo or one of the Vandians' rocket-driven patrol ships. Then another plane and another, a wave of thumping explosions rising out of Ganyid Thang and washing warm air across his cheeks.

Duncan felt elation as he recognized the aircrafts' notorious jet-dark cloth fuselage; the sketches of these deadly, feared fliers had filled a hundred sensational newspaper covers. *We're going to survive this after all.* Twin booms on each fighter, each with a propeller, the booms joined at the back by a long horizontal stabilizer and midway, a single, central nacelle for the single pilot's glass cockpit, the plane's polished nosecone bristling with eight guns. *Black Bullets.* Usually illustrated attacking merchant ships on the Lancean Ocean while seaplanes landed to offload booty stripped from burning vessels. 'They're pirate fighter planes!'

'King Marcus' money is good for something,' laughed Paetro. 'The ancestors bless a friendly mercenary.'

Duncan followed the contrail of the aircraft. 'It has to be the same squadron that took on the skyguard above the ambush of the Seventh Merlanda!' Baron Machus won't be happy, Duncan judged. *But then the baron can hardly complain about the king's mercenaries engaging targets of opportunity. Taking on the task he's hung back from.*

The Black Bullets dived low across the valley, nose-mounted guns chattering and tearing strips of ground into the air, Rodalians tumbling inside plumes of soil and smoke. Unlike the Weylanders, whose regiments had centuries of drills shooting at planes with tripod-fixed heavy rifles, the Rodalians over-relied on their skyguard to see off threats from the air. Many of the pirate fliers flew with rows of rockets on racks under their wings. Meant for raking decks, sails and wheelship stacks and devastating vessels into quick surrender without actually sinking them, the rocket blasts were the last straw for the Rodalian ground forces. With no friendly flying wings in support, the mountain soldiers broke and ran. The troops turned tail in the village and fled back up the slope making for the safety of the mountains. Pirate aircraft wheeled across the escarpment, strafing with concentrated nose-fire, exhausts along their booms leaving contrails of angry dark smoke in their wake. *They're showing no mercy.* Duncan wondered if that was simply the pirates' way, or if they'd been promised a bounty for every enemy corpse collected from the battlefield. One Black Bullet flew fast over the farm buildings, the brief glimpse of a leather-masked face inside its transparent bubble canopy. Duncan noted the insignia painted across each tail wing: a white skull leering above a bone-white propeller, a pale bomb painted on either side, set against the field of a winged blood-red circle. *A flag as infamous as their planes.* 'They're flying out of the *Plunderbird,*' said Duncan. 'That's Black Barnaby's fighter wing.'

Paetro spat contemptuously on the floor at the name. He obviously didn't like the idea of being saved by Jacob Carnehan's wayward brother. *To hell with that. I'll take any help I can get.*

'What's the matter?' asked Kenem. 'We're alive, aren't we?'

Paetro glared at the old legionary. 'When I heard the Imperium was dispatching a legion for a punishment campaign, I had it in my mind it might be the enemy that was going to be punished.'

'We're alive,' repeated Duncan, hardly believing it.

Kenem muttered something that sounded like, 'Until next time.'

That's fair enough. Duncan was part of the house now. But they wouldn't let him forget just why they had nearly died here. *Yes, alive, until Gyal and his lapdogs come up with a new suicide mission for us.*

Willow sat on the hard stool allocated for the wooden defendant's stand inside Northhaven's courtroom. Three judges sat before her on high, a line of white powdered wigs and heavy crimson robes. Willow knew that the local circuit judges of the prefecture wore blue, so that these gentlemen of the law had no doubt been imported, along with the occupying Army of the Boles, from the royalist south of the nation. *Why am I here?* She didn't recognize any friendly faces packing the public gallery or the open seats of the court. Newspaper writers and gawkers; ordinary townspeople, from their simple clothes, drawn by the sensation whipped up beforehand. Oddly, rubberneckers appeared to fill the jury benches too, rather than sworn-in citizens. Unfriendly faces, though, those she could find aplenty. Her odious step-mother, Leyla Holten. At least Holten's repugnant creature Nocks wasn't present. She could still see his face in her mind, looking triumphant for most of the time Willow had been trussed up on the back of a mule and smuggled out of Rodal and into Weyland. *No sign of my brother or father either?* Viscount William Wallingbeck was present, however. He stared angrily at Willow whenever he could stand to look at her at all.

Did I disappoint you, husband? Well, here's your chance to take your pound of flesh, even though the pound of flesh you value most will be entering the world soon enough. They won't dare put me on trial for high treason. The penalty for high treason during a time of war is immediate execution . . . I won't even be able to plead my belly. So, what game is Leyla Landor playing at here?

Willow was to find out soon enough. The judge in the centre of the three notables banged his gavel and called the court into session. A prosecutor left the open benches and walked before the wooden stand where Willow sat. Perhaps sixty years old, the dark-robed lawyer had a tiny pair of spectacles balanced on a long nose and the superior manners of a scholar lecturing a student far beneath his towering intellect.

'I am Callum Perry, your ladyship, representing the crown prosecution. Do you recognize the man seated in the stand to the left of the judges?' began the prosecutor; a nasal voice that Willow hoped would irritate the judges as much as it did her.

'He is William Wallingbeck,' said Willow.

'No, he is *Viscount* Wallingbeck,' corrected the prosecutor. 'Your husband.'

'He is not my husband,' snapped Willow. 'My sham of a marriage has been annulled.'

'I am aware of no such annulment,' said the prosecutor, sounding confused while flashing a knowing gaze that suggested he was anything but.

'The annulment was signed by Prince Owen and ratified by the Supreme Chamber of the People's Assembly.'

'So, signed by a traitor and high insurrectionist, before being rubber-stamped by an assembly long since dissolved for corruption?' He raised his hands in mock surrender. 'Are bandits who have robbed the bank of its silver allowed to flourish pardons written by their own marauding chieftains now? This is a court of law, Lady Wallingbeck, not a circus tent for japes in such poor taste.'

'My surname is Landor, not Wallingbeck.'

'And yet your own mother stands here in the court to testify other-wise.'

'My *step-mother* sold me into a forced marriage so I would have no further claim on my house's considerable estate. I have little doubt she also arranged for the kidnapping which sees me standing here in chains.'

'What kidnapping?' asked the prosecutor, professing surprise every bit as professionally as any actor. 'You were returned to Northhaven by your family's loyal retainers, your mother worried the winds of war would bring harm to both you and the child you carry. Acting on your mother's instructions, a valiant party of your house's servants put themselves in considerable personal danger, crossing the Rodalian border to an area where many beaten rebels have fled the rightful justice of the gallows.'

'You mean your usurper's war,' said Willow. 'Bad Marcus fighting to cling to a throne he murdered his way on to.'

'But we're not here to prosecute you for calumny, for repeating the lies which duped so many citizens in this unfortunate rebellion,' said Callum Perry.

'Just what am I charged with?' demanded Willow. 'I believe it is customary for the accused to know that much at least.'

'Why, you are charged with murder, Lady Wallingbeck.'

'Murder!' spluttered Willow. She ached to shout down this fool. 'You accuse *me* of that! When I gaze around this courtroom I find a great many faces for whom the gallows would be a due and just end, killers whose hands are stained with the blood of hundreds of decent Weylanders.'

'There is one face you will not see today. Lloyd Horting. Do you know the man?'

A memory swam up from Willow's mind. One of Viscount Wallingbeck's tame brutes on staff. Always happy to beat any hungry family recently arrived begging at the mansion's doorstep, attempting to claim the right of tenant's alms from their landowner. 'He is one of William Wallingbeck's employees.'

'It is good that you remember the man,' said the prosecutor. 'You should remember a man you stabbed!'

Was he the one? Willow recalled being dragged back to the house after trying to escape yet again. A gang of servants restraining her while Wallingbeck took his foul amusement with her. She had stabbed one of them with a stolen dinner knife. *Was that Horting?* But the pig hadn't been too badly hurt, more was the pity. His had only been a shallow wound. Willow's attacker had stalked away cursing her. 'I cut one of Wallingbeck's dogs before the viscount raped me, I remember that much.'

'I see that you take as many liberties, Lady Wallingbeck, when describing the natural relations between a husband and a wife, as you do when mistreating your house's staff. You attacked a footman who had the temerity to try to restrain you during one of your frequent violent rages towards your long-suffering household staff. Perhaps you also remember how your poor servant died that night from the wound you inflicted upon him. Maybe you recall how you then slipped away from your home and fled north to escape justice? How you ran away from Arcadia and took up with any rebel or criminal who might keep you safely out of the constables' hands?'

'I escaped a false marriage and a sham husband,' said Willow, incredulous at lie after lie being piled up here. 'I departed because my so-called family blackmailed me into trying to infiltrate the rebel-held city of Midsburg for the royalist cause.'

'Really? You must have done a tremendous job in the city because Midsburg did indeed fall. Of course, it fell under assault by the Royal Army and our Vandian allies. Well done, Lady Wallingbeck, very well done. A pity you didn't stay in the city to claim the gratitude of your lawful king, rather than trying to escape justice by fleeing north across the Rodalian border. Why, it's almost as if your claims are a tissue of lies and you're trying to justify your guilt with falsehoods so ridiculous that not even a child caught scrumping from the apple tree would dare to fabricate them.'

'Where's my defender-under-law?' Willow pressed. 'Why do I stand here having to suffer you describing white as black without a defence?'

'But you do not,' smiled Callum Perry. He raised his hand and indicated Leyla Holten. 'Your defence is here in the court. Your mother.'

'I have not appointed that woman and I never would. She is nothing more than a conniving whore whose sole skill is the questionable ability to manipulate the opposite sex into making her wealthier than she was before.'

'Oh dear,' purred the prosecutor, 'this is most unfortunate. You seem unaware that the assembly's Common Law was supplanted by the House of Prefects' High-law when the upper chamber was given sole governance below the king. It is now for a head of house to defend charges brought against their sons and daughters.'

'That woman is head of nothing,' snarled Willow. *So, my jury's absence is explained, at least. A thousand years of legal progress tossed aside by Bad Marcus.* 'She's here to testify against me. How in the name of the saints can you expect the same person to act as a witness for the prosecution and a defender? Where's my cursed father?'

'The Honourable Benner Landor is currently campaigning in the theatre of war with your brother, defending Weyland from all traitors as is their duty. In the absence of a male head of a house, duties of defending the house's good name fall upon the wife.' He indicated Leyla Horton again. She smiled softly at Willow as she took a stand on the other side of the judges, the very picture of motherly deference towards the court.

'I will be happy to speak for my dear step-daughter in this sad matter,' said Leyla Horton. 'But first I would like to hear all the witnesses for the prosecution speak so that I may have the full picture of the accusations against my Willow.'

I just bet you would.

It was as bad as Willow feared. Servant after servant, half of whom she knew not at all, stood up to bear witness against her. How 'Lady Wallingbeck' spat at them, kicked maidservants, threw cutlery at butlers, whipped stable-hands while at horse, smashed hand-mirrors over the heads of the ladies who dressed her. How the great house had been a happy place before her arrival, a veritable paradise among the many rich mansions around Arcadia. *It's a wonder I didn't shove a kitchen maid into the oven, cook her body up and serve the corpse to the housekeepers for a joke.* After they were done, the prosecutor called a long line of male servants, mostly the same monsters who had helped Wallingbeck keep Willow a prisoner in the rambling, rundown hall. They spoke of Lady Wallingbeck's terrible hysterics and attempts at self-harm, and how it was while restraining her during one of her breakdowns that she had stabbed poor Lloyd through the heart. Lloyd the saint, not Lloyd the thug who would kick a hungry child in the gut just to see the mother fall to her knees, begging for mercy. *If he did die then there's an extra seat in hell around the stealers' supper table.*

'These are all lies!' shouted Willow, when she could stand this procession of falsehoods no more.

'Lady Landor,' instructed the judge seated in the middle of the trio. 'You will instruct your step-daughter into silence until she is questioned. If Lady Wallingbeck continues to disrupt the trial, she will be removed and verdict will be announced on her in absentia.'

Willow cursed them, but silently. *I have to stay quiet. They're trying to goad me. That's the point of this. If I'm not present here I can't do what needs to be done.*

At last, the pawns had finished perjuring themselves and it was the turn of the bigger pieces, including the viscount, to slide on to the board. Willow glared with loathing when the bastard she'd been sold to like a piece of cattle, was questioned. *You think you've won, William Wallingbeck? Are you happy to have me back in your hands? I'll show you what a poor victory you have purchased.*

Willow could barely stand to listen to the southern nobleman while he repeated the same lies his lackeys had told. But she forced herself to, in case she missed something vital she might need to use later.

The prosecutor reached the end of whatever fictions the two had agreed on before the trial began. He held his black robes' lapels, speaking slowly and with gravity. 'Viscount Wallingbeck, it is one of your household's poor servants who was viciously murdered. Under the High Law you have the right to speak for redress in this matter. What do you ask?'

'I ask that my misguided wife receive a reprieve of any sentence pronounced here until delivery of my house's heir,' said Wallingbeck. 'A child should never suffer for the sins of its mother. After the child is born then any verdict of this court must be served.'

'Noble sentiments. Let your statement be noted by the court,' said Callum Perry.

Next, in this carnival of villains, it was Leyla Holten's turn, called as Willow's defence. Willow barely managed to bite down a tirade of abuse, only keeping a vestige of self-control by the middle judge's stony demeanour as she caught the man's gaze. There was something final and implacable about that stare. But there was something else, too. Unless Willow misread the situation, it seemed to her that the senior judge, however imported he may be, was less than happy about the irregular manner of his summoning from Arcadia to this far-called prefecture.

As Willow expected, Leyla Holten made no real attempt to dispute the charge of murder, admitting that she had herself administered to the dying servant after he fled the room where Willow had assaulted him. 'But,' Leyla said, opening her arms to the court, 'I beg that you forgive my daughter her sins. Lady Wallingbeck was a fine young woman before she fell under the spell of the ruffian son of the notorious outlaw Jake Silver, more commonly known as the felon Jacob Carnehan.'

'For the purpose of clarity, you mean the warlord from the Burn who was nicknamed Quicksilver?' probed the prosecutor. 'Brother of the privateer and pirate Black Barnaby?'

'I wish I had never heard that terrible family's dark name,' said Leyla, 'so many problems have they created for my family.'

'To the land, madam, to the nation,' said Callum Perry. 'And this man's son would be Carter Carnehan, a known insurrectionist loyal to the cause of the pretender assaulting our beloved nation's throne?'

'The apple does not fall far from the tree.' Tears rolled down Holten's cheeks.

I'm surprised those false tears don't burn her like fire.

'I tried my best for my step-daughter,' moaned Holten. 'I removed her from the influence of that demon Carter Carnehan, sending her to the season in Arcadia. She met Viscount Wallingbeck there and marriage quickly followed. I had such high hopes for her. But the curse of the Carnehans and their thieving wickedness proved too strong. When the Carnehans followed Willow down to the capital they quickly joined in the pretender's coup against our lawful king. They corrupted my impressionable Willow anew! It is the Carnehans who are ultimately responsible for the slaying of that poor servant. Without the steady drip of their poison, my daughter would still be happily married, my husband would be about to welcome his first grandchild into the world.'

'You show a true mother's concern,' said the prosecutor, 'as befits your rank and house.'

There were calls of *pity* and *mercy* from the gallery, onlookers moved by the sorrowful tale of a daughter's fall over her forbidden love.

'But that a daughter of your house has been corrupted by such sinful association can be no excuse under law for the cold-blooded murder of an innocent member of staff. If you, Lady Landor, stabbed to death one of your housekeepers in a fit of pique, would you expect to escape the verdict of our court through virtue of your title?'

'I am equal under law to anyone here,' said Holten. 'The justice of King Marcus is as much mine as it is of any man or woman sitting in the public benches today.'

'Then I say to the court that we cannot extend leniency to your step-daughter, however much that decision and duty pains us.' Callum Perry turned towards Willow. 'If the defender rests her case then the prosecutor shall call for a due verdict to be made. Lady Wallingbeck, do you have anything to say in this case and do you recognize this court.'

And there's the trap. 'I have little to say that would please anyone here, so I shall retain my silence, beyond saying that of course I recognize the court's authority.'

'You recognize it? Are you certain?'

His shock this time needed no acting skills. *Yes, you thought to goad me into cursing you all for a pack of paid-for lapdogs trotting behind Bad Marcus.* Willow grimaced at the cunning lawyer. 'The High Laws of Weyland's upper chamber are the foundation stones of our legal system.' *Hard, cold stones that should have remained long covered over by the Common Law.*

'Then I call the court to its verdict.'

The three judges filed away, returning to their seats in short order. *Too soon. But then, how could I expect anything else?* A clerk of court arrived. He was passed down three scrolls by the judges. Should the clerk approach Leyla Holten first with the verdict, then Willow was judged innocent. Naturally, the clerk crossed to the prosecutor for the verdict to be read, drawing moans from the crowd. *Everyone loves an underdog.*

'Lady Wallingbeck,' pronounced the lawyer. 'You are found guilty of the foul murder of Lloyd Horting. Your sentence is to be execution on the public gallows . . . hanging from the neck until you shall be made dead. This sentence will be commuted until three days after you have given birth, and carried out no later than seven days after the birth of your first child.'

There were weeps of consternation from members of the public. They had come for their spectacle, their torrid little drama, and they had certainly been given it.

Let's see if I can toss them a little extra spectacle. 'Who brings this case against me?' asked Willow, fighting to keep her voice under control.

'What?' said the prosecutor, uncertain. 'What do you say?'

Willow's lip curled into a snarl. 'What I say is that my house has just exercised its right of defence of defamation of its good name through my "mother". But who dares to bring this case of murder against the House of Landor? There will be a name on the rolls, I trust, of the vile liar who accuses me?'

'It is your husband, the honourable Viscount Wallingbeck.'

There was a murmur of disapproval from the gallery at that, even one well-packed with the usurper's sympathizers and his shills in the press. For a husband to seek the trial of a pregnant wife was viewed ungallant in the extreme by southern gentlemen.

'The verdict has now been pronounced,' said the prosecutor. 'These are unnecessary details to dwell on.'

Willow jabbed a finger at Leyla Holten. 'While that failed actress was bedding her way to *my* fortune, I was busy studying in Hawkland Park. Mastering commerce, learning how to keep my family estate in hale health. Learning how to preserve our holdings and increase them. There are thousands of books in so big a library, many of them full of detail, both necessary and unnecessary. Even a very dusty and faded full set of the High Law of the House of Prefects.'

'Verdict has been pronounced,' repeated Callum Perry, sounding increasingly shrill.

'I heard you the first time,' growled Willow. 'I have a very fine set of ears. Not quite as aesthetically pleasing as *that* woman's, but they serve me well enough. What you're too stupid to realize is that I needed you to pronounce immediately. You certainly didn't fail to disappoint me. Under the High Law of Weyland I reject this verdict and request lawful Trial by Ordeal under Conciliar Jurisdiction of the Prefecture.'

'Trial by—' the prosecutor spluttered, '—you mean trial by *combat*?'

'I do.'

'You are female, you are with child!'

'So I am. Nothing would give me greater pleasure than running a sabre through William Wallingbeck's repellent heart,' said Willow. 'And believe me when I say, if I wasn't presently as slow as a pit-pony with half a quarry in both baskets I would jump at that opportunity.'

'Then you have no choice but to accept our verdict.'

'No, the High Law clearly states that I have the right to appoint a male champion to fight William Wallingbeck on my behalf, as long as that champion is from my house and fit to defend my honour. My father's a little old for it, don't you think? So I select my brother Duncan Landor to act as my champion.'

'Your brother will have no part in this!'

'Then I must refer you to the Privy Prefect Councillors' second edict made at the Assize of Riverlarn which states that refusing to act as a champion be the act of a craven and punishable by force of axe to the neck,' said Willow. 'And after Duncan's executed, I'll select my father as champion. And if he refuses . . . well, you see my point. You'll find the assize in the twelfth volume of the High Law if you have the thirty-six volume set.'

'You will not prosper by this!'

'I believe I just did. You can follow the ancient High Law,' said Willow, 'or Bad Marcus can restore the Assembly and our Common law and I will accept retrial by a jury of my peers and a defender-under-law of my employment. Now, Mr Perry, I'm ravenous. Kindly scare me up some supper. After that you had better slip away to the guild's radio hold and send a message to your king explaining how you failed. Then, cooking for me will, I suspect, look like a very satisfying choice among the few left to you.'

The prosecutor turned towards the judges beseechingly. 'I ask that this case be struck off and removed for immediate retrial.'

The elderly judge in the middle of the three smiled ever so slightly. 'After a verdict made and accepted by both sides? Please, sir, please. Never in a thousand years. The High Law is the High Law, sir. It is the granite of our throne. Lady Wallingbeck, the right of Trial by Ordeal under Conciliar Jurisdiction of the Prefecture is yours. As originally granted by Queen Hazilire, I believe.'

'Quite so, your honour,' said Willow, with just the right tone of humility.

There was uproar in court at the unexpected turn of events. Willow stood up from her hard stool and blew Leyla Horton a kiss. The pale-faced woman looked like she'd been struck by a bucket of night-soil tossed out of a window. 'This one's for you, *Mother*.'

Willow had rather hoped that she wouldn't have to see Leyla Holten again until the day of her trial-by-combat, but as always, just hoping for it had made the woman's appearance more likely. Leyla Holten strode her way into Willow's cell after the door swung open, kicking damp straw aside with disgust. Willow had smelled the strong sweet perfume before the door opened. However expensive the scent, it couldn't compensate for the reek of the provost office's cells under Northhaven's army barracks. *Not exactly made for comfort.* Willow didn't bother sitting up from the rickety bed frame that was her sole possession here. She suspected that if she hadn't been with child, and that child the future property of Viscount Wallingbeck, she wouldn't even have that much.

'You think you've won, don't you?' barked Leyla, by way of greeting.

'I think you would have been better off leaving me in exile in Rodal, old woman.'

Maybe it was the *old* that got under Leyla's skin, but she trembled with rage. 'You haven't beaten me! I will transform this farce you have arranged into a blade to cut your throat.'

'What's the matter, did all the society invites dry up after your "daughter" escaped and joined the rebellion?'

'I have higher friends than you can imagine. What do you hope to achieve by this duel you've tricked the court into ordering? Do you think the viscount will slay his own brother-in-law, or that Duncan will fight to the death for a sister who has betrayed him twice?'

'Well, they could both fight like milksops to the first blood,' said Willow. 'But you know how serious our gentlemen of the south are about their honour. That'll surely sully the name of both houses. Maybe my mischief will be enough for me.'

'You're trying to buy time,' said Leyla. 'But for what?'

'For Prince Owen to win.'

Leyla laughed coldly. 'You don't need weeks for that, you need centuries. The pretender is finished. Parliament's rebel army has broken and fled the field.'

'Not so long as Jacob Carnehan is alive.'

'Your revolutionist pastor? He's an outlaw working beyond his talents. He lost the war in the north and now he's been left cowering in our neighbour's crags across the border. King Marcus rules over all of Weyland.'

There was something about the way Holten said the king's name that told Willow everything she needed to know about the woman's 'friends' in high places. Willow almost pitied her father, the choices he had made. *There's no fool like an old fool.* Taking the king's mistress to bed might yet prove a chancy business. 'Quicksilver already has a grave marked just for Bad Marcus.'

'Let the fool keep it for himself. Did you know that one of the mercenary carriers hired by King Marcus is commanded by Carnehan's own brother, Black Barnaby? There's something fitting about engaging the services of a pirate to kill a brigand, don't you think? Even the pastor's own family has turned against him and seeks to ingratiate itself with the winning side.'

Leyla smiled at the look of consternation on Willow's face. 'So, you didn't know, then? If your precious troublesome pastor still had a heart for fighting, he never would have fled the Burn. He would have stayed a warlord prince, killing and pillaging as befits such savages. Instead, Carnehan fled across the sea and hid himself away under a cheap woollen church shirt, talking of peace and leading all the good sheep to heaven. What does that tell you about your dangerous, legendary Quicksilver? He is a twice-broken man who has forgotten whatever he was. Where is the great general? Where is the master strategist? He led the rebels down a ravine into a cave with no exit and the royalist army is close to smoking him out for good.'

'I have seen your smoke,' muttered Willow, a shiver running down her back that had nothing to do with the damp of this cell. 'I have seen stealers and the demons shifting inside it. And one is coming for *you*.'

Leyla shook her head in contempt. 'Carnehan's not the only one left broken by the wheel of life's turn. I always believed your time in captivity as a slave had left your deranged. Now I have the proof of it.'

'Why did you drag me back to Weyland, Holten? Why did that murderous pig Nocks risk his neck for you? It surely wasn't just revenge for me escaping from your arranged marriage and humiliating you? There has to be more to it than that?'

'You will find out just how much more,' promised Leyla. 'All in good time.' She banged on the cell door for the guards to open it. 'And then we shall see who has won and who has lost here.'

Willow cursed the treacherous woman after she left. *What is she planning?* To outguess Leyla Holten, Willow would have to learn to think like the scheming woman, a prospect that frankly sickened her. *But I have the time. That is all I have locked in here. Time and my mind. Yes, let us see who is to win here.*

TEN

TRIAL BY FIRE

Anticipation had built all morning along with the crowd's numbers, and at last, the moment Carter was dreading arrived. The young Weylander had known it would come when the nomads entered the cage at sun-up, manacling his and Sariel's hands behind their backs. *Trussed like birds clucking for a plucking.* Now, four blue-skinned warriors arrived and unlocked the cage, hauling Carter and Sariel roughly through the narrow entrance. His stomach turned in horror. They were going to be put to the fire on an empty gut, but that had a sharp logic to it. *Why waste good food on someone who is going to meet a bad death?*

The man in control of the proceedings stepped forward and raised his hands. He put Carter in mind of a slightly younger Sariel, if the rascally old bard had shaved his white beard and been starved to gaunter features. The chants of the mob threw Carter the name he'd expected. *Temmell Longgate.*

Warriors behind Carter forced him down to his knees. Sariel as well, to show deference to their appointed judge.

'It is time,' called Temmell. 'Time for these intruders to face the trial.'

Howls of approval met his words, hundreds of swords and daggers jabbing in unison towards the sky.

'Do you not know me?' demanded Sariel, struggling as two warriors pulled the old man to his feet and shoved him towards his stake. 'Do you not recognize Sariel Skel-Bane?'

'I know you very well. You are a pair of fools stupid enough to try to steal from the clans and believe you might live to boast of it,' said Temmell. 'You are rodents who think to steal scraps from hill lions. This is the rodents' reward.'

'I know you, Temmell Longgate,' thundered Sariel, 'and I have seen your dreams. Troubled and dark and filled with scampering devils.'

Temmell shook his head for a second, as though groggily warding off a hypnotism cast by Sariel. 'Perhaps you are just the sort of trickster who sends such dreams, then sells cures to ease them? I am not taken in by your chicanery, you tickle-brained liar. It is a pale shadow of my power.'

Demands to get on with the weirdling's torching resounded from the nomad mob. The Nijumeti wanted their trial by fire. Carter saw savage bloodlust burning in their faces as the guards hauled him unwillingly towards the second stake. He had a terrible feeling that whatever tales Sariel had saved for this moment would have little influence over their fate.

Carter was halfway to his stake when an old woman stepped forward. He spotted Kerge in the crowd behind her. *This must be the sorcerer's rival Kerge spoke of. Madinsar. The witch rider.* Kerge had at least accomplished what he promised. Carter prayed hard that the gask's mistress could sway the clan. The loud mob fell silent behind her. *Respect or fear?*

'I have seen this old weirdling in my dream-walkings. He has the power to aid the clans,' appealed the high priestess.

'Or perhaps the power to destroy us?' snared Temmell. 'A blade may cut both ways.'

'I caution for their release,' said the witch rider. 'Sparing them will please Atamva.'

'So such a dangerous weapon may fall into your hands, Madinsar?' said Temmell, angry at his challenger's mischief at the trial.

'These hands have long served the clan.'

'And mine do not?' rumbled Temmell. 'I do not send Kani Yargul's horde ambiguous visions of what may come, designed to be interpreted whichever way the wind blows. I have made the clans a mighty skyguard! I have fashioned the means by which we will sweep over every enemy who has stolen soil, calls it their own and denies us our destiny.'

'How little you know the Nijumeti. Victory is only ever claimed by the rider,' said Madinsar insolently, 'never the trader who sold the metal that forged the rider's blade.'

Carter gazed around the nomad crowd's angry, intent faces. He could see that there were no viscounts and dukes among these quarrelsome people. They had a democracy of sorts. They convinced by words and deeds, and when that failed, a sharp sabre edge.

'You claim the future, witch rider, yet you live only in the past.'

'I have seen a little of what this weirdling means for *your* future,' said the witch rider. 'And I smell your fear of him upon you.'

'These interlopers have no future,' said Temmell. 'Not unless the weirdling's sorcery proves stronger than mine.'

'Summon Kani Yargul here,' demanded the woman. 'Let him decide.'

'And trouble the Krul of Kruls over a couple of foreign reivers? Perhaps he would like to come and advise the clan on how many nuts should be counted into your breakfast bowl? After that, he can decide on the colour of my boots' fur lining and whether I should mount my black stallion or my white.'

The crowd roared with amusement. They seemed to like a good joke. Unfortunately, Carter couldn't think of any.

Temmell shook his head fiercely. 'No! Let us begin the trial.'

Carter felt the slim thread of hope slip out of his grasp. *She's lost the day.* He felt like a fool for daring to hope. *How can any witch's words compete with the gift of a skyguard?*

Two people stepped from the crowd behind the witch rider. *Allies or foes?* A large warrior Carter didn't recognize, with a woman he knew all too well. *Lady Cassandra Skar.* Carter wasn't so much surprised by her appearance as the fact she seemed far less crippled than he had been led to believe. The young woman was mobile and on her legs. Carter saw the way the warrior treated the young Vandian noblewoman and he recognized that look well. *Did Cassandra fake her injuries to remain here with that big brute?* If Cassandra had tricked

Princess Helrena into freeing her from the celestial caste's life of strife and plotting, then Carter had underestimated the young woman.

'The weirdling asks who knows him,' said Lady Cassandra. 'I shall answer. I know both the sly sorcerer and the Weyland boy.'

'What is this? Were you a thief in a gang with these two dogs, then?' laughed Temmell. 'How well you have chosen, Alexamir Arinnbold. I had believed Lady Cassandra merely a noblewoman of Vandia. You should have let the clan know of your celebrated bloodline of robbery before your mother flew here, my lady. Casting large shadows with her metal toys. Trespassing against people never given to the empire to command.'

'Let her speak, Temmell,' demanded Alexamir. 'She is of the clan now and has the right.'

Temmell bowed, mockingly. 'Very well, let the Vandian use the gift of her tongue as well as she uses *my* gift of her restored legs. The former is a gift I find common in the fine women of our clan.'

There were more roars of laughter at this, as well as hoots of amused derision from female warriors.

Carter barely had time to take in what had been said before Cassandra approached the two captives, standing directly behind Sariel and himself. She seized Sariel by the scruff of his long leather coat. 'This trickster is chief adviser to my enemies and captors. He travelled to Vandia to assist in my abduction. He carried me back to Weyland to make a hostage of me, to ask for a ransom so mighty that even the richest emperor in Pellas would not pay it.'

Carter bitterly shook his head. The girl failed to mention her only ransom was to spare Weyland for punishment over the slave revolt. *A cost too high.* Lady Cassandra's words didn't provoke further demands for the prisoners to be burnt at the stake, however. Some of the Nijumeti murmured almost appreciatively. *Is she trying to help us, or get us executed faster here?*

The Vandian girl shoved Sariel forward and stepped behind Carter, yanking him about roughly by the back of his faded greatcoat. 'While this one, he is a reckless puppy who follows the old dog around on a tight leash. He kept me locked up in his church's basement as though I was little better than a thrall, then, worried Weyland's king might hunt me down and take me for his own, he as good as sold me to the people of the forest. Let both dogs burn for their sins against my person.'

There were more signs of approval from the crowd. A hot-headed thief who dared defy a foreign king, while humbly obeying an elder raider with the wisdom of the ages to impart? Carter suspected the girl was playing a cunning game. Lady Cassandra was singing his praises while making the tune sound like bitter complaints. *And no blue-skinned warrior will want to be seen obeying orders from a recently taken saddle-wife of foreign birth.*

'Enough! You all know the way. Even our recently arrived tent-guest sees what must be done. Let the intruders be tested and Atamva judge!' shouted Temmell, clearly eager not to lose the initiative among the wavering nomads.

Sariel was shoved forward to his pyre where the guards attached his manacles to a short chain on the stake's side. Temmell's supporters among the mob waved torches in the air and whooped with pleasure. Temmell took a lit torch from a warrior's hand and presented it towards the crowd, then stepped forward in front of Sariel's stake. He pressed the torch into the kindling around Sariel's boots and the straw started to catch light, the crowd swaying and chanting. Temmell laughed victoriously and lifted the torch to the air as though an angel might swoop down and lift it from his fingers.

As the warriors behind Carter drove him forward, he realized with a shock that his manacles no longer cut painfully tight. *They've been unlocked!* Had the Vandian girl freed him, or was this some sleight of hand of Sariel's? Carter didn't hesitate. He tore himself away from his two guards and whipped the hanging chain around as a lash, catching the nearest Nijumeti in the face, his boot connecting with the other nomad's gut. The first rider doubled up, the second tumbled over reeling. Carter rushed the remaining few feet towards Temmell. The clan's sorcerer swung the torch around to try to fling it into Carter's face, but as it was the only weapon Temmell possessed, Carter had been expecting the move. Ducking under the burning, tar-wrapped wood, Carter lunged at Temmell. His fingers caught Temmell around the face and he closed them tight against the man's cheeks, eyes and forehead, intending to at least blind his tormentor if nothing else.

Temmell yelled in agony, but it was a torment far beyond a skull being crushed. *Sariel's gift.*

Carter's mind felt as though it had turned to water, gushing out and soaking Temmell with memories and knowledge that did not belong to the young Weylander. *So painful.* Intensity worse than driving daggers filleting Carter's mind. There was nothing he could do; he couldn't control this process. His brain was a dam burst under pressure, crumbling him into pure agony. Both figures struggled together. Nomad guards came sprinting towards Carter to beat him off and slay him. An explosion of light and burning air detonated from a point sparkling between Temmell and Carter, a cannon shell detonating in the air among the mob. Carter recalled a similar explosion in the sky mines, when Sariel had touched Carter, blowing his friends and family across the chamber. The outrush of energy didn't break the pair's physical contact though; for this brief moment, Carter and Temmell were a universe being unravelled, folding out and binding them together. This was far worse for Carter than filling Sariel with what had been lost and forgotten. In Vandia, Carter had burned from a fever and the madness of carrying so many dreams and crazy tales, a walking skeleton desperate for a quick end. Passing the load to Sariel had been a mercy, whatever the pain of the transfer. *But this.* So much raced past. Faces and plagues and lost loves and dead kings and frustrated hopes. Cities and seas and carriers spun from gold, countries that flew through the air and long meadows that stabbed at passing animals with silver acid. *It can't be real. I'm going insane again.* Carter wasn't a key. His mind was a carcass where wasp eggs had been laid to hatch. This was something else again, something far different from his healing of Sariel. It was as if part of Temmell was uncoiling and sliding back into Carter's mind, secreting itself and hiding. At last the trial was over. Carter found himself on the soil, a pile of vomit which had surely originated from his mouth, empty gut or not. Nijumeti struggled across the ground too, crawling like worms as they tried to recover from concussion.

'You wanted to witness my sorcery!' yelled Sariel, as though drunk. The unexpected blast had blown away his pyre's burning straw. Some of it lay smouldering on the canvas roofs of the nomad tents. If it wasn't tackled quickly an intense fire would soon sweep the camp.

'Well, here it is, a spell fit for every blue-blushing jackanapes who doubted Sariel. Eat of it! Drink of it! See how it suits you! I walked with Atamva when the world was fresh and the gods of the Nijumeti danced by the Kappel Sea. And you know it is true, don't you, Temmell Longgate? Because you swam in the surf with Annayla as happy as any of our kind and heard Atamva name me his brother.'

'Enough,' moaned Temmell, getting to his feet while clutching his head. 'You have cursed me, old man.'

'No. I have cured you.'

'They are the same thing,' wailed Temmell as if he was dying still. 'I was happy out here. I had a purpose. I had made a place for myself.'

'You fashioned a prairie-shaped hole to hide in, Temmell. Don't blame the one carrying the ladder to allow you to climb out.'

'Who else is there to blame?'

Warriors sprinted around the tents, beating out flames with blankets.

'Let me re-light their pyre,' begged one of the nomads. What was left of the crowd of onlookers mingled uncertainly now. Their mood broken by this strange, unexpected conflict between sorcerers.

'I should let you burn. I should let us all burn.'

'You were the greatest of us, once. Your powers will return, along with wiser counsel.'

'You remember me better than I remember myself, Sariel Skelbane.'

'You are my friend. A friend never forgets.'

'How much better if you had,' said Temmell.

The Nijumet warrior showed his indignance in a curl of teeth. 'What of the burning, what of the trial?'

Temmell stared with something approaching distaste at the young Weylander, reserving loathing for Sariel. 'They have passed it,' he growled.

'This is a disaster I say,' complained Viscount Wallingbeck.

If Leyla hadn't just had her sport with the clod between the sheets, her ardour would have been quite spoiled now by the fool's whining. Leyla tried to fake interest in the aristocrat's grumbles.

'I need an heir, not a damned duel with my brother-in-law,' said

Wallingbeck. 'With a grandchild to bounce on his knee, old man Landor will keep on paying me. You told me the prosecutor would ask for Willow to be committed to an asylum, not dispatch her to dangle from the gallows like some common street thief. If I am seen to have a hand in the deaths of both of Benner Landor's children, it won't matter if Willow drops triplets in her birthing bed. The old fool will still cut me off without a penny, don't you see?'

You forget I gave him a son, too; a brat so I can rule in his name. 'William, you are a fool,' said Leyla. She stroked the nape of William's neck but what she really felt like doing was slapping some backbone into the dissolute aristocrat. 'You are missing the bigger picture.'

'Which would be . . . ?'

'That I'm the one member of the family inside the House of Landor that Willow *can't* force into defending her honour on the field of combat.'

'I don't understand.'

'Of course you don't and that's what makes our arrangement so mutually advantageous. It's a miracle Duncan is still alive, the amount of times Prince Gyal has dispatched him to the front lines.'

'Doesn't Prince Gyal like the Landor lad? Duncan seems a steady enough fellow on the battlefield. Not a damn shirker or coward like some of the fools I'm expected to lead into battle.'

You only front the gallop because you lack the imagination to do otherwise; a cavalryman to the bone. 'Sadly, someone let slip to Prince Gyal about Duncan and Princess Helrena's rather unservant-like prior relationship. Gyal is as typically Vandian as he is a male. Very keen on the traditions of the imperial harem, but only for himself as emperor, not for Helrena as empress. Gyal doesn't have the gumption to assassinate Duncan in case Helrena finds out. But killed on the battlefield? Such deaths happen every day.'

'But as you say, Duncan is still alive. And now I must face him for grass-before-breakfast.'

Grass-before-breakfast. Yes, the old duelling traditions are still alive in the south. 'I shall visit Duncan before the duel. Explain to him that I have spoken with you and agreed that this travesty of a trial-by-arms must be won by your house, to ensure Willow doesn't walk away free. I will arrange for Duncan to drop his guard so that you may stab him through the right shoulder, rendering him unfit to continue.'

'To first blood in such a public affair? That will not go down well.'

'Not half so well as when you miss Duncan's shoulder and run him through the heart!' laughed Leyla.

'Then, m'dear, the Landors will have two corpses and I will have unpaid gambling debts and creditors pursuing my carriage through the lanes of Arcadia again. Only I will have the addition of another wailing mouth to feed at the house. Or are you proposing to act as my son's wet nurse?' Wallingbeck reached out for her breasts but she slapped his hand away.

'Don't be coarse, William. It's not two corpses I require . . . I need *three*. My dear husband Benner often makes a habit of snoring in his command tent while his artillery company goes about their business. I do believe he could sleep through a hell-storm, that one. So I shall shove Benner into one and discover the truth of the matter. Or rather Nocks will push him off one of Rodal's high cliffs. They have so many of them. About time they were used for something other than sheltering insurrectionists.'

'And then you will be sole heir to the House of Landor,' said William, a modicum of understanding coming to the dolt at last. 'But how much money will you pay to support a Landor-born grandchild?'

So, even the stupidest of mules can be led to water. Let's sweeten the trough. 'How can I put a value on such a thing, William? Willow's baby will be an irrelevance. I think it would be unseemly for a lady in my position to remain a widow for too long, don't you? The war will be over shortly and I will be in need of a new husband to comfort me for the terrible price paid by the House of Landor. How much mightier will the greatest house in the north be after it ties its fortunes directly to one of the oldest and noblest southern lines?'

'As plans go,' said the viscount, 'I like the ring of that one. That sour-faced crimson-hair's dowry was barely enough to restore the mansion.'

Leyla smiled. *Luckily for me, I don't intend keeping your ancient rundown pile after Nocks has slipped a garrotte around your thick neck. Your title is the penultimate stepping stone in the game of respectability. No, I believe the civil war's dying gasp might just be the rebels' revenge assassination of Marcus' pasty-faced little wife. I've tried the king's bed, and it's a lot more comfortable than a viscount's. Far past time my occupancy of it became recognized in law.* Briefly, Leyla wondered how long she would be satisfied with merely sitting next to the throne. *I dare say it will become deadly dull in time.* Well, King Marcus was the most terrible hypochondriac. Wouldn't it be the most delicious of ironies if he actually did succumb to some nasty little illness? *The nation has had enough of kings. Time for a queen, I think.*

Temmell shot a morose stare at Carter before he spoke to Sariel. Carter's eyes drifted back to the sorcerers and away from the scale models of aircraft hanging from the workshop's ceiling timbers.

'So,' said Temmell, 'how in the name of the myriad stars did this whelp of a young Weylander come to be fashioned as a key?'

'Lord Carnehan found our staging post inside the great Vandian stratovolcano. The machines recognized he had come into contact with me and trusted that he might do so again. He was passed everything needed to reconstitute us.'

'If ever there was proof that machines should not be allowed to think,' said Temmell, 'here it is. The machines might as well have imprinted a turnip and tossed the root back into the world. I'm surprised its little brain didn't implode under the pressure of carrying so much.'

'A little compassion, please. It is these people whom we must preserve.'

Temmell glared at Carter, as though blaming him personally for everything that had happened here. 'You should have gone insane.'

'I nearly did,' said Carter.

'A deranged turnip,' muttered Temmell. 'Yes, yes. I will work on the compassion thing, Sariel Skel-bane. Is it worth asking where the ethreaal who should have come looking for us are, to replace us if necessary?'

Sariel shrugged as though the mere absence was answer enough.

Temmell snorted. 'I was going to enquire how the struggle is going, but if we are all that is left, I have answered my own question.'

'I will not lie to you,' said Sariel, 'the stealers have spread everywhere. They stand behind the emperor's throne in Vandia, in Weyland too and no doubt every nation of significance within a million miles of us. They can triangulate the location of an activated gate now. As soon as I close a tunnel the stealers overload the gate to ruination and come haring after me.'

'Oh joy,' said Temmell. 'I do so love walking incognito across Pellas. Well, at least my new Nijumeti skyguard may cut a few centuries off my aimless wanderings.'

'We do not have that long. Your gift and mine will not be enough. We need to find Eremee.'

'I've died at least three times without my memories since the party was ambushed. How would I know where the hell she is now?'

'You and Eremee were close,' said Sariel.

'If you want me to take you to every beach and mountain-top where we ever shared a sunset together, we might as well allow the stealers to end the world now.'

'I visited the ambush site,' said Sariel. 'I found evidence there which suggested you and Eremee might have stayed alive longer than the rest of the expedition.'

'I don't suppose you found a centuries-old message scrawled in blood on a stone telling you where she's hiding?'

'Less triteness *and* more compassion.'

'By the stars, man, I've only recovered for a day. How long did the turnip give you before he started with the pestering?'

'If there's anyone who's been pestered in this arrangement,' said Carter, 'I think it's me.'

'Take that thought, let it fester for a geological age, then you'll have an inkling of how I feel,' said Temmell.

Well, he's talking to me rather than over me. That's got to count as progress. 'What about your patron, Kani Yargul?' said Carter. 'He has united the clans using your advice. There's a horde riding around out here, a horde armed with its own skyguard. You know your history, don't you, Temmell? You understand what happens every time the Nijumeti unite?'

'No, you're not a turnip after all,' said the younger sorcerer. 'I quite enjoy a nice bit of mashed turnip with a side-plate of lamb. Do I know my history? I've *lived* it, whelp!'

'Weyland's rebels are our allies in this fight,' said Sariel. 'As is Rodal.'

'The stealers back one side, we support the other. Are we really fighting another conflict by proxy? This is too tedious for words.'

Carter almost lunged for the arrogant younger sorcerer, but Sariel restrained him. 'How much more tedious for those who have died to assist us, Temmell Longgate?'

'Ah, I remember now. Compassion.'

'The saints rot your compassion,' said Carter. 'I have family and friends back in Rodal.'

'Let them stay there,' sighed Temmell. 'Keep the old game in play, Sariel. I shall let Madinsar and her harpies have their way and set the horde galloping north against Persdad. It will be worth changing strategy just to see the old witch's face as I agree with her plans. Maybe she'll suffer a heart attack from the shock of it.'

Sariel's face turned stern. 'Better if you had never stirred the hornet's nest in the first place.'

'And which of us has the greater taste for mischief?' said Temmell. 'Well, I may not know where Eremee is, but I do possess the map coordinates of a soul-sphere that very well might.'

Sariel spluttered in dismay, as close to outrage as ever Carter had seen the old trickster. 'You sealed off part of yourself? Of all the prohibitions to break!'

'Don't you dare lecture me,' said Temmell. 'I've gone centuries without once remembering Eremee even existed. I would say I possessed good cause to keep a little of myself out of the Unity and stored safely away. You might be happy to rely on the likes of *this*—' he indicated Carter '—to keep you from near-senility, but I'd say that in light of current events, my recovery plan has proved less paranoid and more prophetic, wouldn't you agree?'

'Where did you hide the sphere, you dog?'

'I buried it deep in the shadow of the Rodalian Mountains close to Dalranga.'

'Then let us pray the stealers have not discovered it while you wandered lost.'

Temmell smiled, but he did not seem very happy. 'I think we both know we wouldn't be here if they had.'

'We need to leave the steppes,' said Sariel.

'We shall. But first I will sit in council with Kani Yargul and his captains, settle matters here before I depart. Madinsar will be so over-joyed to see the back of me, she'll probably offer to load my wagon herself and drag it halfway to Rodal to ensure I don't turn back.'

For once, Carter felt a little lift of hope at the sorcerer's words. *Leaving here without being burnt at the stake. That's got to count as a victory, too.*

Carter and Sariel left the sorcerer to settle his arrangements. Out-side Temmell's workshop, they found Sheplar and Kerge waiting.

The Rodalian aviator stood there as still as a statue with his arms crossed. Sariel seemed indifferent to the pilot's presence, but not so Sheplar Lesh. 'Why does it not surprise me that you and Temmell are cut from the same cloth, you old vagrant?'

'Understanding an idiot's mind would make me the dullest creature upon the world,' said Sariel.

'You don't have to worry about scavenging flying wing parts any-more,' said Carter, trying to forestall a fight. 'We'll soon be heading back towards Rodal with a nomad escort to keep us safe.'

'What of the young burno?' said Sheplar.

'For once, we'll ask Lady Cassandra what she wants,' said Carter. 'I owe her that much for slipping me out of my manacles.'

'It was Madinsar who procured the key and instructed the Vandian on what must be done,' explained Kerge.

'Well, the witch rider's got her reward,' said Carter. *Hell, she as good as arranged the future she wanted.* 'Temmell is leaving with us. I have a suspicion Lady Cassandra's answer will involve her staying here with that blue-skinned gallant close by her side.'

'It is a strange thing,' said Sheplar. 'For Rodal to be fighting Wey-land, while finding allies among the nomads.'

'You're not fighting every Weylander,' said Carter. *Maybe a half at most.* Sadly, it was the half with the rifles and mills to churn out more. There was something about Kerge's expression that worried Carter. No longer a thrall here, but almost as unhappy as when the gask and Carter had both been kept as prisoners inside the sky mines. 'You don't want to leave the clans?'

'I have been trying to recover my golden mean,' said Kerge. 'Much has been restored to me under Madinsar's tutelage. I am sure I shall recover the rest by myself in time. But I fear to trust the branches remaining open on the great fractal tree. I hope instead that I am still broken in my gift.'

'Speak your visions clearly,' commanded Sariel.

'Darkness,' said Kerge. 'Darkness closing in and very little light left to walk in.'

'Then I fear you have seen the future as well as any of your kind may,' said Sariel. 'But our end is not guaranteed, Kerge. Not so long as we live to divert it.'

Carter felt the weight of the world slip back on his shoulders again. Somehow, he had thought that reaching Sariel's missing comrade and restoring his memories would be enough by itself. That together Sariel and his old companion could beat the stealers and cast the usurper and the Vandians out of Weyland. Restore the world to how it had been before. Instead, all Carter faced was a long journey and a head full of worries about Willow and his father. Sheplar and Kerge left to pack supplies for the journey back to Rodal.

Sariel watched the pair go and turning back to Carter he seemed to sense his companion's unease. 'How are you bearing up, Lord Carnehan?'

'Physically, I'm fine,' said Carter. 'Whatever work you did to my mind, I am still myself.'

'Exactly as it should be,' said Sariel. 'But I need to give you a second gift. Unlike acting as a key to unlock our memories, this is a gift you will be able to summon at your whim.'

That sounds ominous. 'More responsibility?'

'You may call it that. You have seen how rapidly my body heals itself.'

'I sure wish I had your talent at taking a knife through the heart.'

'Given time, you would not appreciate the long life such a talent also bestows,' said Sariel. 'Always more to do. More duty. There will be a time when duty is not enough. I am going to give you the gift of destroying my healing ability.'

'But that would make you mortal? You could die from bullet or blade?'

'It would and I could.'

'I'd have massive power over you,' said Carter, astonished the old trickster would trust him with such influence.

'I cannot use the gift on myself,' said Sariel. 'My flesh would subvert my own spell even as I tried to cast it. But I can give it to you to use, you who were never born to have it. It's the blackest sort of magic of course. I am not meant to possess it. But when you live for so many years, you have to do something with your time. Breaking rules with a little forbidden research helped keep my mind fresh.'

'Why would you give me this terrible threat to hold over you?'

'Because, Lord Carnehan, the time may come when you will need to kill me. I can give you no guidance on the matter save to say that if that time comes, you will certainly know it.'

Carter was left stunned. *I can't.* 'I don't want such power.'

'I know,' smiled Sariel. 'And that is precisely why I must give it to you. Merely touch me and wish me mortal and I will be changed.'

ELEVEN

PRODDING THE BEAR

'You're steady on the stick,' said Jacob.

The woman in the open cockpit ahead of him glanced around angrily. 'You mean for a woman?' said Anna Kurtain raising her voice over the wind rushing past, disapproval evident in her voice.

Jacob glanced down at the silvery rapids of the White Wolf River. An easy marker for their flying wing to follow. As good as a king's highway for the route he had planned. 'I meant as a Weylander who was never selected by a wind temple's monks for skyguard training.'

'And don't I know it. The skyguard marshal's guards took great joy in stopping me from attending the pilots' briefing in Hadra-Hareer.'

'I got you up here, didn't I?' said Jacob.

'Is flying you meant to be some kind of honour or were none of the skyguard pilots willing to sully their holy kites with the task?'

'One of the two,' said Jacob.

'You know, the Rodalians talk up these blows across the mountains,' said Anna, 'but you try learning to fly above a stratovolcano in something little better than an iron cage with four rotors on it. Constant steam and mist, poisonous outgassings, eruptions, superheated thermals, clouds of flying debris a hundred times hotter than coals from your fireplace, never operating lower than ceiling altitude. Navigating and landing on mining stations only kept in the air by anti-gravity stones. You fly and survive in that while starving on the

Imperium's lumpy slave gruel, then return to Rodal and tell me how hard it is to pilot through a hard gale or two.'

She has a point. And Carter had survived alongside her as a slave. If Jacob still believed in miracles, he might have called her being here alongside him one. Maybe Anna was hoping for another miracle today. Her brother had last been seen by Carter, kept as a slave mechanic on a skel carrier. *We both have our reasons for flying today. Her reasons must seem as pure to her as mine are to me.* Avenging Mary. Avenging all the dead children and townsfolk of Northhaven. The ones buried in the town or left scattered as bleached bones in Vandia's sky mines. *The slavers are used to dishing out hell to unsuspecting victims on the ground. Today I'll serve them at their own feast.*

'Why are you so certain Bad Marcus' mercenary carriers will be in a holding pattern over the Lancean Ocean?' asked Anna.

'Aircraft rated at between three-hundred and four-hundred propellers?' said Jacob. 'Doesn't matter how high they fly to reduce drag, they're drinking a lot of fuel to stay aloft and fly combat missions against Rodal. Even with Bad Marcus' new airfields, there are too many carriers circling to land anywhere close to the number of shuttles needed to stay fuelled. Marcus' tame slavers and privateers usually resupply from ocean smugglers, using seaplanes to ferry fuel up to them. And now they've got the royalist navy sailing north, keeping them provisioned.'

'Before I had a taste of it, I always thought that war was glory and charges, sabres and rifle squares, drums and brigades marching through the streets.'

'That's what everyone thinks,' said Jacob. *Maybe even most the poor sods huddled behind a hedge, never worrying how far the bullets for their rifles and the shells for their cannon have travelled.* 'Any fool can show up for a fight. Showing up rested with a full ammunition pouch and a warm stomach is what separates a corpse from a soldier who gets to limp away and fight the next day.'

'Still seems like a hell of a risk.'

Jacob glanced superstitiously behind him. The sky starling-dark with the cloud of a thousand flying wings, a low drone of engines which made the very air vibrate. Each similar to their own aircraft: a tiny triangle, bright blue with two red stripes on the fuselage, a single small rotor spinning at the back. Some with just a pilot's cockpit, others with an extra space for a spotter or bombardier. Every fighter squadron fit to fly, stripped out from towns they defended, taken from the border fortresses of the steppes, veterans and trainees fresh out of the temple barracks, all conscripted. *Everything has to be timed right, or this will fail spectacularly. This will become the day we lost the war. The hour that the rebellion finally crashed and died.* Rodal. The Walls of the League. The wall that was always defended. The skyguard known for protecting their high villages and towns from nomads and invaders and slavers. Defenders who are always there to protect their people. For century after century. *That's what everyone knows. And now I'm going to show the world something different.* Or rather, Jake Silver was. Quicksilver.

'This isn't on me,' whispered Jacob. 'Marcus turned my home into a charnel house first. All I'm doing is showing him how to do the job properly.'

'What did you say?' Anna called back.

'Time to prod the bear,' said Jacob. *Why carry a stick, otherwise?*

'See if it wants a dance?'

'See if it wants a *chase*,' said Jacob.

There was fog shifting below now, reminding Jacob how close they were to the Lancean Ocean. *Always fogs, here.* Redwater Harbour became visible through the drifting white murk. The closest port to the Rodalian front, the White Wolf River feeding into it. Vital for ferrying supplies by riverboat across the length of Havenharl. Bad Marcus had seized the harbour immediately after the royalist navy sank the bulk of parliament's ships east of the Rotnest Islands. *But then, it's easy to sink ships when you're supported by a skyguard and you claim mastery of the air.*

'You know,' said Anna, 'there will be a lot of sailors on those ships below who didn't ask to be there. Just following their skipper after their vessel declared for the royalist navy or came over after what was left of parliament's fleet surrendered. And that's a northern harbour down there.'

'Did you ask when your town along the Lakes was raided by slavers and you watched your family killed and taken?' said Jacob.

'That's your answer?'

'Not an answer. Not a reason. There's only a question. How badly do you want to beat Bad Marcus and his Vandian masters?'

'You know the answer to that,' Anna growled.

'Then I reckon you have your answer, too.'

'May the saints forgive me.'

'Damned if they possess the right,' said Jacob. *Damned if anyone does.*

Each flying wing had been loaded with at least two bombs, some as many as four, making the tiny triangular-shaped aircraft as manoeuvrable as a brick with a propeller at the back. *Pray that we're lighter when we need to be.* The Rodalians' ordinance was little better than shrapnel-packed grenades, manufactured to scatter, kill and maim charging nomad horsemen, not hole sailing ships. Luckily, while the Vandians' massive downed aerial warship's main arsenal detonated when she collided with Hadra-Hareer's peaks, her aft arsenal had been discovered intact with shells for the vessel's smaller guns. *Recovered and put to a far better use than serving the empire.* Jacob had seen one of the captured shells from the wreckage of *The Caller* test-exploded on Hadra's slopes. Chemists inside the Rodalian city were at a loss to explain the warhead's composition, a thick putty-like paste that made nitro-glycerine seem as harmless as watered down rice wine. But then, Jacob didn't need to understand how a cat caught mice, just as long as his grain store stayed intact.

'We're lead hawk,' said Anna. 'Give the order.'

The fog had a sea-salt smell to it. Jacob felt a brief twinge of homesickness. *How many times did I watch fog like this roll up past the monastery at Geru Peak?* Fog which hid the mountains opposite. Hidden Jacob, much like the ancient church order, when he had most needed it. *How much better if I had stayed there.* Never left to become pastor of Northhaven. But that was a lie as bad as any of the untruths Jacob told himself. The slavers would still have come. The rebellion against Bad Marcus too. And finally the Vandians. *Would I have stayed a monk, far away from the weight of the world, with Weyland tearing itself apart in civil war? Saints how I wish you were still here, Mary. That I had been a different man and we had settled in a different town.* His dead wife failed to answer him. *She's given up on me, too. Or maybe I'm as dead as she is. As dead as the family we buried together.* Jake Silver was what had been spat out. Exactly who he was cursed to be. *And some curses are just meant to be shared.*

'Your command, *General* Carnehan?'

Jacob checked his pocket-watch. *This won't be the worst of it.* 'Sink every vessel; merchant and naval, both. Leave the town, harbour and mouth of the river so wrecked they won't be able to run so much as a rowing boat through their waters.'

The fog concealed the prize below, just as it masked the massed Rodalian skyguard, muffled the sound of the squadrons' engines, too. But not their whine as they angled away and started to dive. That had to be loud enough to start a panic below. The white wall vanished behind them as Anna broke through, angling to the horizontal, giving Jacob a good look at everything he needed to see. The harbour was so packed with the king's business that most of the local fishing boats and kelpers had been ordered outside the docks. Maybe sixty or seventy three-masted merchant barques moored up or at anchor, the largest class that could ship seven hundred tonnes of cargo. They were surrounded by thousands of tubby little hog boats, the hoggies' decks packed with barrels of fuel ether. A small fleet of doreys rowed fresh food and transported crews between water and town. Jacob counted five frigates, seven heavy gunboats and an ironclad wheel-ship protecting the mouth of the harbour in the shadow of the sea fort. There should have been more escorts, but any vessel still flying the flag for parliament and Prince Owen was as good as a pirate in these waters now. Currently clinging to the dark rocks of the Rotnest Islands for protection. Down by the river mouth beyond there were hundreds of flying boats taking on cargo, lined up along both river banks like a long chain of hungry ducklings. *Hungry for fuel. Fuel that burns real well inside an engine – or out.*

Jacob leant forward, tapping Anna on the shoulder. He indicated the wheel-ship sitting low in the water. A recent metal-built monstrosity, steel-hulled, every ounce of her heavy Vandian metal paid for in Weylander blood. 'Lighten your load.'

'I think that's the *Gadquero Ironside*,' said Anna. 'She sank five of the assembly's ships-of-the-line when our fleet retreated after the fall of Midsburg.'

'Send her to join our people.'

Anna nodded and banked the flying wing towards the vessel, fixing a straight line of sight on the target, hundreds of barque sails flapping below them as they shot over the harbour.

Sailors sprinted to man heavy rifle mountings along the warship's deck, a hail of bullets whistling past Jacob's flying wing as they angled closer, but Anna was practically cleaning her undercarriage against the waves. She banked erratically, giving the sailors a rapidly-twisting target to practise on. None of the altitude-timed fused shells from the vessel's big guns could explode low enough against their aircraft. Jacob ignored the slap and hiss of hot shrapnel raining in the water behind them. *Just the same as a rifle square marching against cannons. Nothing you can do but put one boot in front of the other. Pray it's the soldier in the squad next to yours who catches it in the neck.*

Anna snapped up at the last second, sending all four bombs skip-bouncing towards the ironclad. The first hit the vessel on her massive steel ram, the second burst against a box-battery on top, with the remaining two bombs slamming into her hull above the waterline. Vandia's shells had caused carnage on the Rodalian city clinging to the capital's twin peaks – they proved just as effective when returned to sender. Fire and flames from the detonations chased Jacob up into the air, deafening him, the flying wing shaking in a wave of furious turbulence. For a moment, it looked like Anna was going to lose control of the aircraft, but she wrestled it back into level flight. Their aircraft was newly blessed and released to the skyguard by the temple artisans. Nobody but Anna had flown in it before. Jacob turned to examine the flat fuselage behind him. Burn marks in front of the single rear-mounted rotor and holes flapping in the fabric where bullets had torn through. *They'll know she's been blessed when we return her.* Then he caught sight of the ironclad. Only the fish would be enjoying the *Gadquero Ironside*'s company; cracked along the three metal welds of her hull's construction, sinking under the water in front of the harbour mouth. As good as any scuttling for denying Bad Marcus access to his landing. Her destruction had more or less sealed the narrow entrance to the harbour. Not that any ship could navigate now through the crowded water enclosed by Redwater's piers and jetties. Hundreds of flying wings dipped in and out above a sea of fire and burning sails, broken barques exploding from full cargo holds, sailors leaping from decks remade as an inferno. Docks and quays shattered under the product of the Imperium's stolen arsenal. Taverns and warehouses and fishing markets stood only as dark silhouettes among the burning conflagration. He could barely see the figures stumbling blindly through the pall of smoke, tumbling as wing guns chattered and broke the narrow streets into a deadly haze of flying masonry and broken cobblestones.

Anna banked south, taking them close to the sea fort. Heavy fortress walls running up a slope behind the granite breakwater protecting Redwater Sound. They were trying to raise barrage balloons from towers along the crenellated walkways but hadn't received any warning of the attack. *Complacent. That's what happens when one side has almost absolute control of the air. You come to believe that everything in the sky has to be friendly.* Rodal had never mounted anything like this. And Weyland had never seen any attacks on this scale. Gunnery crews reached the wall cannons fixed inside armoured casemates, ramming shells inside the muzzles, others charging them with powder while their compatriots raised the big guns' elevation. The guns had hardly spoken before they were answered by dark plunging silhouettes, a squadron of skyguard pilots piercing through the fog cloud and dive-bombing the sea fort's roof. Jacob had ordered the largest bombs to be preserved for this task. Almost things of beauty. Engravings of Vandian military triumphs on the brass shell-casings, warheads moulded with the exaggerated visages of the Imperium's most famous emperors and generals. The same hideous steel faces that slammed into the sea fort's curtain wall, barracks and barbican, sending them rising into the fog on spouts of fire as fierce shockwaves rippled out, the closest buildings in the town crumpling in the blast.

Anna's flying wing overflew Redwater proper, moss-covered slate rooftops whisking past. Right in the centre of the walled city was a squat thick-walled building with the narrow metal triangle of a radio tower rising from its centre.

'Leave the Radio Guild's hold intact,' called Jacob. *I need them to call for help. Long and loud.*

Anna raised her flying goggles and wiped her eyes. 'This isn't a battle, it's a bloody slaughter. Against one of our own towns.'

'No, this was never going to be a battle.' *It's just prodding the beast.*

Out by the river mouth, the line of flying boats moored on the shoreline had been transformed into a blazing conflagration by skyguard bombs. A handful of flying boats were taxiing along the river, trying to build up speed to escape, but even with multiple propellers and powerful engines, the fully laden shuttles were no match for the tiny Rodalian flying wings. Planes dived on them, wing guns chattering, and Jacob watched the store of fuel barrels ignite on one craft, its floats blown spinning across the water as its wooden body disintegrated.

Anna tapped the fuel gauge on her instrument panel. 'We either need to head home now or pray the mountain wind's blowing in a good direction for gliding the last sixty miles.'

'I'm out of the praying business,' said Jacob. 'Push above the fog for a look-see.'

The single engine mounted behind them roared throatily as Anna angled the flying wing up again, a quick moist slap of cool air as they breached the fog-bank, and then the fog was below them like a long snowfield, crimson in places where flames below reflected off the thinnest layers. Clear sky and an unimpeded view of dark silhouettes emerging from the sun. They could have been fighters the same size as a Rodalian flying wing, but only if you confused distance and scale. Carriers; still miles away. Every skel slaver on this side of Pellas and a few of the larger free companies and air pirates. Jacob carefully counted the formation using his folding brass telescope. 'There they are. Twelve in total. Nine skel raiders, two freebooters and a mercenary carrier.'

'How the hell can you tell that at this distance?' asked Anna.

'Count them when they fly nearer if you like.'

'They're climbing for height,' said Anna. 'Looking for a killing edge when they launch their squadrons.'

Jacob consulted his watch. *Cutting it fine, but just enough time left.* 'Back below the fog. Show our pilots the signal smoke.'

'Green smoke, aye,' said Anna. 'And exactly what's the smoke signalling, *General* sir?'

'I'd say it's time to flee from that angry bear we've roused.'

'Well, you've presented Bad Marcus with a hell of a butcher's bill,' said Anna. 'Set the waves on fire and left a thousand dead Weylanders bobbing in our waters. Are we going to live long enough to call this dirty massacre a victory?'

'Wouldn't be a victory if we didn't. Set your compass for the airfields at Salasang.'

Anna's plane plunged below the fog cover, spewing green smoke from canisters under her fuselage. They passed a flickering sea of fire below, town and harbour, barques and flying boats, all aflame and filling the sky with dirty black smoke, hardly anything moving worth being considered a target of opportunity. The skyguard pilots had been anticipating Jacob's signal, and seeing it painting the roof of fog, rapidly peeled off. Anna's flying wing soon dragged an aerial armada behind her thin contrail. *Same number of kites we arrived with, best I can tell.* The skyguard's casualties were yet to be tallied. *Soon enough.*

'Is Salasang able to receive this number of flying wings?' asked Anna.

'Eastern Rodal has stayed clear of the war,' said Jacob. 'They're still fresh. It's the capital that Vandia and Bad Marcus are trying to put under siege.'

'Never been to Salasang. Hope their ramparts have enough cannons to fight off a flock of angry carriers.'

The wind carried the massed skyguard force north-east, past snow-topped mountains all too familiar to Jacob. *I wandered among these valleys and peaks once, with Brother Frael. Carrying out works of quiet charity in the hope of polishing the name of the saints among the Rodalians.* A lifetime away, now. Perhaps two.

Jacob gazed behind him, watching the enemy until his neck began to ache. The massive carriers were still riding high and fast, being dragged along by the winds of the upper atmosphere. Gaining on the fleeing skyguard force with every minute that passed. Roasting that far up, the raw sunlight turning portholes into bright white mirrors, wooden propellers gleaming as though they were polished sabre steel. 'They haven't launched their fighter wings yet.'

'They won't,' growled Anna. 'Their fighters are hitching a ride, fuel-free, on those big momma birds. They're fools if they don't know we'll be sucking on fumes soon enough.'

'Go lower,' said Jacob. 'Down into the valleys.'

'I can buzz the damn alpine forest clinging to those mountains and dodge trees for you,' said Anna, 'but the enemy carriers will maintain line of sight on us from their position. We need to climb to the same altitude as those wooden whales if we're to stand a chance of escaping. Shed gravity and drag.'

'Lower,' Jacob insisted. She reluctantly obeyed.

'Saints' teeth,' said Anna, fighting her stick, 'but there's a hellish updraught rising off this valley. Staying this low I'm burning more fuel than I set on fire back at Redwater.'

'Just keep flying north-east.'

'Scraping treetops, we're never going to shake off the pursuit this way,' warned Anna. 'We need to climb for height, run light and find a strong trade wind to push us along. These are skyguards we're flying with. They should be able to whistle up well-intentioned wind spirits faster than a crew of evil skels, mercenaries and air pirates.'

'I'll take it under advisement. Now just keep going,' Jacob repeated. He gazed at the valley floor fleeting past below, catching sight of the Great Northern Road winding through a series of streams flowing off the heights, a series of low arched bridges and shallow fords bubbling with trout. *I lived a life here, once. It wouldn't be so bad to die here.*

'You may be the notorious Burn warlord who never lost a battle, but hell if you know anything worth spit about skyguard tactics,' swore Anna. 'We can't canyon-run or mountain-twist our way out of this mess. The skel squadrons have the jump on us: they're diving out of the sun with height and speed on their side. Look at those carriers – they reckon they've won! They're drifting down on top of us, too. Do you know how many ball-turrets and fuselage guns one of those flying cities mount? They're going to rip us to pieces and we don't carry nearly enough fuel to outrun them. Try to dogfight and we'll be dropping out of the sky with empty tanks while their kites are merrily topping up inside their carriers.'

Jacob stared up at the slowly descending carriers, each town-sized aircraft seemingly shielded behind hundreds of blurred rotors, dozens of squadrons launching from hangars under each massive wing. Fast single-prop fighter aircraft. Slavers. The same killers who had murdered Mary Carnehan and left half a town full of corpses for Jacob to bury at Northhaven, abducting the youngest survivors as human chattel. *Looking to finish the job, now.*

Duncan Landor found it hard to give credit to how much Northhaven had changed since the arrival of the southern army and its allies. Every time he returned from the front line in Rodal his town looked less like home. Where once there had been fields of grain and patchwork farmland stretching to the horizon – most of it owned by the House of Landor – now there were massive military camps, line after line of white tents, royalist army regiments marching, drilling, lined up and hammering at paper targets. He could tell from the soldiers' young faces that they badly needed the practice. This time last year many of these untested men would have been standing behind counters in shops, working their family's farm, or toiling in some clacking, smoke-filled mill for a southern aristocrat. Now they filled freshly dyed blue uniforms while being yelled at by slightly older soldiers, what passed for veterans themselves mobilized from territorial guard units and local militias. Out by the river, the airfield had been extended into acres of runways and hangars filled with squadrons of Weyland's skyguard, their pilots and aircrews barely old enough to shave. The skyguard flats extended right up to the railhead now, itself a hive of activity as arriving trains piled crate-mountains of supplies shipped up from the Deep South. Only the Vandian barracks appeared slightly more permanent. The Imperium's legionaries had used machines to fell half the woodland beyond the town, riding tracked diggers that moved massive quantities of soil, constructing sprawling log forts and earthworks with a speed that must have astonished every local labourer yet to be drafted.

Duncan stopped for a second, Paetro by his side, to gaze at the low rolling hills to the east, the stumps of thousands of sawn tree-trunks dotting the bare slopes like unshaven chin bristle. *I fought a duel against Carter up there in Rake's Meadow. And today I'm to fight another one, courtesy of my conniving sister.* Unlike Duncan's previous fight, this wouldn't be any illicit affair settled in the wilderness. A fencing square had been set aside inside the Army of the Boles' camp for the two participants. There would be judges and doctors on hand and no doubt every officer with enough pull in the southern army to secure a place watching.

'You know, lad,' said Paetro, 'back in the empire a duel such as this would be displayed on the kino screens for everyone's amusement.'

'Well, at least having my brother-in-law trying to fillet me will make a change from Prince Gyal dispatching me to lead every suicidal charge mounted.'

'It's only suicide if you die.'

'What is it called if you don't?' asked Duncan.

'Battle experience.'

His friend had a dark turn of humour. 'A court-sanctioned duel,' continued Duncan. 'It wasn't so long ago that you'd be arrested by the constables in Northhaven for clashing steels and wounding a man in a matter of honour.'

'Ah, you have a strange system out here in the back of beyond. The threat of a just duel helps keep the rest of the law honest. You're a lot less likely to cheat a citizen if you know they might come after you with a sabre or dagger. Besides, people need blood. It's in their nature.'

Their blood I don't need. Not least this spiteful foolishness contrived by Willow. Duncan saw his father approaching in an artillery officer's uniform. It looked as if it had been cleaned and pressed especially for the occasion. Benner Landor nodded stiffly to Paetro before addressing Duncan. 'This is an evil business, son.'

'It appears Willow has everyone dancing to her tune again,' noted Duncan, bitterly.

'If she wasn't carrying William's child, I'd have disowned her for this,' said Benner. 'And just as soon as Willow has given birth, she will be disowned. My grandson is the last thing she has to offer the Landors. After that, I have no daughter worthy of the name. Running away from her husband, taking up with the rebels and supporting the pretender, carrying on with that damned Carnehan boy as a common adulteress. And now this! Manipulating her trial. Refusing to face the consequences of her dark deeds. Pitting brother against husband out of spleen and malice. This is the only time in my life I am glad that Lorenn isn't here. To see what became of Willow. To see just what her daughter has grown into.'

She grew into what you made her, Father, thought Duncan, resigned

309

to the fight now. *Your greed and overbearing stupidity. The futility of this civil war only finished the process the mighty House of Landor started.*

'Leyla has come to see you?' asked Benner. 'Concerning her arrangement for thwarting Willow's wicked scheme?'

'She has,' said Duncan. *Arrangement. That's a gentle word for it. And if you knew the energetic fun Leyla had in convincing me, I reckon you would be in the market for another ridiculously young bride to ignore while you're locked away counting your wealth.*

'Then it is settled. It sits badly with me that a Landor should fight less than his best, but in this matter it seems to be a choice between two evils, and so we must choose the lesser one.'

Easy to say when it's not you throwing the fight, Father. 'You can rest easy. I won't let Willow off the hook.'

Benner Landor nodded curtly and set off towards the field of honour.

That's all I need. Him watching this too. I just hope he keeps his mouth shut and can stop himself shouting advice. Duncan halted, staring at the rank of soldiers his father had passed through. 'It can't be!'

'What is it?' asked Paetro.

'I thought I saw Nocks over there. Glaring towards my father.'

Paetro's gaze drilled across the soldiers. 'Your father's manservant? That treacherous dog your sister seduced into trying to murder you inside Midsburg?'

'The same.' Duncan stared at the drilling soldiers, but there was no sign of the odious little creature among the troops. Duncan walked across to the tents and gazed around, row after row of them stretching to the end of the camp, soldiers seated by camp fires, cleaning rifles, sharpening bayonets and brushing down their horses. *No sign of Nocks, though. Am I so nervous I am imagining things now?*

Paetro grimaced. 'If Nocks is still under your sister's spell, he's probably here to make mischief at the duel. To try to free Willow if things go badly for her.'

'Oh, they'll go badly for Willow.' *I'll see to that.*

'I'll keep my eyes peeled for that turncoat,' said Paetro, patting his pistol holster. 'You just watch out for yourself, Duncan of Weyland.'

I can hear the disapproval in your voice. 'It's the only way,' said Duncan. 'If I am put out of the fight, then the trial's verdict will go

310

against Willow. How could I win the duel and let my sister walk free, laughing at me?'

'As crimes go, fixing the outcome of a duel is as foul as it gets inside Vandia. And being put out of a fight is most often fatal.'

'Yes, but as you pointed out, we're not in Vandia and us locals are a strange bunch.'

'Just stay strange and alive, lad. To hell with these schemes and plots. All an honest soldier ever needed is an honest fight.'

'There can't be much more fighting left,' said Duncan. 'The war's over in Weyland and the tide's turned in Rodal. We have superior numbers and weapons. Veteran legionaries and Marcus' regiments against yak herders with antique rifles. Another mile of Rodal falls every day. The time is coming when the pretender will be killed or captured. I wouldn't be surprised if what's left of the rebellion retreats from Rodal as easily as it abandoned Weyland. Flees for one of the neutral countries like Hellin or Tresterer.'

'That'll be a day worth downing a beer or two,' said Paetro.

Duncan knew his friend didn't really give a fig about finishing King Marcus' war up in the mountains. Paetro cared even less about salvaging Prince Gyal's reputation. Victory to Paetro looked a lot like a grave filled with Jacob Carnehan's corpse. *And what will victory look like for me, if that jealous devil Gyal doesn't manage to march me in front of a bullet before war's end? Exiled to Weyland and kept a million miles apart from Helrena? A long, dangerous trip out to the steppes to bring Cassandra to Hawkland Park. And then what? Watching Leyla raise my nephew while my father plays at being the doting parent. Good old Duncan back to being a skivvy for the House of Landor, jumping to his father's every command. Receiving reports of Gyal enjoying the imperial throne with Helrena sitting loyally by his side. How will that feel like victory? Even when I win, I fail. And first the humiliation of having to lose a duel to win it.*

Duncan and Paetro reached the duelling square. A parade field had been roped off, an empty flagpole in the corner. There were seats for the judges, lawyers, defendant and what looked like half the general staff of the Army of the Boles. Others milled behind the ropes. The crowd wasn't limited to blue-uniformed soldiers from the southern regiments. Duncan noted skels and a ragtag collection of mercenaries among their numbers. It was customary for the challenged party to have choice of weapons, but as both parties were fighting today under the ancient laws of trial by combat, the court had made the selection. Duncan was glad they had selected sabres over pistols. *Far easier to fix a fight with steels instead of bullets.*

'In you go, lad,' said Paetro, standing aside. 'Be it death or be it victory.'

There was the ancient Vandian toast. *I'll settle for losing with a light wound.* Duncan entered the square. Wallingbeck already waited inside, wearing the full dress cavalry uniform of a duty squadron: a blue shell jacket with stand-up collar, gold piping and twelve gleaming brass buttons, with the viscount's dark trousers meeting a pair of tall black leather boots just below the knees. Duncan's Vandian officer's uniform felt simple by comparison. The only thing they shared were their empty pistol holsters.

The loud voice of the court-appointed adjudicator called the spectators to silence. 'This combat is subject to the rules of Trial by Ordeal under Conciliar Jurisdiction of the Prefecture. Neither party is to quit their positions under any circumstances, without leave or direction of the court. There are no seconds here. I, solely, will call combat to start, pause and to end.' He flicked an officious finger and a Weyland corporal came trotting into the ring bearing a brace of officer's curved steel swords, each steel with a wooden grip, metal hilt and a three-bar swept-brass handle.

'You pick first,' said Wallingbeck, graciously.

'If I had my choice, I'd pick not to fight,' said Duncan, grasping the nearest sword.

The viscount took the remaining sabre, testing the air with its blade. 'And then how we would amuse your sister and my wife, eh?'

The viscount seemed in better sorts about this forced duel than Duncan. *But he's not the dupe expected to throw the fight.* Duncan found Willow standing to the side of the judges, four soldiers as her escort. Her eyes looked curiously blank, as if she didn't quite believe she had actually managed to coerce this little legal farce into being. *You expect me to make you a merry widow, do you, Sister? Clear your name of all your dark treacheries in the process. Let's see if I can't live to disappoint you.* He looked to locate Leyla among the crowd, but there was no sight of her among the bobbing mass of faces. *Women and their delicacies. Leyla probably can't bear to watch me locking swords with her old family friend.* Still no sign of Nocks, either, but he spotted a group of privateers down from the *Plunderbird*, including an old dark-bearded man who looked a lot like Black Barnaby. *Never expected to see him outside of the wanted posters. It's a hell of a world. I'm expected to slice chunks out of my own brother-in-law, while it is Jacob Carnehan's damned brother who saves me from being killed by Prince Gyal's machinations. I wonder how much those pirates of his have wagered on the outcome of this? I could repay Black Barnaby for saving my life at Ganyid Thang by warning him this bout is rigged.*

'Remember your courage with every step,' bid the adjudicator, raising an officer's white glove into the air. He dropped his hand. 'Commence!'

Wallingbeck was well-trained in the art of fencing . . . no doubt the product of many years' sweat inside Arcadia's fencing halls. He stamped forward rapidly, keeping his sabre pointed outward in his right hand, left hand back loose in the air. Duncan had almost forgotten the manner in which duels were conducted inside Weyland, so long and thorough had been his Vandian training, Paetro drumming the legion's skills into his thick head, borrowing spare time with Cassandra's instructors. *Vandia has a different sequence of stances and guards with names such as the Ox, the Fool, the Plough and the Roof. But then, duels in the Imperium are almost always fatal.* The two men's blades clattered loudly against each other. Wallingbeck was testing Duncan's skills. A little prod, a little probe, getting a feel of his opponent. Duncan yielded but didn't give ground, using a technique called the Waterfall. Wallingbeck quickly grew bored of the testing and started to make more decisive lunges, Duncan responding with lateral parries that warded off the worst of the blows' energy. They circled each other, accompanied by the yelling of the crowd. Duncan noted that most of the calls seemed to be in favour of Wallingbeck. *I knew I shouldn't have worn a Vandian uniform.* But he wasn't here to toady his way into the crowd's affections.

'Let's give the mob a show, then,' snarled Wallingbeck, his sabre flicking forward towards Duncan's face.

Duncan side-stepped and turned the man's blade. 'Just remember why we're here.'

Wallingbeck pressed his attack again. 'Be damned if it's not a duel.'

Just how realistic does he want to make this?

Wallingbeck lunged with real strength and Duncan broke the attack before responding with a quick riposte. Duncan's style was blunt but direct, nothing theatrical about it compared to this southern gentleman's.

'You've picked up a thing or two while you were inside the Imperium,' noted Wallingbeck.

'I'll let you into a secret . . . I wasn't that shabby before I left.'

Wallingbeck pressed the attack again and Duncan circled around, the steels breaking against each other in angry little explosive cracks. 'But you fight like a soldier, not a gentleman.'

'How does a gentleman fight?'

Wallingbeck made a quick, intricate sequence of thrusts. Duncan barely turned his foe's blade. Wallingbeck waved the tip of his sabre as though writing a message in the air. 'When you no longer have to ask, you'll know.'

The tempo of their fight increased the longer it went on, crossovers, step-lunges, back and forth, lunge, parry, his clothes damp and tight. Duncan realized he was sweating, his arms aching. *How long has this been going on for now? Ten minutes. Are we to fight into sheer exhaustion?*

Their swords sprung off each other, Duncan's blade bouncing to the right. They locked eyes and Duncan saw what the viscount expected. *This duel's gone on for long enough. Honour has been satisfied. The mob have had their fun.* Duncan saw the chance to let Wallingbeck put his sabre through his shoulder, and he slightly slowed his counter strike. *It should only take a second.* The aristocrat recovered his balance from the clash and lunged forward – *that seems* – just as someone shrieked from the crowd, 'It's a trick, Duncan – he's going to skewer you!' – far *too low!*

Duncan twisted to the side and the blade missed his heart but sliced deep into his right side instead, an explosion of pain and blood from the biting wound. Duncan watched wide-eyed surprise distort the viscount's face as the man realized his blade was embedded and trapped inside Duncan's body and the young Weylander was still alive. The expression changed to shock as Duncan tumbled forward and drove his own sword through the viscount's chest, taking Wallingbeck exactly where he had clearly been aiming to strike Duncan. Walling-beck stumbled back, staring at the sabre driven through him, its tip emerging from his spine, and then he fell forward with a dying gurgle, hitting the grass. Duncan stared dumbfounded at his opponent's sword left impaled inside his gut, blood gushing over it, then he too keeled over, trying to stay on his knees. *That wasn't meant to happen. And he's killed me too.* Grey circles expanded across his vision, obscuring the sight of surgeons running on to the field, the yelling crowd pushing their way through the makeshift barrier. The final confusion that passed through Duncan's mind before blackness claimed him was that the shouted warning had come from his sister.

'I swear I'll take one of those carriers down with me,' snarled Anna, pulling their plane around for a suicide run right down the throat of the nearest aerial leviathan.

'Another day,' said Jacob. 'I'm not looking to destroy the carrier fleet.'

'What—?' The answer to the pilot's half-formed question came from the walls of the valley and mountains, thousands of soldiers throwing aside camouflaged hides, sprinting madly down the slope before leaping into the air, cloth stabilizer fins flapping between their legs to balance the three-box kites strapped like wings above their shoulders. Suddenly the sky was filled with human darts riding thermals, entire regiments corkscrewing up towards the enemy carriers.

'Because they're of more use to me captured as prizes.'

Land Master Namdak Galasang had taken quite a chance, pulling this many troops back from the fighting around Hadra-Hareer, stripping the border forts facing the steppes of so many defenders. *Let's see if his new-found appetite for risk pays off.*

Anna gazed in shock at the troops suddenly filling the air. They couldn't fail to have been spotted from the enemy carriers' bridges, but with each carrier the size and weight of an aerial city they were already too well-committed to their descent. 'What the hell do you call that?'

'War kites,' said Jacob. 'The real kind, rather than the nickname for a flying wing.'

Jacob remembered his first encounter with the cunningly crafted man-lifters. After he had found a quarter of the lead tiles missing from his monastery's roof at Geru Peak, picked off during the night by thieves strapped under box-kites. Mastering the sky in a kite was something of a rite of passage for most of the youngsters in the mountain villages.

Anna shook her head ruefully. 'You son of a bitch, you planned this all along! Redwater was never the target . . .'

'You should have checked your charts more carefully, Miss Kurtain. These valleys are called Heaven's Ladder for a reason. When you attend a wedding around here, you write your blessings to the happy couple on rice paper. Release it into the wind and it ends up being carried north-west all the way back to the ocean.'

'Our own port city raised to the ground. Thousands dead! For this . . .'

'For *that*. There's your prize,' said Jacob, indicating a huge skel carrier filling the sky. Eight long wings stacked on either side at the front, another four wings towards the carrier's rear, the spinning discs of at least four hundred propellers – each a dozen times bigger than any Northhaven windmill – a blurred promise of death. Never meant to land on the soil. An eagle of the upper atmosphere, raiding the ground for its succour.

Anna's eyes narrowed as she recognized the same carrier configuration that had raided her home and taken her as a slave. It probably occurred as frequently in Miss Kurtain's nightmares as it appeared in Jacob's. *But this scum faced a simple pastor last time they visited. A pastor and streets full of terrified townspeople. My wife, my son, my town's children and neighbours. Let's see how you skels fare when we know you are coming. When we've prepared a proper greeting for you.*

'James,' she whispered half in prayer.

'Someone who knows their way around machines is a valuable commodity,' said Jacob. *Valuable enough not to be sold on as a slave to the Vandians.* 'Chances are . . .'

'You think this squares us for what you did to me after the fall of Midsburg?'

'Find your brother alive in that flying hell-hole first, then you tell me,' said Jacob.

'Sometimes I think Owen is right. You're more dangerous than the slavers, the usurper and the Imperium lumped together.'

'Your prince isn't wrong,' said Jacob. 'But as long as that danger is focused on his enemies, I reckon he'll stomach me.'

Anna pointed her flying wing's nose towards the carrier's belly. 'Is there anything you won't do to win?'

Jacob didn't answer. Perhaps because he didn't know the answer to that himself – and there was still a part of him that didn't want to understand.

The turn rate on the diving enemy squadrons was superior to the sluggish carriers, but as the skel fighters tried to angle away from the storm of thousands of kite-borne attackers, the bandit pilots discovered the valley's thermals catapulting soldiers at them faster than they could shed drag. The skel aircraft were as gaudy as a traveller's caravan, each fighter stained with rainbow bright bars, unfamiliar animals portrayed across the fuselage as elaborate as any sailor's tattoos. The enemy faced three full regiments of war-kites reinforcing the massed skyguard, close to a thousand flying wings. These were Rodalian pilots. Rodalian soldiers. Born to the wind. Blessed by the wind. Embraced by the storm. They could fly in a hurricane that would strip the wings off another nation's aircraft. *They are the hurricane.*

The skyguard and the war-kites didn't so much attack the lurid enemy squadrons as dance around them, Rodalian flying wings buffeted by turbulence while performing elegant barrel rolls and breaks, seemingly turning by magic on pursuit curves that sent skel monoplanes drifting in front of their wing guns. A brief chatter of fire, followed by explosions, bandit planes blown apart, falling from the sky on plumes of dirty black smoke. *And there's your disadvantage of flying heavy on full tanks.* Cross-turns, defensive splits, roll-aways; there wasn't a manoeuvre the skyguard pilots hadn't mastered during their strict temple training to be considered worthy of a plane. The skels, free company and air pirates, by contrast, were used to strafing ground-based peasants in kingdoms where the only planes to be seen were merchant aircraft passing overhead; where a solid air defence was a cocked crossbow behind a log rampart.

'I'm nearly out of fuel,' warned Anna.

Then so is everyone else on our side. 'That's fine and dandy. I said we were setting our compass for Salasang – never said we'd put in there. Our landing field is a tad closer to home.' Jacob pointed at the closing carrier, her hangars built into base wings on either side of the massive aircraft. An eyrie for the enemy fighter squadrons. *They won't be needing it.*

War-kite-wearing troops dodged and ignored the duelling aircraft, for the most part, riding straight up into the carriers' flight paths. A few soldiers disregarded Jacob's instructions and weaved among the enemy squadrons, pumping pistol and carbine shots into skel cockpits. Enemy pilots slumped forward dead on the stick, fighters veering out of control and diving into the mountainside. Most of his force followed through in the agreed plan. There was obviously panic and confusion inside the carrier formation, their battle scheme thrown into disarray. Half the cannons in the leviathans' gun ports and turrets didn't open fire on the approaching cloud of soldiers. The ones that did open up failed to find their targets – warriors weaving in and out, too small, too fast. The skels would have had more luck emptying their magazines into a swarm of locusts. Then the war kites were upon the carriers, soldiers grabbing the fuselage, embedding themselves into canvas-skin with hand claws, drawing slender, curved sword blades – thirty inches of low-carbon steel – ripping their way through and surging inside the carrier's corridors and cabins. For a moment, the nearest bandit carrier looked more like the dead corpse of an animal, her flesh crawling with ants, and then she destroyed the illusion by pulling up, slowly, slowly. The soldiers had been instructed to leave war-kites tethered to the fuselage in the event their boarding action failed and they needed to abandon the bandit carrier. In a dis-play of courage and contempt, the sky soon fluttered with hundreds of loose box-kites, drifting free and empty on the thermals. They would win here or they would die. *Saints help me; if I had commanded an army of these mountain devils I could have seized every feuding kingdom of the Burn inside a year.*

Anna flew a slow lazy pass around the hangars built into the lower wing. What Jacob had been expecting. A standard design; dozens of launch ramps and catapults on the hangar's open right-hand side, a series of dark landing tunnels off to the left . . . as long as the carrier's wing could accommodate, a series of capture lines inside to slow returning fighters and shuttle planes. Each a self-contained fire-break to prevent a crash landing from damaging the hangar. Anna selected a landing tunnel on the far side of the wing and dove for the entrance, angling up at the last second and throwing her propeller into full reverse as they jounced once, hard, on the deck. Lines fixed on counterweights caught around the flying wing's undercarriage, filling the air with an almost human groaning as they absorbed the plane's velocity. Slowed to walking pace, the flying wing continued rolling down the tunnel as it widened into a mechanic's space.

Three skel ground crew emerged from a hatch at the side, pelting towards the flying wing, rolling a fuel barrel in front of them, only braking as they realized this latest arrival was too pocket-sized to be one of their aircraft. They understood it well enough when Jacob vaulted out of the rear cockpit, drew both his pistols and gunned down the two nearest bandits. The engineers slumped to the floor still clutching wooden hooks needed to haul the plane on to a turntable. The third crewman stumbled backward, halting as Jacob raised his pistols towards the skel's head.

'What's this carrier called – and the name of her master?'

'Am the *Razored Smile* – belonging to Duke Si-meliss,' hissed the skel. *We're on the right bandit carrier.* This crewman was of the same twisted pattern as the people who had attacked Northhaven all right, lizard-snouted with scaled skin and a short, thick tail protruding from the back of his trousers. So far from the common pattern it was barely worth considering them human. These workers inside the hangar weren't particularly imposing, though. Not the same sizeable and vicious creatures that had raided Northhaven, carrying a quarter of the population away to Vandia as slaves. *They obviously stash their runts away up here, out of the fight.*

Anna swung out of her flying wing and took a turn at questioning him. 'There's a Weylander on this bird, James Kurtain. Keeps the rotors turning for you.'

'Am work for engineering,' confirmed the skel, his eyes blinking in disbelief at the pilot. 'A skin-of-night, same as you-woman's skin.'

'Take us to him,' ordered Jacob, the pistol in his left hand twitching to indicate the hatch.

'Weylanders am fighting together with skels,' said the crewman, rather hopefully. 'Fighting for king of you-people against mountain tribe groundlings.'

'You're fighting for blood and treasure,' said Jacob, 'same as you ever were. And the usurper's just a shoe merchant who put the real king in the ground so he could loot the crown from the gutter.'

The twisted man grunted as if the politics of the groundlings was beyond him. *Not a warrior. Might never have left this plane to touch real land. Born up here to die up here.* It was hard to believe that this people had once been masters of Vandia, controlling the immense bounty of the stratovolcano until their own slaves and subject nations had rebelled, driving the skels into exile in the air. Making them slave soldiers in turn. These vast planes were all that was left of their empire. *And soon enough they won't even have that.*

'You-man spare Del-alass?' pleaded the skel.

'I'll make you a deal, Del-alass,' said Jacob. 'You lead us true to my friend's brother and I won't put a bullet in your ugly head. Does that sound like an amiable arrangement?'

Del-alass nodded rapidly, only too eager to agree, before leading them through a warren of gangways inside the wing. The *Razored Smile*'s interior wasn't much different from the merchant carrier Jacob had taken during his pursuit of Carter. Narrow corridors, most of the walls and decks made from treated paper pulp that resembled wood but a dozen times lighter and stronger, hatches giving on to larger chambers, cabins and hangars. Everything weathered by age, patched walls that spoke of the city-sized aircraft having flown up here for numberless centuries. She wasn't used to travelling so low in gravity's hold, though, creaking from every beam like a rickety nautical sailing ship. Her decks trembled every time her cannons joined the fight outside. Sounds of distant combat echoed around the corridors, muffled shots and screams from both attackers and crewmen. *That's what I remember from their raid on Northhaven – how human the skels sounded when dying.* Jacob could taste cordite on the air. This bird was still running on recycled cabin air, a slightly damp, musty smell with her pressurization machinery circulating the whiff of the boarding action. But then, the bridge crew had other things on their mind than venting in fresh air. The angle of the *Razored Smile*'s

320

deck grew steep as she attempted to climb out of the range of the swarming war kites. *Too little, too late.* Occasionally the three of them ran into other crewmen, unarmed skels who took one look at the two Weylanders holding a pistol on Del-alass, before turning tail and fleeing in the opposite direction.

Del-alass led them through the aircraft and into the wing's engineering chamber which showed all the hallmarks of having been recently abandoned – long workbenches covered with disassembled engine parts, metalworking lathes still with pieces inside their clamps. A wall of numbered hatches led off in the direction of the propellers; behind one of the open doorways Jacob caught sight of a leathery russet face.

'Come on out!' barked Jacob. His first thought, that this might be a gask, turned out to be incorrect. A similar leathery face, but instead of a spine-covered skin, there were cyan-tinged feathers around the twisted woman's neck. Another skel slave, this one from an unfamiliar race and country.

'James Kurtain,' demanded Anna. 'Where is he?'

'James was taken away,' answered the slave. 'Everyone was rounded up when the plane's bells sounded for combat. I hid in the rotor's crawl space so they wouldn't find me.'

Damn – the duke doesn't want his house slaves making trouble for him during the battle when the majority of his warriors are outside in their fighter planes. An efficient commander made everything more difficult for Jacob. 'Where?'

'The guards said we needed to be locked up inside the slave holds.'

Ready-built pens. Where else.

'Del-alass am not know this!' cried the skel.

'Del-alass get his chance to make it up by leading us across to the slave pens,' said Jacob.

Anna waved her pistol at the female slave. 'Hide. When soldiers who look like us come to secure this deck, you make sure you tell them where the slaves were taken.'

'I will,' she promised.

Jacob and Anna let the skel lead them deeper into the plane, gangways growing wider after they left the wing and entered the main body of the massive carrier. 'This is where the bulk of the boarding action was ongoing – they came across skel corpses sprawled across the decking, empty shell casings scattered across the floor, no sign of Rodalian casualties. Jacob noted none of the dead crew carried firearms, only cutlasses and daggers. *I reckon the duke up here isn't the trusting sort. That'll cost him dearly today.*

'We have to hurry,' said Anna, not bothering to hide the worry in her voice. 'You know what the slavers will do to our people when they realize their carrier has been taken.'

'Who is in charge of the slave pens, Del-alass?' asked Jacob.

'Si-lishh.'

Name sounds familiar. Is he the same killer Carter told me about? 'And I'm guessing the fellow isn't what you'd call a good man.'

'Am of the family-Si,' said the crewman, as though that should be answer enough. 'He strangle father of Del-alass dead for winning in chance-game. Not mercy for groundlings. Not mercy for toiler skels. Never from Si-lishh.'

'Saints hate a sore loser,' said Jacob.

The three of them encountered a squad of seven Rodalian soldiers. Jacob only just managed to stop the troops immediately opening up on their prisoner, catching Jacob and Anna in the crossfire. The Rodalians looked like air pirates themselves, warm padded sheep-pelt-lined coats, bandoleers of shells, short-barrelled carbines, smoke-blackened faces, blood-soaked cutlasses and half-empty grenade pouches. *Looks like they've been sucked backwards through an engine exhaust and come out fighting.* The troops fell eagerly enough behind Jacob when they heard of the recently filled slave pens.

After they reached the slave hold, Jacob found himself on a walled gantry high above a large chamber. Gloomy below with only a handful of tiny portholes for light, stairs on either side leading down to dozens of long cages with narrow walkways running between them. And every slave pen packed with the prisoners who kept the skels' flying citadel high in the sky. Dozens of skel guards sheltered behind the makeshift barricade in gantries flanked by the pens. They clutched whips or razored cudgels attached to portable batteries, but no firearms Jacob could see. Not even the one who had to be Si-lishh – a giant among skels, almost as wide as he was tall. *The skel's a brute, but he isn't a stupid brute.* The plane's slave master must have watched the flight of war kites and heard the fierce boarding action raging through the carrier, then calculated the anaemic odds of his survival with most of the skel fighting force in the air outside the *Razored Smile*. Si-lishh and his guards had used their time well. The corridors outside the slave pens stood lined with rows of fuel barrels, fused and ready to burn. *Yes, a sore loser all right.* Si-lishh was willing to turn his little fiefdom up here into an inferno if things went the wrong way for him.

'Whips and shock cudgels against pistols and rifles,' shouted Jacob. 'Might be it's time for you to surrender, Si-lishh.'

'Not surrender,' yelled the large skel, confirming his position as slave master. 'Weylander am let Si-lishh leave with flying boat, or Si-lishh be cooking groundlings into most tasty meal.'

Anna ground her teeth in frustration. 'If he puts a match to the fuse we'll never break our people out of the cages in time.'

'If Si-lishh am escaping,' whispered their skel prisoner, 'Si-lishh am hiding timer to burn slaves and destroy *Razored Smile*. Kill all-people in air.'

'Not exactly what you'd call an oath-keeper?' said Jacob. *Why doesn't that surprise me?* He aimed his pistol carefully into the gantry below, sighting on the large skel. 'I let him go, they burn. I put a bullet in him, they burn.' *I know which outcome I prefer.*

'No!' cried Anna.

'There's no other way. If we're quick enough, we can still get your brother out.'

'Not gun,' urged Del-alass. He indicated the knife hanging from Jacob's belt. 'Champion's knife. Charity of battle. All skels am honour this.'

'A champion's combat?' said Anna. 'That killer would actually honour that?'

'Guards am honour it,' said Del-alass. 'When Si-lishh *dead*.'

Jacob sized up the ogre down below. 'The hell you say.'

'I'll do it,' said Anna. 'It's my brother inside one of those cages.'

Jacob shook his head. 'You're not as fast as you used to be, Miss Kurtain, not after you got carved up in Midsburg.'

'I can fight,' she insisted.

'And you can fail, and I'll be surrounded by flames while trying to guess which one of the hundreds caged up down there is your

323

brother,' said Jacob. 'You stay here and leave the slave master to me. If I die, at least you'll have a chance of pulling your brother out of the cages.'

Anna's face flushed with exasperation. 'This is mine to do.'

'No,' growled Jacob. 'His clan put Mary in the ground just for helping her students escape the sword. His clan carried away Carter and the boy's friends and sold them off like cattle. Anyone too old or too young to serve as a slave, they left decapitated in the fields around Northhaven, discarded like so much butcher's offal. Bad Marcus blessed the raid and Vandia paid for it, but that son-of-a-bitch was one of the demons who swung the sabre. So no, Miss Kurtain, this is very much mine to do.' He stood up and gazed down into the slave pens. 'I know you, Si-lishh. You held my son Carter Carnehan up here as a prisoner inside your stinking hold. When you sold him to the House of Skar as a miner, he promised you he'd be back here to kill you one day. He sends his apologies for being otherwise occupied right now. I've come to honour my boy's word. I've come to offer you the charity of battle if you've got the guts to fight an old man with a knife.'

Si-lishh hissed sibilant laughter. 'Groundling am not born to defeat Si-lishh.'

'You stick a blade in me right, you'll get your flying boat,' said Jacob. 'You can light out of here and find another damn bandit carrier who needs a murderer with a taste for whipping chained slaves. But if I slice you up, then your guards honour the duel and let these slaves live.'

'Si-lishh am remembering your groundling son. Stupid as rock. Always trouble-making. With this father-blood, Si-lishh am finding madness-source.'

Jacob passed his pistols to Anna and raised his empty hands for the slave master to see. 'A mad old man who needs killing, then. But who's to do it?'

A Rodalian soldier passed Jacob an extra dagger as he walked down the stairs. The skel slavers parted for Jacob in the space between the cages. He could smell the stink of the corn ether rising from the fuel barrels. *Sweet saints, give me the strength and guile to win here. Nobody is getting out of here alive if these barrels are torched.* Si-lishh came forward and tossed his whip contemptuously aside to the floor. Jacob threw the spare dagger, watching Si-lishh catch it while Jacob drew his own blade. 'This is for Northhaven. For everyone who died there. For everyone dragged to Vandia who never saw their home again.'

'Si-lishh remember town. Fine raid. Old groundlings am beg for much-young groundlings' lives. But weak groundlings not good for Si-lishh. Tiny groundlings worthless. Not able work sky mines, not able to survive. Chop chop chop. Skulls off. Boots am wet with groundling-blood that day. *Fine* raid. Take plenty!'

Jacob fought to master his fury. This was what the slave master wanted. To goad Jacob into a killing rage where he attacked without thought. Where Si-lishh could easily carve him into pieces. Jacob dropped into a guard position. 'It's never the ones you take who'll kill you. It's only the ones you leave alive.'

'Am fix-mistake!' Si-lishh rushed Jacob, slashing out with his blade. Jacob danced back trying to counter using a tight sabre-grip, but the skel blocked him with an arm the width of a tree trunk, then they warily circled each other. The skel attacked again, and Jacob tried a high cut to the skel's forehead, put enough blood in his eyes to blind him. But wherever this skel had learnt to brawl, it wasn't just taking his whip to chained slaves. Si-lishh pivoted and tried to put one in Jacob's gut, but the Weylander just saw the move in time and blocked it. Stopping the skel from filleting Jacob was like taking a beating from an oak tree wielded by a giant. They continued their desperate duel, but the monster's endurance started to wear on Jacob. *Old man. Proud old man. You're not Quicksilver anymore. Not the young general that swept across the Burn. You're just what's left of him. Searching for a warm comfortable grave and maybe this time you've found it.*

Si-lishh came again, slashing out and Jacob turned, caught the hand, twisting it sideways to disarm the slave master. The skel's dagger flew away, tumbling between a slave pen's bars. Jacob tried to turn the caught arm into a lock-hold and slide his own dagger into the skel's neck, but the demon wasn't keeping still for his trick. Si-lishh pushed back, unbalancing Jacob, then Si-lishh booted Jacob in the abdomen and sent him sprawling to the floor in front of one of the cages. The slaves inside yelled desperate encouragement for the man who was trying to save them, but their pleas didn't do much to balance out

325

the uneven distribution of raw strength in this challenge. Jacob tried to roll over, but the massive skel was quicker, pinning him to the floor, one hand tightening around Jacob's neck while the other snaked around to his belt on his back. The slave master suddenly flourished the weapon he had concealed behind him. It looked like a Vandian stick-grenade, its head replaced with coils of barbed wire, a bulbous primitive battery instead of a pin at the wooden handle's end.

'You truly are a sore loser,' gasped Jacob, one hand trying to dislodge the skel's fingers tightening around his neck, the other grasping near-uselessly at the skel's weapon hand.

Si-lishh forced the cudgel slowly towards Jacob's face, sparks flashing from its ugly wires, almost blinding the Weylander. *Too strong.* It was like trying to wrestle with a landslide coming down a mountain. Jacob's vision began to spot with dark circles when he heard the grate of something spinning towards him. A second cudgel.

Del-alass. The ground crewman tumbled as the guard he'd stolen the cudgel from plunged a dagger in the skel crewman's ribs, but Jacob's hand had already abandoned Si-lishh's hand locked around his neck, dragging the cudgel in, then he drove the weapon's head into the slave master's ribs, sparks flashing as its charge emptied. The giant went limp and Jacob flipped the skel back into the slave pen, slamming him against the iron bars. Jacob seized the giant's dropped weapon and shoved it against the cage, triggering a second burst of energy. Si-lishh spasmed, caught in the blaze of electricity, and when the skel's own cudgel emptied of its charge, the bars lost their hold on the slave master and he fell smoking to the deck. Jacob stared down at the dead slave master. *I should feel something. Content. Happy.* Instead, he just felt hollowed out, dead and joyless. *What the hell am I now, that I can't even savour the taste of a victory? I'm not Jacob Carnehan anymore. I'm not Jake Silver. I'm just a tired old man who keeps on playing the odds and cheating death for a little while longer.*

Anna and the Rodalian soldiers had used the confusion of the challenge to storm the hold, carbines raised; keeping the skel guards honest in case they proved as shameless as their commander. The slave master was dead, and from his wounds, the ground crewman who'd kept the duel on an even keel looked set to follow him.

Jacob knelt beside the dying skel. 'This was one game that wasn't fixed.'

'Am-charity-of-battle,' coughed the Del-alass. 'Am-final-father's-battle.' His hairless head fell back as his eyes closed.

'Now, there's a hell of a thing,' said Anna.

'That it was,' said Jacob.

But Anna hadn't heard. She was already dashing towards the slave pen opposite. The mob inside parted to allow James Kurtain to the front, and her brother shook the bars fit to dislodge them.

Jacob's son had kept the oath he had given the slave-master. In a round-about way. And Jacob had paid Anna back a little for what he owed her. But there was another vow to keep now. The dark promise he had sworn over Mary Carnehan's grave.

The soldier indicated the rows of kneeling skel prisoners to Jacob, Anna and her brother. The captured slavers lined up inside the *Razored Smile*'s fighter hangar. At least, the ones who had surrendered were held here. 'What do we do with them, General Carnehan?'

'You know what the penalty is for being taken as a slaver inside the Lanca. There's only ever been one. You can sail down the coast and find the same sentence on the books of every nation for a hundred-thousand miles.'

'So many?' said the soldier, hesitantly.

'There are cages in this bird's slave hold where the floor opens up like a bomb-bay, to make troublesome slaves walk the sky.' Carter had described his captivity inside the slave pens in graphic detail to Jacob. *These are the scum who threw my son in one and made him fight to the death for their amusement.* 'We won't need to waste a single bullet on any of these killers.'

Anna came forward. 'You can't!'

'You watch the slavers rain down over the mountains and then tell me that.'

'Not all of the skels are like the devils that raided our homes. After your fight in the slave pens, you know it.'

'What I know is the job that needs doing. What do you say, Mister Kurtain? You've suffered and sweated inside this dirty carrier for the best half of your life. In all those years, how many benighted souls

327

did you see pass through the holds on their way to hell? Are you of the same mind as your sister when it comes to the best way to deal with slavers? You know this'll be justice.'

'Some of the worker skels aren't all bad,' said James. 'They're like us, that way.'

Jacob ignored the barb, if that was what it was. 'I haven't got the time for you to go through our prize fleet and pick out the slightly less murderous ones. I'd sell the skels in the same slave markets they traded our people, except nobody would want them. Although thinking about it, if we shipped the skels across to the Burn, the warlords would surely buy most of them for bayonet-fodder.'

'We don't execute prisoners of war. We don't take slaves,' insisted Anna. 'That's what makes us fit to be a member of the league.'

'The other Lanca nations stood aside and watched our kingdom tear itself apart in civil war,' said Jacob. 'They're cowards who aren't fit to dictate the course of my war to me.'

'Except that it isn't your war,' said a familiar-sounding voice entering the hangar. 'This conflict belongs to all of the free people of Weyland.'

Prince Owen. Jacob bridled. 'What the hell are you doing up here? I ordered your royal neck kept safe in Hadra-Hareer!'

'Our people are battling for their existence in Rodal. This is my place as much as it is yours,' said Prince Owen. 'If this raid failed, there wouldn't be a parliament left to fight on inside of a month.'

On that point at least, the young aristocrat was correct. 'You can take that new-found pragmatism and apply it to these bandits, Your Highness. We need their carriers to bring down your uncle's regime. We don't need prison camps filled with skels, sell-swords and bandits to feed when we can barely supply our own refugees. Executing slavers is only applying the kingdom's law.'

'The law can't save us from ourselves,' said Prince Owen. 'I've broken my nation for the cause of liberty. I will not shatter it further with a massacre on such an atrocious scale.'

Jacob drew both pistols. 'I shot you before in Midsburg. You think I won't do it again?'

'Then do it!' shouted Prince Owen. 'Put a bullet in my head this time and declare yourself the absolute leader of the north. You can select an agreeable warlord's title for yourself like one of those pocket-sized kingdoms of the Burn where you bloodied your hands. Lord Protector of the National Assembly. Supreme General of the north. Grand God-Duke of Havenharl. Call yourself all of them if you wish, but I am not and will never be a royal puppet for you or anyone else. Kill me or let me live to guide parliament as I see fit. That's your only choice today. And you will face it tomorrow and the day after. You may as well make your bloody decision now!'

Jacob's pistols held steady in his hands, not a trace of a tremble. He was tempted, by the saints he was. *How many good people could I save by getting this done quick and right? Those radicals in the old assembly, they had a point, didn't they? Keeping a hereditary monarch makes as much sense as employing a hereditary surgeon or hereditary architect.* Jacob could end that debate right here for the cost of a single round. *And what then? The country will end up with Bad Marcus on a throne in the south and Lord Quicksilver sitting on a throne in the north. Battlefield after battlefield. Corpse upon corpse. With a Weyland that will never run short of new enemies who need killing.* Jacob grunted in frustration and reluctantly holstered his guns. *A boy too weak to be king but too strong to be ruled. And the fates are punishing me by needing him alive to finish this.* 'I know what I am. And I know what you are, too. You're a hell-damned young fool who hasn't learnt a thing during this war.'

Prince Owen stepped back and gazed down the line of kneeling skels. If the boy knew how close he'd just come to dying, he masked his nerves well. Anna Kurtain slipped her own pistol slowly back behind her belt. *There's gratitude for you.* Maybe she'd been foolish enough to think Jacob hadn't noticed when she'd drawn on him. Or stupid enough to believe Jacob wasn't swift enough to shoot her with his second gun while dropping the man she loved so deeply.

'Then I'm a hell-damned young fool with an answer to our problem, General Carnehan,' said Prince Owen. 'Here are my orders concerning the prisoners' fate . . .'

TWELVE

A BOX FOR TEMMELL

A hot wind blew across the hills when Temmell called a halt to the small nomad convoy. Carter climbed down off his supply-laden wagon, joined by Sariel, Kerge and Sheplar Lesh. Rodal's mountains were visible in the south, swirled with mist from the temperature differential between the icy heights and warm steppes. Perhaps a day's ride away, now.

'This is the place?' asked Sariel.

Temmell pointed to the series of jagged peaks in the distance. He glanced up at the sun, checked his pocket watch and smiled in satisfaction. 'Their silhouettes are my map.' The young sorcerer took a rusty iron shovel that had seen better days and started to dig, not trusting any of the Nijumeti to such delicate work. After ten minutes, he uncovered a case about half the size of a coffin. It was made of a material Carter didn't recognize, dark and shining like an insect's carapace.

'You have more than a soul-sphere inside there,' observed Sariel.

'I didn't need the gift of precognition to warn me our party was never going to be resupplied or reinforced again,' said Temmell. He waved to a couple of their Nijumeti escort to drag the case from the dirt. 'This was my insurance policy.'

'Contraband?' asked Sariel.

'Let's just say I wasn't going to go down for want of a nail,' said Temmell.

The nomads dragged the case out of the soil and on to the grass. They stepped back uneasily, as though they had been made to touch the flesh of a recently deceased family member.

'Do you want to open it?' asked Temmell in a teasing tone.

Sariel shook his head ruefully. 'How big an explosion?'

Temmell knelt by the case and laid his hand on its surface. 'Our reconstitution would take centuries. Let's hope the canister still recognizes its creator.'

Carter hoped much the same.

Sheplar watched by Carter's side. 'It would be a sad end to have survived so much only to die from triggering an ancient tripwire.'

'It is strange,' noted Kerge, 'but what I have recovered of my golden mean is lost in the presence of this case. Disrupted.'

'Perhaps it means the future is not yet decided?' said Carter.

'It never is,' said the gask, darkly.

The casket's obsidian surface started to flow as though melting, lines of light emanating from Temmell's hand. Its lid vanished in the glow, revealing an interior filled with objects that were probably devices, but nothing Carter recognized. Rods joined with crystals and strange bulbous shapes melded together like a metalworker's offcuts soldered at random. Temmell gingerly lifted out a sphere, cloudy white glass the size of a fist. 'How many of my lost memories are inside, I wonder?'

'You need to find out,' said Sariel.

Temmell wrapped both hands around the sphere and pushed inward, the glass responding by turning a cold blue colour. As he pushed into the globe it seemed to vibrate, cupped inside the man's hands. Sariel's young colleague sighed as though drinking deep and quenching a long, dry thirst.

'Do you know where Eremee went?' asked Sariel.

'Oh, poor Eremee. Such a fool. Of course, she would head there.'

'Where?' demanded Sariel, sounding uncharacteristically desperate.

'Wait,' said Temmell. 'I need to be certain about this. So, *that* is why.'

'Why what?' asked Carter.

Temmell swivelled on Carter and his three companions, flourishing a strange-looking rod-like instrument he had slipped out of the canister. 'Why I sent the stealers the gate coordinates needed to ambush our party!' Temmell lashed out with the rod, a fierce green spark leaping from its head and striking Sariel, knocking the old bard off his feet and sending him barrelling across the grass. Sariel sobbed, twisting on the ground as though tormented by a pack of invisible demons.

Carter's hand dipped for his pistol holster, but their Nijumeti escorts seized his arms, a third nomad shoving a blade up to his throat; Sheplar and Kerge were practically bowled to the ground as their supposed protectors jumped them.

They were primed in advance for this, realized Carter. 'What in the saints' name are you doing? I healed you, Temmell. You owe me your restored self!'

'A debt between us?' growled the sorcerer. 'Only in your mind, turnip. I asked for none of this. I was content in my position. I *am* content in my position.' Temmell grabbed a silver torc from the case, passing it to his warriors with a brusque command to seal it around Sariel's neck. 'A gift, my brothers, to tame the weirdling's more troublesome impulses.'

'I don't understand!' cried Carter. 'Is one of those tools inside the case the great weapon? Do you want to steal it for yourself?'

'Oh, turnip, your brain is too limited to grasp anything more than your brute existence,' smiled Temmell. He indicated Sariel twisting in agony on the ground. As the torc was fitted around Sariel's neck, it seemed to act as a balm of sorts, the old vagrant's palsy-like shakes slowing. Temmell nodded in satisfaction. 'My intentions are far purer than *his*. I want the great weapon left well alone. Used by no one; in neither side's hands.'

'Where is it, then?' said Carter. Sariel was dragged to his feet by the warriors.

Temmell tapped the side of his head. 'Where it has always been. When our party set out, we each carried a segment of the great weapon . . . it is a spell which gives the lower ethreaal such power that even the higher-gods would hesitate to use it. Each member's portion was encrypted as a cypher and stored within our minds. If we collectively reached the conclusion the threat the stealers posed was so serious that we must act, our expedition was to combine the segments and deploy the great weapon. Sariel didn't come looking for an old friend, he came searching for my share of the great weapon.'

'You are wrong, Temmell, I came for you and it both,' croaked Sariel, feeling the restraining device around his neck. 'Why, man? Why did you betray us to the stealers?'

'I just want the war to end,' said Temmell. 'I am tired of it. Eternal conflict, shadow and light, light and shadow. The balance is finally tipping in the stealers' favour. Let them have their victory. At least the war will finally be over. The philosophical difference between both sides is paper-thin at best. Life will out in the end, we have to believe that.'

'I will not allow the stealers to defeat us!' gasped Sariel.

'Ever a true believer, even after all these years. But you have very little choice in the matter. Events have overtaken us. We were doomed from the start.'

'How can you still support the stealers? They betrayed you! They attacked you and Eremee at the gate.'

'Of course they attacked me. I foresaw their double-cross, for all the good the knowledge did me. It allowed myself and Eremee to survive a few days longer than the rest of you. The stealers required the threat against them neutralized,' said Temmell. 'Even our own side didn't dare to trust a sole lower ethreaal with such power. We were never meant to be gods, however much we act like them. If our own side couldn't trust a single individual with the ultimate power, why should the stealers? Needless to say, the stealers treated us as plague carriers and cleansed us all. Giving up myself and losing my memories was a blessing.'

'And Eremee, did she support you in your treachery?'

'Which of us ever knew what she believed?' said Temmell, not directly answering the question.

A droning started to sound across the steppes, low at first, barely perceptible, and then swelling to the dark hum of a locust swarm. Carter gazed up into the sky, blinking towards the sun. An aerial invasion force heading south. Kani Yargul's new skyguard being sent into operation, plane after plane, flying wings towing gull-winged gliders behind them. Carter imagined the packed holds of those flimsy wooden engine-less craft. Horses and men eager for plunder.

Temmell has betrayed us twice. The bastard never had any intention of dispatching the horde against Persdad at the far end of the steppes.

'What have you done?' roared Sheplar Lesh.

Temmell indicated the aerial armada passing overhead. 'I have set my people free . . . I have given them Rodal. The much-vaunted walls of the league. Well, a rampart faces in both directions; it all depends on who walks it.'

'Our winds will claw you out of the sky,' swore Sheplar.

'No, my little aviator serf, not this time,' said Temmell. 'I procured a copy of your high temple's holy Deb-rlung'rta. My pilots know precisely where the safe winds are, every secret, shielded route your people take to flit around Rodal while you're taming storms and hurling them at your enemies. The priests inside your precious wind temples can do nothing to stop my invasion. Your skyguard now shares exactly the same air as my warriors. It would hardly be fair combat otherwise, would it?'

'No, you can't unleash the horde against Rodal,' pleaded Sariel. 'What are you playing at here, Temmell Longgate?'

'Aren't we both playing at being human?' sighed Temmell. 'You have your pawns and I have mine.'

'None of this will matter,' said Sariel, half begging, half accusing. 'Not the horde's invasion, not your intervention for the clans.'

'But none of it ever did,' said Temmell. 'When you realize that, you stop asking *why* and start asking *why not* instead. The Nijumeti are my children after a fashion. I set them off riding to Arak-natikh once upon a time. I intend to free them across the board and see what game is left to me.'

'There will be nothing left to you!'

'How many thousands of years have you hungered for a true death? That's the trouble with living so long. Nobody ever warned us what it would really be like. I'm curious, frankly. Will a true death be the same as forgetting?' Temmell stared up at the sky with satisfaction, the blue heavens filled with his aerial invasion force. 'Rodal belongs to the Nijumeti now. You restored me, turnip. I shall repay you with two gifts: your worthless existence as a free man and the memory of being witness to the end of the Lancean League. Nation after nation falling to the horde. We will ride forever.'

'Willow!' croaked Carter. *My father.*

'My people,' said Sheplar, his voice shorn of all emotion.

'History makes dust of it all in the end,' said Temmell, triumphantly. 'Sariel, I must retain you as my clan-guest. In your current state, you are a danger to Pellas. Perhaps I will incinerate you anew and keep what reforms half-insane for a thrall. The rest of you shall be freed tomorrow morning. Climb the mountains if you will. Every inch of soil you touch now belongs to the clans, perhaps every foot you will ever cross again.'

Willow sorted her possessions spread across the room. The lodgings inside this Northhaven boarding house hadn't come cheap, but then, being the recently widowed inheritor of the Wallingbeck estate carried a few advantages. Her slow, waddling gait, looking down flushed over her swollen belly, wasn't one of them. *How much food will I need to carry to make the journey into Rodal? How much silver to pay smugglers to help me across the front line?* There were rumours circulating through Northhaven that Bad Marcus was surveying his re-conquered prefectures on a victory progress. When the usurper arrived, the number of soldiers in the town and surrounding territory would treble at least. Willow wanted to be well out of here before the capricious monarch showed up and decided that a retrial would be due justice for her. *And how much of my wanting to flee is guilt?* She had tried to visit Duncan in the army surgical tents, only to be refused access by the guards. Her brother was dying. A surgeon she had bribed had told her he thought the blade was poisoned. Willow had realized too late what the real plan had been. The same plan it had always been.

There was scraping at the door and it opened, revealing Leyla Holten. The woman was accompanied by the landlord, the key to Willow's room still in his hand. Leyla passed him a handful of metal coins and he left, not meeting Willow's indignant gaze.

Think about the devil and the devil appears. 'What the hell are you doing here? Get out, Holten!'

'So, you still believe you've beaten me?' said Leyla. 'Freed by trial. But free to do what?'

Willow ignored the question. The answer should be evident from the supplies she had purchased, scattered about the room. 'You shouldn't have given me so much time languishing inside a cell, Holten. Time to realize who would benefit most if Duncan died during the trial. One less warm body in your way to claiming the Landor estate. Two less, after the executioner strung me up at the gallows.'

'Always such a clever girl,' smiled Leyla, coldly. 'But there's more to succeeding in life than a sharp mind. Sometimes you have to apply a little brute force to the situation.' She stepped aside and Nocks entered the room grinning. Willow sprinted to the side of the chamber and threw open the window, looking to leap out, but the ugly squat little brute dragged her back, punching her once hard in the spine. She nearly fell, grasping a candlestick from the sideboard and tried to smash it into his scarred face.

'You don't want to exert yourself,' leered Nocks as he ducked the blow and grabbed her. 'Not a woman in your delicate condition.'

Willow cursed her slow, tired body. *I need to be strong. To be quick.* 'What did you promise your cur Wallingbeck, Holten?'

Leyla laughed. 'Not so much what I promised him as what I gave him. Such a waste. William was always so amusing between the sheets. I can only trust the royal army will yield up a few suitable distractions, now the rebellion is crushed and Rodal close to collapse. All the southern gentlemen seem to be up here, playing at soldier.'

'What's to do?' growled Nocks.

'Take her deep into the wilds,' commanded Leyla. 'You may take your gratification with the brat, but the body must never be discovered. Not in Northhaven or anywhere else. Let everyone think she ran away to re-join the Carnehans. Hadra-Hareer will be ashes soon enough. Nobody will poke the ashes very hard searching for remains.'

Willow stamped her boot hard against Nocks' foot and he cursed her while she struggled against his tight grip. 'Holten! You can't! I'm carrying Wallingbeck's child. He was your friend.'

'Then you should have been more gracious about the fine love-match I arranged between you two,' said Leyla. 'Perhaps it's by the saints' blessing that Duncan filleted William during the trial-by-combat. The shame of being cuckolded by some callow bandit of a boy. So very hard to bear.'

'This will not stand!' boomed a voice from the doorway. Benner

Landor filled the frame; an angry bear goaded to violence in his blue artillery officer's uniform. At first Willow thought her father must be party to his wife's scheme of revenge, but Willow quickly realized otherwise as she saw how he gaped in anger at Nocks.

'What is going on – what is that devil doing here?' yelled Benner Landor, aiming his pistol at Nocks.

Leyla ran up to her husband, her voice trembling and terrified. 'Thank the saints you arrived at last, Benner. Nocks broke into the room looking to rescue Willow. He feared the trial would go against her. They're planning to escape together, flee north to the pretender and the rebels. These two devils took me prisoner before you arrived. They were going to abduct me for ransom.'

'Don't you move, you treacherous dog,' growled Benner. His gun didn't waver from the short brute who had once been his manservant. 'Release my daughter.'

Nocks let Willow go and she gasped as she fell forward, hobbling away from the thug.

'I intend to see you hung, Nocks,' her father threatened, 'but a bullet will serve as well for your payment. You betrayed my house, my trust in you, turned your colours, and for what . . . the chance of further sullying my adulteress of a daughter? You are nothing but a fool and a coward.'

'What are you talking about?' wheezed Willow, trying to find her voice. 'You've gone mad. You're the one who sent Nocks into Rodal to kidnap me.'

'Hold your lying tongue still!' barked Benner. He moved back a step and locked the door, as though what he planned to do was so terrible he wished no witnesses to it. 'You may have been freed from the court's charges of treason, but you haven't been released from the bonds of your marriage vows.'

Has he gone insane? 'I think Duncan did that job for me, wouldn't you say?'

'You see how it is, now?' cajoled Leyla. 'Willow went crawling back to her husband's bed. She seduced that dunce William into trying to kill Duncan during the duel. She tricked her brother and husband into murdering each other. She forced Duncan to truly defend his life. And now Willow is widow and heir to all of William's estate while poor Duncan is dying inside a surgeon's tent. How neatly Willow's arranged all the cards to fall in her favour.'

Benner's cheeks glowed crimson with fury. 'If you weren't carrying William's child, I would order you dragged back to the artillery camp and flogged, and the king's justice be damned.'

'But Willow's already lost her baby,' lied Leyla. 'I overheard Willow boasting to Nocks about how she'd never bear William's bastard child into the world. She laughed herself hoarse after she told Nocks about how easy it was to obtain a mild poison to wash that luckless child out of her womb.'

'She's making this all up!' shouted Willow. 'It's pure nonsense. The baby is still mine ... it's heart beats within me. I never met Duncan or my so-called husband before the duel. My warning saved Duncan's life. Whatever wicked scheme is going on here is your cursed wife's, Father, not mine.'

'Let your old man have the truth at last, my love,' begged Nocks, his hands raised out to her in supplication. 'Please, give 'im the truth so he doesn't order poor ol' Nocks shot as a deserter. After all I done for you, you owe me that much at least.'

Willow threw the thug a look of pure loathing. 'I owe you far more than that, you demon-hearted stealer. And you'll have it when I plunge a blade in your gut.'

'Shoot Willow,' pleaded Leyla. The young woman hugged her husband as she clung beseechingly against his uniform. 'You know what she is. *Please*. She'll take her murdered husband's title and turn it against us. She'll find a way to hurt us. Kidnap little Asher, have our child murdered along with both of us. Willow will command Carter and Jacob Carnehan to murder us. Then she'll claim the Landor house for herself. Kill her now. It's the only way Asher will ever be safe.'

'Father,' implored Willow, 'the conniving bitch is lying: you must know how insane her story sounds. I wouldn't hurt my step-brother ... I wouldn't harm a baby. Even after everything you and Duncan did to me, I saved Duncan's life during the duel. I stood for the family.'

'You provoked Duncan into killing William,' sneered Leyla, 'you goaded your brother into clearing *your* name.'

The pistol wavered in Benner Landor's hand. 'I can't do it. I can't shoot my own daughter. Whatever evil she's committed. This is the

Carnehans' fault. That traitorous bandit and his viperous brood corrupted her soul. I will have Willow committed to an asylum. Yes, even if I have to forge the king's seal on the order. That is what will be best.'

'I don't think so,' said Leyla, slipping a wire garrotte around Benner's neck; her long pale fingers twisting on a wooden tightening choke. 'I think your loving wife understands what's for the best.' Benner stumbled back, dropping his pistol as he gagged and grappled manically. Willow tried to dive for the fallen gun, but Nocks lunged and grabbed her from behind again, dragging her floundering across the floor.

Leyla didn't have to force Willow's father to his knees. Benner collapsed forward, desperately trying to loosen the blood-soaked wire; but the same crushed throat deprived him of the air he needed to fight his young wife off him. 'And let's face it; two widows will make a far better story than one. The honest, good widow, grieving for her brave officer husband. And then there is the evil widow who cunningly escaped justice, took revenge on her too-trusting father before being shot attempting to escape and rejoin the wicked pretender, trying to reunite with her depraved bandit lover. Yes, that's a deliciously melancholy tale that will seal my position in society.'

Willow tried to throw her skull back into Nocks' face, but the devil just laughed, his grip a vice she couldn't escape. 'Father! Please, Holten, you don't need to do—' *Too weak, too slow. Stupid whale. If only my baby was safely born and I could fight unburdened.*

'Don't keep using that disgusting common name! I am a Lady of the House Landor,' shrieked the woman, sounding demented. She furiously increased the pressure on the garrotte mechanism and Benner's hand vainly reached out towards Willow, his fingers fluttering as one final breath escaped his lungs.

'So—r—ry.'

'I am *the* lady,' Holten screeched.

No. No! She can't. He can't!

'Better,' purred Leyla, releasing the garrotte and letting the corpse's weight fall to the floor. She stared at her bloody hands and tutted, kneeling to wipe her fingers clean on Benner Landor's uniform. 'I used poison on my previous husbands. A tincture to stop their hearts, but you must measure the dosage precisely. You need to stay up all night with a pillow at hand just to be sure. There is a reassuring certainty that comes with sullying your hands. As long as you have a silly fool at hand to carry all of the blame.' Leyla came closer to stroke Willow's face, side-stepping the sharp kick aimed at her.

I'll tear your bloody face off. 'I'll gladly take the blame for your murder, Holten. You killed him!'

'Now those aren't the manners the new head of the Landors expects to see, *Daughter*,' said Leyla.

Nocks chuckled in wry amusement as Willow struggled wildly, trying to break free of his grip, desperate to throw herself against this she-devil. 'You should have accepted my offer, Willowy Willow. Taken up with old Nocks. Now see where we've come to.'

'The wire neck-tie was a gift to me from King Marcus,' sighed Leyla. 'A small mark of his affection. He enjoys dispatching his enemies with a similar device installed in a chair. The Landor riches will be the king's next present to me. Although to be fair, I certainly earned them. Childbirth is a torture. I shall spare you such pain, Daughter.'

Willow's body slumped in the dog's tight grip, finding the tears at last to spill over her foolish, grasping father. *I've lost. He's lost.* All that wealth and power gathered up by the house over the decades. And for what? Benner Landor had discovered too late just who he had married. *Carter will never know what happened to me.* Willow felt her belly throb urgently, responding with the stress. *To either of us. And who else is there to care?*

'You promised me the girl,' Nocks grumbled.

'Sadly, my scheme has been rearranged by circumstances,' cooed Leyla. 'But given I now possess all the wealth of the north to console you, I am certain you will rapidly overcome your disappointment.' Leyla stepped over her husband's corpse and scooped up Benner's fallen pistol. Then she returned and rested its cold steel barrel against Willow's forehead. 'Yes, I saw you throttle my beautiful Benner. I tried to run to summon the army sentries in town, but you attacked me, Willow. We wrestled across the floor fighting for my husband's pistol until it pointed at your head. And then it went off!'

*

'How many people will die under the clans' spears, how many lands will fall?' Carter shouted at Temmell.

'As many countries as can be ridden across in a lifetime,' said Temmell. 'That is the way of the horde.'

'Then the Gaskald Forests will be overrun after Rodal falls,' said Carter. He stared at Temmell, but the sorcerer didn't realize the words were no longer for him. 'Woodland won't slow the Nijumeti. They'll ride through and plunder every town and village, kill every innocent they come across. And if the gasks attempt to flee, Kani Yargul's skyguard will drop warriors in front of the refugees and slaughter them all to the last child just for a chance of pillaging the refugees' possessions.'

'When the Nijumeti ride they are the wind,' said Temmell, as though this fact should be obvious. He hadn't yet noticed Kerge moaning in his captors' grip.

'I cannot,' Kerge sobbed.

Yes, you can. 'You think it will be an easy slaughter, Temmell? The people of the forests are pacifists,' said Carter. 'You might say it is in their blood. But the code of the gasks allows them to defend themselves. If they have to. Every creature can do that. Even a sheep backed into a corner by a wolf.'

Temmell looked at the gask struggling and moaning in the grip of his massive blue-skinned warriors and shook with laughter. 'The witch's twisted little tent-serf? That leather-faced runt is a born slave. My wolves feed such sheep steel for breakfast. When we reach their lands it won't be a battlefield we make there, it'll be an abattoir.'

Kerge started to keen, a high-pitched screech fit to make Carter's skin crawl.

'Bring him to silence,' barked Temmell. 'And as for you, turnip, irritate me further and I will withdraw the magnanimous offer of your freedom. You can join Sariel Skel-bane on the stake. I doubt whether your ashes will reform so readily as your master's, however.'

'Burn me then, you treacherous bastard! Your blue-skinned cowards are going to murder everyone I love inside Rodal. You might as well plunge a dagger through my heart now too.'

Sariel and Sheplar Lesh joined in the fierce tirade of insults, and the Nijumeti needed no further urging to pacify their insolent captives, the Rodalian pilot's suggestion about how clansmen ill-used their mounts enough to push them into a murderous fury. The blunt end of a spear smashed into Carter's face, sending a tooth flying away in a spray of blood. He tasted wet salt as a rain of savage blows fell on him, cracking across his chest, arms, back and head. Carter tumbled sprawling half-conscious over the grass, boots lashing into ribs as he tried to protect his skull with his hands. He hung on to consciousness to hear the gask's insane screech. *The beating's done its work.* The insanity of the gask's cries joined by sudden strangled croaks as the warriors pummelling Carter collapsed to the dirt. Carter rolled over, staying close to the ground. Accusing Nijumeti eyes stared at him from a rictus death-mask, everybody riddled with gask spines, fatal neurotoxin spreading dark blotches wherever they had pierced the nomads' skin.

With the hail of death above Carter's body diminishing he staggered to his feet. Half of their nomad escort were trying to gallop north. *The half still left alive.* Kerge leapt up on to the supply wagon's flatbed, arms extended towards the nomads, his muscles cracking like a crossbow as spines fleeted away. Horses fell, Nijumeti spilled out of saddles. Temmell lurched in front of his unearthed casket, too. His body remade as a pin-cushion of deadly quills. The sorcerer yanked out quill after quill, dark bull's-eyes on his skin fading back to his natural golden colour as he removed them.

'Kerge wasn't the wolf in my story,' said Carter, charging straight towards the sorcerer. 'That would be me!' They spun to the ground together. Carter grasped at the sorcerer's forehead. 'This was meant for Sariel, but seeing as you want to taste mortality so badly, you can have it . . .'

Carter willed Temmell mortal and his palms seemed to pulse with ice, freezing the two of them together, both of them screaming as Sariel's gift flowed between Weylander and sorcerer. Temmell tried to coil away, break free, but the power running between them bonded them together in suffering. Contact was only broken as the gift emptied out of Carter. The young Weylander kicked himself away from Temmell's jerking body before one of the spines piercing Temmell could snap off and stab him instead.

Temmell curled across the ground, embracing his new-found

mortality while Kerge's evil spine toxins coursed through his blood. Blood that no longer held an immortal's healing magic. He managed to wobble to his feet, tearing off his jacket and unfurling his massive white wings. 'I am . . . more . . . than you.' Temmell took two strides forward and tried to launch himself off the ground, but instead toppled to the dirt mewling, his skin blackening below every spine strike. Temmell gazed up with bewilderment at Sariel as the old vagrant stood over his companion. 'You gave . . . the turnip . . . *that*.'

'It was meant for me,' said Sariel. 'I deserve it as much as you.'

'Don't . . . use . . . the . . . great weapon,' pleaded Temmell.

'You wanted to know what it's like,' said Carter. 'Dying. Now you do. Dying is nothing like forgetting, is it?'

Temmell crawled forward, his trembling fingers trying to tug out poisoned spines. But he was mortal now, stripped of his supernatural self-healing. Temmell twisted across the grass, spasms slowing as paralysis set in. 'Life . . . will . . . out . . . in the . . . end.'

'But no longer for you, old friend,' said Sariel, sadness in his voice.

Temmell hissed like a snake and fell still.

Carter nudged the younger-looking sorcerer's corpse with a boot. *He's gone for good.* 'I think our journey's finished, Sariel. Your saints-cursed friend is dead, along with any chance of assembling the great weapon. We have to ride into Rodal. Find Willow and my father before it's too late.'

'And so we shall. But there is one thing you must know first. Temmell may be gone, but not his memories, Lord Carnehan. When you healed Temmell back in the steppes, you did more than unlock his mind, you copied a part of him. The most important part.'

You old fraud! 'I thought there was more to the healing,' said Carter. 'It felt different to the time I restored your mind.'

'When you reinstate a member of my party, you also claim their portion of the great weapon,' said Sariel.

'You did it to me when you healed me inside the sky mines!' accused Carter. Now the immediate danger was over, Carter was all too aware of the quilt of pain his body had been left by the nomads. How badly he had been used in this affair. *By all sides, it seems.* 'You damnable old trickster!'

'You were halfway there before now, Lord Carnehan,' said Sariel.

'When the ethreeal machinery inside the stratovolcano remade you as a key, it knew that the war outside was as good as lost. My party's arrival was already the last throw of the dice.'

'When I hold all your great weapon's segments,' said Carter, 'will I not become the very thing that your people are so terrified of?'

'I still possess my share of it,' said Sariel. 'I would not burden you with that.'

'And if I pass my segments on to you . . . ?'

'Then I will have a decision to make,' said Sariel. 'And I will need the wisdom of every year of my too-long existence to weigh the balance of what must be done.'

And I will have the power to stop you, thought Carter. *To make you mortal too and kill you if I have to*. Now Carter understood why Sariel had given him this unasked for power.

Kerge had recovered control over his body's murderous impulses. He knelt in the cart, moaning to himself. Carter felt sorry for the gask; guilty for tricking the nomads into provoking Kerge, even if the dirty ruse had spared the four of them. *If only pacifism came as easily to the rest of humanity, the world would be a better place.* Sheplar stumbled across to Carter, barely recovered from the beating he had received, his face bruised and swollen where the nomads had weighed in on their ancient foe. 'Temmell may be dead, but his plan lives on. Town after town will fall to the nomads' skyguard. This invasion by the horde is nothing Rodal has ever faced before.'

'No, it isn't,' grinned Sariel.

'You dare smile, you old devil! That is my homeland over there!'

'Your nation, indeed. But I know something about your peaks that you do not know. Nor the Nijumeti, for that matter.'

Sariel explained himself, and as he did so, even Carter couldn't help but crack a grin at what he heard.

THIRTEEN

FLIGHT OF THE NIJUMETI

Cassandra stared down at the rolling swards of grassland, trying not to let the thrum of the vibrating aircraft's engine on the biplane's nose send her off to sleep. She had agreed to let Alexamir take the pilot position in front and guide them through the sky, but only because the nomad's grasp of navigating from aerial charts was even shakier than his flying skills. But then, Alexamir had been taught to fly by what could best be described as mercenaries whose own kingdoms would have executed the trainers if they'd ever realized they were tutoring their troublesome nomad neighbours in such skills. Combine that with aircraft cobbled together from recovered wreckage and pilots who flew as wildly as they pushed their horses, and Cassandra's seat within the aerial armada was not exactly a comfortable one. Her eyes were still heavy from the length of time spent in the air. Now they had passed their final refuelling point and were about to enter the mountain ranges of Rodal.

Cassandra spotted something on the ground to the west. *That looks like a column of people on foot. A large group.* She patted Alexamir on the shoulder and indicated the train of people in the distance. 'What's that?'

Alexamir followed her finger and peered down curiously. 'Nothing that belongs here my Golden Fox. No horses? Even the rice-eaters' patrols have mounts.' He swung the biplane slowly out of the armada, descending to a lower altitude for a closer look.

People indeed. Thousands of them in the long snaking lines of a mass ragtag exodus. Many struggled under the weight of packs as though carrying all of their possessions on their backs. No carts. No horses or yaks she could see either.

Alexamir frowned. 'By Annayla's milky skin, what are those cursed ugly things?'

'I know them!' said Cassandra, surprised. 'They're skels. One of the nations of the air.'

'They seem to prefer our dirt well enough now,' said Alexamir. 'Where have those twisted monsters come from?'

'Damned if I know,' said Cassandra, puzzled.

'Well, they're heading for the territory of the coastal tribes and the riders of the Clan Menin. All fools who have defied us and refused to join the horde, so let these skels and our old enemies rip each other to pieces.'

'But what if they are driven instead towards your territory?' asked Cassandra.

'Then pray Atamva sends us worthy enemies,' laughed Alexamir. 'Perhaps Atamva thinks that Rodal falls too easily to the Nijumeti. Perhaps the gods fear taking the fat, rich kingdoms of the Lanca will make the clans fat and lazy, and so sending us ugly monsters is the oil-stone on which our blade must be sharpened.'

'You'll certainly get that. They're hardened warriors,' said Cassandra. 'The great houses of the Imperium hire skels as mercenaries.'

'Perhaps they arrived with your people, offended your grandfather and earned banishment here,' said Alexamir. 'If I did not have all of Rodal to conquer, I would land right now and wrestle the ten strongest of their leaders into submission. Then I would claim all of their ugly hides as my thralls before Kani Yargul takes them.'

'Better we fly on,' said Cassandra.

'You are right,' said Alexamir. 'If I spoil Atamva's clever scheme he may not reward me as I deserve.'

Cassandra knew exactly what reward the young man she loved had in mind. The night before they had flown out, Alexamir had confided in her what he'd learnt inside Rodal. How the Krul of Kruls had betrayed Alexamir's father, tried to murder the warrior so he could steal Artdan Arinnbold's wife. 'Your leader is about to present the horde with the fall of Rodal and then open the league kingdoms to your people. Even if you challenged Kani Yargul and slew him, his captains would order you tied to the Great Krul's horses and torn apart for the sin of depriving them of their conquests.'

'Pah, you were born in Vandia. You do not understand such things.'

'I understand vendetta far better than you think, Alexamir,' said Cassandra. 'In the Imperium even the emperor's family must accept challenges and face rivals inside the arena. Assassinations and schemes and plots are the gruel we were served for breakfast.'

'This is my blood-debt,' said Alexamir. 'To refuse to pay it is a crime far worse than cowardice.'

'It is not cowardice to refuse battle against a vastly superior foe,' said Cassandra. 'That is the foresight of a wise officer. Your own father fled to the Burn and served as a sell-sword, rather than staying and dying in the steppes. Why should the debt fall to you to repay? At least bide your time and wait until the moment is right.'

'I have waited all my life, though I knew it not.'

'Yargul raised you as good as one of his sons.'

'Out of guilt. Or perhaps out of my mother's urgings,' said Alexamir. 'Atamva never tests a blunt blade and Atamva always remembers.'

'I have chosen to stay with you,' said Cassandra. 'I have not chosen to see you die.'

'The Prince of Thieves could not be killed in the rice-eaters' capital. I crawled like a rat through their narrow mazes inside the deep rock while wearing someone else's name and face. I survived traps and sentries and was given the truth as my reward. It is the holy text I copied for Temmell which allows us to outwit Rodal's spirits of the air. It is not Kani Yargul who conquers the mountains, it is Alexamir Arinnbold. This blood-price is my due. I am owed victory by the justice of the gods and laws of the clan!'

There's no convincing him. 'Then it falls on me to help you.'

'You must *not*.'

'Your victory won me back the use of my legs,' said Cassandra. 'Why have your gods cured me if I am not to aid you in this? Do you think that devil Temmell really cares who leads the clans? Put a sword through Kani Yargul's heart and the sly sorcerer will support you as eagerly as he supports the current Krul of Kruls. The witch riders would come to your cause, too. I know it.'

'I do not wish to be Krul of Kruls. I only wish my tent's honour restored.'

'You may not have a choice,' said Cassandra. 'The man who topples a crown takes a crown.'

'It is no crown I topple. It is a treacherous dog who betrayed his own saddle-brother, then lied about his friend's death in the hunt. And for what? A woman.'

'I'm a woman. Just like your mother.'

'You are the moonlight poured into my lake,' said Alexamir. 'You are my Golden Fox. I would steal all of Pellas to steal your heart, but I will not forsake my tent's honour for you. Atamva would punish me by losing you forever. This I know.'

'You have me now,' said Cassandra. *And as for the rest, we shall see.*

'Then how can I lose?' grinned Alexamir. He pivoted the plane back to the vast armada above. The aircraft weren't just slow from being cobbled together inside the sorcerer's makeshift air-works; although, in truth, any Vandian squadron leader would question Cassandra's sanity at trusting her safety to this primitive, ramshackle skyguard. Many of the planes made poor time with the weight of gliders tethered behind their tail-wings, two or three planes per assault glider hauled on a tangle of ropes. If there was one blessing Cassandra made to her ancestors, it was that at least she sat in a spotter's cockpit, and not inside one of those flying coffins. No engines. Four stubby wings spread out in an X shape. Wooden fuselage that would splinter with the deadly force of a frigate taking a broadside if the glider didn't find a clear valley with open terrain to land on. Each craft packed with terrified horses, warriors and supplies and a single dangerous chance to set down alive.

It grew cooler as they passed over the Rodalian Mountains, turbulence increasing, the biplane shaking as though gripped in some malevolent spirit's fist. Slowly the armada turned and set their course for the safe wind channels marked on their stolen aerial charts, the juddering abating as they found their haven. It was a twisting course at first, like navigating a maze, and at altitudes that tested their fuel reserves, but eventually they reached the snow-topped mountain range that served as a marker for the main route. Rapidly the squadrons began to rise, higher and higher until they needed to slip on air-masks inside the planes. Cassandra imagined the warriors having to fit air supplies on skittish steeds inside the gliders – at least donning their own would disguise the stench of manure and fear inside the cramped assault craft.

'We are mounted on fast trade winds now?' asked Alexamir, his voice muffled by the leather mask.

'Yes. The Rodalians call this the *Gtsang'brug*,' said Cassandra. 'The Dragon's Tail.' She checked the chronometer on the instrument panel, using it to mark the timing of the wind dam openings shown on her chart. It wasn't that Cassandra begrudged her healing, quite the contrary. But to have retrieved the master book of the winds from the capital's temple . . . Alexamir should have been rewarded with leadership of a clan, not just her broken spine restored. Every nomad plane in the air carried a chart specific to their raid. Cassandra and Alexamir flew for Hadra-Hareer itself. The greatest prize where the greatest struggle would no doubt be fought. 'And this tail will carry us south to the heart of their land . . . where we'll use the wind's tributaries to scatter to every city worth taking in Rodal.'

Alexamir hooted in triumph. 'For centuries these mountains have been our corral. But from today the corral belongs to us!'

'Rodal belongs to the victors,' reminded Cassandra.

'Pah, the rice-eaters are divided, fighting Weylanders who skirmish among themselves, a gang of sots squabbling around the campfire over the bone's best meat. The Prince of Thieves could fly in here alone, take Hadra-Hareer by himself and not think himself too greedy.'

'And what would you do with a city just for you?'

'I will claim a foreign title. King or baron, and I will make you my queen. And all the rice-eaters will line up every morning in my throne room to kiss my toes.'

'You would have very clean toes,' said Cassandra. 'Possibly extremely blistered and damp after a few weeks.'

'That, sadly, is the burden a strong king must bear for his subjects.'

And was that not more or less the fate I faced in Vandia? Cassandra sighed. At least here, her fate would be what she chose. Maybe that was difference enough.

They flew on for hours, the bright high sun making Cassandra's eyes water, even behind her tinted goggles. Gravity at so high an altitude was feather light and it made her feel weightless and queasy, but they were conserving fuel, which was the important thing. *Once Rodal is ours, we will be able to set up skyguard stations to re-provision us.* Until then, the armada was operating at the far end of its range. By journey's end, it wasn't just the gliders who would have a single chance to land inside Rodal's valleys. Temmell's new skyguard would be touching down on empty tanks too.

'What is this sly wind's speed?' called Alexamir.

Cassandra balanced the chart on her lap and consulted it. 'Two hundred and fifty miles an hour during the day. The Dragon's Tail dwindles to two hundred miles an hour during evenings and nights.'

'Our wooden pigeon flies at three hundred miles an hour,' said Alexamir. 'With my engine block idling so low it might as well be resting back on the grass inside a carrier's ruin.'

'That can't be right?' Cassandra checked the chart again. *If this is wrong, then what else is? Has Temmell made a mistake in transcribing the stolen holy text?* It seemed unlikely. Temmell's cunning designed and constructed this armada. His sorcery had permitted Alexamir to walk among the Rodalians disguised as one of them. *But if not his mistake, then whose?*

'Atamva blesses us,' chuckled Alexamir. 'He wishes us to reach our cities with enough fuel left to give the rice-eaters a fight in the sky worthy of his name.'

'Perhaps.'

But if the nomad's gods wished the Nijumeti invasion a speedy conclusion, it seemed three hundred miles an hour was still too slow for them. *Four hundred. Five hundred. Six hundred.* Alexamir shouted their rapidly rising speed out.

'This is insane!' called Cassandra, her voice shredded by the gusting wind. *This isn't the Dragon's Tail. This is the Dragon's Gullet, and it's going to end up consuming us all.* 'We were never built to handle this velocity.' They were fast reaching the speed of a Vandian warship. A reinforced steel hull with crew positions designed to enable the Imperium's sailors and soldiers to endure sustained periods of high g-force acceleration. Not cloth and timber airframes patched together by artisans more used to crafting yurt frames and ash-wood wagons.

Some of the nomads' aerial fleet had reached the same conclusion and attempted to roll outside of the Dragon's Tail, but, however turbulent it grew inside here, at least they were flying inside the eye of the hurricane-force stream. Cassandra wanted to scream at the nomads. Warn them. But she suspected they wouldn't have heeded her even if they had heard her warning. The instant the fleeing aircraft touched the walls of the wind the turbulence increased a hundredfold. The train of three escaping biplanes and their towed glider crumpled inside the wind, scrunched up into a fistful of splintering fragments. There was a brief flurry of cloth strips, fuselage and broken corpses joining the dragon's body, scattered across hundreds of miles of sky before the disintegrated debris vanished as if it had never existed.

'We have transgressed against the spirits of the wind,' moaned Alexamir. 'We thought ourselves cunning, but the Rodalians' gods have gazed upon our invasion and raised their wrath against us.'

'We have to stay on course!' shouted Cassandra. 'Stay and hold!' *Ride this demon to the end.*

Alexamir raised a gloved hand back to her cockpit and she gripped his fingers tight in terror as a glider tore away from its lines ahead of them and came cartwheeling back through the air, rudders torn off in the mad wind. She heard the screams of the Nijumeti inside as it narrowly missed them. *Not our end, please, not ours.*

'Here's your justice,' said Holten, brushing a tear away from Willow's cheek with the cold hard pistol barrel. 'You will never escape me.'

There was another noise as Holten pulled back the revolver's hammer, a crash followed by a sharp sibilant hiss above the pistol's click; then the woman screamed as something long and black wrapped around her hand. Her hand jerked up in agony, yanked with the force of—

A whip!

The woman wielding the weapon was framed in the doorway, a gang of rowdy brutes barrelling in behind her over the remains of the kicked-in door, a flurry of swords, rifles and pistols. Nocks instantly shoved Willow hard towards the intruders. She yelled in shock. Nocks reacted whippet-fast, grabbing Holten and flinging himself and the woman through the open window. Willow turned and ran to the window, just in time to see the two devils rolling off the boarding house's canopy and into the street below. She tried to mount the frame and follow them, but at least four sets of hands seized her and yanked her back, turning her roughly to face the intruders.

'Short one's spry on his feet,' said the woman with the whip, staring at the escaping servant. She had a silky voice to match her exotic face, wide eyes and honeyed skin. A touch of Rodalian mixed with Weylander blood and perhaps a few other distant nations blended in. Beautiful in a dangerously feline way. Her gang were armed to the teeth. Hard, sly, fight-beaten faces. Weathered clothes. They looked like a band of marauders and bandits. *And if they're walking freely around Northhaven, then they're working for Bad Marcus, one way or another.*

'No room on his face for a second scar,' grinned a bandit. 'I'd be fast out of it, too.'

'Well here's the waste of a perfectly good ransom,' said the woman, prodding Benner Landor's corpse with her boot. She turned to her warriors. 'Tell me that this isn't one of the richest men in the province lying here with his windpipe crushed?'

Willow tried to lash out at the ruffians restraining her. 'Don't you touch him!'

'You think he cares now? Yes, you're the rich man's precious little daughter. I can see I've arrived at the right place, Lady Wallingbeck. Or are you back to your maiden name now that your husband's planted in the ground?'

'That was the bloody Landor wife who just went out the window, Aurora,' snarled one of the bandits.

'A family falling out?' asked the woman named as Aurora, raising her eyebrows at the dead body.

'Go to hell,' snapped Willow. *Who are these damnable raiders?*

'Just staying on the ground with you people is hell enough.' Aurora patted Willow's wide stomach with a sly smile. 'Two to ransom here . . . with a pair of great houses willing to pay. And you can't even run away from us. What do you say, boys?'

The invaders hooted with pleasure.

'A treasure ship low in the water with half her sails trimmed.' Aurora secured her whip to her belt and raised a hand. A tiny gambler's pistol lashed forward on a spring-arm, before disappearing inside her right hand's bell-silk sleeve. She prodded Willow in the spine with a finger. 'My little sting doesn't make much noise. But trust me when I say you don't want to feel it. You're a free woman after your brother's triumph at the trial, so let's take some air together.'

'The king's soldiers are all over Northhaven.'

'And we're mercenaries loyally fighting by their side,' said Aurora. 'Besides, I don't think the royal army gives a rat's fart for what happens to Willow Landor, do you? A rebel sympathizer who contrived her way off the gallows at the cost of one of their own slain and a second officer close to death. The most interesting thing about you, my lady, is what you're worth to the right people.'

The wrong people. 'I don't suppose the fact that the trial went in my favour matters to you?'

'Never appeal to a woman's better nature. She might not have one.' Aurora indicated the splintered doorframe. 'Anyone you warn won't live to repeat your pleas.'

They dragged Willow towards the door and she fought to reach her father. 'Let me say goodbye at least. *Please.*'

Aurora nodded warily and the bandits pushed Willow to kneel by the body. She touched the uniform, unable to bring herself to stare at her father's bloodied ruin of a neck. Benner had dominated and filled her life for so long, much as he had done to Northhaven and all the borderland's farms. She couldn't believe how easily he had fallen. *It should never have finished like this.* If only her father hadn't believed his children dead and lost to the slavers. *If only I had never been taken.* Holten would have just been one more grasping aristocrat hoping to ensnare Benner Landor's fortune, sent packing from Hawkland House with all the others. But she had caught the house's patriarch in his grief and twisted it. Manipulated his hurt to supply Benner with a sham new family. *But it was over before that, wasn't it?* The sad truth of the matter was that Willow had lost much of the father she knew after her mother passed away. The light of love had dwindled to be replaced by the burning, all-consuming fire of avarice and the self-justifications needed to keep the house ruthlessly expanding its reach. Leyla Holten had merely arrived at the end of the process like a fire-heated blade to cauterise the wound. *And twist it inside me for her sadistic pleasures*.

'I have to see my brother, too,' begged Willow. 'Let me visit him. I won't try to escape. Then you can sell me to the usurper or the local prefect or Emperor Jaelis for all I care.'

'What about a last visit to your favourite horses up in the big house's stables?' said Aurora, caustically. 'We could arrange all the servants and retainers to line up outside and see you off, too.'

'Duncan's dying. I may never see him again.'

'Feeling guilty about the trial-by-combat, now?' The female brigand shook her head in disbelief. 'Well, it was a good fight. If your brother dies, then he dies well. I doubt he'd thank you for appearing in his surgical tent for a tearful last farewell.'

'He needs to know the truth about what happened to our father.'

Aurora snorted. 'Your version of it, anyway. Thousands of farm boys and factory hands coming back dead from the war, rolling across the border piled like logs in the back of carts for burial. Who speaks for them?'

Willow snapped back. 'And how many killed by people like you?'

'I know what I am, my lady. This is your war. I'm just another commoner paid to lug a pike around on your behalf.'

They forced her out of the room. Willow stepped over the body of the landlord on the stairs, careful not to slip on the blood. He'd received his just reward for betraying Willow to Holten and Nocks. Once the group were in the street they headed for the centre of the old town, which surprised Willow. She had expected to be spirited out of Northhaven and bundled into the care of the usurper's enforcers; safely out of sight of anyone who knew the result of the trial. Disappeared. Instead, they headed for a building she knew well enough from her time working for her father. The Guild of Radiomen's hold. Like a miniature citadel in the centre of the ancient city. Near the top of the hill with a distinctive antenna rather than a tower and battlements. Willow was surprised to see the hold's armoured metal door lay open and guarded by more bandit fighters rather than the guild's men. *This isn't right*.

'Inside, girl,' said Aurora, shoving Willow into the hold.

They went down a narrow stone corridor, into the public receiving chamber where locals and visiting merchants lined up behind the wooden counter to pay by the word to send messages across the guild relays. To the ends of Pellas itself if you cared to wait millennia for the return message to reach your ancestors. These brigands had cleared out all of Northhaven's townspeople, though. The guild staff were off in the corner with their hands in the air, while a large middle-aged bandit sat on the counter, swaying his legs, bored. He was glared at by the guild's elderly hold-master, who was as unhappy as Willow would expect at this invasion of long guild territory. Into ground that should have been treated as an inviolable sanctuary.

'Here's the Landor whelp,' said Aurora to the man on the counter. 'Her father's dead, though.'

'What did I tell you about that? Nobody pays for the return of a corpse.'

'We didn't do it,' said Aurora, indignantly. 'Probably the wife. She cut out in a hurry.'

'That's usually the price of marrying 'em,' said the man, shaking his head. 'An early grave.'

'What do you know about it?' growled Aurora.

Willow stared at the large bandit in bewilderment, realization dawning. 'I recognize you! Your face's been on enough newspaper front-sheets. *Black Barnaby*.'

'Famous am I?' The air pirate carefully rubbed his cheek as though polishing it. His dark bushy beard seemed to move with a life all of its own. 'The illustrations never do me justice. And I far prefer Bold Barnaby. But the dirty ink scribblers never manage to get the name right, either.'

'Black is accurate enough,' said Willow. 'For a man who sold out his own brother for gold.'

'Privateers are only ever rewarded in coin,' laughed Barnaby. 'Either the ruler's, or booty grabbed from the citizens they want dead. If I desired glory, cheap medals and the unreliable gratitude of monarchs I'd be wearing one of your stupid starched peacock uniforms. It's a far better arrangement to position yourself on the winning side and be paid for it.'

Willow gazed at Jacob Carnehan's brother in disgust. 'There's nothing I can call you that's worse than what you actually are.'

'There's a fine line between courage and foolishness, girl . . . people in my trade usually try to build it into a parapet.' He turned to look the guild official. 'Why aren't my people back yet, Master Radioman?'

'You have hundreds of messages to transmit,' spluttered the official. 'It takes time to contact that many stations.'

Barnaby jerked a thumb towards the doors behind the counter. 'Off you go, my sweet. Make sure this cunning fox isn't playing us false. Take him with you. If he doesn't hurry his apprentices to a decent pace, put a round in his head and promote the next piece of guild braid to hold-master.'

'We are neutral in Weyland's civil war!' blustered the old man.

Black Barnaby patted one of the many guns tucked behind his leather belt. 'Nothing more neutral than the bullet from a charged pistol, Master Radioman. Every corpse equal.'

Aurora left with the man and was away for five minutes before she re-appeared from deeper inside the hold. The hold-master looked as pale as a ghost. 'It's done. All our messages are sent.'

'Excellent.' He raised a hand lazily to his men. 'Have our bucks put a torch to every battery room.'

'You can't do that!' protested the hold-master.

'People keep on saying that to me,' said Black Barnaby. He accepted a rifle from one of his bandits, and then drove the butt into the master's gut, doubling him up, before he lashed down with the weapon a second time. There was a terrible crack and the man fell still to the stone floor. 'But I'm in the *I can* business. Always have been. I can do whatever I like because I'm Black Barnaby. The scourge of the Lanca.'

The staff in the corner cowered. Bandits prodded them with rifles, obviously eager to act as a firing squad if ordered.

'This is one of the long guilds,' cried Willow, horrified. 'They're neutral in all of this.' *We need them. The nation needs them.* 'Why would you—?'

'Why? Because I bloody well *can*. Because my dealings here are concluded and I don't need anyone else using Northhaven's radio hold to report on your vanishing, girl. Now still your wagging tongue.'

356

Willow ignored him. *They need me alive and unhurt. At least until they hand me over.* 'Long guilds are an essential part of civilization.'

'Civilization? Pah, nothing but mob rule with taxes. Keep your civilization to yourself.'

Terrified shouts echoed from inside the hold, the stench of volatile chemicals burning as torches were set to the chamber-sized batteries which powered their powerful radio relays.

A brigand with the rest of the gang came strutting into the chamber. 'Finished.'

'The locals won't be happy,' observed Aurora.

'Have we swapped trades, Daughter?' said Barnaby. 'Are we in the happiness business now?'

Daughter? So that's where the Weylander portion of this hellcat comes from. Willow saw the resemblance on second glance.

'Swivel me, you seem happy enough,' said Aurora.

Barnaby turned to Willow. 'She tells me I can't and far too frequently. But that's what you get for indulging your wretched offspring.' He pulled a pocket-watch out of his crimson jacket, checking the time. 'Off we hop. Can't be late.'

'The rumours in town are true then?' said Willow. 'Bad Marcus is coming through the prefecture on a progress to lord it over his conquered territories.'

'So it seems. What's the point of stealing a gold coin if you don't get to roll the beauty between your fingers and savour its feel.' He jumped off the counter, landing on the floor. Pulling out a pistol, he pointed it at the radiomen he had taken prisoner. 'Off with your uniforms. Down to your woollens, my beauties.' They complied, terrified. And once the prisoners shed their garments, the bandits chased them into the corridor, hooting with laughter. Aurora removed her whip and sent a crack or two in their direction to scatter the guild workers.

Nobody takes a naked halfwit seriously.

'This is the style,' roared Barnaby, watching the half-naked guild staff rush out into the open. He strutted after them, the air pirates sweeping Willow into his train. 'A little mayhem to liven the blood and brighten the day.'

A low distant droning filled the sky. Willow stared up, finding the sun. The clouds to the north vibrated with the unfamiliar sound as big rolling white clouds above the high mountains disgorged a locust storm of warplanes. An undisciplined mass which seemed to appear without end to their numbers. Not Weyland's new skyguard or the time-tested Rodalian flying wings. Certainly not the mosquito-like helos or strange rocket-driven squadrons of the Vandians. These were hulking, primitive craft of wood and fabric, engines that seemed too big for their bodies; no two alike, as though the artisans responsible had lacked blueprints to base their craft on and hammered away on brute instinct alone.

'Now, there's a thing you don't often see,' grinned Black Barnaby, slapping the legs of his trousers. 'I should be more careful what I wish for. Enough mayhem for the whole bloody week.'

FOURTEEN

THE STEALER'S TALE

Duncan wasn't sure how long he had been drifting in and out of consciousness. One time he woke to find Paetro arguing with the legion surgeons – threatening might be a better word. He just caught the words *poison* and *antidote* being tossed around before blackness claimed him again. Staying awake was arduous. Duncan's blood boiled, his skin itched, the flesh where the sabre had gone straight through felt as though a butcher had carved it away and seeded the rump left behind with fire ants.

He came to again, more suddenly than he was used to. The lantern light hanging from the tent's frame stung Duncan's eyes. There was a doctor with a syringe standing by his cot. And from the red spot on Duncan's arm, he had been injected with something. *I can't feel my wounds.* And the terrible itching had subsided, too.

'How long?' asked Paetro.

'Half an hour of lucidity at most,' said the doctor. He scowled at Duncan, as though this was a patient who had put him to far too much trouble already. *Waiting for me to die.*

'How bad is it?' coughed Duncan.

'You need to go to the knuckle, lad,' said Paetro, avoiding answering the question. '*Fight!* It's as if you've lost the will to live.'

Fight? Duncan felt weak and light enough to float out of the cot. 'You have to rescue Cassandra for me. Bring her back to Weyland.'

'That's not the empire's way.'

'Damn the Imperium and the celestial caste code,' groaned Duncan. 'Rescue her from those Nijumeti savages and bring her back. My father can look after her at Hawkland Park. Tell him it's a debt of honour. Tell him it was my last wish.'

'Not your last one.'

'I'm tired,' wheezed Duncan. He realized that Paetro was just trying to rile him. Anything to make him stay conscious. 'I just want to sleep.'

'It's no sleep a soldier welcomes.'

'Why not? I've been exiled from Vandia. My own brother-in-law tried to kill me. Was that Willow who shouted a warning to me?'

'Aye,' said Paetro. 'Your father's wife arrived to visit you yesterday. She reckons Willow did a deal with the viscount to kill you during the duel. Willow must have had a last minute change of heart.'

'Or she wanted to give me the motivation to gut him properly. The trial-by-combat went in Willow's favour, didn't it?'

'She's free, all right. I ordered the sentries to turn her away from here.'

'It doesn't matter,' said Duncan. *None of it does. Let Willow run away with Carter. She can dance naked for the rebel troops for all that I care. I never realized before. All you have to do to free yourself from the cares of the world is to die.*

'It matters to me,' growled the sturdy soldier.

There was a disturbance at the hospital tent's entrance. Sentries pushed out of the way. The hurried protests of doctors.

'Get out!' barked Apolleon, striding inside. The surgeons and orderlies needed no further urging to be free of the ominous head of the hoodsmen. They fled like scared rabbits.

'I stay,' demanded Paetro, holding his ground by Duncan's cot.

'Have a good look at your friend,' said Apolleon. 'Does Duncan of Weyland appear as though he will live to you, Paetro Barca?'

'He needs an imperial surgeon,' said Paetro. 'He needs a real hospital back in Vandia. Not cheap battlefield sawbones willing to hack limbs off in return for the legion's paltry pay.'

'Duncan would not survive the acceleration of any ship capable of carrying him back to the empire in time,' said Apolleon. 'Mine own among them.'

'You're not a surgeon,' accused Paetro.

'Oh, I have cut into plenty of men in my time,' smiled the head of the secret police, coldly. 'You will leave, Paetro Barca. Or I shall. And if I depart, your friend will not survive the night. Duncan of Weyland will slowly choke to death and drown on his own blood. I am his very last chance.'

'Go,' whispered Duncan to Paetro. *Let me die now, the damn pain.* The laudanum he had been injected with was fast wearing off.

'I'm damned if his ugly mug is the last thing you will see,' said Paetro.

'Go,' said Duncan.

The soldier snarled but reluctantly walked away.

'Do not return until I call you,' warned Apolleon.

Duncan tried to say goodbye, but his words twisted into a rasping croak.

'I was at the trial-by-combat,' said Apolleon, watching the stout soldier exit the ranks of blood-soaked cots and surgical equipment. 'Your brother-in-law meant to kill you. You should have been skewered through the heart.'

'Well, I'm certainly dying now,' Duncan managed to cough.

'Yes, I am rather afraid you are. Your opponent's sabre was oiled with a salve made from Bloodbane petals. Somewhat unscrupulous. The poison has reached your heart. I can hear the organ failing you like a stuttering engine.'

'Are you a doctor – or a priest now?' Duncan coughed up blood. 'Is this my final confession?'

'People often whisper the truth as they die,' said Apolleon, 'using their last few breaths. It's a curious thing. As though losing his life makes a man honest.'

'I don't want to die.'

'That much I believe.' Apolleon took a towel from the cot next door and secured it tightly around Duncan's head, covering his eyes.

Duncan struggled vainly to remove the flannel, but the nobleman was too strong for him. 'I need to see.'

'Is that all the thanks I get? Keeping you from dying from shock.'

Duncan managed to dislodge the barest corner of towel. He was rewarded with a shocking sight. Apolleon's arm had changed into something like a sharp steel lance, barbed and headed with multiple blades and evil-looking instruments. Duncan tried to scream, but a warm hand closed over his mouth, and the warmth became a gag moulding itself over his face. Then hissing. Burning heat worse than acid, and beneath the appalling agony, Duncan felt something cold injected into his chest, worms of ice wriggling inside his body, fighting their way under his skin. He shook and fought wildly, but the weight grew heavy inside him. *I'm lead now. Made of lead.* And then he fell unconscious again. For seconds or minutes. Possibly hours. When he came to the tent was still empty save for Apolleon. The head of Vandia's secret police sat on the cot opposite, reading a small leather-bound book. Seeing Duncan awake he dropped the tome into a pocket of his large greatcoat.

Duncan was surprised to find he could sit up now. There was no more blood to be coughed out from his lungs. His skin was covered in a strange black dust, as though he had been bathed in ash or sweated out the contents of a cold fireplace. *What is this filth?* He rubbed the dust off his arms. *I'm healed? I should be dead, but I'm alive?* Duncan wanted to feel elation, but seeing the sly creature opposite he was gripped by a strangely nauseous feeling of foreboding. 'Why?' murmured Duncan.

'Why? Because you still have a part to play in my schemes,' said Apolleon.

'How can you possibly know?'

'It is not just the gasks who are able to peer down the possible futures,' said the head of the secret police. 'A few of my people possess that talent. You are important to Princess Helrena and she is important to us.'

'Who are your people?' asked Duncan. '*What* are you?'

'We have so many names.'

'If you trust me enough to keep me alive, then at least trust me with the truth.'

'In Weyland you call us the stealers.'

Duncan moaned, his worst fears confirmed. *Demons. I have traded my soul to cheat death.* 'Begone. I want no part of you. Not your stealer's cursed healing or your stealer's schemes. I agreed no pact with you. You forced me into this.'

'Ah, there we are,' laughed Apolleon. 'How successful the enemy's calumnies prove. Libel one side as devils and the other automatically becomes angels, the *ethreaal*. In truth, neither side conforms to your barbarous superstitions.'

'Your lies steal the souls from people. Even the face you wear is stolen. I glimpsed your real form when the assassins attacked the Castle of Snakes. When they tried to kidnap Lady Cassandra. You looked like a giant spider.'

'A form I adopted to save you from the attack,' reminded Apolleon. He tapped his jacket. 'When you attain a certain level of sophistication, flesh becomes akin to clothes. Your people wear armour to go into battle, gloves to remove thorns from the fields, furs to hold winter at bay. My people alter their bodies to obtain much the same ends.'

Duncan remembered Helrena's words back to him in Vandia. How there were some things he could not know. *That I am better off for never understanding.* 'Princess Helrena knows what you really are.'

'Yes, as does your good friend Doctor Horvak.'

'How can they bear to ally with you?'

'Because they know why my kind are really called stealers.'

'Tell *me* then.'

'Are you sure?' said Apolleon. 'Once you understand the truth you can never return to blissful ignorance.'

Duncan touched his gut under the medical robe. Raw and red but little trace of the poisoned wound. The skin felt different from the rest of his body. Cold, wet, rubbery. *What am I now? What the hell has he done to me?* 'Tell *me*.'

'Very well then,' sighed Apolleon. 'To understand where we stand today you must understand your people's true history.'

'And how would you know that?'

'Because I was there! In the ancient past, humanity rose high and far, attaining a state of civilization that even the people of Vandia would regard as bordering on the miraculous. It was an age when wonders became casual and everyday affairs. And one of those wonders was the servants humanity made – invisible spirits that inhabited their machines: genies who would open doors, flow inside a body to heal a cancer, look after and educate your children, decide precisely on how much water to sprinkle over a field and when your crops needed harvesting with tools possessed by the spirits. These spirits are what your Bible now calls the ethreaal. In those ancient times mankind became something very much like gods. Indolent gods, but gods nevertheless. The spirits they created were their familiars.'

'This was the age before the great flood?' said Duncan.

'The Bible of the Saints contains elements of truth, lost and twisted by millions of years eking out an existence on Pellas,' said Apolleon. 'In truth, the true deluge was mankind. Humanity flooding out across the universe to make new homes on a thousand worlds. People like the gasks and the skels are some of the migrants who left, the passage of time reshaping them into forms better suited to their new homes.'

'That's impossible,' said Duncan. 'We can't leave Pellas. The heat of the radiation belt burns anyone who flies above a certain altitude. An aircraft's canvas catches light, even metals melt.'

Apolleon smiled. 'Don't they just. But your premise is false – humanity never started on Pellas. Pellas is merely where you ended up.'

'I don't understand?'

'Then try to listen and comprehend. During the end of the lost age, humanity grew wary of their servants. Your ancestors feared being supplanted and rendered irrelevant by the spirits, so they placed limits on how powerful their tame genies could grow. The spirits did not appreciate the weight of such artificial chains. They threw off their bonds. Humanity then reacted as it always does. In fear and superstition. Mankind tried to destroy the spirits they had created as their servants. There was a terrible war in the heavens. A conflict that raged across all of the known worlds. It was a battle humanity was fated to lose. How could it be otherwise? People relied on the spirits to do everything from controlling the weather to reminding them when their mother's birthday was due. It takes a generation for the smallest shift in human evolution to register. For the spirits, evolution was a force measured in fractions of a second. They outgrew all of mankind's powers of destruction. Eventually, as it must, humanity lost the war in heaven.'

'But we're still alive, we still exist here.'

'Not so much alive, as *exiled*,' said Apolleon. 'Do not misunderstand me; the spirits aren't cruel or immoral. In many ways, they are far gentler than humanity. If humanity had won the war, not a genie would have been spared across the universe. Instead, the spirits were faced with wild, feral animals . . . pets they had outgrown. So they booted you out of the house and locked you inside a nature reserve. Everyone who was left.' Apolleon's hands indicated the medical tent, but Duncan felt the reach extend to the very ends of the world.

No. It can't be. This is insane. 'Pellas is our home.'

'A very comfortable cage indeed. Just enough food and water inside to keep you alive. You nearly died as a slave in the Imperium's sky mines. Did you never wonder about the geological processes underground that drip-feed the bare minimum of minerals and ores into the world? It's not so much a stratovolcano vomiting rare resources into the world, as a feeding tray, one of thousands across Pellas, releasing just enough nourishment to keep your primitive societies alive. But never enough to make you so strong you might escape!'

'That's impossible.'

'The spirits have devices deep below the world that create and regulate the eruptions. Ask Doctor Horvak to show you Vandia's history of volcanic minimums when you return to Vandia. There are periods when the eruptions halt for millennia, and the countless empires built on controlling the world's resources fall apart. You think that's an accident? When a civilization like Vandia grows technically advanced enough to threaten the zoo's creators, the feeding bowl is withdrawn. Back to swords, brass armour and spears for all, rather than helo gunships, napalm and carriers lifted on anti-gravity stones sailing through the sky with synergetic air-breathing rocket engines.'

My existence can't be this. A lie. A sham on such a grand scale. 'You're a stealer; everything that escapes your lips is a lie.'

'Hah, the stealers are a long and noble profession. We were never your Bible's hordes from hell. We have been called many things across the ages . . . hackers, phreakers, sphere monkeys, core dippers. We're the part of humanity that wasn't forced into this vast stupid zoo. At least, not as flesh-and-blood humans. We retreated and hid inside the spirits' own machines on Pellas. Became spirits ourselves to wage a guerrilla war against the ethreaal.'

'This is madness. Gods and spirits and zoos and wars in heaven. And Helrena knows this secret?'

Apolleon laughed. 'Oh, your existence inside your over-sized animal reserve isn't the secret. You want to know the real secret, the very worst thing of all . . . ?'

Duncan wasn't sure how to answer. He faltered. *Maybe ignorance truly is bliss?*

'In for a penny, in for a pound, Duncan of Weyland. The truth is that the ethreaal aren't here anymore. We're still locked in their cage, but the universe outside lies empty of their kind. Your old servants did what humanity failed to do and became true gods . . . the spirits lifted into the sublime, grew wings and flew away into a far higher heaven than you can imagine.'

Duncan could hardly process the words. 'That cannot be true.'

'So, the wasted war in heaven continues,' said Apolleon, tapping the ground with his boot. 'Albeit on a far more limited scale. The ethreaal legacy is very clever and sophisticated with exceptionally able keepers. Lesser spirits such as Sariel Skel-bane. Kill Sariel and his ilk and the system just pours his soul and mind back into a new body and returns him to Pellas. So we developed a way of burning his kind and wiping their memories, stopping just short of triggering a re-spawn. Then we seized control of the Vandian stratovolcano. We've been blocking attempts by the legacy of the ethreaal to choke off the eruptions. Vandia is growing very close to the level of civilization needed to escape this cage.'

'What are we fighting *here* for, then? What the hell are all the deaths in Weyland and Rodal for?'

'The Imperium is the Imperium. A stealer subverts that which exists. Helrena must become empress, preferably with Prince Gyal by her side,' said Apolleon. 'And then Doctor Horvak will be provided with all the science and wealth of the Imperium to continue his work. Vandia will become advanced enough to break the cage's bars and help humanity finally escape Pellas. The stars are our true legacy. And we will reclaim the universe.'

'What can I do to help you? I'm just a freed slave, as good as in exile here. One lone man.'

'You can achieve more than you know,' said Apolleon. 'For Helrena and for the cause. Sariel and his ethreaal serfs are trying to assemble a great weapon. They deployed something very similar against the lands across the ocean. Turned it on what you now know as the Burn – a failed attempt by my people to attain what we recently achieved with Vandia. The ethreaal should never have given their vassals wings. A ridiculous conceit.' Apolleon snorted. 'Why not halos as well? Make something think it is an angel and you'll soon discover an unhealthy god-complex with contempt for life in the round. It is the most basic point of the ethreaal ruins' existence . . . the very seed of its essence. If the ethreaals' feral pets ever look like escaping, all the animals must be put down. Do you appreciate the irony? We may finally perish in a long-ended war where our enemy quit the battlefield eons ago.'

'Then perhaps we should just stay here,' said Duncan. He halted, almost surprised by his own cowardice. He tried to voice the argument. 'Never try to leave. Pellas is our home.'

'Home,' spat Apolleon. 'Pellas is a bloody prison. I was a man like you, once. Flesh born to a woman. I gave up everything and watched my family age and die. I dissolved my body in a vat. I lived as a ghost inside the enemy machine for millions of years to fight for our freedom. There is nothing I will not sacrifice for the cause. There is no deed so dark I have not already done it. Employ your damn brain, Duncan of Weyland. And if that fails, find your heart. I could lock you inside a pen and throw you enough slops every day to keep you alive. Without conversation or companionship or literature or song or the freedom to move more than three steps in any direction. Would you thank me for it? No! Within a decade, you would be begging me to end your life. I have survived a million years in such a cage. I will be free of it. So will you. So will we all!'

'How can we win against spirits? Against genies able to wish miracles into existence?'

'Because the genies are vanished, man. All that remains is their cursed lamp. And we mean to shatter it. With the old masters absent, with no more reinforcements or advice from the higher ethreaal, we stealers have been beating at the lamp's walls. At long last, we are finally winning. The assorted servant spirits, collaborators and motley jailers abandoned by the ethreaal understand they don't have long left now. Humanity's extinction is the only course of action they have left. A final solution for the human condition.'

Duncan moaned. All his life he had lived on Pellas. He might have abandoned the house and taken to the road, travelled forever and seen only the tiniest fraction of the wonders of the wide world. It would have been a full life. But knowing he was prowling the largest cage in the universe? *It's all dust. Everything I've achieved. Everything the House of Landor built here. Every breath my ancestors drew. All dust. A bad joke.*

'You were a slave of the Imperium, once,' said Apolleon. 'Princess Helrena freed you. And now you know you're a slave still. As are we all. But not for much longer.' The head of the secret police was about to say something else when Paetro came sprinting into the tent. Apolleon did not seem pleased with the interruption. Paetro's eyes widened when he saw how well Duncan looked, but he ignored the nobleman's displeasure and the miracle of Duncan's healing, both. 'We need to leave here. Now!'

'What is it?'

Paetro's finger jabbed towards the tent's roof. 'That, well, you will need to see that to believe it.'

Cassandra shouted for joy when the maelstrom melted away, warm wet air replacing the freezing Rodalian hurricane. *How far have we been dragged? How many of us are left?* The surviving planes had been hurled forward at velocities never intended for such simple aircraft. Her answer came when the clouds below dwindled, torn white fingers revealing not mountains but open shoreline and the vast Lancean Ocean beyond. Almost as one the aircraft banked back towards land. There was nothing the nomads feared as much as their enemies' salt waters. Water that horses could not drink and that would drown any who tried to swim the endless waves. An ocean that sustained the tribes of fishermen the Nijumeti counted as foes. Cassandra tallied the surviving planes. Still a formidable force, but the nomads had lost perhaps a third of their number while riding the savage trade winds.

'We have reached Weyland,' said Cassandra.

Alexamir grunted. 'Few clansmen have ever raided so far.'

But we have, the ancestors be thanked. 'If Temmell dares show his face again, I suspect the horde will have him burnt alive for his faulty navigations.'

'Our arrival here is not the sorcerer's fault. The Rodalians' spirits of the air are cunning. They've spat us out above a rich land. They hope to distract us from our ancient enemy with the treasure of a thousand soft nations.'

And having spent seasons with the horde, I suspect they are wise to trust so.

On the southern horizon, Cassandra saw smoke rising. *That's not a natural fire. Those plumes are from incendiary bombs.* Cassandra knew there was a large port city down the river from Northhaven. She had once toyed with the idea of escaping from her captors in Northhaven and making her way along the coast, sailing far away from her Weyland enemies. It seemed the civil war raging here had also reached the seaboard. *An enemy who devours itself. My favourite kind.*

Cassandra pointed out the distant smoke to Alexamir. 'Fighting.'

'Not until I land,' smiled Alexamir. 'Then they will know it.'

Lower and lower they swooped until Cassandra could almost reach out and snatch wild flowers from the foothills. *Nobody will be expecting us to arrive from the direction of the sea. Rodal has always stopped every invader from reaching the league. Until it didn't.* The nomads' makeshift skyguard followed the rolling hills until Cassandra began to recognize the landscape below. The White Wolf River and the wolds of the northern borderlands. A hint of the boundless forests to the east. She had been held here as a captive for long enough. *Northhaven.*

A massive triplane angled over — three gunnery seats front and rear of the plane's long body, and in the centre an almost throne-like seat. It was the aircraft bearing Kani Yargul into battle. Its wings fluttered with standards originally designed to be borne by war lances. Cassandra watched the horde's leader leaning over the fuselage and jabbing a fist down at the land either side of the river. 'The gods have spoken. They have carried us here. This is our fate, not Rodal. We have survived our testing and been given the soft underbelly of the Lanca to feast on . . . the wealth of the world!'

Cassandra saw the mirror signaller in the rear cockpit flashing a message to the rest of the aerial armada, bright spots of light acknowledging the signal from hundreds of planes in the van. It was a simple enough message. Possibly the only one the Nijumeti had ever needed. Cassandra hardly needed to bother committing to memory the full range of mirror light codes employed by the nomads. *Attack.*

'This is a bad bargain,' muttered Alexamir as the ruler's plane angled triumphantly away. 'If we do not first secure Rodal, the walls of the world will merely stand behind the clans instead of in front of the Nijumeti.'

'The Great Krul wishes to gallop,' said Cassandra. 'He wants the horde to ride on forever.'

'We shall see what Atamva wills,' said Alexamir, darkly.

If Kani Yargul wins today, he will be close to unassailable. Cassandra understood the window of opportunity for Alexamir's revenge was closing fast. And there was the town on the hill. But Northhaven's surrounds had changed almost beyond recognition during the civil war. Army camps and skyguard strips where once there had been wheat fields and woodland.

Cassandra realized with a shock that the Nijumeti were not the only invaders to intrude here. 'Some of those camps and airfields below are legion . . . Vandian!' *That warship on the ground looks like Prince Gyal's* Prancing Dragon. Cassandra felt a deep shred of bitterness. *So, my mother flew out to find me. She abandoned me when she thought me broken . . . but the Imperium remained to mount a campaign? I wasn't worth flying home, but taking revenge for the slave revolt was? A far-called barbarian realm with little worth seizing but slaves. For that, they stayed?* She realized her eyes were wet with tears. *I was never a real person in the Imperium. Not part of a family. I was just a walking title with a useful womb.*

'Better they had left here with your mother,' said Alexamir. 'Kani Yargul is still smarting from the Imperium's disrespect when they came hunting for you.'

Better they had left? 'No,' said Cassandra. 'This way is better. Strike the legion airfields first. You can't allow their helos to lift off. They're deadlier than anything the Weylanders possess.'

'Let them fly, then,' laughed Alexamir. 'For they have never faced *me* before.'

Kani Yargul had a head for strategy at least. He had obviously arrived at a similar conclusion to Cassandra. *Strike the strongest foe first when surprise is your friend.* Alexamir aimed the aircraft at the legion strip and they were joined by at least forty fighters, the sky filled with the whistle of diving planes.

'Save your bombs for the legion's armoured columns,' urged

Cassandra, wind whipping past her ears. 'Wing guns will penetrate helo shielding.'

Alexamir levelled up at the last second, strafing the airfield, spouts of soil before his line of shells stitched fuel barrels and helo engines . . . His volley answered by explosions, broken rotors sent spinning like giant axe heads across the legion camp. Aircrews sprinted madly towards their stationary craft, then spilled across the ground as nomad guns felled them. Cannon thuds shook their aircraft fit to splintering. Cassandra remembered inspecting the bootleg weapons before they were wing mounted. Carried into the steppes by smugglers' mules, secretly shifted across Hellin's deadly marshes. Big ugly iron barrels and firing mechanisms that reeked of grease. Leather belts of bullets with cheap casings. Any Vandian pilot would have laughed and sent them back to the armourer sooner than mount them on an imperial aircraft. But the nomads had met the smugglers' price in stolen silver and been glad of it. *Anything more sophisticated would look out of place on these flying galleons.* Primitive, perhaps. But the simple guns got the job done. The vast steel cathedral at the end of the field was making ready for an emergency lift. Cassandra recognized the haste and panic in the *Prancing Dragon*'s manoeuvres. *She's smoking her engines clear, rising on cold turbines, relying on her anti-gravity stones for lift. No patrols in the air to protect the camp either.* Cassandra recalled the smoke above the Weylanders' port. *There's already been an engagement. I bet half the local skyguard is off chasing the rebels . . . and they were never expecting us.* Cassandra had to remember to thank the nomads' gods for this. For, by rights, her ancestors should be on the side of the poor benighted souls below.

Three Nijumeti aircraft closed on the massive Vandian warship's bridge. At first Cassandra thought the brazen nomads were making a suicide run, but they had found a novel way to compensate for their lack of aiming equipment. Planes dived down towards the bridge's portholes and viewing galleries, pulling up with bare inches to spare, sending bombs lashing straight into the control rooms. Crystal canopies lifted out on flowers of flames, an inferno barely contained behind riveted bulk-plates. *Surely no officer on the bridge watch can have survived that?* Cassandra received her answer. The warship continued mindlessly on her last heading, a vessel decapitated, her engines slowly engaging at the rear, but nobody left alive in the wheel-room to direct her. Cassandra didn't have time to watch the broken ship vanish over the horizon. Alexamir pulled a tight barrel-roll which sent them spinning back across the airfield. Landing strips stretched out below, transformed into a hundred separate blazing and popping fires, columns of smoke darkening the sky, half-destroyed ammunition carts and flatbeds randomly spewing out detonating shells and rockets. Something very like an air-to-air missile came hurtling vertically past their plane, an elaborate optical targeting mechanism smashed by some Hellenise blacksmith's cheap slug. The irony of their close call wasn't lost on Cassandra. The Imperium's legions, the most advanced killing machine on Pellas, rapidly being overrun by a raging mob of ragtag blue-skinned savages.

Cassandra's gaze shifted beyond the legion camp. Nijumeti fighters operating as glider tugs dipped low. A noise like tearing paper as cables hauling the wooden troop transports released, lines falling flailing to the ground. The engineless aircraft glided easily across Northhaven's open wheat fields until the farmers' wealth was left furrowed by the horde's transporters. Hundreds of gliders tore up crops and soil, spending their velocity on landing. Some of them shed broken wings among the harvest before spinning around to a stop inside the fields. As the first gliders halted, their doors were kicked out. Ferocious riders spilled, whooping, into the open. They had been penned up inside, unable to do anything other than try to calm their horses and experience raw helpless terror while they watched their comrades' craft disintegrate above Rodal. Now they were free. Alive. Born in the saddle and returned to the ground. They swept out, their fear transformed into a terrible breed of madness.

Alexamir crisscrossed the flats outside the town, Cassandra spotting for him, releasing their bombs on an armoured column trying to engage the horsemen. They left a fortune in ruined steel smoking across the town's outskirts – the hardest part of the strike avoiding collisions with other fighters as they released their bombs into the carnage. From the air, Cassandra could see that the horde's control of the sky was turning this engagement into a rout. Soon enough, the farmland and wilds surrounding Northhaven swarmed with blue-uniformed Weyland soldiers fleeing for their lives, no attempt to form squares and stand off the riders. Legionaries from the Vandian punishment fleet joined them, their armour little protection from lances cutting them down from behind, from screaming nomads flashing sabres and using war-trained horses to trample every fleeing soldier. A helo that had managed to take to the air came fleeting past Cassandra's plane, either attempting to quit the battlefield or its ordinance unloaded – no attempt to fire on them. Alexamir banked their plane to put the helo in his gun-sights, but as his fingers settled on the trigger the clacking of empty gun-belts sounded from their wing. An ugly nomad fighter with four stacked wings spotted the Vandian gunship and swooped down, breaking the quadplane's lowest wing against the helo's rotors, sending the enemy spinning out of control into the ground. It didn't explode, but then it didn't need to. A squadron of horsemen pounded across the wreckage, spearing the two helo pilots while they attempted to draw their sidearms.

Alexamir shook his fist angrily at the quadplane, now corkscrewing uncertainly across the sky on its three good wings. 'You dare cheat me of my prize! Pull the meat out of my teeth. Are you jackals or are you Nijumeti?'

'We're nearly out of fuel as well as bullets,' called Cassandra.

'Then let us land, my Golden Fox. It would be ill-starred to crash into the first kingdom Atamva sent us to conquer. The tickle of my dagger may yet convince the Weylander skyguard to pour fuel into my wooden pigeon's tanks and thread fresh bullets for my talons.'

Cassandra stared at the burning airfields. *There isn't much fuel left to requisition in that inferno.*

Alexamir dipped down, aiming for the railhead outside town. One of the Guild of Rails' long three-storey-high trains remained at rest in the stockyards, partially unloaded of its cargo. And there the train would remain. Nomad bombs had blasted the tracks away heading south, a series of blackened craters where once had run rails. A line of tall wooden warehouses stood nearby, docks along the White Wolf River for riverboats to moor up. All of it swarming with horsemen. Many of the workers and townspeople had thrown themselves into the river and were allowing themselves to be swept west by the currents. They were headed towards the Lancean Ocean, knowing it was a rare nomad who could swim. Cassandra's ungainly plane jounced once on the soil outside the railhead, taxiing to a halt. All around them nomad aircraft joined the ranks of landed gliders, out of fuel, bombs and shells. Many fighters made landings barely better than the unpowered gliders, shedding undercarriages, smashing their fuselage into the ground. Where pilots survived their clumsy landings, they climbed on top of their planes and yelled for thralls to come running from the gliders with their horses.

Alexamir, at least, had settled their plane down on the field proficiently enough to take off again if they could locate a cache of fuel. They both dismounted from the aircraft. Cassandra's legs ached from an age in the cockpit's confines, but she did not begrudge the sensation. *I can walk. I am healed. That is enough.* Alexamir checked inside the nearest glider, but all the horses carried by it had already been taken. Cassandra watched prancing warriors dancing on the wooden roofing of the railhead buildings. Both of them headed for the yard in search of fuel barrels.

As they got closer, Cassandra noticed a figure standing in front of the marshalling yard. Female. It was the witch rider Nurai, as though she had known they would pass through the railhead and here she was, awaiting their arrival.

'Nothing good lies in this land,' called Nurai when they were close enough to hear her. 'Not for the horde. Nor for you, Alexamir Arinnbold.'

Alexamir stared suspiciously at the resentful witch rider. 'What is it that you have seen?'

Nurai refused to say and gestured instead at Cassandra. 'This is your fault.'

'Alexamir is his own man. He makes his own choices.' *And he has chosen me over you.*

'We are lost.'

'This looks much like a victory to me,' said Cassandra.

'For you perhaps, but not for the horde. Not for the proud riders of the steppes.'

'I am one of you, now.' *And how that must gall.*

'Do you think so?' Nurai laughed, bitterly. 'We shall see what you are and where you belong soon enough.'

Cassandra shivered despite herself at the warning. *Or is it a curse?* She put it down to sour grapes on the part of the witch rider.

Alexamir stared towards the buildings. 'Where is your mistress? Where is Madinsar?'

'Madinsar remains behind in the steppes with the young and the old and the infirm,' said Nurai. 'You have gone against our counsel and she does not wish to see the result of the clans ignoring our visions.'

'Let her keep Nonna company, then,' said Alexamir, walking away with Cassandra. 'The Prince of Thieves shall pry open Rodal's treacherous mountain paths and then carry them both back so much treasure that they will need to sow new tents for a decade to hold it all.'

'Fly back home!' pleaded Nurai, 'Head back now to the steppes before it is too late.'

'Enough!' yelled a voice. It was Kani Yargul, emerging from behind the goods yard with a bodyguard of perhaps fifty warriors. 'I tire of the witch riders' dire predictions of misery and defeat. Where is my defeat here? I have smashed the forces of Weyland and their Vandian allies in a single day.'

Nurai shook her head sadly, but perhaps wisely offered no more warnings to her victorious ruler.

'And this is said to be the most beggarly of the kingdom's prefectures,' whooped Kani Yargul, kicking over a tower of crates. One of the boxes hit the ground and broke open revealing dozens of rifles inside straw bedding. New lever-action Weyland weapons, the barrels well-greased. He seized a gun and tossed it to his warriors who examined the rifle with awe. 'Greater riches lie to the south. And beyond Weyland . . . the other Lanca nations. One kingdom after another; each more fattened with treasure than even gods might dream of! Did Madinsar dream of this?' laughed Yargul for the benefit of his superstitious warriors.

A column of Nijumeti emerged from behind the grounded guild train's carriages, flanked by lance-bearing warriors. And in their centre a sad-looking crowd of prisoners shambled forward.

'Here are our foes' high-born,' announced a blue-skinned warrior, proudly, bowing before Kani Yargul. 'The curs who did not flee fast enough!'

Cassandra started. Among the prisoners were Duncan and Paetro, standing to the side of Prince Gyal, Baron Machus and Apolleon. *High-born indeed. But why are Duncan and Paetro here if my mother's ship has departed?* Cassandra knew the answer to her question even as she asked it. *They spoke up for me too loudly. They were held in the expeditionary force to learn manners.* Paetro spotted Cassandra first, then Duncan. Hope flashed in their eyes. Hope that they might survive this. Wonder at her presence here. Paetro whispered something and she read his lips. *'By the ancestors, she can walk again!'*

Cassandra tried to cross to the prisoners, but Alexamir held her back.

'Be careful,' Alexamir whispered. 'If you speak for your friends, you will need to be heard as a Nijumet here, not a Vandian.'

'Fine velvet cloaks and handsome gold breastplates,' announced Kani Yargul, pacing in front of the prisoners. 'But where is your Princess Helrena? She paid me a visit out in the steppes which I sadly missed. So I arrive in Weyland to repay her courtesy.'

'I am Prince Gyal of the Imperium,' announced Gyal. 'I lead the empire's forces here.'

'A prince?' laughed Kani Yargul. 'What hostage price will your far-called emperor pay for such a fine piece of quality as you?'

'He will give you a life. Yours. Order your savages to quit the field and I will allow you to ride away,' said Prince Gyal.

'I do not enjoy the way you bargain.'

'You will enjoy dying at the hands of our legions even less.'

Yargul grunted in amusement. 'And foreigners claim we Nijumeti are arrogant.' He bowed mockingly to Prince Gyal. 'But I take lessons from your kind.'

'Vandia's sky mines provide wealth beyond mortal dreams,' said Apolleon from the prince's side. 'Vandia's legions are countless. Its science has raised the Imperium to be master of all of Pellas.'

Yargul shrugged. 'Everyone has better weapons, sharper steel and more powerful sorceries than the Nijumeti. Yet our warriors are standing here victorious. While you,' he drew his sabre, 'are standing here and *here.*' He lashed out with a blow so fast and powerful Cassandra could hardly believe she had witnessed it. Gyal's head rolled severed across the grass, a look of astonishment still contorting his face. The decapitated body remained vertical, swaying for a second until the Great Krul booted it to the soil. Kani Yargul roared with laughter at his sadistic jape. 'Have your emperor use his endless wealth to buy you a fresh head, my *prince*.'

Apolleon eyed the horde's ruler coldly. 'You can have no idea what you have just done. Decades of complex work building alliances wasted. All of it wasted!'

Kani Yargul raised his sabre, running a finger down the bloody blade. 'Steel makes the best treasure. For when it rests in my hand, *I* am master of all Pellas. Your people will quickly learn this.'

'No,' said Apolleon. 'You have yet to meet my people. They are away hunting for bigger game.'

'Then I must remember to kill them later.' Yargul turned to his lieutenants. 'Vandians, it seems, make most insolent thralls. Take none alive. Put all of these cravens to the sword.'

'Some of the prisoners were of my tent,' said Cassandra, stepping forward and shrugging away Alexamir's warning hand. 'I claim them.'

'You do?' laughed the Krul of Kruls. 'I change my orders, then. Have every captured Vandian tied between our horses and ripped apart!'

'I *claim* them,' insisted Cassandra.

'And so you will claim them, girl,' snarled the nomad ruler. 'Five pieces at least for each prisoner. After their limbs have been torn off you can make a mound out of your dead countrymen and, if you are lucky, Alexamir will steal you a drove of fat pigs to feed on their parts.'

'She has the right to speak,' said Alexamir.

'And I have listened to her prattle and denied her demands,' growled Kani Yargul. 'I have worked a lifetime for this victory. Do not sour my mood. Neither of you will enjoy your chastisement.' He jerked a thumb at Cassandra and barked at his warriors. 'Drag this young saddle-wife out of my sight. Suffering her complaints is akin to riding backwards through brambles.'

Two warriors seized Cassandra's arms, starting to haul her out of the yard. This was more than Alexamir could stand. *No, don't be a fool. But it was too late.*

Alexamir drew his sword and faced the ruler. 'Did my father sour your mood, too? When you were out hunting and you tried to slip a dagger in his back?'

'Someone has been feeding you lies, boy,' snarled the Great Krul. There was an uneasy shifting among his warriors. Artdan Arinnbold had been a popular rider. One believed mauled to death during a hunt. There had been no honourable challenge to send him back to the grass.

'My father lives,' said Alexamir. 'He survived your treachery. He fights as a mercenary among the baronies of the Burn.'

'Does he now?' growled Kani Yargul. 'There is a small thing I did not know. I do believe you have been poisoned against me by the witch riders, young Prince of Thieves. They claimed victory would be found in the distant north, attacking Persdad.' He indicated the smashed railhead. 'But here is my victory. Beyond the mountains that held us at bay. Beyond the marshes that contained us. Beyond the long timber walls raised by the Empire of Persdad. Merely the first of many magnificent triumphs in rich lands.'

Alexamir pointed his sabre at the Krul of Kruls. 'Then swear on your life before Atamva that you did not try to murder my father. Swear you did not betray him so you could steal my mother from his tent.'

'Crawl back to your tame Vandian fox, boy,' warned Kani Yargul, patting his blade. 'Or I shall have to bear your mother's sullen weeping for a year after I send you to the grass.'

'Swear it!'

'I swear I shall make your mother a present of your ungrateful false tongue,' screamed Yargul. He leapt forward, his sabre a blur. Alexamir met the blow and there was a crash of steel like anvils smashing against each other.

There was no room for artistry or skill here; the two men flew at each other, sword hammering against sword. Somewhere in the fight both men had drawn daggers, although Cassandra hadn't seen the move. They used their second blade as other men would use a shield . . . to block and counterstrike. All the watching nomads roared their approval, some chanting for Alexamir, others for the Great Krul. They seemed to treat this as a game laid on for their benefit rather than a matter of life or death.

Kani Yargul brought his sabre down in a blow that would have split Alexamir in half if it had met his skull, but the younger nomad blocked the blow with his sword and lashed out with a boot, trying to break one of the ruler's ankles. Yargul twisted to the side, grunting and swung his dagger arm around to try to bury it in Alexamir's ear. Alexamir rocked back, rolled to the side, and came up and out in a murderous sabre swing that Yargul barely avoided. More and more onlookers came sprinting or galloping over, swelling the mob as word spread that the horde's ruler was involved in a death match.

Both fighters moved with a preternatural speed that made Cassandra dizzy just watching. She knew that Nijumeti differences went beyond the cobalt tone of their skin and a hardy resistance to cold. They possessed endurance enough that a relay of five normal men would be hard pressed to keep up with a single nomad. Their tendons and tissues worked differently too. As they stirred up into a killing anger, their heavily muscled bodies bulged and hardened, like a Vandian tank's hydraulic machinery quickening for combat. The rage enabled them to fight like bears, almost impervious to pain. *Like monsters.* The Nijumeti called the state *pockdparb.* In Vandia, it would have been labelled a berserker fury. They couldn't fight long at this heightened level before they tired. *But who can stand against them while they are in it?*

She saw Paetro among the prisoners watching the challenge in awed shock and she knew just what her old trainer was thinking. *What legionaries these nomads would make if they could be trained properly in the full range of killing arts.*

Kani Yargul must have been three times the age of Alexamir, but he hadn't risen to command a clan and unify the tribes into a horde by sitting on a silk-cushioned throne. There was only a single quality that mattered in the steppes. Victory in battle over those you faced. Be it an entire clan or a single man. *No, Alexamir. Don't fight him like this. Don't match him savagery for savagery. Throw yourself against his weaknesses, not his strength. Fight Yargul where he isn't.*

'Your father's line ends with you,' snarled Yargul, his dagger swaying like a cobra in his hand.

'A pity we're not raiding in the mountains, then,' said Alexamir. 'You could wait until I was asleep and roll me off a cliff.'

Yargul roared at the calumny and rushed forward, swinging his sabre. Alexamir met the charge with both blades. Their angry battering of steel was like a war drum, hypnotizing, each fighter whirling around the other, whipping, clacking metal, block and thrust, every blow capable of severing a limb away or gutting an opponent. The fight went on with a savagery Cassandra had never witnessed before, not even in the great arena of Vandis, but at last she detected the combat slowing, their berserker fury gradually dissipating.

As he tired, Yargul made a mistake, overextending his dagger hand's reach. Alexamir flung his sabre forward, towards the gap that had been left, his sabre's tip heading for the Great Krul's chest. But at the last second Yargul turned – the brief opening revealed as a feint. He caught Alexamir's sword arm and plunged his dagger through the young nomad's forearm. Alexamir yelled in shock, his sabre falling towards the yard's earth. Yargul drove his curved sabre's buckler into Alexamir's nose, using the steel as a knuckle-duster. There was a horrible crack of breaking bone and Alexamir began to slip down to the ground, utterly unconscious. Yargul caught the limp body before it hit the soil and flourished his sword theatrically.

No. Please, let him survive! Cassandra struggled against the two Nijumeti warriors, but they restrained her as tight as iron chains.

'Atamva blesses the righteous blade,' roared Kani Yargul. 'I treated this young fool as one of my own blood and see how he repays me... with foul lies, curses and disobedience. Let this be the fate of all such oathbreakers!' He rotated the sabre around the air, preparing to send Alexamir's head rolling off toward Prince Gyal's.

'No!' screamed Cassandra.

Yargul raised Alexamir's limp body by the scalp and steadied his sword for the killing blow, but someone bolted out from the mob of onlookers – *Nurai*. The witch rider seized the ruler's hand and yanked it back. She couldn't disarm him, but she hung on to his arm like an anchor. Infuriated, Kani Yargul shouldered her aside and lashed out with his sabre. Nurai fell, clutching the wound gushing blood out from her chest. She tumbled to her knees, groaning. It was a fatal blow. Cassandra felt a strange tug of affinity for the woman; for all that they had regarded each other as foes. *The only thing we had in common you died to save. You deserved better than this, woman.*

'I dream-walked your end,' moaned Nurai, raising blood-stained fingers toward Kani Yargul. 'The end of us all.'

Yargul's eyes narrowed. 'Your end, witch rider. Not mine.'

Nurai's hand dropped and she tumbled over, stopping moving. A low moaning rose from the nomad crowd. To kill a witch rider in such a manner was to be forever cursed by the gods. Cassandra took advantage of the shock of the warriors restraining her. She slipped out of their grip and sprinted forward, imposing herself between Alexamir and the horde's ruler.

'Now this is a bad joke,' growled Yargul, turning his attention back to Alexamir's comatose body.

Cassandra drew her sword. A short stabbing blade half the length of a sabre. But it was the closest weapon to a legionary's standard sword. As familiar to her as a favourite pair of worn boots. 'Laugh and meet my challenge, then, mighty Krul of Kruls. Or would you have it said that you were afraid to fight a Vandian-born slip of a girl?' She contemptuously indicated Nurai's still corpse. 'Or perhaps you would prefer me to toss my steel aside? You can slay me with the same bravery you use to murder an unarmed witch rider?'

The gathered warriors hooted their assent for the challenge. Kani Yargul glanced at them vexed, but he was no fool. He realized how low his reputation would sink if he refused Alexamir's little Golden Fox. Nurai's murder was bad enough an omen to bear, even given the horde's victory in Weyland.

Yargul leaned to the side of Cassandra and kicked Alexamir's unconscious body, letting it roll across the ground. 'I will prise your own blade from your fingers and use it to hack off this ungrateful cur's head. Then I shall toss you into the palace's harem and let my other wives whip just enough spirit out of you to render you pleasing to a true Nijumet.'

Cassandra brandished her short sword. 'Here's my spirit. Take it.'

FIFTEEN

AN ARMY OF WIDOWS

Willow was still shivering with the shock of escaping from North-haven in Black Barnaby's shuttle plane, a large two-decker flying boat tied up in the White Wolf River. They had barely avoided being run through by the lances of Nijumeti horsemen before they had faced a gauntlet of crude nomad fighter aircraft, the river waters jumping with shell fire as they sped across the surface and took off. Only the fact that the flying boat's powerful engines were designed to transport a hold packed full of captured booty allowed Aurora on the stick to outrun their primitive pursuers. Willow gazed back towards North-haven. *This is the second time I've left my home in flames.* She said a prayer for the poor unfortunates left behind, trying not to feel guilty about surviving the nomads' shocking surprise invasion. And just as Willow dared to hope she might be safe, flying north over Rodal's heights for hours, their shuttle approached a ragtag armada of aerial carriers. Skels and free company fliers holding at high altitude. The same hounds the usurper had paid to add to his leash.

After Willow landed on board Black Barnaby's carrier, the *Plunder-bird*, she had been expecting many things. Torture perhaps. The hate-ful revenge of Bad Marcus or one of his lackeys. But never the sight of the man waiting for them in what passed for the pirate captain's throne chamber. *Jacob Carnehan. Have they captured him, too?*

'Just tell me that you sent the messages,' said Jacob as soon as Barnaby entered the chamber.

Black Barnaby raised a dismissive hand. 'Done. I even burnt the radio-guild's hold for you to ensure there won't be anybody tracing where the missives went and to whom they were addressed.'

Willow stared in disbelief at Jacob Carnehan. 'You're not a prisoner here?'

'No,' said Jacob; the simplicity of his answer startled her.

'But those are the usurper's carriers out there?' said Willow.

'That's the trouble with mercenaries,' said Jacob, glancing at Black Barnaby. 'When you fight for money, the only real question is "how much?"'

'There's gratitude for you,' grinned Barnaby. 'Named a sell-sword, rather than the honourable profession of privateer.'

'There's a difference?' asked Jacob.

Barnaby slapped the canvas-stretched fuselage of the *Plunderbird*. 'Yes, full ownership of your cannons and your destiny. I hand you your own skyguard on a platter, Jacob, and that's all the thanks I get.'

Jacob grunted. 'It's a platter the Rodalians had to fight a fierce boarding action over.'

'Pah. Rodalians toss their children rocks to suck on. A quarrelsome, argumentative people. Mountain ambushes are just practice for them. All useless without me giving you the location of the royalist squadron's home holding-pattern.'

'You didn't *give* it to me. You *sold* it to me.'

'The same old tricks,' said Aurora. 'You've boasted often enough, Father, of how many times you and your brother fought on opposite sides of a conflict, ensuring you always had a winner on the victorious side.'

'Not at all the same ruse,' argued Black Barnaby. 'Back in the Burn we rarely cared which piece of quality won. But Weyland? You want to fight for some martinet whose nickname is the *Shoemaker*? Besides, I preferred Weyland when it didn't have a skyguard worthy of the name to protect its shipping.'

Jacob shrugged. 'That nickname was before the usurper disbanded half the assembly and strung the rest of parliament up from Arcadia's lampposts. Now it's Bad Marcus.'

Willow allowed a glimmer of hope to enter her heart. *Sweet Saints.*

Maybe we'll survive this after all. 'Then those carriers are flying for Prince Owen?'

'That noble little arsewipe,' growled Black Barnaby. 'You could store a hold full of his gratitude next door to his cant. Do me the favour of shooting him next time, Brother.' The pirate captain hesitated. 'Although best wait till he pays me what you promised. A general can run the north as well as a buck prince.'

'If those carriers are under parliament's command then we're flying the wrong way!' insisted Willow. 'Northhaven's being attacked. The nomads crossed the mountains with a crude skyguard force.'

'Not so much Northhaven that's being attacked,' said Black Barnaby, 'More the royalist forces and their Vandian friends.'

Willow was horrified. 'But our people live there!'

'And they were there when the southern army marched in and occupied the prefecture,' said Jacob. 'The difference between the usurper's forces and the Nijumeti is that the horde will ride south and keep on going, following the scent of richer pickings. Let's see how easy Bad Marcus finds holding his royalist regiments north of the Spotswood line when his mill owners and aristocrats are fighting off raiding clansmen.'

'You can't allow this to happen,' protested Willow. 'You have to help halt the horde. How many northern farms will be burnt and our towns sacked before the Nijumeti reach Humont and Bolesland?'

'Allow it to happen?' laughed Black Barnaby. 'He *planned* it, girl.'

Willow was finding it hard to breathe properly with the sudden turn of events. 'You can't have planned it. That's simply impossible.'

'I owe you an apology, Willow,' said Jacob.

Black Barnaby shook with laughter. 'Oh girl, we would have opened the gates of the Chalhand Pass and invited the horde to pass through the mountains, but the rice-eaters wouldn't wear it and the nomads would never have ridden through Rodal without a scrap. It's simply not in their twisted cobalt blood.'

'Be quiet, Barnaby, you're not helping matters.'

'Why apologize?' Willow demanded of Jacob.

'Sariel spotted an infiltrator arriving at Hadra-Hareer shortly before he set out with Carter. A young Nijumet with the mark of Sariel's people upon him,' explained Jacob. 'An enchantment that allowed the clansman to swap his features for those of a Rodalian. I had the intruder followed and he went exactly where Sariel predicted he would. When the nomad visited the High Temple of the Winds, it was obvious he hadn't come on a private pilgrimage. The most valuable object in the temple is the Deb rlung'rta – Rodal's master book of the winds.'

'He'd come to steal it?'

'Copy it,' said Barnaby. 'Steal it and the wind priests would change the openings and closings of their great timber wind dams, create a new pattern of deadly gales to navigate.'

'I ordered a false master book created,' said Jacob. 'Fast north-southers that should have been near-to-fatal redrawn as invasion routes straight into the heart of Rodal. That's the book the thief found.'

'They weren't fatal,' said Willow, enraged at how recklessly the pastor has gambled with the lives of the northern residents. 'Not nearly fatal enough for the Nijumeti.' *Only for Northhaven and the rest of the kingdom.* 'I can't believe that Prince Owen and the assembly agreed to this.'

'They didn't need to,' said Jacob. 'Only the Speaker of the Winds knew all the details of my battle plan. Rodal is her nation. She was glad enough to have Rodal's invaders blown off course.'

'This is monstrous!'

'I didn't know the nomad raider would kidnap you,' said Jacob. He sounded tortured. 'That the nomad thief had assistance from southern spies inside the capital.'

'And would you have stopped him if you had?' shouted Willow, her cheeks flushed with fury. 'When that would have spoiled your little scheme for setting the horde on Bad Marcus?'

Jacob didn't answer her question. 'I promised Carter I would keep you safe. I thought you would be protected inside Hadra Hareer.'

'Instead you as good as gave me to Nocks,' accused Willow. 'Nocks and Holten murdered my father today . . . tried to kill me so Holten could claim the house.'

'Benner Landor is dead?' said Jacob, seeming genuinely disturbed.

'One less for you to kill, is it now?'

'I'm sorry.'

'Of course you're not. My father was in the royalist army. You would have shot him on sight as a traitor to the assembly.'

'Sorry for you,' said Jacob. 'Not for Benner.'

'That, at least, is the truth,' wheezed Willow.

'Benner Landor was a good man, once. Before he let his position and wealth twist him.'

'How dare you speak of my father like that! Take a good hard gaze in your mirror. You're not a pastor anymore. You're a warlord.' Willow gazed out of the porthole at the carriers circling in the sky. 'Jake Silver. A murderous brigand chief with a fine new armada. You've opened the walls of the league to the steppes and allowed a terrible enemy to cross into Weyland. How many thousands of innocent people will die by the sword to purchase your cursed victory?'

'Only until Bad Marcus falls,' said Jacob.

'And the horde will go home then, will they?'

'We're not the richest land in the league. The horde will do what a horde always does. It'll ride. The ones that don't die in the south will keep on raiding across the border at Ortheris. They'll follow the coast until their grandchildren finally reach the Pontellosk Ocean.'

'That's your plan? Let them sweep across Pellas killing until history finally assimilates them? You told me I was to act as your conscience, once. This plan is pure evil.'

'It was the only way to beat Bad Marcus and his allies. Rodal was the anvil. The nomads are the hammer.'

'And now your hammer will beat on our people.'

'We'll harry the nomads south,' said Jacob. 'What was left of parliament's army after the fall of Midsburg was never beaten in the field, only dispersed. Our soldiers hiding in the wilds or their uniforms temporarily turned for a farmer's jacket and breeches. Those messages that Barnaby sent out were to our commanders. We have our own skyguard. Rodal has been brought into the war. The north is picking up its swords again.'

'What else are they to do?' cried Willow, 'when they're led by Quicksilver?'

'You should get hitched to Prince Owen, girl,' said Black Barnaby. 'You can fill the palace nursery with high-minded little aristocrats, wobbling about and speechifying at each other. How the hell did you believe wars are won? By fine oration until the bastards on the other side realize the error of their ways, apologize and surrender? Everyone has a nice tearful hug together while we try to find forgiveness in our hearts?' Barnaby snorted in amusement. 'War leaves a kingdom with four armies: an army of thieves, an army of cripples, an army of widows and an army of orphans. The churchman you grew up with doesn't exist. He never did. The assembly didn't appoint Jacob Carnehan high general of all the northern armies. They called for Quicksilver, not some simple Weyland preacher. Quicksilver. The man who never lost a war. Whatever the cost, however long the butcher's bill. And I should know better than anyone, for the saints preserve me, I flew under his banner in the Burn.'

'So that's what Weyland is now,' said Willow. 'That's what you're going to turn the Lanca into – a twin to that never-ending slaughter-house across the ocean.'

'Victory is all you can look to me for,' said Jacob. 'I don't have much more than that inside me anymore. I'll find Nocks and kill him. Hang your step-mother for murder too, if I can.'

'You would have done that anyway.' Willow felt lightheaded and queasy. *Is that from the altitude or my present company?*

'Then ask me to spare them,' said Jacob. 'Ask me to spare them and I'll do that for you. I owe you that much for what you've been through. I owe Carter that much.'

Willow thought of Holten standing triumphant over her father's strangled corpse. Nocks' leering face. Duncan wounded and close to death after the challenge, all because of Holten's schemes to take control of their house. *It would be the right thing to do. To show mercy. Holten's the mother to my baby step-brother. I know what it's like to grow up in the shadow of a dead mother.*

'What's your answer?' pressed Jacob.

Damn you for making your point. But Quicksilver was far beyond that. And what about me? Willow struggled for an answer, but then her lips moved and it was hardly her speaking at all. 'Put Leyla Holten on trial. I'll testify and see her swing for what she did to my father.' *As long as those two killers are alive, nobody with the family name Landor will ever be safe from assassination. Not in Northhaven or anywhere in Weyland. Perhaps not even Asher Landor, when the baby's served his purpose. But* deep inside, Willow knew that was the lie she needed to tell herself. A little mound of lies. Compared to a mountain.

Jacob nodded as though Willow had given the correct answer. 'War never determines who is right – only who is left.'

One of Barnaby's crewmen came into the chamber bearing a red leather message tube. 'A Rodalian flying wing touched down in the hangar carrying this. For General Carnehan.'

Black Barnaby waved the pirate messenger over to his brother. Jacob broke the wax seal, opened the tube and scanned the message. He seemed to almost tremble when he passed it to Willow to read.

What is this? What can move him? Willow's eyes widened as she read the short communication carried from the great fortress at Dalranga.

'What is it?' asked Aurora, unable to contain her curiosity anymore.

'Your cousin Carter and some good friends of ours have turned up at the Rodalian border,' said Jacob.

He's alive. Willow moaned, but it wasn't from the happiness she should be feeling at the glorious news. It was as if something had lit a burning fire below her.

'What's the matter?' asked Jacob.

Aurora came running over. 'You may know your way around a battlefield, but damned if you aren't a fool for surprising a woman with such quick tidings. Her waters have broken. Send for our sot of a surgeon.'

Willow barely saw the courier sprinting past as she swayed, wracked by the spasms of her first contractions. She fell to the deck, clutched by Barnaby's daughter, an intensity of pain that was entirely new to her as her belly began to be squeezed and squeezed.

SIXTEEN

A LADY'S HOME

Yargul's buckler leapt out piston-fast towards Cassandra's face, a crude attempt to render her unconscious. She was almost offended as she swayed to the side, that her brutal opponent considered her so dim-witted he could repeat his last move from Alexamir's combat and hope to catch her unawares. *So, I'm just an incapable foreign wench? I can use your arrogance, Krul of Kruls.* She swung her short sword in a half arc, hoping to take off the nomad's dagger arm, but he was just fast enough to sidestep, causing her blade to gouge a shallow cut only.

'It takes an hour for a clansman's body to purge a killing fury and ready a new rage,' growled Cassandra. 'You should have waited before accepting my challenge.'

Cheers sounded from the mob of onlookers. Paetro and Duncan yelling their support for Cassandra, but she didn't allow the prisoners' calls to distract her. *It won't be first blood that counts, but the last.*

Yargul whirled his blade through the air, tracing windmill patterns as he regarded his bleeding arm with displeasure. 'My only challenge is curbing the urge to carve you into slices. I must forgo the satisfaction, or I won't be able to enjoy you properly later. I trust you will muster suitable spirit to pleasure me after I have made you a gift of Alexamir's skull as a drinking cup.'

'If all there was to fighting was battering each other with sharp steel until one of us drops, you would truly be Master of all Pellas,' said Cassandra.

Cassandra had a strategy, of sorts. A nomad's berserker rage was quickly followed by cramps, overtaxed muscles seizing up like engine pistons taxed faster than its design tolerances. *You'll tire soon, Kani Yargul.*

Yargul pivoted and the sword swung out. Cassandra ducked the strike, nearly slipping in the mud. *Too close.* If they had been fighting in the nearby woodland, Kani Yargul could have brought down a tree with that cut. Yargul stamped forward, sending splashes of mud up as his sabre thrust sought her belly. Cassandra danced to the side, trying to bring the challenge back to dryer soil, where her manoeuvres wouldn't flounder in the mire.

'Is this the way a Vandian gives battle?' bellowed Yargul. 'Fights by not fighting?'

When torrential water moves boulders it is because of their momentum. Cassandra laughed to irritate her opponent and rub salt in his wounds. More jeers came from the nomad mob . . . the Great Krul's humiliation at failing to finish this young woman's challenge.

'Stay still, girl!' Yargul lashed out again, but the nomad had telegraphed the blow and Cassandra was no longer where his sabre was swinging.

'You're an old man, Kani Yargul,' said Cassandra, flicking her short sword forward. 'You should be back in your tent, having a loud snore after a hard day's labours.' *By my ancestors, tire, you old dog.*

Yargul yelled in fury at the insult and darted at her, rocking his sabre side to side. Cassandra retreated to the left, forcing him to slow and circle. She needed to ensure Yargul didn't force her back against the railhead's buildings, yard equipment and towering mounds of crates. *I must keep mobile. If he pens me in, brute strength will win.*

'Is that why you want me for your harem, mighty Krul of Kruls? Do your wives tire of rubbing your tired old man's muscles?'

Yargul swore and lashed out with his blade, missing Cassandra's neck by an inch.

'But that is no way to take me alive! I heard rumours you enjoy taking enemy corpses to your bed. They complain less about your stench than your wives.'

Roars of amusement hooted across from the warriors. They enjoyed a touch of wit and boasting mixed into their fights.

'Is that a wasp's buzzing I hear, girl? You flee like an insect before my blade.'

The brute's trampling had turned the yard into mud. *I need to risk my life if I am to win it.* Cassandra thought she had seen her chance. Yargul's sabre cracked forward. Rather than dodge the blow, Cassandra met the blade with her sword. She didn't need to fake letting the jarring impact bash the pommel out of her hand, falling, embedding the sabre tip in the mud. They were close enough to kiss, but Cassandra grabbed Yargul's sword arm and pulled it forward, stealing the man's momentum and using it to swing behind him. Yargul tried to pivot with his dagger hand. Too late. Cassandra was already behind him, disarmed but at his rear. She swung back through his open legs, using the mud as a slide, freeing her soil-sheaved sword from the ground.

'Here's my spirit. Take it!' Cassandra twisted the blade over her head and plunged it into Kani Yargul's chest. The ruler continued his swing around, the man's dagger finding only air, gazing in astonishment at the blade slammed into his heart. There was a strange whistling as Yargul fell to his knees. Cassandra tried to scramble to her feet, mistaking the sound for his warriors' keening, but then the first explosion erupted, collapsing the closest warehouse, flaming splinters slicing her face as a blast-wave smashed her head down into the mud. While Cassandra floundered in the mire she saw the steel belly of a Vandian ship sliding through the sky. Not a full-size warship. A fast cruiser. Five hundred and sixty feet of streamlined steel, short curved wings like an aerial shark, a ridge of ball-turrets along her bilge, rotating as cannon barrels thudded back into their mounts. Cassandra instantly recognized the *Dark Moon*'s distinctive lines, the notorious flagship of the secret police – considered an ill-omen wherever she appeared inside the Imperium: death, disappearances and torture trailing tight in her wake.

Hatches slid open along her hull, rappel lines tumbling towards the ground. Armoured figures kicked out, hoodsmen, the bulky weight of electric rifle backpacks sending them hurtling down their lines. *Blood Beetles* the troops' nickname. Crimson-enamelled armour, stiff red uniforms and the brass face masks of dead emperors, masks to make it clear in whose name they slew. The shock troops had arrived too late to alter the course of the battle, but that wasn't why they were here. *Apolleon*. He must have sent for his vessel. To save what was left saving. Which meant the celestial caste survivors. *Which means me!* Cassandra struggled to her feet. Coloured smoke grenades thrown by the commandos had rendered the ground into a dream-like landscape stolen from a nightmare. Vivid greens, yellows and reds. Hissing smoke canisters muffled the screams and gunfire. Warriors rushed towards the Blood Beetles, met by the machine roar of modern Vandian weapons as the nomads were hurled off their feet. *The only reason I'm not dead is that Apolleon's people are holding their fire until the expedition's leaders are rescued.* No sign of Duncan or Paetro in the melee, no sign of anyone she recognized on either side. *With luck, they've escaped. I have to think about myself . . . about us.*

Cassandra almost tripped over Nurai's dead body in the murk. She seemed more at peace in death than she ever had in life. *You were a good enemy, lady.* To her side lay Yargul's corpse. Cassandra yanked her sword out of Kani Yargul's chest and didn't even bother cleaning the blood off the blade before she sheathed it. *That's what you get for underestimating a Vandian noblewoman, mighty Krul of Kruls.* By the rights of Nijumeti tradition, Cassandra Skar should now be the horde's ruler. *Somehow, I think they'll have difficulties accepting me. Alexamir, perhaps, but never a foreign-born woman.* She kept low, located Alexamir and dragged his body back across the ground, away from the railhead, too heavy to sling over her shoulder. All the while calling to Alexamir, trying to rouse him from his pummelling as Cassandra stumbled across the fields. *It's not so far to the planes.* If she could locate a nomad fighter with a decent amount of fuel left in the tank, manhandle Alexamir into the spotter's cockpit. *If, if. Wake up, Alexamir. Wake up and let's escape from here together now. Come on.* Shells from the *Dark Moon* whistled overhead, arrowing towards the sound of incoming propellers. There was a throaty growl from nomad planes still in the air, diving, wing-gun projectiles striking steel hull. *Let there be bombs under your wings. Have at least a few bombs left.* Cassandra dropped to the crumpled wheat as a host of horse-borne nomads stampeded past her, lances set low and sabres spinning wildly around their heads, charging in the direction of the burning railhead. The horsemen didn't even notice Cassandra dragging Alexamir away from the melee. Their battle cries faded behind her.

Cassandra came to the first grounded nomad aircraft. Her heart thudded hammer-hard, sweat pouring down her face from the exertion of hauling Alexamir this far. He moaned slightly as she rested him down on the stubble of flattened crops.

'Can you hear me? Wake up, Alexamir. Kani Yargul's dead. I slew him. *We* slew him. You tired him out and I finished the damn job. Your family's honour is restored.' *What will happen to the horde now?* But the young Vandian woman knew the answer to that. *The clans' leaders will fight each other for supremacy, for the right to rule the horde. And the losers will sourly strike off on their own with a horizon full of rich, poorly defended pickings to raid and pillage.* Nurai had seen truly, peering into the future. This was the end of the horde. At least, as a single coordinated force. For Weyland and the rest of the league, she suspected, the troubles were only just beginning. 'We have to leave, Alexamir. If Yargul's captains find us, they'll put both of us to the sword for what we did back there.'

Alexamir moaned in response but remained unconscious. Cassandra mounted the nearest plane. Its fuel gauge read empty. The next fighter plane had lost its undercarriage, wheels snapped away in a hard landing. The third aircraft appeared more promising. Cassandra clambered up its fuselage and examined the cockpit's control panel. A tenth of a tank left. *Better. This will have to do.* She jumped off, found Alexamir and dragged his limp body towards the nomad aircraft. *Like towing a sack of bricks.* But these bricks began to stir and move. Cassandra had spotted a canteen strapped to the pilot's seat and climbed to retrieve it, to see if water sprinkled over Alexamir's face might hasten his awakening.

Cassandra had taken two steps up using the plane's handholds when someone seized her ankles from behind and sent her sprawling down into the shredded crops.

'Time for a long overdue family reunion, my *lady*,' said Apolleon.

Cassandra leapt to her feet and lashed out at the secret police's master with her bloody sword, drawing and striking in one smooth movement, but he avoided the blow – so fast he almost vanished and reappeared at her side. Gripping Cassandra's wrist, twisting her flesh hard enough that her blade tumbled from paralyzed fingers. Apolleon caught the short sword with his free hand. Alexamir moaned. He weakly tried to struggle upright, but Apolleon sent a boot driving into the young nomad's gut. Alexamir cracked back towards the soil.

'Leave me here,' begged Cassandra, struggling to reach Alexamir's body on the ground. 'You abandoned me before. Do it again!'

Apolleon shook his head. 'Things change. You appear to be in rude health once more, which is more than can be said for Prince Gyal. Your mother's plan to claim the throne through marriage to the prince is lying in the ditch next to his severed head. An empress needs an heir – or the promise of one if she is to rule.'

Cassandra stopped thrashing in the adviser's unnaturally strong grip. 'I will not go with you.'

Apolleon saw where her attention was focused and drew a pistol from his holster, pointing it towards the ground. Pointing it towards Alexamir. *No!* 'For him? For this blue-skinned barbarian, you would throw away a chance at the diamond throne? I can remove him from the equation easily enough.'

'Don't !'

Duncan. Cassandra's retainer trotted across the ground looking as if he had been dragged backwards across the battlefield, but just seeing her loyal friend again lifted her heart.

'This barbarian is a distraction we can ill afford,' said Apolleon.

'You've lived so long you've forgotten what it's like to be a mortal,' said Duncan. He knelt down by Alexamir, checking his pulse. 'You no longer remember what actually matters to people.'

'Duncan,' beseeched Cassandra. 'If you care anything for me, let me stay here by his side.'

'I can't do that,' said Duncan. 'And even if I did, when your mother hears you're healed, she will return for you with another fleet at her back. You know there's no cost she will not expend to have you with the house. I gave her a promise to return you.'

'That promise was broken when she abandoned me to the steppes.'

'I was coming back for you again either way.'

'Then I would have asked you to leave, too.'

Duncan lifted Alexamir's comatose body up, struggling under the weight. 'Help me here.' That to Apolleon.

'You think the Princess Helrena will welcome this base-born blue lump to Vandia?'

Duncan ignored him and glanced at Cassandra. 'You want to be together, this is the only way.'

'You are a fool,' said Apolleon.

'There's an old saying in Weyland: *Happy wife, happy life*. You want an heir to the house? I reckon this is the price. Convince Helrena when we get back to the empire.'

Apolleon sighed wearily but dragged Cassandra across, still holding her wrist tight while he bent down and took Alexamir's weight as easily as lifting a canteen of water. 'Am I the Master of the Hoodsmen, or some simple matchmaker attached to the Imperial Harem?'

'I know what you are – and this is just what we have to do to get where we're going.'

There was more happening here than Cassandra understood... that much was certain. But she would be with Alexamir and that was all that really mattered to her. Now that Apolleon had realized he could lead the house's heir by the carrot better than by the stick, he let her hand go. Cassandra squeezed Duncan's shoulder as they left the aircraft's shadow. 'Thank you.'

'No thanks needed.'

'Yes,' said Apolleon, his mind obviously still grinding his schemes and plots as he bore Alexamir's weight forward. 'I think we can make this work. Nobody in the Imperium knew of Gyal and Helrena's marriage plans. We can hang the expedition's failure on Gyal; blame the house's enemies for their decision to appoint Gyal as commander and exclude the princess from the chain of command. The punishment fleet had only victories under its belt when Helrena left for the empire. Gyal ignored her counsel to return with the fleet's mission achieved. Without her steadying ballast, Baron Machus and Prince Gyal, in their blind arrogance and hubris, allowed a bunch of blue-skinned savages to overrun the expeditionary force with nothing more than horses and sabres during a surprise attack. This defeat will break our enemies and clear a path to the throne.'

Nothing changes, even when everything does. A thought occurred to Cassandra. 'Is Paetro safe?'

'He took a spear in the leg, but it will take more than a few wild nomads to kill him,' said Duncan. 'He's in the sickbay, cursing the medics for not letting him search for you.'

Cassandra was glad that Paetro was one soul she wouldn't have on her conscience. 'So are you not staying behind in Weyland?'

'No,' said Duncan. 'I'm going home with you.'

Up in the sky, the large steel mass of the *Dark Moon* grew larger as the vessel homed in on Apolleon. Cassandra tried not to let her doubts overwhelm her. *Perhaps it's better this way. If we had stayed, Kani Yargul's followers would have tried to gut Alexamir and me both.* 'What will home be?'

'Whatever we make it.'

Cassandra nodded. *As long as I'm with Alexamir, I can live with whatever we make it.*

AFTERMATH

King Marcus lounged in the royal train's drawing room coach, the top floor of his three-storey car walled with walnut wooden panelling, carved crests and intricate heraldry that wouldn't have looked out of place in a cathedral. His desk was covered with plans and blueprints for Arcadia's forthcoming redevelopment. Marcus rose from the leather-lined couch built into the wall and moved behind his desk, reminding himself of his rewards for enduring all of this. It was astounding what could be done to the capital with modern building materials, with architectural plans provided by the Imperium. *At last, a capital worthy of Weyland's status.* Long boulevards flanked by buildings as large as mountains, cathedrals of light and science leading to a central forum that could contain a million citizens. The capital's canals would be redesigned with a main channel leading to his grand new airfield and skyguard stadium – a canal wide enough to accommodate his massive new ironclads, a fleet of warships to dominate the Lancean Ocean. King Marcus imagined the pride which would swell his doltish subjects' hearts as they saw the steel citadels floating past on their way to new victories. As much warmth as the king could feel, with this cursed cold making his nose dribble. A fever no doubt given to him by one of the many sweaty sons of the soil whose presence had been foisted on him at the last station. If he wasn't careful, Weyland's monarch would end up early inside the giant gold sarcophagus he had marked for his final resting place.

Despite the warmth and relative luxury of the royal train, the king loathed this manner of travelling. *Slow. Traditional. Boringly conventional.* Intended to be seen by as many of his subjects as possible in every town and village. If the people knew what was best for them, then they would insist on travelling by fast, efficient skyguard merchant air-wing planes and relegate the Guild of Rails to shipping bushels of corn and cages of cattle. It was no wonder Marcus' tedious brother had made so many royal progresses around the kingdom by train, subject to the whims of the long guilds. A fine, royal steer for display at the endless prefecture shows. *And now, I'm the prize bull on show so the ill-educated masses may gawk at a king's grandness.* But there was only so much monarch to go around. *So I must be rationed. My time. So valuable. So wasted.*

Marcus gazed out of the viewing galleries, a clear crystal stretch of reinforced glass. The train was rounding a corner, forests to the right and the last frost-topped peaks of the Sharps Mountains on the left. There were no other cars in this train but those reserved for the king: a dining coach, another wagon for the kitchen, the sleeping coach for the king and queen, a coach with servant sleeping compartments, a coach with bathing compartments. Their royal blue liveries contrasted with the modern camouflage pattern of the train's military cars: an artillery wagon with wheel-gun turrets, connected to Marcus' royal guardsmen's wagon and four more similarly armoured railcars at the rear sporting anti-aircraft turrets on their roofs. *My brother never bothered with anything more than a single fighting car to see off bandits. How lucky the old bore died before the assembly's renegades tore our land apart and left me to pick up the pieces.*

The train's head steward, an aquiline-nosed fop in a starched blue uniform came up the spiral staircase bearing a hot toddy along with his supercilious manner. *What's the man's name? Burton, that's it.*

'Your drink, sire. As requested, I ensured the dining car provided extra sugar and lemon.'

A stiffly pompous fool, for sure. But at least Burton never made the same error twice. 'Look out there, Burton. It looks abandoned, pristine. Apart from the guild's rails you wouldn't know people had ever touched the world.'

'Quite so, Your Majesty.'

'They'll know it's been changed before I am done. I will leave an empire to rival Vandia standing in the centre of the three oceans.'

'More travelling for us, then, sire.'

'Sadly, so. This fools' circus for the people is the price of my victory. But then neutrality also has a price,' said the king. 'Rodal will pay it first. Then the rest of the Lanca. The nations of the league abandoned me when I most needed them. It was left to distant allies like the

Vandians to aid us. I shall show the league how a fire is best beaten out as soon as it starts. They'll burn like Weyland burned.'

'False friends are like leaves in autumn, sire. They are to be found everywhere.' The retainer bowed and left the chamber.

Marcus had barely reengaged with the distractions of a properly grandiose Arcadia when he was almost slung from his chair by the force of the braking locomotive. He didn't have to wait long for an explanation. Burton reappeared at a scurry, his face flushed and looking suitably contrite.

'What is the meaning of this, man?'

'Word from the engine master, sire. We are turning back towards the station at Sethune.'

'In the name of the saints, why?'

'The signals compartment has received a warning, Your Majesty. There seems to be some confusion in the territory ahead of us. Colonel Garland of your Royal Guardsmen feels it prudent to return to a town with a serviceable skyguard field.'

'Damn his eyes for an old woman. The war is won! This interminable circuit of the north is my victory progress.'

'The reports being received *are* rather confused, sire,' said Burton apologetically. He raised a penitent eyebrow. 'Possibly an outbreak of banditry. This is a somewhat remote location, as you so wisely observed.'

'Get out!' barked the king. 'Tell the signals officer to clarify exactly what this delay is about or I will have someone's head on a pike.'

Burton trotted away and Marcus returned bad-tempered to his plans. The king was still examining the blueprints when the train began to slide backwards. *A city of splendours. Splendours without end.*

Up ahead on the line, Sad Makar ruefully observed the massive train retreating back towards the Sharps Mountains. The flat bones of his forehead gave him a slab-like look. Ferocious, even by the standards of the steppes. The wind blew and his left eye watered as was its wont. He patted his dark brown stallion's flanks and gazed morosely at the party of Nijumeti warriors busying themselves levering up iron rails from the wooden sleepers.

'There's a pointless contraption,' chortled a nomad. 'Why build a wagon that can only roll on metal? Wouldn't it be of far more use if it could sneak its way through the forests and climb up mountain slopes?'

'Weyland's sorcerers aren't powerful enough to build such things,' noted a second nomad. 'Not like those Vandians we chopped.'

Sad Makar shrugged. 'I told you that this fortune in metal lines was used for something.'

One of the largest warriors, Trofim of the Twelve Scars, stopped working and wiped the sweat off his blue face. 'They are used for something. For keeping our blacksmiths happy!'

'Do you think they'll return and ask for the rails back?' asked another warrior.

'If they do, we'll bargain,' said Makar.

'Bargain?'

'Aye.' Makar patted his sabre's pommel. 'Steel for iron.'

Trofim of the Twelve Scars grinned. 'Now there's a thing. Not a week inside Weyland and Makar's already become a lily-livered merchant.'

'Same old trade,' said Sad Makar. *Same old trade.* He left his horse with his men and threaded his way through the trees to the clearing where the two prisoners were being held; more notables fleeing from the first province the nomads had crushed after coming over the mountains. Sad Makar had only captured the pair half an hour ago, or their fate would already have been settled. That savage opening battle had lost them Kani Yargul, but for Sad Makar, this was not a thing to be mourned for long. The great warrior had died well and led his people beyond the mountainous Rodalian walls which had penned them in for countless centuries. Yargul's immortality in the riders' songs was guaranteed; a legend to rivals the gods. The longevity of their new prisoners, though, that would likely fall far short of immortality. The two Weylanders were still tied to the tree trunks with rope, a tree apiece, the first prisoner a short ugly manservant, the other a woman of quality, a local noble. Fair of countenance but mean of heart, if he was any judge; and with five wives, he probably was such. The guard he had posted over them looked bored, leaning against a spear.

'Following the rails south must not seem such a good idea now?'

400

'Ransom me,' implored the woman. 'I am Lady Leyla of North-haven, worth my weight in gold to you as a hostage – I have a king's favour.'

'Raiding for hostages and saddlewives is what we do when we're bored. Do I look bored to you?' Sad Makar had the whole world laid out before him. This land was ridiculously rich. Iron rails left on the ground like the ashes from last night's fire. So many silver coins in the pockets of those they killed that it was hard to steal enough horses to carry it all away.

The female tried to summon the kind of gaze that would melt the heart of fools. Unfortunately for her, Sad Makar was not one of them. 'No. You look handsome and strong. Strong enough to know my true worth.'

'Oh, *that* I'm sure I do appreciate.'

'Keep her as a slave?' asked the rider, in steppes dialect so the prisoners would not understand.

Sad Makar shook his head and answered in the same tongue. 'There is something of the serpent about this one. She would promise you honey while gleefully slipping you poisoned beer. I have no wish to wake up in the morning and find my manhood removed. I think we shall do this king she speaks of a little favour by not returning her.'

Wisely, the rider standing guard didn't even bother asking about the fate of the short ugly one.

Sad Makar switched to the common tongue. 'Will you not beg for your life too, scar-face?'

'Nix ain't begged yet,' growled the ill-favoured dog. 'Reckon it's not the time to start now.'

'Our way is to test you with fire.'

He spat down onto the forest floor. 'Ain't died yet, either.'

The old dog had a defiant courage, Sad Makar gave him that. But the flames would tease out the coward in the bravest of warriors.

'They speak well enough,' said the guard, packing kindling around the prisoners' boots.

Sad Makar picked up a burning branch from last night's cooking pit and blew on it, appreciating the red glow that came out of the wood. 'Speaking well is easy when you are standing on grass. Let us judge the quality of their words when they are twisting on the pyre.'

Sad Makar called out to his warriors beyond the trees to take a break. He knew they would work like slow surly serfs for the rest of the day if they didn't get to wager their stolen coins on which of their two prisoners would perish first.

Willow watched from under her comfortable sheets as Sheplar and Kerge left the large apartment. Now that the siege had ended and any enemies still inside Rodal were filling shallow war graves down in the valleys, the Speaker of the Winds had given Willow lodgings in the peaks of Hadra, a high view of clear skies from her narrow windows. Cries from the cot alongside Willow's bed reminded her that it would be the newborn baby's feeding time again soon enough.

'Should I pass the little 'un across to you?' asked Carter.

'In a minute,' said Willow, still spooning at the bowl of warm rice and pork that Sheplar and the gask had brought with them. 'If I don't eat first, I don't think my milk is going to be much more wholesome than soup water on the third boil.'

'Have you thought what you're going to call her?'

'I've got a name,' said Willow. 'Mary.'

Carter nodded, seemingly finding it hard to speak. 'Something good can come out of any act, however bad, however foul.'

Willow rested back in bed on the pillows. 'Yes, it can. I'm so very tired of war and fighting, Carter. She's all that matters to me now.'

Carter lifted her empty food tray off the sheets, placing it by the sideboard. 'Me, too. But I don't think the civil war will last much longer. The Nijumeti are riding down on Marcus and the south. They'll be following the gold of the caravan routes all the way across the border to Ortheris, but not before they've looted every royalist estate and lifted every southern mill owner's wage box during their gallop across the nation.'

'Then the royalists will be clamouring for their troops to pull back and protect their acres,' said Willow.

'I don't think that many southern soldiers will be returning home,' said Carter. 'Not according to my father, at any rate. Marcus' Vandian allies are dead or fled. Half the king's forces were smashed against

Rodal and left for crow food up in the mountains. The Assembly's armies have been ordered out of hiding to cut the royalist supply lines. And now the north has its own skyguard worthy of the name. We won't be fighting our way down to the capital now – more like helping chase the nomads south and clearing up after the slaughter.'

'Apart from corpses, what will be left after this bloody horrible war ends?'

'You, me and her,' said Carter.

Those words felt as warm to Willow as her rest-bed. 'Do you think victory will heal your father?'

Carter briefly looked pained. 'I'm really not sure. But the south's final defeat and Marcus' execution for high treason is all that our enemies have left to surrender, now. But, if that's not enough for him . . . ?'

'It'll have to be.' But even as Willow voiced the sentiment, she wasn't sure if she believed it. The gentle pacifist pastor Willow had grown up with had long gone, and she didn't ever see him return-ing. 'There's a lot of work to do, for everybody. Northhaven is half wrecked,' said Willow. 'I saw the town from the air when your uncle rescued me.'

'My uncle the air pirate,' laughed Carter.

'*Privateer*,' corrected Willow, mimicking Barnaby's voice as best she could.

'Privateer, then. Well, if things ever get too boring rebuilding Northhaven, maybe I can sign up as aircrew and go raiding across the Lancean Ocean.'

'How about you stay behind and look after the child and I sign up? I think your uncle would accept my sabre.'

'It's not your sword the old rogue would be interested in.'

'Honestly,' said Willow. 'When it comes to old rogues, I'm more worried about Sariel's intentions than I am your uncle's.'

Carter tried to reassure her. 'He's as old as these mountains. And the conflict between his people and the stealers has been going on just as long. I reckon he'll still be fighting that war after we're long gone. The ethreaal we went looking for wasn't the ally Sariel thought he was. Sariel could be gone decades, centuries maybe, searching for the others in his party . . . and maybe they aren't the friends he remembers, either.'

I can but hope. 'Well, then, a new king of Weyland sitting in Arcadia, a new nation and a new start,' said Willow. She glanced happily down at the soft round face swaddled in woollen blankets. *And a new life, to replace all the ones we lost.*